WITH ONLY ONE KISS . . .

"I think I deserve a reward of some sort for what I just did," Shawn said. His gaze slowly roamed over Karissa, eager to take in every detail of her stunning beauty. With part of her long brown hair tumbled from its pins and her almond eyes stretched to their limits, she was the most exquisite woman he had ever seen. Everything about her spoke of perfection.

"I think what I deserve is a kiss of appreciation," he went on to say, and waited to see what her reaction would be. He could tell she was not the sort to share her kisses with just anyone.

A delicious shiver of awareness cascaded over Karissa while she studied him. "Is that *all* you think you deserve?"

"Well, no, but it will do for now."

"All right, but only one kiss. . . . I don't even know you."

He leaned closer until his lips were almost touching hers, then gazed deeply into the large, round eyes that peered up at him apprehensively.

"Then I think it is time we got to know each other a little better," he said, and finally dipped forward to claim her lips in what turned out for Karissa to be the most powerful and the most persuasive kiss she had ever experienced. It was as if he possessed some invisible energy that when transferred to her had left her feeling momentarily weak yet at the same time vibrantly alive—and left her more breathless than ever . . .

ROSALYN ALSOBROOK

Passion's Bold Fire

Melissa Burke:
Hope you
enjoy!
Rosalyn
Alsobrook

ZEBRA BOOKS
KENSINGTON PUBLISHING CORP.

ZEBRA BOOKS

are published by

Kensington Publishing Corp.
475 Park Avenue South
New York, NY 10016

First Printing: January, 1993

Printed in the United States of America

Chapter One

May 1873

Karissa Caine sighed heavily when she paused to look through the large, multipaned window at her father napping in the sun-dappled garden. If only he had not awakened that morning feeling so much better than usual then perhaps she would not regret having promised to meet her friends for lunch at the Hotel Royale. Clearly, this was to be one of her father's better days, and because such days had become a rarity during the past few months, she did not want to miss a minute of it.

But what could she do? He was the one who had insisted she go and she did so want to do everything she could to please him during these final weeks of his life.

"Madison," she called out to the butler just before she turned and headed again toward the front of the house. She did what she could to push aside her sad thoughts, although not an easy task. "I'm ready to leave."

She tried to think of several plausible excuses to keep from having to join her friends on the shopping part of that day's plans when she stopped in front of the large gilded mirror in the entrance hall. She checked to make sure her stylish blue satin and white lace hat was perched at just the correct angle atop the luxuriant pile of brown curls while she considered the problem further.

She hated the thought of pretending to have yet *another* debilitating headache, knowing how needlessly concerned her friends had become over her health during the past few weeks. But if she could think of no better reason to part company with them soon after they ate, then another headache it would be.

"Here are your gloves and parasol, madam," Madison said when seconds later he arrived in the entrance hall beside her.

Karissa glanced at the immaculately dressed butler while she quickly retied one of the tiny bows attached to the brim of her hat. She noticed he held a pair of white summer gloves in one hand and her favorite blue parasol in the other. "Has Franklin brought the carriage around?"

"Yes, madam, he has," he answered in his usual, dignified manner while he stared at some point just above Karissa's left shoulder.

"And does he have the top down as I requested? It is such a beautiful day. I'd like to get as much sunshine as I can today." Which was the same reason her father now napped in the garden. He also loved to feel the sun's warmth against his skin, especially this time of year.

"I made certain of it," Madison responded, moving

8

nothing but the facial muscles that worked his mouth while he waited for her to accept the lightweight gloves from his outstretched hand.

That was the way it was with Madison, who was part French but mostly British. He was so fastidiously proper about every aspect of his job, he was the only servant in the house who refused to call her "Missy." Having been a butler for nearly thirty of his fifty years, he knew a great deal about service protocol and proclaimed it highly inappropriate for the domestic help to speak to the mistress of the house in such an informal manner. He had tried repeatedly to discourage the other servants from treating her with such familiarity, but as usual they paid little attention to him.

"Then I guess I'm ready to leave." She sighed dejectedly when she stepped away from the mirror then took the gloves from Madison's hand. "Oh, and Madison, tell Shelly there'll be no need to press my new gown. I don't think I'll be attending the opera with James tonight after all."

"Planning another headache?" Madison asked. He dared one quick glance at her before he gazed off into the distance again. All the while he continued to stand as tall and erect as his five-foot-eight-inch height would allow.

"I think so," she admitted, looking almost eye level with him as she slipped on the gloves he'd just handed her. She felt no remorse in planning such a lie. Her father's last days were far more important to her than a frivolous night out with a friend. Truth was, her days of being one of Pittsburgh's most celebrated socialites were long past. She would much rather stay

9

home now and enjoy life's simpler pleasures than attend all those grand balls or see the latest opera.

"Although I do plan to follow through with my luncheon plans, for Father's sake, I doubt I'll go shopping afterwards and I *know* I won't be accompanying James tonight. Not with Father feeling so much better. I'll have Franklin carry a message to James later this afternoon explaining my reasons."

"But you still plan to be gone for an hour or so this morning?" Madison wanted to know and again stared at some obscure spot just to the left of Karissa's right ear.

"Only because Father has demanded I go." She pursed her pretty mouth into a tight frown. Even though she understood his reasoning why, it frustrated her to have to leave for even those few hours. But her father did not want anyone other than her brother, John, and his wife, Lana, and those servants living directly within the house to know he was dying.

That was why she was forced to keep alive the painful pretense that everything was normal by continuing to meet with her friends for lunch several times a week and accompanying them on afternoon shopping jaunts whenever she could find no clever reason to get out of them.

It was also at her father's request that she continue putting in several hours each week reading stories to the children at the orphanage across town. Because she loved her father so dearly, she proved willing to do anything he asked of her, especially if it meant keeping her friends from questioning the inordinate amount of time she spent at home these days.

"Then I should expect you back by early afternoon?" Madison asked. He next handed her the parasol, keeping his back perfectly erect.

Karissa smiled while she watched Madison's rigid motions, remembering she had once accused him of sleeping on a board instead of a bed. How else could he keep his shoulders and back so stiff? "Yes, I should be back here by one o'clock. But don't tell Father. I want to surprise him."

"As you wish," Madison responded. Although he did not return her smile, his blue eyes sparkled with the knowledge of what a happy fuss Lawrence Caine would make when he found out what she had done. He loved his daughter's company but did not want her setting aside her normal activities because of her extreme devotion to him. "I shan't breathe a word."

Karissa's smile widened until a tiny dimple appeared high in her cheek. "Thank you, Madison."

Before the graying little butler could respond, there was a sharp knock at the front door and he promptly moved forward to answer it. He paused just long enough to brush a piece of imaginary lint from his lapel before finally reaching for the brass handle.

Thinking it was either a tradesman unaware of the side entrance or her father's lawyer, who had agreed to stop by sometime that day to discuss some personal matter, Karissa glanced at the mirror again. She wanted to make certain that particular parasol went with her new dress.

"Oh, it's *you*," Madison admonished in an extremely hushed voice as if hoping not to be overheard by Karissa, who stood only several yards away. "How many times must I tell you that you are not to come here?" Then in a much louder voice, he said, "I am

11

sorry but Mr. Caine is very busy and is not receiving visitors today."

"But I'm not here to see Mr. Caine," a soft-spoken voice with a distinctive Irish lilt said pleadingly. "I am here to see his daughter, Karissa. 'Tis *very* important that I have a word with her."

"I think perhaps you should come back another time. Madam is preparing to leave for the day," Madison responded with a sharp, forward thrust of his jaw, already stepping back to close the door in the woman's face.

Karissa thought such behavior a little odd even for Madison and hurried forward to find out who wanted to see her. She was surprised to see an unfamiliar red-haired woman who looked to be in her mid-thirties dressed in a gray and black cloak that was frayed at the collar and tied snugly just above an immense, protruding stomach.

It was obvious by the roundness of the bulge that the woman was about seven or eight months with child. Karissa also noticed that the woman wore an abundance of face tint on her cheeks, eyes, and lips which did nothing to enhance her appearance. If anything, the stark colors detracted from any natural beauty she might have had.

"Who is it, Madison?" she asked, and grabbed hold of the oversized door in time to prevent him from closing it further. She continued to stare at the woman curiously, certain she had never seen her before.

"No one with whom you should concern yourself." Madison spoke with a significant lift of his chin, clearly provoked. It was obvious he found the woman's appearance disturbing. "Just another vagrant looking for a handout she does not deserve."

"I am not!" the red-haired woman shot back with that unusual, lilting accent. Her green eyes narrowed with resentment when she glared at Madison but then widened with concern when she looked again at Karissa. "Please, ma'am, I must have a word with ya." Her gaze cut back to Madison, who stared at her icily. " 'Tis a matter of grave importance."

Karissa studied her visitor's troubled expression for several seconds before deciding that although the woman was clearly upset about something, she meant her no harm. Stepping back to let her guest enter, she immediately started tugging out of her gloves, one delicate finger at a time. "Then come in and we'll talk. But I really do have only a few minutes. I am scheduled to have lunch with friends in about twenty minutes. I'll probably be late as it is." But then that was probably expected of her. Ever since she had learned about her father's illness, she was always arriving to places late.

"All I ask is a very few minutes of yer time," the woman promised then cast Madison a contemptuous glare that more than equaled his before she politely stepped inside.

Grinning at Madison's chin-thrusting reaction to that, Karissa handed her gloves back to him then motioned that her unexpected visitor should follow her into the front parlor.

After entering the room, the woman glanced around at her eloquent surroundings, but they did not hold her attention. Clearly, she had come to deliver a particular message, but waited until Karissa

13

had closed the sliding door to give them more privacy before stating anything else.

"Hello. Me name is Jacqueline Lawler, but me friends call me Jacque, which is what I hope ya will be callin' me," she said as a way of introduction then paused to see if the name registered. "I am presently from a small Pennsylvania borough called Black Wall, but lived for a long time in Sun's Wake just outside Pittsburgh." Again she paused to see if the name of the town had caused a spark of recognition in the young woman's almond-shaped brown eyes — eyes so very much like her father's. But there was nothing to indicate Karissa had ever heard of the village before.

"Please make yourself comfortable," Karissa offered with a polite wave of her hand, indicating her visitor should select one of the six chairs that had been arranged into a small conversational cluster near one of five bay windows. She waited until she had done so then took the chair across from her. "I guess it is pretty obvious that you already know who I am."

"That I do," the redhead responded with a firm nod as she removed her dark gray cloak then placed it across what remained of her lap. "And I must say, ye're every bit as beautiful as yer father claimed ya to be."

"Oh, so you are a friend of my father," she responded with a questioning lift of her eyebrow. Although she had not meant to sound insulting, she had been unable to hide the skepticism from her voice. Still, she decided she would rather hear the woman out than call her on the validity of such a ludicrous statement.

"That I am," Jacque replied and seemed pleased

14

that Karissa had not responded more adversely. "The truth is I am a very *close* friend of yer father's. I am also a bar maid at a place called the Lucky Choice tavern there in Black Wall." She waited to see what Karissa's response would be to that and when Karissa did nothing but continue to listen attentively, she found the courage to finish what she had to say.

"The reason I wanted ya to know where I work is because last night, while servin' drinks and stew to the customers, I overheard four men I'd never seen in there before quietly plottin' two murders. Curious to know more about their ill deeds, I turned me ears to them for the rest of the night and eventually learned that Lawrence is one of the men they plan to see murdered."

Any other time, Karissa would have questioned the woman's easy use of her father's first name, but the rest of what had just been said had been too startling. "You *what?*"

"Overheard the men say that they wanted yer father dead by nightfall tonight. That is why I have come. Ya have to keep yer father inside the house and protected at all times," she said. Her tone was frantic and her hands trembled violently. Tears had filled her green eyes but had yet to spill. "I know these men, or at least I know their type. They are nasty and vicious, and I feel like they probably belong to that treacherous lot of Irishmen known as the Molly Maguires. If that's so, then they truly do intend to see yer father and some man by the name of Clay Jones dead as nails before this day is through."

Karissa recognized the other name immediately and the small knot twisting inside her stomach tight-

15

ened with increased apprehension. Clay Jones was the man her brother had hired several months ago as the new supervisor for most of their father's Pennsylvanian mining operations. "But why would anyone want to kill them?"

"Because of the grave injustices they claim the two have caused them."

"But what could my father have possibly done that would warrant anyone wanting to kill him? He happens to be one of the most sympathetic coal owners in that entire region." Which was true. Unlike the other owners, her father saw no advantage to having sick or frightened workers, and because of that, he had gladly spent the extra money to ensure the safety of his coal mines. His were the only mines to install secondary emergency shafts and an adequate number of ventilation tunnels. He was also the only man to pay his men a fair wage and rarely worked them more than ten hours a day. "There is no reason for these men to be *that* unhappy with my father."

"The way I understand it, some of yer father's coal mines are startin' to neglect many needed safety standards until it has again become a dangerous thing for the men to be goin' down inside the mines — especially if they 'have to work in the newer shafts. Why, just last week two men were killed when one of the new sections of the mine right there in Black Wall collapsed due to the meager bracing. I might add that both miners were Irishmen."

Jacque's expression remained somber. "That accident sparked off a lot of ill feelings among all the workers, not just the Irish. The miners who have to work there, they be a-claimin' that all yer father cares about these days is makin' an extra dollar. Not only that, but the company stores at your father's mines have more than doubled their prices in recent months, makin' it impossible for the men to be feedin' their families on what little they earn. And just last week, a few of the miners I know caught rumors that their wages were about to be severely slashed for the second time in just a few months. All because yer father suddenly seems to care more for himself than his workers, or so they say. It is obvious that the Maguires are angry about what has happened and have decided to rid themselves of the men they consider most responsible for their latest woes."

"But none of that is true," Karissa told her, terrified by what she had heard. "My father has always cared about the men who work for him. I know that to be fact. Those men in that tavern must have been discussing the owner of another mine. There have been no accidents reported in any of my father's tunnels in quite some time. I would know. I am always right there when my brother, John, and my father go over the ledgers and the work reports every Friday afternoon." Because her father had so little faith in John's ability to keep his different business concerns thriving for very long, he was secretly grooming her to take over a large part of the family holdings after his death. That made her privy to everything involving his many investments.

"I just know what the men say," Jacque responded then held up her hands as if to indicate she was there only as a messenger, not to start more trouble at the mines. "And I do know for fact there were two funerals in Black Wall last week. Both for dead miners."

"They must have died from natural causes, because there have been no fatal accidents at my father's mines in a long time," Karissa repeated, and crossed her arms to show she refused to believe otherwise. "And there has been no price gouging at my father's company stores, nor has there been any discussion of cutting the workers' wages. Nor has there been a word said encouraging the use of substandard materials for bracing. My father would never allow any of that."

"Oh, but the raisin' of prices at the company stores is true. That much I know because I've seen proof of it meself. As for benefit cuts, I also know for fact the company has all but done away with the widows' pensions because I meself was set to receive a small but set amount each month for the rest of me life. Then suddenly the bank drafts were cut short and I was told widows were now given no more than two months' wages and a plain coffin to bury her dead husband in, of which I had already received. I've since been forced to move from me home and go in search for a job, which is why I now work where I do."

"You lost your husband to one of our mines?" Karissa looked at the woman's protruding stomach and felt immediate compassion.

"Something like that," Jacque answered vaguely. "The point here is that there *have* been some serious benefit cuts brought on by the mining company. I have seen it meself."

Karissa frowned while she considered what Jacque had said. "If what you have told me is true, if the store at Black Wall has raised its prices or if there have been cuts in the widow's pension, or discussions of cutting wages or skimping on building materials, then my father knows nothing about any of it." She wished she could be as certain about her half-brother, who had been placed in charge of those mining operations shortly after her father had been told that his illness was terminal.

His headaches had become so severe and his body so weak so quickly thereafter, he'd had little choice but to have John handle most matters. But he did so with the clear understanding that John confer with him whenever there was an important decision to be made.

An eerie feeling washed over her. "The truth is my father hasn't been able to visit any of his mines in well over six months."

"I suspected as much," Jacque said, nodding. "Not with him being so ill and all."

Karissa's brown eyes widened. "How do you know about my father's illness?" The secret had been too carefully guarded. They wanted to avoid a panic among the stockholders who shared ownership in his two corporations.

"Yer father told me himself."

Karissa looked at her with a arched eyebrow. *"Who* are you?"

"I told ya that already. Me name is Jacque Lawler and I am a very close friend to yer father."

"But why would he tell you about his illness when he has ordered us not to speak of it to *anyone* outside the family other than his lawyer and the more trusted members of the house staff?"

"Because I am a *special* friend," Jacque emphasized, then aware Karissa would not believe her without knowing the whole story, she went on to explain. "I met yer father several years ago. Back in the spring of 1867. Just two and a half years after yer dear mother died."

Karissa tested the date in her mind and realized Jacque was correct on that point. Her mother had died on November 6, 1864, just a few days before Karissa's sixteenth birthday. Her father had in turn become so distraught after her death, he not only forgot about Karissa's most important birthday, he withdrew into himself for several months. "And just how did you two meet?"

"Yer father came into the tavern where I was workin' at that time," Jacque answered with a wistful smile. "His carriage had broken a wheel and he was passin' the hours until it was repaired. We took a likin' to each other right away. He asked to know why I looked so sad most of the time and I explained that I was not happy havin' to work in such a place. A real rats' nest it was. But because of me lack of education and me very real need to eat, I explained I had little choice but to work wherever someone would let me." Her eyes sparkled at the memories her words caused. "Before yer father left that day, he handed me a fancy leather pouch containin' two hundred dollars and told me to find somethin' else to do with me life."

"Just like that?" Karissa asked, though in a way it sounded just like him.

"Just like that." Jacque's green eyes teared. "Yer father is a kind and generous man. To assure that I continued to have enough money to live on so I

20

wouldn't have to go back to such unhappiness, he had me name put to the widow register. I didn't know about it until that first bank draft arrived in my name. And he did that even before we had started seein' each other."

"Seeing each other?" Karissa slumped back in her chair and worried with her lower lip, not certain she wanted to hear any more. "In what way were you two seeing each other?"

"Within a week after I'd quit me job at the tavern, I moved to that small town just outside of Pittsburgh where life was not so coarse and set up to do some mendin' to help me get by. Soon after I wrote to thank yer father for what he had done for me, he started payin' call on me." Her smiled widened. "Nice and proper he looked, comin' to call at me door with his hat in one hand and a dozen yellow roses in the other. Yellow, because he knew it was me favorite color. He stole me heart right away. After that, we continued to see each other regularly for nearly six years." Her adoring smile fell into a look of pure sadness. "Until the day he found out how serious was his illness."

"Which was when?" Karissa asked, still testing her, still not certain she believed her father had taken up with an Irishwoman who had once worked in a tavern. Not when he was so eagerly sought by the most beautiful and gracious women society had to offer. But then, too, he *had* cut back on much of his normal socializing during the past several years.

"It was nearly six months ago. He came by to see me the same afternoon he left the hospital. Right after those examinations. He wanted to tell me what

21

the doctor had told him about a mass growin' in his head so I would know what to expect."

Jacque turned her tear-filled eyes away. Her whole body trembled when she told the rest of it. "He stayed the night with me, weepin' in me arms like a young lad. When he left the mornin' followin', I knew that was the last time he would come to me. I could tell by how pale he looked and how shaky he stood that his illness had already progressed to the point he would soon be unwillin' to leave the house. Yer father is such a proud man. He wouldn't want others to see him once the sickness became too much to bear. It was a painful moment for me because when I told him goodbye that day, I knew it was for the last time."

Glancing down, she rested a quivering hand on top of her rounded abdomen. "And if it weren't for the baby, I'd have slipped quietly out of his life forever. But I felt he should know. That's why I have tried to see him twice since, which is also why yer butler became so angry with me when I appeared at the door again. He sees me for what I am, a common woman not fit to enter this house. It is his desire to protect yer father from the likes of me because he does not know that Lawrence and I were once lovers. None of his employees do."

Karissa leaned forward, skeptical of that last remark. If he had spent so much time with her, how could *none* of the employees know? "But if you really are carrying my father's child, why haven't you tried to catch me away from the house to tell about it, or even my brother? We are easily accessible."

"Because it is not somethin' a daughter or son would want to be knowin' about their own father.

22

And I know how very much yer father adores ya both and enjoys yer respect. I didn't want to do anything that might be causin' either of ya to think any less of him in these final months."

"Then why are you telling me now?"

"Because I have to find a way to make ya believe me. To make ya understand that I love yer father as much as ya children do. His life, or what there is left of it, truly *is* in danger. Ya must warn him and keep him safe." She reached for Karissa's hand and gazed beseechingly into her dark eyes. "Don't let his last days be taken from him."

Karissa's skin prickled with awareness when she realized the woman had told the truth. Of all the many women who had pursued her father since her mother's death, this was the one who had stolen his heart. "But who are these men? You said you didn't know them but surely you caught their names. What were they?"

"I cannot be tellin' ya such as that. I've already put me life in grave danger by just comin' here. It is dangerous enough that I have chosen to discuss this with ya at all; but if it were also to come out that I had named names while I was here, then they would surely kill me—and me unborn child. These are ruthless men. No one must know I was ever here, and if they do somehow find out about me visit, they must believe no names were ever spoken. Besides I only heard mention of their given names. Hardly anyone ever offers their last names at the Lucky Choice." She continued to look at Karissa pleadingly. "Dona tell even yer brother because he might by mischance let me name slip to others who work for him who in turn

23

might let me name slip to those who would pay good money to know."

"Don't worry. I won't tell *anyone* you were here. And I'll make certain Madison doesn't either," Karissa vowed, grateful the woman had shown the courage to come there at all. The Maguires were known for committing the worst kinds of violence and murder—even against women.

She had already risen to call Madison and have him help her father back indoors when she gazed at the woman's rounded stomach again. "I promise your secrets are safe with me, Miss Lawler. Both of them. To everyone except Father. I think he should know that you are the one who saved his life and I think he should also know about the baby. It will make him very happy to see you carrying his child." She also hoped that Miss Lawler might be more willing to tell her father the men's first names so they would have something to go on when trying to track them down.

"Then ya will allow me to see him?" She asked eagerly then winced when she forced herself out of the plush chair. She swallowed back her excitement while she quickly brushed the wrinkles from her pleated dress and adjusted her sleeves just so.

"Of course I want you to see him. I think it will do him a world of good," Karissa answered, having already forgotten about the awaiting carriage and the fact she was late. "Wait here near the door while I have Madison escort him back into his study." She paused with her hand on the servant's cord. "When will the child be born?"

"Should be in about two months," Jacque an-

24

swered, and stroked her stomach proudly. Clearly she did not think of the coming baby as an added burden. "About the first of July I should think." Her expression took on a distant sadness again when she turned her gaze away from Karissa's. "I don't mean to be sorrowin' ya none, but I'd like to know if ya think Lawrence will still be alive to hear whether I have given birth to a son or a daughter?"

"I don't know," Karissa answered honestly. She ignored the sharp twinge in her heart while she tugged the bellcord that would summon Madison. This woman did not need to see her cry. "Some days, like today, he seems so much better that I think the doctors must have made a mistake. But on other days, he is so ill and in so very much pain, he doesn't even know who I am." She pulled on the cord a second time to make sure Madison heard the summons. She knew he liked to slip off into the kitchen to badger their head housekeeper and could not always hear the bell from there. Especially not if Lizbeth had a lot of pots boiling on the stove. "I hope and pray Father lives that long, but I just don't know what the future will bring for him."

Letting go of the bellcord, Karissa stepped back and turned her gaze toward the door where Madison should appear.

While waiting, a gunshot sounded. Then another. Her heart leaped with horror, drawing her hand to her throat. Both gunshots had come from somewhere near the back of the house.

Breathlessly, she threw the door open and hurried down the carpeted hall toward the closest door leading to the backyard. Jacque came only a few yards be-

25

hind her and Madison hurried only a few yards ahead.

Karissa disappeared from sight, and when Jacque realized she had no idea where Lawrence might be in that huge maze of plush gardens, she froze just inside the open doorway.

Meanwhile Karissa, who was too concerned for her father's welfare to consider the danger, followed Madison out into the area of the garden where her father lay.

Chapter Two

Karissa's heart drummed in her ears, drowning the clamor of their boots while she and Madison ran head-long across the brick terrace toward the padded lounge chair where her father had lain napping in the sun. She knew even before they reached his slumped body that he was dead, and she steeled herself against what she would see after she circled in front of him.

But nothing could have prepared her for the sight of her father lying hunched to the side with one gaping hole in his forehead and another in his neck. Shimmering trails of dark red blood poured from both.

"Father!" she screamed, her voice so strangled with horror she had barely recognized it as her own.

Her stomach clenched into a hard, tight spasm of fear and dread when she then sank to her knees beside him to feel for signs of life, futilely hoping that there was still a chance. First, she pressed her fingers against the pulse point at his wrist then reached for the one on his neck. She found nothing to indicate even a faint heartbeat.

When she sat back, she placed that same hand over

the constriction at the base of her throat and felt the sticky warmth of her father's blood against her neck. Her whole body convulsed at the realization she had her father's own blood on her. Suddenly, it was too much for her. She screamed hysterically, shaking so violently with rage and horror that her carefully placed hat tumbled off her head and into her father's lap, where it, too, became spotted with his blood.

As if the reason behind Karissa's sudden hysteria had not yet registered, Madison bent forward and patted Lawrence's cheek. "Mr. Caine," he called loudly. Clearly he thought there was still a chance, however remote, that Lawrence could hear him. "Mr. Caine. Wake up."

Jacque felt her legs grow weak. She leaned against the door frame and took several needed gulps of air while, desperately, she tried to come to terms with the painful fact she had arrived too late. The four men must have already been in place before she ever arrived. They may have even been hiding where they could watch whoever arrived or left through the front door. If that was so, they had to have seen her enter and were probably out there waiting for her to come out, so they could put an end to her meddling. *Or* they could have their rifles aimed at Karissa and Madison at that very moment.

Fear gripped Jacque down to her very soul, making her want to run away from there as fast as she could. But when she saw Karissa crumpled to her knees, sobbing hysterically at her father's side, Jacque shoved her own fears aside. She rushed outside to pull Lawrence's daughter back into the house and away from further danger.

"Karissa!" she shouted at the top of her voice, then ran as quickly as she could toward the others. "Get back in yer father's house before they decide to shoot ya too."

Just before she reached the area where Lawrence lay dead, she heard another shot ring out. She screamed with outrage when it knocked her off balance and caused her to fall to the ground.

Karissa heard Jacque's scream above her own and jerked her head up to see what had happened. She watched in horrified disbelief while the pregnant woman who had wanted so desperately to save her father from an early death tumbled backward.

Madison was the first to snap out of the bewildered state that had followed finding Lawrence so suddenly dead. Aware now of the danger that still surrounded them, and with a strength he did not know he possessed, the small man gathered his employer's body into his frail arms and hurried toward the house while Karissa rushed to Jacque's side.

She knelt to have a better look at the crumpled woman who had not moved since she had fallen, and noticed that not only was there a large bloodstain spreading around a tiny tear in her dress front inches above her right breast, there was another trail of dark red blood trickling down the side of her head. It flowed from somewhere within that thick pile of red hair where she must have struck the brick with her head when she fell.

"Miss Lawler? Can you hear me?" She tried to wake her then glanced in the direction where that last shot was fired. Her eyes widened with renewed fear when only a few hundred feet away she saw the dark shape of a man kneeling on top of the brick wall, hidden within the shadows of a low, overhanging branch.

All she could really tell about the man from that distance was that he was tall, muscular in build with very broad shoulders, similar to the shoulders one might expect to see on a lumberjack; but this lumberjack-looking man held a large rifle in his hands instead of an axe.

Karissa drew in a sharp breath. Although he did not aim the rifle at them at that particular moment, she knew it would take only seconds for him to swing it up against his shoulder and fire again.

"Miss Lawler—Jacque! Please! He can see us. We have to get away from here."

Panicked, she glanced toward the house to see where Madison had taken her father. The side door to her father's study had been left open. Hoping to carry Jacque to safety in much the same manner Madison had just carried her father, she slipped one arm beneath Jacque's shoulders and the other up under her skirts behind her knees. She then tried to stand, but found it impossible to lift her off the ground.

"Please wake up," she wailed, and next tried to drag the unconscious woman toward the house, but even that was impossible. The woman was large-boned anyway and with the added weight of the baby, she was too heavy for Karissa to move.

By that time, Franklin had heard the shots from the carriage where he still waited for Karissa and had rounded the house as fast as his long legs would carry him. The twenty-two-year-old did not stop to ask questions. He dipped down, scooped the unconscious woman into his strong black arms, and carried her im-

30

mediately toward the house. Karissa ran ahead to make sure no one closed the door in front of them.

When the three entered the elaborately furnished study, Karissa noticed Lizbeth Mitchell kneeling beside her father's body, trying desperately to bring him awake with a small bottle of smelling salts. Lizbeth had obviously heard the commotion and come running from the kitchen, where she'd been preparing Lawrence's lunch.

Being the head housekeeper and the only one to have been with the family since before Karissa was born, Lizbeth was responsible for the entire house and for all the other servants, except for Madison, who answered to no one but himself. She was also Franklin's mother and the only one in the house with any medical sense.

"Where do I put her?" Franklin asked once they were safely away from the door and windows. His dark face was wrenched with confusion and fear.

Although Franklin had asked the question of Karissa, it was his mother who answered.

"Over there on that other couch," she said, and waved him farther into the room. She put the lid back on the smelling salts when she stood and looked at the injured woman with an empty expression, as if none of this had really registered with her yet. "Is she dead, too?"

"No," Karissa answered, and stepped to the side while Franklin placed Jacque lengthwise on the plush, blue velvet sofa near her father's large desk. She kept her gaze fastened to Jacque's face because she did not want to as much as glimpse her father's lifeless body for fear of what that would do to her temporary calm.

"She's not dead, but she is unconscious and I could not make her wake up."

Believing it was her duty to take care of anyone hurt, Lizbeth hurried toward them while Madison continued to stand vigil over Lawrence's body as if he still held to the foolish hope that Lawrence would yet open his eyes.

Lizbeth paused beside Karissa then grimaced when she saw Jacque's injuries. "Look at all that blood. She been shot, too?"

"Yes, she has. And she's also hit her head on something," Karissa answered, then promptly stepped back to give Lizbeth more room. She knew from experience that the large Negress liked plenty of working room when taking care of those who were sick or injured.

While Lizbeth continued to study Jacque's injuries, she pulled the lid off the smelling salts again. She then sank quickly to one knee, her thick black skirts puddling around her. "Why, this woman has to be seven months with child. Who is she?"

"A good friend of Father's," Karissa answered. She felt a catch in her throat when she glanced at Madison to see if that comment had registered. "She came to warn me that some men from Black Wall were coming here to kill Father."

"She *what?*" Lizbeth and Madison responded in unison, then after slipping a hand beneath Jacque's head, Lizbeth went on to question, "So she knew ahead your father was going to get shot?"

"Yes. She'd overheard four men talking about it last night." Karissa decided not to mention that those men had been in a tavern at the time. She did not want to cloud whatever opinion would be formed of this very

32

brave woman by letting them know that Jacque had worked as a bar maid. "And because she cares for Father so much, she put her own life in danger by coming here to warn him."

"She got a name?"

"Yes, but I promised her I would not tell it."

Lizbeth's eyebrows lifted a notch, causing her forehead to wrinkle beneath the black turban she wore to hide her graying hair. "Why? She still in danger from that gunman?"

"Yes. Especially now that she has been seen."

Lizbeth lifted Jacque's head off the padded arm of the sofa and waved the tiny blue bottle beneath her nose. Jacque winced and tried to jerk away from the smell. When Lizbeth refused to let her turn away from the pungent fumes, she coughed violently. After a few seconds, Lizbeth set the bottle aside and watched attentively while Jacque struggled to open her eyes.

Karissa leaned forward so Jacque would see her right away and not be frightened of Lizbeth's scowling face.

"Are you all right?" she asked when she thought Jacque was awake enough to speak.

"I-I think so," she responded in a questioning voice, then looked to see who held the back of her head. She blinked several times as if to further clear her thoughts when she saw Lizbeth's dark grimace only a few inches away. The black turban she wore on her head instead of the white mobcap most housekeepers wore made her look all the more menacing.

Seeing Jacque's fear, Lizbeth lessened her scowl while she gently lowered her head back against the scrolled arm of the sofa. Even that slight movement caused Jacque to suffer a sudden shaft of sharp, throbbing pain.

"I must have hit me head on somethin' when I fell. I remember feelin' a hard jolt of pain just before everythin' went dark."

"You've been shot, too," Karissa pointed out, thinking perhaps she did not know.

Jacque lifted her head to see where the bullet had struck her and grimaced from the sharp pain that resulted from the abrupt movement. She kept her eyes closed for several seconds, letting the tiny sparkles of white light settle in her vision. "Me head feels like it is about to split wide open."

"You lucky it ain't done that already, what with the way the side of it swole up so fast," Lizbeth told her then reached for the blood-soaked area of her blouse. "Franklin, you and Madison turn around. I got to have a look at where this woman was shot." She waited until the two men had obliged then gave the material a sharp yank that tore both the blouse and her chemise wide open. She gasped when she saw how much blood still flowed from the small bullet wound.

"That's a nasty one," she muttered more to herself than the rest then slipped her arm under Jacque's neck. Again she lifted Jacque's head and shoulders several inches off the sofa so she could see her back. "Appears it went clear through. That's good. Won't have to go looking for no bullet. Franklin, run to the kitchen and bring me the medical box and some ice. I've got to stop the swelling on the side of her head before it bursts wide open and get those other wounds cleaned up and bandaged."

Franklin bolted immediately from the room. He

34

looked relieved to have been given something useful to do.

"Do you want me to bring you anything?" Madison asked, still standing close with his back to them.

"Yes. Hand me your 'kerchief so I can try to stop some of this bleeding."

Stepping backward toward her, he thrust his arm out and handed her a neatly folded white handkerchief. "Anything else?"

"Might be a good idea to go get Dr. Owen."

"No!" Jacque responded with a gasp that sounded so frightened it caused Madison to glance at her briefly. But as soon as he noticed that her blood-streaked shoulder was still exposed to his view, he quickly turned away again.

"Please don't bring a doctor. I don't want anyone else to be knowin' I was here. Too many people know already."

"Including one of the gunmen." Karissa thought she should be told the full extent of the danger. "I saw him up on the privacy wall just before Franklin carried you inside."

"Do you think he was the same man who shot me?"

"I don't know. I was staring at Father when you were shot. I didn't notice the man until later."

"Oh, dear Saints preserve us," she said, her eyes round with renewed fear. "Listen, you must help me to get away from here now. They saw me and now they *know* that I came here to warn ya."

Karissa could not give her much hope. With that head of brilliant red hair and that well-rounded stomach, they had to have recognized her.

"They also *know* you were shot," she added, already

35

piecing together a plan. "For all else they know, you are already dead."

"That's why you must help get me away. I canno' trust hidin' here will be safe."

Franklin returned at that moment with a small brown medical box in one hand and a kitchen towel filled with large chunks of ice in the other. His eyes were wide with fear, having overheard the last of the conversation. "If I jumped out one of the parlor windows, I might could make it to the carriage without getting shot. Maybe I should make a try for it and go get the police."

"No," Karissa said then placed her hands on either side of her face to help her concentrate better. "She thinks the Molly Maguires are somehow involved in this and everyone knows those men have a strange way of getting their hands on police reports — even those reports that are supposed to be marked confidential."

"Then what should we do?" he asked, clearly ready to do *something.* Because Franklin was not brought up with the same strict proprieties as Madison, he did not bother turning back around to face the wall again. He continued to stare at Karissa while he talked. "We can't just sit here and wait for those men to come busting down that door and shoot the rest of us."

"They wouldn't do that," Madison told him, although he did not look quite as convinced as he sounded. "Now that we are in the house, they have no way to know whether we have armed ourselves or not."

"Still, I think we'd be a lot safer if I went for the police," Franklin stated, looking as worried as ever.

"No police yet," Karissa reiterated.

"Then what're we going to do?"

36

"I'm thinking, Franklin. I'm thinking."

Lizbeth glanced at the two with a curiously raised eyebrow. "First thing we need do is stop this woman's bleeding and get some of that head swelling to go down," she said, already hard at work in her attempts to do both. "I also want her to drink down some of those pain powders the doctor sent for your father. Fetch over a glass of water."

"Maybe I ought to run over to Mr. John's house and get him," Franklin suggested, still thinking they needed to do something else. He continued to frown darkly while he watched Karissa pour a glass of water from her father's drinking service. "Your brother, he'd know what to do."

"Wouldn't do us any good to go after him now," Karissa said while she singled out a small packet of the pain powder. "He's not at his house. He's not even in Pittsburgh today. Besides, I gave her my word I would never tell my brother that she was here. No one is to know she was ever here. Not even the other servants when they return from the market, or Father's nurse when she comes back from visiting her mother. It is possible those men don't know our friend by name and I'd like to keep it that way."

Jacque looked at her gratefully, then winced when Lizbeth began scrubbing her front shoulder wound with hard, brisk strokes.

While Karissa considered their options further, she stirred the gray powder into the water with her finger and handed it to her. Then suddenly it dawned on her that the mining supervisor was still in danger. With her father now dead, those men would surely go after him next, if they hadn't already.

Fearing the worst, she headed immediately toward her father's desk and scribbled a message on a blank piece of paper.

"Franklin, if you really are willing to chance going outside, there is something you can do to help after all," she told him as soon as she had folded the paper twice. "Change out of that blood-stained coat so as not to attract attention then take this message to the telegraph office and have it sent to Mr. Clay Jones at the Caine mining office in Black Wall. Explain to the telegraph operator that this is an emergency. Tell him that this message has to go out right away."

She reached into the top drawer of the desk and flipped open her father's cash box. As usual, it was unlocked. She extracted two coins and handed them to him. "Pay the man twice the going rate if you have to, but make sure he sends that message while you are still standing there. Then come right back so I'll know it was done." She did not bother reminding him to keep their secret. She had known Franklin since childhood and trusted him to understand the seriousness of Jacque's situation.

Franklin did not ask questions. He simply tucked the paper and the two coins into his uniform pocket then headed toward the west end of the house to change out of the stained coat. Though the blood was not that noticeable on such dark material, the smell was obvious even to him.

Meanwhile, his mother continued to do her best to cleanse and bandage Jacque's wounds while Karissa tried to decide what to do next.

Madison left long enough to find a sheet to cover

Lawrence's body, then stayed in the room facing the windows.

Fifteen minutes later, Franklin was back. By then Karissa had decided how to solve their present dilemma. She ordered Madison to bring her one of his older uniforms, which he did in near record time.

"Miss," she said to Jacque; having found that the only way to get around calling her by name. She held out the butler's uniform to her. "I want you to put this on."

Jacque nodded, understanding that to be smuggled out without being recognized, she would have to be disguised. As the pain powders started to take effect, Jacque sat up. She tilted her head and looked at the uniform doubtfully but held out her hand. "Ask the men to leave the room."

Madison was already headed for the door and Franklin quickly followed. Once the door was closed, it took only a few minutes of Jacque trying to squeeze her rounded body in the small man's clothing to realize Karissa's scheme would never work.

"Guess we'll be needin' a different plan," she said when she tried to pull the front edges of Madison's shirt together over her protruding stomach and failed miserably. Because of the size of her baby, there was a full twelve-inch gap.

"Perhaps we *should* try to hide you here," said Karissa.

"No!" Jacque exclaimed. "They'll find a way to get in. They'll discover me. Please you must get me away."

"But are you well enough?"

"I'm healthy and strong. I'll be fine."

Lizbeth, who had been quietly scrubbing blood

stains out of the sofa and carpets with a stout mixture of vinegar and soap, spoke next. "We could try smuggling her out of here disguised as you."

"Me?"

"Sure. If those men had intended to kill you, they would have done so when you first ran out into the garden. But they didn't even take one shot. So why not put her in one of your mourning dresses and an oversized cloak a different color from her own? That way we could pretend she was you. I could even call out your name to her when she leaves the house so anyone watching and listening would think for sure it was you."

Karissa considered the idea. Although her dress would be a little long on Jacque and would need to be pinned to keep her from tripping—and would probably not fasten together in back—all that could be concealed beneath a cloak. A *hooded* cloak, so it could also hide that brilliant red hair. It just might work. "Bring down that gown I wore to Aunt Mary's funeral last fall. It was a little short on me anyway. And bring one of my largest black cloaks. We'll have her safely out of this house in no time."

To everyone's relief, the clothing fit well enough to give the plan a try, and because the cloak had an unusually large hood, it fell far enough forward to cover most of her face.

"Turn around." Karissa wanted to see how the outfit looked from the back. She smiled. "All you need is a black handkerchief to dab at your eyes and they will surely think you are the grieving daughter setting off to get the police."

As soon as she said the word *grieving,* Karissa real-

40

ized she should be crying her heart out right now. She had just lost her beloved father. But the truth was, she did not have time to grieve just yet. She had to see to Jacque's safety first; and to the safety of her future sibling. "But where can you go? You certainly can't head back to Black Wall. They'll be waiting for you there."

Walking back to the desk, she reached into the cash box and counted out a small handful of bills. She waited until she had returned to Jacque's side before she held the money out to her. "Here, take this cash and go as far away from here as you can. Go to friends or relatives if you can, and as soon as you've settled somewhere, I want you to find a good doctor and have him keep a close watch on those injuries. They could easily become infected."

Jacque pushed the hood back and looked at Karissa with gratitude shimmering from her green eyes. "I'll pay ya back somehow. Every last cent of it. I swear to ya."

"No you won't. That money is not for you, it is for my half-brother or my half-sister." She ignored Lizbeth's sharp intake of air as she slipped a supportive arm around Jacque's trembling shoulders. "That baby is very important to me. And I don't want his mother in any danger. All I ask is that you send word of the baby's birth shortly after it is born. Use a false name and go to a neighboring town to mail the letter so it can't be traced back to you if you like, but I must know if I have a little brother or a little sister."

Jacque looked at Karissa, her eyes still brimming. "I hate to be askin' it of ya after all else y've done, but would ya be kind enough to do me one more favor?"

Karissa held her head high in a very real attempt

41

to keep from crying herself. "Certainly, what is it?"

"Would ya place a dozen yellow roses on yer father's grave for me." She smiled a tearful smile. "He was always bringin' me yellow roses."

"Of course." Karissa blinked several times to clear her eyes and called Franklin and Madison back into the room. Both had waited in the hall. "Drive her to a train station across town and see that she boards one as soon as possible, but don't ask her for her destination. If none of us know where she went, then none of us can accidentally let that information slip."

Both Franklin and Madison nodded that they understood.

"As soon as you both have seen her off, head next to the police station to tell them that my father has been shot." She felt a sharp stab of pain at having spoken those words aloud, but she quickly forced the grief aside and continued to talk in a calm, controlled voice. "Tell them we will need the coroner."

She stepped forward to hug Jacque one last time and felt the woman's whole body tremble and sway. "Madison, offer her your arm. She's far too weak to walk to the carriage unassisted."

Madison smiled and stepped forward. "It would be my pleasure."

Jacque's eyebrows arched questioningly as she accepted the arm, and after pausing beside Lawrence's body long enough for her to tell him a tearful goodbye, they headed toward the front of the house.

Lizbeth waited until Franklin had taken his usual place on the front seat and Madison and Jacque were nearly there before she shouted after them in a tearful voice. "Don't worry about nothing, Miss Caine. I'll

42

stay right here with your father's body until you get back from that police station. I won't move even an inch."

Karissa stood back well away from the door and watched through a window while Madison helped a trembling Jacque into the carriage. She waited until Lizbeth had closed the door again, then spoke in a soft, quivering voice. "I hope she makes it to wherever it is she decides to go."

"She will," Lizbeth said reassuringly. She erased any signs of worry from her face. "Her kind has God Himself watching out for them. She'll be fine."

Together Karissa and Lizbeth turned and headed toward the back of the house. It was not until they had returned to Lawrence's study to finish cleaning away Jacque's blood as best they could that the tears they had held back suddenly burst forth.

"What we going to do without Mr. Lawrence, Missy?" Lizbeth said, staring down at his ashen face with heart-wrenching remorse. "What we going to do?"

"I don't know," Karissa admitted with a choked sob, finally giving her emotions their reign. "I just don't know."

Trembling with grief, the two women went into each other's arms and wept bitterly, knowing that life in the Caine house would never be the same.

Chapter Three

Franklin and Madison remembered their promise to Karissa. They waited outside the station on the platform near a large, hissing passenger train while the woman who had tried to save Lawrence Caine's life went inside to purchase a ticket. They did not want to overhear her destination. But even so, they realized it was still possible she might faint from having lost so much blood so they kept a close eye on her trembling form through a large window.

"She sure has done an awful lot of crying since we left the house," Franklin said in a voice low enough only Madison could hear. "She sounded like her whole heart was breaking. You think maybe she was Mr. Caine's mistress?"

Madison cut a questioning gaze at Franklin, having wondered the exact same thing. "Could be. As you recall, he did rather enjoy taking one of the carriages out by himself quite often."

"And was sometimes gone for days at a time," Franklin added, aware that meant there had been ample opportunity. He pushed his driver's cap to the back of his head while he thought more about those trips. "I guess now I know why he didn't want me to drive him even when he knew he would be gone overnight. Always told me he'd be gone too long and would rather I be here to drive Missy wherever she needed to go. But now I think maybe he just wanted to be able to go to places we didn't know nothing about."

Madison nodded and offered a distant smile while he watched the woman in question reach into her handbag and bring out the money needed to pay for her ticket. He knew she had to be at least twenty years younger than Lawrence, but also knew such an age difference would not have mattered all that much if they had truly desired one another.

"Business trips he called them." He cut his gaze to Franklin. "Now I think we finally understand the true nature of some of those business trips. Do you suppose that child she carries is his?"

"Could be. I didn't see no wedding band to indicate there might be a husband waiting for her somewhere. And she sure is pretty enough." Franklin, too, offered a cheerless smile while he continued to study her through the window. "And brave. She sure must have loved him an awful lot to risk her life like that to try to save him."

Madison's distant smile faded into a tight, grim line. "To think I didn't want her inside the house." His voice filled with regret while he watched her hand the ticket agent part of her money and return the rest to her handbag. It worried him that she had to hold on to the counter's edge while she waited for her change. He knew if she fell, it could hurt both her and the baby. "When I first met her, I thought she was up to no good. I tried to send her away."

"You had no way of knowing," Franklin reminded

him, then leaned back against a brightly painted wooden support. He was too emotionally drained from all that had happened to continue standing on his own. "You didn't know she was such a good friend of Mr. Caine's."

Madison looked down at the planked flooring, overwhelmed with remorse. His face had turned as pale as his hair was white, making him look more like a withered ghost than the proud butler of Lawrence Caine. "Still, if I hadn't tried to turn her away at the front door the way I did, she could have told Miss Caine what all she had come say a few minutes sooner. And had she done that we might have been able to get Mr. Caine back inside that house in time to save what was left of his life."

Franklin ran his large black hand over the lanky features of his face while he thought about what Madison had just said. "I don't think a few minutes would have made no difference. Those men were probably already out there picking their spots before she ever even arrived."

"Still, if I'd let her in and let her speak her mind right away, we might have gotten him inside before they fired that first shot."

Franklin shook his head, not seeing the logic in that. "They'd have seen when you come out, and as soon as they realized you were there to try to help Mr. Caine back inside, they'd have shot you both."

For the first time in Franklin's memory, Madison's narrow shoulders slumped forward and his pale eyes glistened with tears.

"In a way, I wish they *had* shot me, too. Mr. Caine was more than just an employer to me. He was a friend."

"We all liked him and had good reason to. But look at the comforting side of all this. At least now he don't have to suffer those terrible headaches of his no more. I know he still had a good day now and then, but it was hurting my heart to see him suffer like he did whenever he was having one of his bad ones." Franklin stood erect again when he noticed that Jacque was on her way back outside. "Here she comes."

Both men glanced at the other people milling about the busy train station to see if there were any suspicious-looking men lurking about. When they spotted no one who looked sinister enough to belong to that murderous labor group, the Molly Maguires, they headed toward her, eager to offer their supportive arms.

"When does your train leave?" Franklin asked, prepared to stay however long it took. He knew Missy would skin them both if they left there before she was gone.

"It leaves now. Since it does not really matter to me where I go from here, I bought my ticket for this very same train." She headed immediately toward the third car while the two men flanked her on either side. Seconds before she reached for the railing outside the rear door, she came to an shaky halt and turned to look at them with a suddenly solemn expression.

"Gentlemen, this afternoon after ya finally return to the house, I want ya both to tell Miss Caine four names for me." She then pronounced each one slowly and carefully, and with great effort because what strength she had left was nearly gone.

With a trembling hand, she reached up to wipe away the last remnants of her earlier tears for what she had to

47

say was important. "Now remember," she said again. "The names to tell her are Shawn, Joey, Thomas, and Jack. Do ya think ya can remember all four of those?"

"Of course we can, but whose names are they?" Madison asked, thinking it odd to be giving out just those four names and nothing else.

"She'll know," Jacque told them, then smiled at their baffled expressions. "And she'll know what to do with them. Just be sure no one else is around when you tell her, and don't tell her until the police have already gone. She might decide to tell them the names before really thinkin' it through and I don't want them askin' how she came by such information for her only answer could point back to me." She patted her stomach lovingly. "And until my baby and I are safely settled somewhere, I don't want the police out there searchin' for us."

Franklin and Madison looked at each other, clearly perplexed, but agreed to wait until Karissa was alone and the police had gone. They then waited until Jacque was safely inside and the train had pulled way from the platform before heading toward the carriage.

"Why do you suppose she wants us to give Missy those four names?" Franklin asked, glancing at the train one last time before it disappeared behind a row of tall buildings several blocks away.

"I don't know, unless maybe the names have something to do with Mr. Caine's murder."

Franklin's expression became even more pensive while he considered that possibility. "What do you think *her* name was?"

Madison flattened his mouth as if thoroughly annoyed with himself. "She gave it to me when she first came to the door this morning, but for the life of me, I can't remember what it was she said."

"Just as well," Franklin admitted as he swung up onto the driver's seat. "That way we can't accidentally tell no one who she was." He waited until Madison had settled beside him, sitting ever so erect on the black leather bench, before he admitted the rest of what was on his mind. "I liked her. I hope she don't find more trouble wherever it is she's going."

"I just hope she gets there without fainting and hurting that baby. She has to be in terrible pain — which proves how truly courageous that woman is," Madison said then looked at Franklin. "And as long as we don't tell anyone exactly where it was we took her and at exactly what time she boarded that train, I think she should be safe enough."

"Nobody will hear either fact from these lips," Franklin said and gave the reins a quick snap. He spread his mouth into a wide grin. "Especially since I can't even tell time."

Shortly after Franklin and Madison returned with news that the police should be there within the next few minutes, Karissa sent Franklin back to the telegraph office to wire her brother, John, about the shooting. She also asked Madison to bring up a bottle of red wine to pour over the sofa where Jacque had lain to disguise the dim bloodstains that remained. She and Lizbeth had had a good long cry while they were gone, which had left her feeling much better. She was now ready to take on whatever would happen next.

"My brother should still be in Johnstown trying to

49

negotiate a contract with the men who run Cambria Iron," she explained so Franklin would know where to send the message. "That means it will be at least two hours before he can get back here. Fortunately, the police should have come and gone by then." With her emotions still so raw, and her mind partially numb, she preferred to deal with each problem individually.

"You want me to stop by Mr. John's house on the way back from the telegraph office and tell his wife about the shooting?" Franklin asked as he tucked the message and two more coins into his pocket.

"Don't bother," Karissa answered grimly. She watched while Madison followed through with her orders and splashed red wine on top of the remaining bloodstains. "I doubt Lana would come without John, and even if she did come on without him, she would just get in the way. I'll have enough to worry about as it is."

Which was true. Lana was the type to want the will read and the money distributed before her father-in-law was even in his grave. Fortunately, there were certain provisions in the will that would not allow any money or property to be distributed to the heirs until the executor had all other debts settled, both personal and business. That alone would take several months, for his business interests were considerable. Poor Lana would have to wait until at least the end of summer before she could start spending all that wealth.

Forcing aside such embittered thoughts, Karissa glanced at the clock on the mantel. She wanted to get the police interview over with so she could have time to think more about what had happened. "I wonder what's keeping the police."

As if by having mentioned them she had in some way

50

summoned them, there was a loud knock at the front door, and while Franklin headed off to see to the telegram, Madison escorted three policemen and the city coroner into the study. Karissa joined them a few seconds later. She had already decided not to say anything about having had a visitor that day so she told them only that information she knew would not harm Jacque in any way.

Within half an hour, the police had finished their preliminary investigation, and after taking a quick look around the garden, they were ready to leave.

But because Karissa's mind was not yet ready to latch on to the fact that her beloved father was now gone from her forever, she had listened to very little of what they said, preferring instead to worry about Jacque. She did not want those gunmen taking off in search of the woman who had tried so hard to save her father. She needed to do something that would convince her father's killers that Jacque had also died. That meant having *two* bodies carried out of that house.

At Karissa's request, the coroner waited until the police had left before calling his aides inside to show them where Lawrence's body lay and the easiest route to carry him. She also waited until the coroner's two aides had gone back out to the wagon to gather a stretcher and drape before asking such an important favor of him.

"Samuel," she began, although she had never before called Mr. Alexander by his given name. "You and my father were very good friends, weren't you?"

"Yes, we were," the large man agreed in that same quiet, consoling voice he used whenever there was a death. "Your father was a kind, generous man. I wish there was something we could have done to save him. But he had to have died instantly."

"He did," she agreed, and fought the tight, wavering feeling that had so quickly enveloped her heart. "He was already dead before Madison and I reached him. But that does not mean you can't still do something for him. Or rather for a friend of his."

Samuel looked at her strangely. "And what would that be?"

Without going into detail, Karissa explained that she wanted him to carry two bodies out of that house instead of just one. "All I can tell you is that by doing so, you will be saving the life of a very dear friend."

Because Samuel was such a close friend of Lawrence's and because he trusted Karissa not to suggest such a thing without a sound reason, he did not question the request other than to ask if the second body was supposed to be that of a male or a female. When Karissa told him it was supposed to be the body of a woman, he studied the different carpets in the room then ordered his aides to help him roll the one in front of the fireplace into a tight cylinder. With their help, he positioned the rolled carpet in the center of the stretcher they had just brought. He then used the fire poker to beat it into shape before covering it with the black drape.

Neither aide asked any questions. They merely carried the weighted stretcher to the wagon and set it carefully inside the small cabin. At Samuel's request, Madison then stood near the back to keep the curious away while they returned inside for Lawrence's body.

"Thank you," Karissa said, choking back the emotions that gripped her as she tiptoed to give Samuel an appreciative kiss. "I'll never forget you for this."

"Don't thank me. If it's saving someone's life, then I'm glad to do it. Just remember to send one of your servants around to my office in a day or two to pick up the unidentified female," he told her then watched while the aides lifted the stretcher that carried her father. "And don't worry about my attendants. If anyone questions them about any of this, they will say exactly what I tell them to say—that it isn't any of their business what went on here." He then grinned at the two young men who were pretending not to have overheard any part of the conversation. "Isn't that true, Andy?"

"Yes, sir," the older of the two answered, then slowly returned his smile. "Besides, I wouldn't want anyone knowing that Tony and I spent over ten minutes carrying a dead carpet out of here anyway."

Karissa thanked them, too. "You will both be well rewarded for being so helpful. I'll see to that myself."

Aware it might upset the gunmen's thinking to see her suddenly appear from within the house when she was still supposed to be gone somewhere, Karissa told the men goodbye from within the house. She waited until Madison had returned inside and had securely latched the door before heading to the west end of the house to find Lizbeth and Franklin. She wanted them all to know what she and the coroner had done and why, because she wanted them to help her think of a logical story to tell her brother that would explain why two bodies had been taken from the house instead of just one.

She worried with her bottom lip while she thought more about the problem at hand. She knew several of the neighbors had watched from their houses and would later ask about that second body, possibly in her brother's presence. They had to be ready with a logical answer.

Eventually, the four of them decided on a half-truth. They would admit that a woman who had come by to warn them of the danger had been shot, but would deny ever having gotten her name. That would coincide with Samuel Alexander's plan to claim to have picked up an unidentified female body of average build and average height should there be any inquiries.

"I just hope no one asks the police those same sort of questions since they know nothing about a second body," she told them. "But if they do find out about the second body, I will just pretend to have been too shaken to tell them."

"And we'll state that it wasn't none of our business to mention it," Lizbeth said with a defiant shake of her head.

Franklin and Madison waited until after they had all rehearsed what John would be told before giving Karissa the four names Jacque had wanted her to have.

Karissa then spent the next hour changing out of her bloodied clothes, all the while running those names over and over in her mind. She tried to visualize what they looked like — already hating every one of them.

She started watching for her brother shortly after dark, but it was nearly seven-thirty before he finally walked through the front door, pale and shaken by the news their father had been shot.

It did not really surprise Karissa that Lana was not with him.

"Where is he? At St. Michael's Hospital?" he asked, not bothering to take off his hat or his coat. He stood near the front entrance, looking first at Karissa then at Madison.

Because Karissa had not wanted John to do anything rash during his attempt to return home, she had been careful not to mention in the telegram that the shot had been fatal. But now the time had come to tell him the truth, and although until he had arrived she had been fairly good about keeping her emotions inside, the thought of having to inform her half-brother that their father was dead became too much for her.

Her eyes instantly teared and her whole body trembled when she opened her mouth to speak the dreaded words. But for some reason she could not force them past the painful obstruction that had overtaken her throat.

Aware of her anguish, Madison took it upon himself to speak for her and stepped forward to gain the brother's attention. "Sir, your father is gone."

"I guessed that much," John said, sounding annoyed with Madison for having said something so inane. "He's been shot, for Christ's sake. All I want to know is where they carried him so I can let him know I'm here for him."

Madison stiffened when he realized he would have to be more specific. Although he did not care one whit what John Caine felt at that moment, for the young man was the most selfish and arrogant man he had ever known, his heart ached for the pain Karissa had yet to suffer. "They took him to the undertakers."

"They *what?* But why?" John glowered at him angrily, as if Madison himself had made the decision.

Madison wished the young man would finally grasp what had happened. For Karissa's sake. "Your father is dead, sir."

John stared at him for several seconds before responding. "But even if that's so, why would you let them take him away? Why didn't they leave him here to be with his family? We'll have people wanting to come by and pay their last respects."

Madison looked at Karissa, and when he saw the steady stream of tears gushing down her cheeks, his heart plunged into the pit of his soul. He decided he would also take away the burden of having to lie to her brother. He would tell the lie for her. "They were both shot through the head. That means there could be no family viewing for either of them."

"Either of them?" John frowned with annoyance and pushed his coat front back so he could plant his fists on his hips. Clearly he was not getting the information he wanted quickly enough. "Who else was shot besides Father?"

"A woman who had come here to warn us that Mr. Caine was in danger."

"A woman who *what?*" John's eyes widened until white had completely ringed the dark brown in his eyes. Looking as angry as he was confused, he jerked his hat off and stepped forward, towering a full six inches above Madison. "I think maybe you'd better start at the beginning. Just exactly what happened here today?"

Not easily intimidated by John's anger, Madison gestured toward the parlor. "I think it would be more appropriate if we all sat down for this."

"I don't *want* to sit," he said, sounding very much like a spoiled, frustrated child. "I want to know what happened."

"Please, sir, it has been a very difficult day for your

56

sister. Hearing it all over again will not be easy for her."

John cut an impatient gaze at Karissa then let out an annoyed huff. "All right. We'll sit. Just tell me what happened here and don't forget *anything* or I'll have you out in the street looking for another job by morning."

Madison waited until John and Karissa were both seated before telling him most of what had happened, relating everything but the name of the woman who had come by to warn them and the fact that they had seen her safely off at a train station across town.

"You mean to tell me the dead woman never gave you her name?" John asked, clearly not believing that fact.

"No. She gave me her name," Madison admitted, but then hurried to finish so Karissa would not have to worry long about what else he intended to say. "But for the life of me I cannot remember what that name was. The truth is I was not all that impressed with her appearance therefore I did not bother to retain such information."

John shifted forward on the couch where he sat beside Karissa. His hands were clasped so tightly together they shook while the muscles in his jaw pumped rapidly. "And the police did not find even one clue to indicate who might have murdered them?"

"Several of them looked around outside, but found nothing," Madison answered firmly, knowing that part was the absolute truth.

John stood and marched out of the room, leaving Madison a moment to console a weeping Karissa. When her brother came back ten minutes later, he carried a small lantern in one hand and a metal bullet casing and what looked like a small coin in the other.

"It looks to me like this was clearly the work of the Molly Maguires," he stated as he tossed his evidence onto a nearby table. His voice revealed more annoyance than anger. "And since that particular token can be spent only at the company store in Black Wall, I think it is fairly obvious *that* is where the killers came from. I can't believe the police did not find any of this. It was all lying right out there in plain sight."

"Where?" Karissa asked, thinking it strange that the police had missed such obvious evidence.

"On the other side of the privacy wall, not far from where Madison said you saw one of them squatting in the shadows."

Karissa stared at the metal casing and the miner's token and felt such a sudden surge of ice-cold rage overtake her, she thought she would surely burst. The names *Shawn, Joey, Jack,* and *Thomas* echoed through the back of her brain, making her more determined than ever to find all four of them. She wanted to see them hang for what they had done.

"I think we should hire a detective to find out exactly who did this," she said when that first swell of anger had abated enough to allow her to speak. "Perhaps a Pinkerton man."

John gave a disgusted toss of his hands. "It wouldn't do any good. The last two Pinks that were hired to infiltrate the Maguire stronghold ended up dead within weeks. Those Maguires can spot a Pinkerton man before he even gets off the train — and the Pinkertons happen to be the very best at what they do. There are no detectives more skilled nor more cunning."

"But we have to do something," she complained, curling her hands into hard fists of frustration. Now that the immediate danger had passed, she was consumed with the burning need for justice. "We can't let them get away with having murdered our own father!"

"And we won't," John assured her. "But the best thing we can do is show the police what I found tonight and let them handle this murder however they see fit. They know what they are doing."

Karissa's contempt was obvious. "If they know so much about what they are doing, then why didn't they find that casing and that token when they searched that same area earlier this afternoon?"

"Eventually they would have," John assured her, having regained his composure with amazing swiftness. "And eventually they will find out exactly who is responsible for the murder."

"I still think it wouldn't hurt to hire someone to help matters along."

"It would be foolish for us to spend our money like that. All we would be doing is hiring some poor soul to mark his own death. Could you honestly live with yourself if someone else died because of all this? It's just not rational."

Karissa pressed her hands against her pale cheeks in an attempt to steady her anger. At that moment her thoughts were too muddled to make any decisions, rational or otherwise. "I want those killers caught. I want them to pay for what they did to Father."

"And they will pay," John assured her, and for the first time in Karissa's memory, he touched her cheek. "It might take a little more time than you'd like, but eventually the police *will* uncover the truth. I won't give them a minute of peace until they do."

Chapter Four

"Di'ya hear the latest?" the huge, middle-aged Irishman known by everyone in Schuylkill County as Big Thomas said as soon as his younger friend, Shawn, had sat down at his table after having ordered his first beer. Thomas reached up to rub his whiskered jaw with his roughened hand while he waited for the younger Irishman to answer.

Although Shawn was known to most of the people in the Black Wall mining community as Shawn Mc-Cowan, Thomas Connolly was one of the few men there who knew for a fact that the handsome newcomer's name was Shawn Larsen. Shawn himself had told him that just a few months ago. He had also told him why he had come to such a godforsaken place. He was hiding from the law for two murders he committed back near the end of 'seventy-one, which made perfect sense to Thomas. No outside lawman in his right mind would come to Black Wall in search of anyone Irish, not with the Molly Maguires to protect him.

"You mean about the murders of Lawrence Caine and Clay Jones?" Shawn asked, his Irish accent evident. Leaning back in his chair, he stretched his long legs in front of him, marveling at how good it felt to be in clean clothes after such a long, hard day in the dank, dusty coal mines just north of Black Wall. "I heard about it just a while ago from Charlie McAllister. He was tellin' us about it at supper."

"Aye," Thomas commented then sat forward and cupped his whiskey glass with his large hands. "But have ya heard who is supposed to have done the jobs?"

"No. But don't tell me yet. Let me guess. One of us did the deeds."

"Not exactly." Thinking Thomas must actually know something for a change, Shawn's blue eyes widened with immediate interest. "Then who?"

"*Both* of us. But this time, Joey and Jack are supposed to have been in on the killings, too."

Shawn shook his head, disappointed. He had never heard anything more ludicrous. He turned his attention to the others in the room for a moment. "Ah, but little Joey wouldn't hurt a pestering fly."

"Doesn't matter. His cousin *is* Jack McGeehan and everyone knows wot a bad one Old Jack is," Thomas said with an exaggerated lift of his brow then leaned farther toward him to be sure he had his attention. "Rumor has it he might even be one of *us*."

"Which one? Little Joey or Old Jack?"

"Both."

"Well, at least they finally got *somethin'* right." Shawn reached up to take off his cap then shook out his long dark hair, which was still damp at the ends from his quick bath. He hooked the small-billed cap over the corner of his chair then slumped back again to make himself more comfortable. "But I heard both the murders happened sometime late Monday afternoon. We were all four workin' the mines late Monday afternoon."

"Seems none of the people who matter remember seeing us after about noon," Thomas explained with a shrug of indifference. "Not the pit boss. Not the breaker boss. No one."

"How convenient for them," Shawn responded with little surprise for this was certainly not the first time the pit boss and the breaker boss had suffered such convenient memory losses. "And when is the trial?"

"First they have to gather a lot more evidence against us," Thomas said, and shrugged again as he tossed the last of his whiskey to the back of his throat. He grimaced hard then slowly relaxed his face while the deep, burning sensation trailed his throat.

"They plan to wait that long?" Shawn glanced around to see where the bar maid who had promised to bring a beer to him had gone. Having had to work an extra hour in the mines that day, he had built a powerful thirst. "I wonder what's takin' Laura so long with me beer?"

Because Shawn and so many of the others suspected of being current members of the Molly Maguires were often being blamed for violent acts they did not commit, he was not all that concerned with what Thomas had just told him. He expected little to become of it. "Do ya happen to know who *is* responsible this time?"

Thomas shook his head. "Haven't a clue."

"Well, I'd be interested in knowin' just in case this thing does get out of hand. I really don't care to end up in jail for somethin' I didn't do."

Thomas laughed a deep, throaty laugh. "Ya

wouldn't be there long. They'd hang you soon enough."

"Now that's certainly reassurin'."

Thomas reached forward and patted Shawn soundly on the back. A thick residue of coal dust was exposed as soon as his arm extended past his sleeve cuff because, unlike Shawn who preferred a full bath after work each day, Thomas reserved his bathing for Saturday nights and had washed only his hands and his face before heading to the Lucky Choice for a bowl of stew and a couple of stout whiskeys. "I'll see what I can find out."

"I'd appreciate that," Shawn said, although he fully intended to investigate the slayings himself. He knew that was exactly the sort of information Richard Porterfield had paid him so handsomely to deliver.

Due largely to his beautiful young wife's constant complaints, John arranged to have the family attorney, Martin Michaels, come to the house and read Lawrence's will only a few days after the burial. At Martin's own request, the family, several of the servants, and the nurse who had helped take care of Lawrence during those final months assembled in the front parlor shortly after noon that following Saturday. Although the servants and the nurse took seats at the back of the room, John, Lana, and Karissa sat closer to where Martin stood near the massive fireplace now hidden behind a decorative summer screen. Because the furniture was arranged in a large semicircle, sitting there allowed them to gaze at each other as easily as at the lawyer.

"I'm glad to see that almost everyone who was asked to be here today has come," Martin said after everyone had settled facing him. Martin was a fairly short man with straight brown hair who looked to be about the same age as John. "I realize how painful this will be for all of you, but it is something that has to be done."

Everyone but John and his wife sat rigidly in the scattered chairs with heartfelt tears already glistening in their eyes. John and Lana shared a small sofette only a few feet from Martin and had yet to reveal any emotion.

"I want to start this," Martin said while he glanced at each person briefly, "by reading aloud a letter Lawrence Caine gave me just a few weeks ago because I think it will explain why he made so many changes in his new will."

"His *new* will?" John echoed, clearly surprised. He reached for his wife's delicate hand as if to comfort her against whatever was about to be said. "What new will?"

Martin scanned the room once more to make sure he had everyone's attention before he looked again at John's stricken face. "Not long after your father found out he was dying, he called me here into this very room and asked me to prepare a new will. He knew he had not updated his old will since shortly after his second wife's death, which was well over eight years ago, and there were several changes he wanted made."

"Such as?" John's tone was both accusing and angry.

"Just be patient," Martin said, and extended his palm to prevent further questions. "Let me read the letter first."

Aware they were about to hear her father's own words, Karissa gripped the arms of the medallion-backed chair with both hands. She hoped to find some form of inner strength in the polished wood while Martin Michaels reached into his pocket and removed a long white envelope, sealed with the Caine family seal.

Martin offered a sympathetic smile to those seated around him while he broke the seal and slipped the letter out of the envelope. He then held the pages and the envelope out for clear viewing. "As you can see, the letter is addressed 'To Those I Leave Behind,' and is written in Lawrence Caine's own hand."

Karissa closed her eyes when a vision of her father seated at his desk writing such a painful letter suddenly struck her. She heard Martin clear his throat while papers rattled and knew he was about to begin the actual reading. Although she hated to behave like a coward, she could not bring herself to open her eyes again. At least not yet.

" 'Dear Friends and Family: Before I try to explain why I made so many changes to my will so soon after I was told I was dying, I want it clear that it was not my choice to leave you with everything so disorganized. Knowing how little time there is, I have tried my best to bring as much order to my affairs as possible. You should also know that I battled my impending death every step of the way. It was not something I readily accepted.' "

Karissa continued to keep her eyes pressed closed while she fought the hard, throbbing ache that filled her heart. She already knew that her father had not wanted to die. Like most men, he had hoped to live a long and fruitful life. Long enough to see a gaggle of grandchildren toddling at his feet. Grandchildren she should have provided for him by now, and probably would have if Robert had survived. The pain from that thought caused her to press her eyes more tightly.

Martin paused after that first paragraph just long

enough for Lawrence's first words to sink in then continued with rest of the letter. " 'It was a hopeless battle. There was no way to stop the black mass growing inside my head. I was doomed to this early death. But perhaps it was for the best. Although I can't yet see the how of it, I truly believe that God had to have a good reason for taking me from you when he did.' "

Unable to bear the ache that pressed her heart and knowing she would rather wait and read such a personal letter in private, Karissa purposely blanked out Martin's voice for a moment. But suddenly he read the name *Jacqueline Lawler* and her brown eyes flew open with surprise. He again had her full attention.

" 'I admit I took an immediate liking to the pretty red-haired woman with the large, sad green eyes and down-turned mouth,' " Martin continued, glancing up occasionally. " 'There was just something about her that made me want to draw her under my wing and protect her. That was why I decided to take her away from such unhappiness.

" 'I handed her the two hundred dollars I had in my wallet the day we met so she could leave that tavern and make a more bearable life for herself. To assure she continued to have enough money to live on, so she would never have to work in such a place again, I put her name down to receive a full widow's pension through one of my anthracite mining companies over in Schuylkill County. It was also a way to help keep our eventual love affair a secret — something *she* wanted more than I did because she was certain such a thing would ruin my reputation.' "

Karissa leaned forward, eager to hear more about the relationship between her father and the woman who

66

had tried to save his life. She did not notice the angry scowl that had settled across her brother's rounded face.

" 'I admit I falsified company records so that she could receive the monthly pension by claiming her to have been the wife of one of the men killed in an explosion we'd had just a few months earlier. It was the only way I knew of making sure she would have some money coming in for as long as she lived.' "

Karissa glanced at her brother and noticed how he shifted uncomfortably beside his wife. She wondered if his discomfort was the result of having just learned about his father's secret love affair, or because he knew that widows' pensions no longer existed.

" 'Granted,' " Martin continued to read, " 'the money she's received from her widow's pension has never allowed her to live in any grand style, but when subsidized with the other money and gifts I have given her through the years and with the clothes mending she takes in from time to time, she has managed to live quite well.

" 'But I don't want any of you to think that she has been using me all these years because it was never like that. Jacque truly loves me, every bit as much as I love her. I know this in my heart. She has always put my well-being first. At one point during our time together, I became so fed up with having to sneak around to see her whenever I could, I came right out and demanded that she marry me.' "

"He *what?*" Lana asked and pressed her hand to her pale cheek, clearly shocked by Lawrence's confession. She looked at Martin with rounded blue eyes. "He asked her to *marry* him? He was secretly married to someone who worked in a saloon?"

Martin held up his hand to silence her outburst because the answers were in the sentences that followed. He continued. " 'But Jacque refused. She claimed it would never do for a wealthy industrialist like me to be married to a woman with such a questionable reputation, which was how she saw herself. Although she never did anything other than serve drinks or food while she was a bar maid, most people believe such women to be promiscuous. She did not want me or my family to have to live with that sort of scandal. She said she was happy enough just being my mistress.

" 'But she has always been so much more to me than that, and if Martin was able to contact her and she is in the room while this is being read, I want her to know how very special she was to me. And I want the rest of you to understand that my love for her was never meant to reflect badly on the love I had for either Catherine or Laura, for I truly adored both my wives, too. It's just that after the grief of having lost Catherine finally diminished, I developed certain needs. Needs which Jacque was able to fulfill. But because she would never agree to marry me, she has left herself with no legal claim to anything that is mine. Which was one of the more important reasons I wanted to change my will.

" 'As the will so states, John and Karissa are to purchase the little house in Sun's Wake where Jacque has been living all these years outright and hand her the title free and clear. She would never let me do that for her while I was alive. Surely she will allow me that now that I am dead.

" 'And even though I realize it will not set well with John, I have also provided my dear Jacque with a generous trust fund that should easily see her until her death. I have made Karissa the sole trustee of the fund."

John stiffened visibly but said nothing.

" 'As soon as the trust fund has been activated, Jacque's name can be taken off the widow's pension for she will no longer need that pittance.

" 'There are also a few other provisions and stipulations in the new will that I fear will not set too well with my son; but he has to understand that I have made these changes because I feel they are in everyone's best interest, including his own.' "

By now John had leaned forward on the tiny sofa, his hands curled into hard fists atop his knees while he listened intently to the rest of the letter. Lana, on the other hand, had sunk back, pale as a ghost.

" 'As you all know, on my better days, when I have virtually no pain and I do not have to take all that blasted medication that makes me so sleepy, I have been teaching Karissa about the family businesses. The reason is that I do not have too much faith in John's ability to keep all my many concerns thriving, and I have worked too hard and too long to establish what I have to allow it to be slowly ruined by John's ineptness. Please understand that I love my son dearly and do not fault him for his inabilities, but I do fear he relies too much on the faulty advice of others. That is the reason I've decided to let Karissa have full reign of all my business interests. As it turns out, she has a very sound mind when it comes to such matters.' "

"What?" John finally came off the sofa and turned to face Karissa with an accusing glare. Like his father in his youth, John stood tall and thin with dark hair atop a rounded face that bore large brown eyes — brown eyes

that now looked almost black.

Martin stepped forward and placed a calming hand on John's shoulder only to have it slapped away. "John, your father wanted Karissa to be the one in charge of his businesses after his death, not you. It was not an easy decision for him to make, especially when he realized the sort of difficulties she will face from being a woman in what has always been considered a man's world; but it's a decision he made all the same."

Lana was next to display her outrage as she, too, came off the sofa and turned to face Karissa with an angry glower. The others watched her with wide, cautious eyes, for the beautiful Lana Caine was known for having a very sharp tongue and a very violent temper.

"I don't believe it! That will is a forgery. Why would Lawrence have put John in charge of everything these past few months if he didn't intend for him to stay in charge?" Though she continued to glare fiercely at Karissa, the question was for Martin.

"Because when he placed John in charge several months back, he was still grooming Karissa for the position, still testing her knowledge and her ability to handle stressful situations. He did not make the actual change in his will until a little over a month ago when he was finally convinced she could handle everything."

Karissa sat dumbfounded while Lana stared sharp daggers through her and John stalked back and forth across the width of the room. Finally he came to a halt directly in front of her. His dark eyes narrowed as if accusing her of something treacherous. "Did you know about this?"

"No," she answered quietly, still stunned by the vast power she now wielded. "I knew he planned to change his will to give me a little more say over the businesses, but I had no idea he intended to put me in full charge of everything."

"He has also made you the executrix to his estate," Martin put in, already placing another restraining hand on John's shoulder.

"This can't be happening," Lana said with a wild wave of her hands, clearly as upset as her husband. So upset that even her perfectly shaped blond curls trembled beneath her feathered hat. "This just can't be happening."

"It's not as if your husband is being left out completely," Martin explained quickly, wanting to calm her before she became hysterical. "He will still have a voice concerning certain investments and he will share equally in any annual profits. It's just that he'll have very little control over how most of those profits are made." He looked relieved when a sudden thought occurred to him. "Look at the pleasant side of all this. Now John won't have to work as hard nor as long as his father did. Think of all the time that will give him to spend with you."

Rather than respond to what she obviously felt was a ludicrous remark, Lana lifted her expensive silk skirts and stalked out of the room with her jaw thrust forward. When John started immediately to follow her, Martin called him back. "John, I think you should stay and hear the rest of this. You'll want to know exactly what you will and will not control."

"Right now, I'm more concerned about my wife," he said, and continued out of the room, leaving everyone but Lizbeth sitting with rounded eyes and gaped mouths. Unlike the others, Lizbeth's eyes were narrowed and her mouth was pressed shut as if worried she might say something she would sorely regret later.

Despite the angry interruption, Martin did not lose his composure. Instead he continued with the preempt letter then followed with the official reading of the will.

As Lawrence had indicated in his letter, the bulk of his estate had been left to his children, John and Karissa, although a large trust fund had been established in Jacque's name with monthly endowments to start immediately. In addition, he provided generously for the more loyal members of his house staff, including the nurse, who he felt had taken extraordinary care of him during his worst days.

By the time Martin had finished reading aloud the last of the legal documents he had brought with him, it was clear to everyone that Karissa Caine had been left in charge of almost everything her father had owned. But Karissa did not feel right about taking over her father's vast fortune just yet, and she knew she would *not* feel right about it until his killers had been found and justice served. Even though her father would not have lived much longer and would have been in pain more days than he was not, it was not fair that someone else had taken it upon himself to end that life so abruptly.

Because she had loved her father so dearly, she could not and would not rest until all four men had been caught, tried, convicted, and hanged. Until then, she would let John continue to run Caine Enterprises. She just hoped it would not take long to bring those men to justice for she was also eager to find out exactly how many of Jacque's allegations were true. She wanted to know if John had really allowed the conditions of their coal mines to deteriorate like that. And if he had, had he also allowed other businesses to deteriorate? If so, she would have had her hands full rectifying matters.

But all that would have to wait. For now, her main priority had to be to find her father's killers.

Even if she had to go to Black Wall and hunt them down herself.

Chapter Five

Shawn ran his large hands through his long, thick hair, unable to believe what Charles McAllister had just told him. Big Thomas was dead. Shot through the heart at close range. His body had been found early that morning in one of the breaker houses of the Black Wall Colliery and, of all people, Thomas's best friend, Jack McGeehan, was the one being blamed for the shooting.

What made the incident even more odd, like with the earlier murders of Lawrence Caine and Clay Jones, a bullet casing and a miner's token were found at the scene. Only this time, a button from Jack's favorite jacket was also found curled inside Thomas's left hand.

Now there was talk in town of a lynching because not only was Jack McGeehan being blamed for the death of his best friend, he was also being blamed for having had a hand in the deaths of Lawrence Caine and Clay Jones as well.

Shawn knew Jack had been set up, but wasn't sure what to do about it. He could not admit to having been with Jack in the wee hours of the morning because of where they had been. Still, he knew *something* had to be done to save him. He could not knowingly allow an innocent man to hang for a murder he did not commit.

Afraid Old Jack might not live long enough to have a fair trial, if there was such a thing as a fair trial for a suspected member of the Molly Maguires, Shawn knew he would have to run the risk of his true identity being revealed to the others. If that happened, he chanced losing not only the good standing he now had with the local miners, but his very life as well. Still, he could not let Old Jack be hanged for something he did not do.

With Richard Porterfield still in nearby Pottsville trying to purchase more land in the Shenandoah area — and knowing he would be there only a couple more days before heading back to Pittsburgh — Shawn slipped out of his room as soon as darkness fell. Taking a little used path over the mountain, he headed immediately for the neighboring town, determined to find some way to have a word alone with the man.

Because Pottsville was a fairly large town for that area and Shawn was not known there by any of his three names, he went directly to the hotel desk where he knew the wealthy industrialist who had hired him usually stayed and asked for his room number. He thanked the clerk who saw no reason to withhold the information then went directly upstairs. When no one answered his knock, he quietly picked the lock and waited for Porterfield inside the elegantly furnished hotel suite.

Knowing it could be hours before his employer returned, he removed his coat and cap then made himself comfortable in a small tufted sofa in the far corner of the room. He chose the sofa over the sturdier-looking lounging chairs simply because it stood where he could more easily watch the door.

Shortly before midnight, Richard Porterfield entered the darkened room and quickly lit the lamp closest to the entrance. He did not seem too surprised when he glanced up and saw Shawn Madden lounging in the shadows but he did hurriedly close the door.

"What do you want?" Porterfield asked as soon as he had checked the windows to be certain the private investigator he had hired to infiltrate the Molly Maguires could not be spotted from the building across the street. It would not do for anyone to see a man who was supposed to be a resistant coal miner talking amiably with the owner of one of the largest mining operations in the whole anthracite region. "It's a little early for you to be reporting in, isn't it? We aren't scheduled to meet until June sixth."

"There's a problem," Shawn answered, having shed his Irish brogue as easily as he had shed his coat. Although he was indeed part Irish and could mimic his Irish grandmother flawlessly whenever there was a need, he had grown up in New York and carried more of a clipped Northern accent when talking casually. "One I thought you should know about."

"Oh?" Porterfield tugged out of his dinner coat and tossed it over a nearby chair then smoothed his short, thinning black hair with his hand before reaching to loosen his necktie. Unlike Shawn, who was tall, muscular, and blessed with a thick head of dark hair, Richard Porterfield was short, soft, and balding. He was also extremely wealthy, which made his physical shortcomings more bearable. "What sort of problem?"

"An innocent man is in jail for the murder of Big Thomas Connolly. And the way some of the locals are talking, if he doesn't get out of there soon, he won't live long enough to stand trial."

"And is this innocent man a member of the Molly Maguires?" Porterfield asked, already heading for the cabinet across the room, where he had stashed an expensive bottle of whiskey.

"Yes, but the fact that he is a member of the Mollies has very little to do with this, except that maybe it explains why he was the one framed."

"Framed?"

"Yes. Someone shot Thomas Connolly through the heart with a rifle at very close range then purposely tried to make it look like his own best friend had pulled the trigger."

"And what makes you so certain he didn't?" Having extracted the bottle, he held it out to Shawn as if to offer him a drink.

Too tired to bother, Shawn shook his head. He continued his explanation from his seated position on the sofa. "There are three reasons I know he didn't do it. The first is that Irishmen don't kill other Irishmen unless there is a very strong reason for doing so. Second, had Jack ever brought a gun close enough to Big Tom for Tom to have yanked a button right off his jacket, he would not have lived long enough to pull the trigger. Big Tom got the name 'Big' because it fit. He was a huge, brawny man with arms like steel. And while Old Jack isn't exactly what *I'd* call old, he is a small man. Probably weighs twenty pounds less than I do. And thirdly, and most importantly, *I* was with Jack most of the night."

"You were? Why?"

"Because I needed a little help breaking into the

Caine offices. I had hoped to find something, anything, that might offer a clue as to who really killed the owner, Lawrence Caine, and his superintendent, Clay Jones, late last Monday. Jack and I were together until nearly dawn. And according to what the breaker boss said right after he'd found the body about six o'clock, Thomas had been dead long enough to have gone stiff and for all the blood to have dried."

"You broke into the Caine offices?" Porterfield wanted to know, the half-filled bottle poised several inches above his glass. Clearly he found that topic far more important than the guilt or innocence of a known member of the Molly Maguires. "Did you find anything that indicated who might have killed Lawrence Caine?"

"No, but that's not why I am here. I am here because Jack McGeehan is being blamed for something he did not do and could very well lose his life because of it," Shawn said, angry at Porterfield's obvious indifference to the man's situation. "It's bad enough that my own name has been linked to the murders of both Caine and that miserly superintendent of his, but at least I haven't been thrown in jail like Jack has."

"*You?* Linked to Lawrence's murder? Why?"

Shawn looked at him, puzzled. "You haven't heard about that?"

"No. What does Lawrence's murder have to do with you?"

"Nothing, actually. But someone is trying to make it look like three others and myself are the ones responsible for both deaths."

"Is it possible the others *were* involved?"

78

"No. We were all down in the mines the day those killings took place."

Porterfield frowned while he splashed an ample amount of liquor into his glass. "Then why do they blame you?"

Shawn sighed with annoyance. That was not what he had come to discuss. "Because we are all four suspected of belonging to the Molly Maguires. My guess is that the authorities have no idea who committed those two murders and someone decided to take advantage of that fact by pinning them both on us. That sort of thing happens all the time."

Porterfield lifted first his eyebrows then his glass. "Oh? And I suppose now you are planning to convince me that the Molly Maguires are actually innocent of all crimes held against them."

"No," Shawn answered, clearly irritated. "Of certain crimes, they are as guilty as Adam was of eating that apple. But more times than not, they really *are* innocent."

"Then focus on those crimes you can prove," Porterfield said. His expression turned rock hard. "Gather the sort of good, solid evidence I'll need to expose them for the ruthless murderers and cutthroats they really are."

"That is exactly what I have been doing," Shawn reminded him, though he did not know why he should have to.

"No," he retorted then gulped the small glass of whiskey down in two successive swallows. "It sounds to me like you are focusing on crimes you *can't* prove. Ones you don't even think those men committed."

"You're angry because I broke into the Caine offices?" Shawn asked, thinking him unfair. "All I wanted to do was find out who is trying so hard to have me thrown in jail. I want to know who is behind all the false accusations that have been going around lately because those people deserve to be in jail every bit as much as the Mollies do. Bearing false witness is still a crime, you know."

Porterfield's eyes narrowed with glowering resentment. "There is a much stronger need here than finding out who has accused you and that is to find out who was behind the murders themselves." His nostrils flared with growing anger. "The Mollies have gone too far this time. No longer are just the pit bosses, the colliery superintendents, and the Pinkerton men being killed or maimed, the Mollies have now started in murdering the owners themselves. Why, *I* could very well be next."

"I'm not so sure the Mollies were involved with Caine's murder at all."

"And I think they were," Porterfield shot back, clearly outraged by Shawn's response. "Who else would want to see him dead?" He paused to take a deep breath but it did nothing to calm his anger. "Lawrence Caine was a friend of mine and I want to know the name of every man, woman, or child who was involved in his murder. I then want you to gather enough evidence to convict every last one of them."

"That will take time," Shawn said, already wondering just how he should go about it, especially when he did not believe the Mollies themselves were involved. The best place to start would be to find out who other than the authorities were asking the most questions about the two incidents. The guilty parties would want to know just how close the police were to honing in on them.

"Fine," Porterfield retorted, and set his glass down but without actually releasing it. "Take whatever time you need to do the job right. Get the evidence I need to convict whoever killed Lawrence and I will pay you double what you've already asked." His voice deepened when he then added, "But fail me on this, Madden, and I just might let it slip who you really are. If the Mollies ever found out that you are really some big-city private investigator hired to expose them for what they really are, you wouldn't live to see another day."

The lines in Shawn's face hardened.

"Porterfield, threaten me like that again and I don't care how worthwhile your cause is or how much more you plan to pay me, I'll head straight back to New York with the information I already have tucked neatly under my arm," he said, leveling his blue gaze at him as he stood to leave. The muscles in his upper arms and cheeks pumped in and out, exposing a carefully controlled anger.

Porterfield swallowed hard when he realized the mistake he'd made. "Don't do that. I apologize for having behaved so childishly just then. It's just that I've been terrified ever since I found out that Lawrence Caine was murdered in his own home. It is very possible I could be next on the list."

"If you think someone might want to kill you, too, then I suggest you hire yourself a body guard."

"I already have," he answered, then let out a quick breath, relieved Shawn had let his foolish threat to abandon him pass that easily. "Three, in fact. One of them is sitting outside my door right this very moment."

Shawn glanced toward the closed door that led out into the main hall.

"Is he now?" he said, picking up his Irish brogue again as he slipped back into his heavy work coat and cap. "Then I guess I'd best be makin' my tracks through that window there and across the narrow ledge."

Feeling the sudden need for another drink, Porterfield bent forward to refill his glass. When he looked up again, he was alone.

It had been only a week since her father's funeral, but already Karissa had pulled herself together enough to have formed two main objectives, neither of which had to do with her taking her rightful place as head of Caine Enterprises. That would come in due time, but she had other more important matters to settle first.

She was as determined as ever to find out who was responsible for her father's death and see that everyone involved was properly punished, but she also wanted to find out where Jacque had gone. She wanted to be sure that the woman who had spent so many years making her father that happy received every penny of inheritance that was rightfully hers.

Accomplishing those two main objectives was all Karissa could think about. All she wanted to think about. And they were what were on her mind when Lizbeth found her standing in the back hallway staring absently through the large French doors that opened out into the area of the terrace where her father had been so brutally murdered.

The bloodstains were gone now, washed away by a violent thunderstorm that following morning. But the

82

painful memories remained. And probably always would.

"Missy, I realize you must be hurting somethin' fierce, but you got to try to pull yourself out of that sorrow," Lizbeth said, standing only a few feet away. "Your father wouldn't want you looking so sad all the time. He adored your pretty smile too much for that. It would break his heart to see you pining away like you are. You've got to stop dwelling on the injustices of the past and get on with the future."

Startled by the unexpected voice, Karissa spun around to face her longtime friend and confidant. Although she was no longer crying at that particular moment, her long dark eyelashes were still damp from the tears she had shed earlier. "I can't help it. I just can't stop thinking about what happened that day. It was so horrible and so unfair."

Her pain and anger grew stronger with each word she spoke. "I realize Father was already dying from that giant tumor and was in pain more days than not, but there was still so much left for him to do. So much for him to teach me. So very much for us to share."

Looking away, her dark eyes filled with yet more tears, making it hard for her to see. "What really hurts is knowing that had Father not been murdered like that, he would have been told that Jacque Lawler is carrying his child. Oh, how he would have loved knowing about the baby." Again, she looked at Lizbeth, her eyes glittering with so many regrets. "You did know that, didn't you? That the woman who came here was carrying his child."

Lizbeth nodded as she slipped a supportive arm around Karissa's shoulders. "I overheard you say something about how that baby was to be your half-brother or half-sister." She took in a deep breath to keep from being overcome by her own deep remorse. She tried to endure the pain as best she could because she knew Karissa needed her to be strong now more than ever. "But I ain't told no one about none of what I heard that day. Not even Franklin."

"I don't think it would matter much now if you had told anyone about it. Father pretty much eliminated any real need for secrecy when he wrote that open letter in which he announced both the affair and her name." Karissa's jaw quivered at the thought of how very much her father must have loved Jacque. Enough to have risked his family's scorn by revealing the truth to them.

"Still I thought it wise not to talk about it," Lizbeth said. "Not when those same men might still be out there looking for her. As far as I'm concerned, we never met her."

"You're right. We did promise that no one would know she was ever here. And that's one promise I fully intend to keep. Anyone who loved my father as much as she did deserves my loyalty." She pressed her eyes closed to clear her vision. "I just wish I had known about her sooner. I would have loved to have seen the two of them together."

"I saw your brother leave a little while ago," Lizbeth said, changing the subject abruptly before she, too, started to cry. "It's pretty early in the day for him to be out visiting, isn't it? What did he want with you?"

In most homes it would have been considered inappropriate for a house servant to ask such personal questions of the house mistress, but Lizbeth was more like family. She had been an important part of the Caine household since long before Karissa was born. That was why after Karissa's mother's death eight and a half years earlier, it was Lizbeth that Karissa had turned to whenever she needed the warmth and strength of a woman's shoulder. Karissa knew she could confide anything to Lizbeth and it would go no further. She was the type of friend who would take whatever secrets had been told her to her grave.

"John came by here for two reasons," she answered, and with a little coaxing from Lizbeth, stepped away from the door. Together they headed toward the front of the house. "He wanted to see how I was faring, but he also wanted me to know that he has everything at Caine Enterprises under control so I wouldn't worry."

"That was nice of him," Lizbeth said, though her dark, glowering expression revealed obvious distrust. "And did he ask when you planned to take over your father's companies?"

"He knows I'm not ready for that yet. He knows I'm still hurting too much to give such matters my undivided attention."

"You're hurting so much because you hardly ever leave this house." Lizbeth pointed out the obvious. "You've been keeping yourself locked away with all his things and won't even let any of your friends pay call on you. You can't keep yourself holed up like this. You have to get away from this house and do things that might help take your mind off your pain."

For the first time in days, Karissa smiled, aware Lizbeth had only her best interests at heart. She stopped just outside the door to the main parlor but did not bother to pull away from her. "John said almost that same thing."

"You mean for once he and I agree on something?" Lizbeth looked appalled.

"It certainly seems that way. Just a little while ago, he suggested that I go away for a few weeks and try to get my mind off what happened. He suggested I take a train up to Cresson and let those hot baths soothe away my troubles like they did when I was a young girl. I guess he didn't realize how painful going to that place would be for me."

Cresson was the resort where Karrisa and her father had gone every spring when he wanted to get away for a few weeks. Lizbeth studied Karissa's sad smile and nodded that she understood the younger woman's feelings.

"To go there now, without Father," Karrisa continued, "would be no different than staying right here in this house. I'd see him everywhere I went and in everything I did while I was there."

"Then maybe you could think of somewhere different to go. Somewhere you never been before. Maybe you could go to Europe. Maybe to that Paris place Missus Lana is always talking about."

"I had somewhere a little closer in mind."

"Then you are thinking about taking a little trip."

Karissa studied Lizbeth's questioning expression for a moment, then decided to tell her the truth. "Will you swear yourself to secrecy?"

Lizbeth's right eyebrow shot up like it always did whenever she suspected that Karissa was up to no good. "Why? What you got up that pretty little sleeve of yours?"

Karissa held up a cautionary finger. "Swear to secrecy first."

Scowling, Lizbeth pushed against her lower lip with her tongue while she thought about an answer. "I don't know if I should do that. The last time you swore me to secrecy like that, you then up and told me about some foolish plan to go with two friends to see that vulgar play down by the riverfront. Can you imagine what I went through knowing you were down there walking around with all those thieves and cutthroats, but not able to tell so I could have someone look out for you? Why, I was worried half to death."

Karissa laughed, remembering that she, too, had worried half to death after they had arrived and she saw just how rowdy a place it was. If she'd had any sense in her then eighteen-year-old head, she would have told Sheila's driver to take them right back home. But Sheila and Veronica had dared her and she had not wanted her two best friends to think her a coward.

"Do you swear to secrecy or not?"

"Only if you can promise me that this secret of yours is not going to worry me like that last one did."

Karissa shook her head. "I can't do that because this one will probably worry you even more."

Lizbeth closed her eyes and let out such a hard, frustrated breath, it ballooned her cheeks. "Now I'll worry more if you don't tell me."

"Then do you swear to secrecy? Do you promise not to tell a single soul what I am about to tell you?"

"Who would I tell? I certainly can't tell your father an I'm in no disposition to say anything to that half-brother of yours."

"Do you *swear?*" Karissa was taking no chances.

Lizbeth tapped her slippered foot a moment, causing the hem of her heavy black skirts to dance with lively animation, then finally tossed up her arms. "Okay. I swear. I won't tell a soul. Now what is this big secret of yours and just how much sleep do you suppose I'll lose because of it?"

Karissa bent low so that she could better view Lizbeth's face, wanting to know her honest reaction. "I've decided to go to Black Wall to see if I can find out who it was that killed Father."

"You *what?*" Lizbeth's eyes stretched to their limits.

"I'm going to Black Wall to find Father's killers. Black Wall is a small mining town up around Pottsville and I have a very good reason to believe that I'll find the men who murdered him there. But what I plan to do is tell everyone else I'm headed for Cresson. It is something I have already decided."

"But you can't do that. It's too dangerous. You'll get yourself killed," Lizbeth said, her words coming in a rush. Her dark forehead furrowed deep. "I know all about that Black Wall. It is one of those throwed-together mining towns that's filled with the roughest sort of men. Why, those men would eat you alive then spit out your bones like they was nothing but a olive pit."

Karissa refused to be swayed. "I am a Caine," she said with a proud lift of her chin. "And because I am a Caine, I have to find out who killed Father." She thought Lizbeth of all people should understand. Karissa had come from a family of doers. A family that did not wait around to see what fate held in store. The Caines had always shaped their own destiny and never accepted any malice or injustice. Her father had been like that and she was like that. Which was probably why he had left her in charge instead of John. He knew she would do whatever it took to keep his interests alive, and do it with pride and integrity.

"And it's not as if I'm planning to go there alone," she continued, hoping to calm Lizbeth yet. "Like Father, I know when to handle matters by myself and when to solicit someone else's help. You'll be glad to know that I've hired a professional private investigator to help in this. That's where I went last Thursday. To meet with several investigators I'd asked Martin Michaels to call together for me. *None* of which were Pinkerton men."

Lizbeth's brow furrowed deeper. "But why not a Pinkerton man? I thought they was supposed to be the best."

"Because I have checked into something John said to me and found that he was absolutely correct. Two Pinkerton agents were recently killed while making separate attempts to infiltrate a secret labor group in that area, a group called the Molly Maguires. That's why I think that the Molly Maguires must have an informant working right inside the Pinkerton Agency. Either that or they have an uncanny ability of spotting a Pinkerton man just by his appearance or perhaps it's his behavior that gives him away. That's why I've hired an older man from New York who had impeccable references but has never been involved with the Pinkerton Agency. I won't bother you with his name, but I can assure you that he will be in Black Wall watching over me and helping me the entire time I am there."

"But why can't you just let the police handle this? Mister John said it's just a matter of time before they will have whoever shot your father arrested and in jail."

"I don't happen to have the same faith in their abilities as John does. Father has taught me to be a pretty

89

good judge of character, and when I talk with them, they just don't seem all that interested in finding out who pulled the trigger. Too many other police matters are always getting in their way."

"But why can't you just send that investigator in there alone to see what he can find out about those men? Why do you think you have to go there, too?"

"Because they are not as likely to suspect a woman of being a spy."

"Not even if that woman is obviously very refined and wealthy — and her last name happens to be Caine?"

"I'm not going there dressed like this and I am not foolish enough to use my real name. I have decided to use my mother's maiden name and pretend I've gone there looking for work."

"But why would anyone go to such a godforsaken place looking for work, especially a pretty young woman like you?"

"I will tell them that my father was a miner so I grew up around the mines and therefore that is the only life I know. And to convince them my name is Catherine Sobey, I will wear the inscribed locket Father gave Mother when they first met and I'll carry letters that were written to her before she was married but with the dates rubbed out."

"It's still too dangerous."

"I don't care." Karissa met Lizbeth's frightened gaze with one of firm resolve. "I have to know who killed my father. I won't be able to live with myself until those people have been located, tried, and found guilty."

"And there's no way I can talk you out of doing such a foolish thing?"

Karissa tilted her head while she continued to meet

her friend's concerned gaze. "What do you think?"

Lizbeth looked as ready to burst into tears as she was to throttle her. "What do I think? I think you are too much like your father, which is why you went to that fancy women's college for nearly two years instead of settling down and getting married like most women that age do. *And* I think there is a good chance that you won't come back from that mining town alive. I've heard plenty of stories about those Molly Maguires and they don't care who they kill or how. If they decide someone has crossed them, then that person is the same as dead."

"I realize the danger. Even to a woman."

"Especially to a woman," Lizbeth corrected. "If they ever suspect the real reason you are there, you are as good as in your grave. They protect their own in anyway they can"

"I am taking Father's derringer and will keep it in my boot at all times," she said, hoping that might reassure her.

"A derringer which I'm sure you don't know how to shoot," Lizbeth retorted with a willful thrust of her chin. "Better that you take your mother's Bible than your father's derringer."

Karissa's eyes brightened. "That's an excellent idea. I'll take Mother's Bible, too. It has her maiden name embossed on the front in gilt lettering. They'll surely believe my name is Catherine Sobey if I keep that Bible lying about."

Lizbeth shook her head, aware her message was not getting through. "Where you planning to stay? Your father has no apartment there like he does some places."

91

"I won't know that until I arrive. I doubt there are any hotels in a town that small. I'll stay in a rooming house, I suppose. I'll have to let you know."

"Then you do plan to keep me informed?"

"As best I can. Just you remember to keep your promise. Not a word to *anyone* about where I've really gone. Not even Franklin."

"But what about Mister John? Won't he have to know?"

"No!" she answered quickly. Her expression hardened at the thought. John was still strongly against the hiring of an investigator and would do everything he could to stop her from meddling in what he clearly considered a police matter. Her brother had always had possessed an incredible knack of trusting the wrong people.

Aware of how sharply she had bitten out that last response and knowing Lizbeth did not deserve such hurtful treatment, she quickly continued in a more friendly tone, "You know John. He won't really care where I've gone or for how long, just as long as I'm not here to bother him. He's angry enough that I've taken away his power to sell anything that belongs to Caine Enterprises. He's certainly not looking forward to having to hand over the rest of his duties to me and knows that the longer I'm off somewhere trying to heal my wounds, the longer he remains in charge of things. Right now, that's all that matters to him. That and finishing that big house for Lana by her birthday."

"That's true. All that young man has ever cared about is himself and that prissy little wife of his," Lizbeth agreed. Her face burrowed into a dark, mahogany scowl. "I never have liked that half-brother of yours.

92

You and Mister John are as different as night and day — both inside and out."

"I'll take that as a compliment," Karissa said with a laugh, feeling much better now that she had told Lizbeth of her plans. She already knew what Lizbeth thought of her brother. "Oh, and I have also hired a second investigator from Philadelphia to try to locate Jacque Lawler. But that, too, is to be kept a secret until the men responsible for Father's death are finally in jail. I don't want them finding out where she is, or even that she is still alive."

"But how's the second investigator going to know where to find you to tell you if he does locate Miss Lawler if you're off in Black Wall pretending to be someone you're not?"

"He's to send any information he uncovers in the form of a letter to a special mailbox I've rented, which I'll check after I return."

"*If* you return," Lizbeth muttered with a snort then abruptly turned to leave. She knew that nothing she said would change Karissa's mind. The girl was too much like her father.

Chapter Six

After a perilous five-hour ride through the lower Allegheny Mountains and an hour and a half ascent up the side of a large, craggy mountain, Karissa was relieved to hear the conductor announce that Black Wall would be the next stop. The sooner she set her feet on firm ground again, the better.

But that eagerness to gather her belongings and get off that clattering excuse of a train proved short-lived. When she glanced out the window and caught her first glimpse of the small mining community, an eerie feeling crept over her.

Black Wall was not at all what Karissa had thought it would be. Nor was the Lucky Choice Tavern, where she intended to ask for work. The tumbledown building looked as if it had been built from odds and ends acquired from the local trash dump. Nor was the land itself what she had expected. The lush green scenery she had enjoyed earlier in the day had at some point turned ugly and black. The whole valley looked charred and sooted. Even the dirt that packed the streets was a dark, dingy black.

When the train shifted its weight forward as it squealed to a slow, jerking stop, Karissa lifted her gaze from the land itself and what few pathetic buildings she could see through her tiny window, and noticed that the even sky was filled with a black, powdery haze that looked as if it had drifted down from somewhere higher in the valley.

She shook her head with disgust and brought her gaze back down to that bleak patch of land that stood behind the train station. The tall trees and thick underbrush that jutted out of the steep mountainsides had been touched by so much black and gray that there was little distinction between the vegetation and the ground itself. Even the tiny stream that snaked across the narrow valley just a few yards north of the tracks looked a dark, murky gray.

"What a miserable place to live," Karissa muttered softly as she reached for her handbag and prepared to disembark. If it was not for her unbending resolve to discover who her father's killers were and have them brought to justice, she might have had paid more attention to the second thoughts she had about stepping off that train.

"You'll find your trunk over there, miss," the conductor said as soon as she had neared the door. He pointed through the windows to several trunks and valises that had been carelessly scattered across a platform only a few yards away. He then abruptly turned to speak to someone who stood directly behind her and left her to step down out of the train unassisted.

Karissa was unaccustomed to such rudeness. Until now she had always traveled in the best coaches and had always dressed in the sort of clothing that let a workman know a handsome tip would be forthcoming. She pressed her lips together to hold back an angry retort.

Knowing why the man had behaved so abruptly toward her, she glanced down at the simple dress she wore. It was one of four she had bought in a small secondhand shop on Market Street. Although the garment was a bit threadbare in places, it was made of a durable pink cloth and fit her curves nicely. It was also clean and freshly mended, thanks to Lizbeth. And to her amazement, the simple garment felt far more comfortable than the elaborate silk or velvet gowns she usually wore.

Spying her trunk—or rather Lizbeth's trunk—for her own had been far too large and had looked far too expensive—she glanced around for a steward and realized there were none. Nor was there a ticket agent in the ticket booth. The offices looked deserted.

Finally, she spotted a tall, heavyset man who stood nearby. Because he looked like a local, she asked how a woman was expected to transport that heavy trunk to one of the town's rooming houses if there were no railroad employees around to assist and was told that for a dollar he would carry it for her.

Karissa's mouth gaped at such an outrageous amount, but seeing that there was no one else around other than the few people preparing to board the train, she reluctantly agreed. Still, she made it a point to complain loudly about his price so he would not think she carried much money. The idea was to appear in desperate need of employment.

Giving a tired grunt, the tall, burly man with well-worn clothing and large dirty wrists slung her trunk up onto his back. Gruffly, he announced that his name was Charles McAllister then headed immediately toward town, leaving her to follow.

"Which of the roomin' houses y'headed for?" he asked, displaying in even a stronger Irish accent than Jacque had used. He stopped in the middle of the street to await her answer.

"I-I'm not sure. I just arrived in town." She glanced off toward the main part of town with a troubled expression. "Which one do you recommend?"

"For a pretty little lass like y'self? I'd suggest y' stay at Mrs. Waylan's," he said with sudden enthusiasm. "She's far more likely to keep the miners from troublin' ya than some of the others might. Besides, I happen to know for a fact that she has a room available. I was there visitin' just a while ago."

"Then Mrs. Waylan's it is," Karissa said, then continued to follow him through the small dank town, if it could be called a town. She frowned when she realized her father would have researched any new place before coming. She should have done the same.

While walking along behind the large man, trying to keep up with his long, purposeful strides, she studied the pitiful collection of buildings that looked as if they had been dropped helter-skelter across the rugged terrain.

As it turned out, Black Wall consisted of a train depot, a company store, a leather shop, a feed store, several large rooming houses that also served as hotels, six rickety-looking taverns, two restaurants, a

97

laundry, two churches, one jail, and a livery stable. As for the homes, there were a few nicer dwellings clumped near the outskirts of the town that looked as if someone at least tried to keep them washed, and beyond that were half a dozen crooked rows of smoke-stained company houses that clung precariously to the jagged hillsides. Each had a tiny yard with a tiny garden. But oddly enough, though it was still midafternoon, there were no people in those yards.

If it were not for the constant chugging and clanking that came from the coal mines a mile or so up the mountain, a few open doors in front of some of the houses, and a half-dozen strings of laundry here and there, she would have thought the place deserted.

Other than the tall, burly Charles McAllister who helped her, the only other people she saw while walking along the narrow muddy street that ran parallel to the railroad track were a gaunt-faced old man wearing rags for clothes and torn leather for shoes and an overweight shopkeeper busily sweeping the boardwalk in front of the company store.

"Where is everyone?"

"This time of day?" He looked back at her with a raised eyebrow, as if she had asked a very foolish question. "Most of the menfolk are still down inside the mines and the womenfolk, what few there are of them, are all inside their houses gettin' a bit of supper ready for their men. I'd be in the mines myself if I hadn't been fired again yesterday afternoon."

He scowled and looked forward again. "But don't go thinkin' we're a ghost town just because ya don't see many people out and about right now. About six

98

o'clock, when most of the men start comin' out of the mines, this town will suddenly spring to life again."

"But what about the children? Where are they?" she asked, still wondering why there was hardly anyone outside. At this hour, the children should be out of school and playing children's games in their yards.

Again he looked at her strangely. "Most of those over nine work in the breakers. Especially if they are lads. Those under nine are home helping their mothers."

"Working in the breakers?" she asked, clearly surprised. "But what about school?" Even before he answered, she realized that the one building she had not seen in town was a school house.

"They learn at home from their mothers," he said. "And on Sundays from the priest or the preacher—dependin' on which church they be goin' to."

Rather than ask any more questions that might seem odd, especially from someone who wanted everyone to believe she had grown up in the mining camps like this one, Karissa kept her mouth shut during the last of the walk to Mrs. Waylan's rooming house. She decided there would be time enough to learn about her strange surroundings later. For now, she needed to concentrate on finding a suitable room. Then she would have to focus on heading over to the Lucky Choice to ask the owner for a job.

As was planned, Frank Neely had arrived a day earlier and had already found himself a room. Fortunately his room had ended up being in the same rooming house where Karissa and Charles McAllister were now headed.

Karissa felt a strong sense of relief when she spotted him sitting on the front porch, dressed in bright plaid trousers and a gaudy yellow vest, and smoking a fat cigar.

"Mr. McAllister, why is that man not in the mines working?" she asked right after she had caught up with the tall man carrying her trunk and just before they had turned down a small planked walkway that led to one of the largest houses in Black Wall. She wanted him to think she had never seen the older man before. "Has he been fired, too?"

"Him?" McAllister asked, and glanced at Frank only briefly while heading for the stairs that led up to the front porch. "Don't rightly know what his story is. He came into town late yesterday and hasn't bothered to ask about the mines nor about any other form of gainful employment." He then bent low and added in a quieter voice so not to be overheard, "Me guess is that he's a gambler man. We get a lot of those in and out of here this time of year."

"A gambler," she repeated, sounding appalled. "Then I will stay away from him."

"Would be wise," the large man agreed, then paused near the front door and rested the trunk between his hip and the outer wall while he reached up to rake his hand through his thick brown hair several times. He then took a few seconds to adjust his shirt collar and the lapels of his dusty jacket just so before he finally reached for the screen door.

When he noticed the odd look on Karissa's face, he

explained while he watched her step inside. "As y'will soon see, the Widow Waylan is quite a looker for a woman her age and filled with lots of spirit." He grinned, revealing one missing tooth. "Wouldn't mind a woman like that lookin' favorable upon me now and again."

Karissa wanted to laugh when she noticed how very much like an awkward young schoolboy the big strapping man acted when he spoke of the Widow Waylan; but she managed to keep a somber expression.

As soon as they were both inside, McAllister set the heavy trunk on the floor then reached for a tiny bell that sat on a nearby table and shook it loudly. Several seconds later a short, amply built, red-haired woman dressed in a flowing dark green skirt with a pale green blouse appeared from the back of the house.

"And what ya be wantin' now, Charlie McAllister? Isn't it enough that I let ya have that free lunch this afternoon? Have ya come after a free supper, too?"

McAllister lifted his bearded chin as if offended by her remark. "I've brought ya new boarder. She just got off the train not more than ten minutes ago and is in desperate need of a place to stay."

"Oh?" Mrs. Waylan asked, her pretty green gaze going immediately to Karissa. "And just who is this new boarder?"

The tall man blinked several times while he tried to remember a name then frowned. "I don't rightly know what her name is." He then turned to Karissa expectantly. "But I'm sure she has one."

"My name is Catherine Sobey," Karissa said to Mrs. Waylan then offered a polite curtsy thinking it might

101

be expected of her. "And your friend is right. I am in desperate need of a room."

"My *friend?*" Mrs. Waylan retorted, looking at Charles with a meaningfully raised brow. "I never claimed this man to be a friend of mine."

Charles laughed then nudged Karissa with his elbow. "Didn't I tell ya? Lots of spirit she has."

"Well, at least I don't go gettin' my spirit from a tall pitcher of beer like some people I know," she quickly shot back. Her green eyes sparkled with merriment beneath sharply raised eyebrows while she extended an arm to Karissa. "Come, Catherine, let me show ya to yer room."

Aware he was about to be dismissed and not yet ready to leave, Charles quickly called attention to the trunk. "Don't y'want someone to carry that thing for ya?"

Mrs. Waylan tilted her head while she thought about that. "I suppose it would be a good idea at that. And since the only room I have left is that one that used to be me attic, that's where ya can carry it if y've a mind to."

Still fighting a strong urge to smile at the way the two carried on in each other's company, Karissa followed Mrs. Waylan up two flights of stairs until she had been led into a small room with a low, slanted ceiling and only two windows. One window looked out onto the street and the other was directly over the door. Inside there was one small bed, a three-drawer dresser with a small pitcher and bowl, and one straight-backed chair.

"I realize it is not much, but it is clean and it is all I

have at the moment," Mrs. Waylan said apologetically. "If ye'd come yesterday early, I'd have been able to let ya have one of my nicest rooms, but as it is, a Mr. Miles rented it just last night."

Knowing that Miles was the last name Frank intended to use while they were in Black Wall, Karissa shrugged then smiled. "This will do fine. To tell you the truth, it's a much nicer room than the last one I had."

Mrs. Waylan smiled, obviously relieved. "Then I welcome ya to my humble abode. Because I own this house, I am now yer landlord and the only one ya report to if there is a problem. My full name is Kelly Elaine Waylan, but ya are to call me Kelly. The privy is out back only a few yards from the chicken coop. I also have a special room for bathin' that stands directly behind the kitchen that ya will be free to use almost any day but Saturday because that's when most of my men tenants prefer to make use of it. Until then, they generally make do with a good face and hand washin'."

Karissa blinked with surprise but tried not to look too appalled to learn that most of the men bathed only once a week and that the privy was not right there in the house where it belonged. It was then she realized how very different her life would be during the next few weeks. "How much do I owe you?"

Kelly looked first at Charles then at the scarred wooden floor as if reluctant to answer. "Four dollars a week, but that includes three hot meals a day and two baths a week. Extra baths will cost ya a nickel apiece or an hour of either helpin' out in the kitchen or else

103

washing some of the coal dust off the house. If possible, I'd like the rent money in advance."

Karissa tried to look very chagrined at what Kelly obviously felt was an exorbitant price. She knew that her father usually paid over forty dollars a night whenever they stayed at Cresson, but then this was a far cry from the opulent suites they stayed in while at the luxury resort. Four dollars probably was an outrageous price for a tiny room like this.

"Oh dear, I had no idea it would cost that much." She chewed on her lower lip for effect, wanting them to believe her destitute. "Can I give you three dollars of the rent money now and the rest in a few days? I plan to go out and find work just as soon as I can."

When Charles heard the troubled tone in her voice, he quickly cleared his throat to get her attention. "Go ahead and give her the full amount, lass. Ya don't have to pay me nothin' for haulin' yer trunk for ya. I'd just go spendin' it on a tall pail of beer and to tell ya the truth, I don't need to be drinkin' it."

Karissa looked at him, surprised by his offering. "Why thank you." She then dug deep into her handbag and brought out a small handful of coins that counted out to be exactly four dollars. "But as soon as I find employment, I will still pay you that dollar, Mr. McAllister."

"A *dollar?*" Mrs. Waylan repeated, clearly aggravated. "For carrying one little trunk? *Charlie!*"

Looking dutifully chastised, Charles pulled his head and took a step back. "I never intended to actually collect that much. I just wanted her to realize what a favor I was doin' for her."

As if no longer aware of Karissa's presence, Mrs. Waylan and Charles McAllister walked out of the room, still bickering over the fact that Charles had thought his paltry services worth nearly a full day's wages.

With very little to unpack, Karissa was settled in and ready to head over to the Lucky Choice Tavern a few minutes before five o'clock. Although a little apprehensive about entering such an establishment alone, Frank had convinced her that the tavern would be the likeliest place for them to happen across those four men Jacque had mentioned. She refused to allow the sudden sinking feeling to stop her. After pausing for a moment to gather the needed courage, she walked right in and asked the owner for her very first job.

It felt strange to be asking someone for work. Because Karissa had grown up in such an extremely wealthy family, she had never had to worry about such matters. Nor had it ever been important for her to become all that proficient in any of the usual domestic arts, like sewing, cooking, or mending. Until now, her few real accomplishments in life had included the fact that she had earned very high marks while taking several courses that had interested her at a local woman's college and that she had been touted one of Pittsburgh's most prominent socialites. Neither of which would help her now.

Unaware of how truly unqualified Karissa was for such a job, and after admitting that he was short-handed because one of his women had suddenly up and quit on him just a couple weeks before, Marcus

Wade hired her on the spot.

"You can start right now," he said in a deep voice that displayed a Southern twang. To Karissa it sounded as if he might originally be from Texas but, for whatever reason, had not been there for a while.

He reached immediately for an apron and handed it to her. "The job only pays three dollars a week but you get to keep any gratuities the men give you, which can sometimes add up to quite a lot. Especially on Saturday nights when they are rested up from having worked only half a day."

Relieved that Marcus had not asked her about previous experience, Karissa took the apron and wrapped it around her slender waist. "What hours do I work?"

"Unless business is slow for some reason, you can expect to work from five o'clock until midnight ever'day but Sundays and certain religious holidays," he said. "I'll introduce you to the other two girls who work for me as soon as they get here, which should be any time now. They'll explain which tables will be yours and which are theirs and I'd advise you not to try to take any of their tables away from them even though it will be obvious that theirs hold the spenders. Hang around here long enough and smile pretty enough, and you'll soon have some of those spenders moving over to your tables."

He paused for a moment as if worried about how to word his next statement. "And even though you have the clear advantage of youth, because Laura and Deborah are both in their thirties now and starting to show it, it wouldn't hurt for you to get yourself some fancier clothes and maybe start wearing your hair down over your shoulders instead of up in a knot like that. Men tend to tip better when a woman wears frilly dresses made from bright colors and combs her hair down."

Karissa thanked him for his advice but told him she preferred her hair up and that it would be a while before she could afford new clothes. She wanted him to believe she truly needed this job so he wouldn't later wonder why she had chosen to work in his establishment.

Ten minutes later, when the other two women entered, one dressed in a crimson satin and the other in an emerald green brilliantine, she was again told the same thing about her choice in clothing. She was told that men liked to see a little ankle and preferred to see that flash of ankle beneath bright, cheerful colors. Especially the Irishmen. It would do her well to dress accordingly.

By six o'clock when the first of the coal miners drifted in, most of them still in their work clothes and covered with coal dust, Karissa was pretty well acquainted with what was expected of her. It had all sounded fairly simple. She was to take down the customers' orders, collect the proper amount, go to the bar, and hand Marcus the money and the order. If it was a large order or if Marcus was busy filling other orders, she was not to wait. She was to head on to the next customer then pick up the last order when she brought in another. If the first order had been filled by then, she was to carry it to the customer and serve it and whatever change he had coming with a bold and friendly smile.

That was one thing Marcus stressed. "Even when you are practically choking on their rancid body smells and they are hacking up coal dust in your face, you always give them a bright smile and call them by their first names. These men have had a long, hard day in the mines, and they come in here because they need their spirits lifted."

"That's sure true," Laura put in, having overheard them while waiting for Marcus to fill her first order. Laura was the older of the two women Karissa now worked with, and the quickest to offer advice. "You do what you can to *lift* their spirits at the same time you do what you can to *fill* them with spirits." When Karissa did not immediately laugh, she looked at her to make sure she was listening. "And if you ever over-hear a fight brewing, be sure to let Marcus know."

"Yes. That way he can step in and try to calm them before they start breaking up his furniture," Deborah added, having come up behind them in time to hear what had been said.

Karissa's eyes widened at the thought of being a witness to actual bar fights, but she said nothing to indicate her fear. Instead, she picked up her pad, her pencil, and her cork-lined metal tray then headed off to take care of her very first customer alone, unaware of the unusual amount of attention she had attracted from the men.

Two hours later, while trying desperately to keep her orders straight and the men's hands off various parts of her body, and while trying to catch everyone's name so she could mentally note those who might have been involved with her father's murder, a tall muscular man of obvious importance walked in. A temporary hush fell over the room while several of the others looked up and waited to see where he would sit.

"Hey! Over here," called out a frail young man with curling blond hair. He looked to be not much older than Karissa.

To make certain he had been heard over all the loud talking and laughing, and the constant coughing that went on, he stood up and waved his hands high over his head until he was sure the newcomer had noticed him.

"In a minute," the man called back with a friendly wink then sauntered over to the crowded bar instead. "Marcus," he shouted over the other men's heads. "Hand me a beer and make it swift. I'm as parched as a desert in July."

Karissa noticed how quickly Laura and Deborah had found their way back to the bar. She really could not blame them for their eagerness to talk to the newcomer, for the man was strikingly handsome. He was also freshly bathed and dressed in a pair of clean broadcloth britches and a partially unbuttoned cotton shirt that was fitted against his tall, muscular shape with a pair of black suspenders.

Karissa could hardly help noticing as well that the man was taller than almost everyone else in the room. He was also much leaner through the waist and hips, and had an abundance of dark brown hair that made him look more roguish than the other men. The hair was long enough to touch his unusually broad shoulders and it looked as if it had been freshly washed, for the ends were still damp.

The man also had a pair of the palest blue eyes Karissa had ever seen, eyes so sultry a woman could easily become lost in them. And even though he looked to be several years younger than either Laura or Deborah, Karissa certainly understood the women's obvious interests in him and did not fault them for flocking to him like mindless geese.

"Miss? My beer?" she heard one of her customers call to her, breaking her concentration. Obviously he was ready for her to turn in his order.

"Yes, sir. Right away, sir."

For reasons she could not quite understand, her heart fluttered and leaped when she realized she would have to go to the bar to turn in that order. Though she had no idea why she would want him to, for he was certainly not her type man, she wondered if the handsome stranger would speak to her while she was there. Or if, like so many of the other men, he might try to touch her. For some reason she did not find the thought of his touching her quite as repugnant as she should.

While trying to avoid as many strayed hands as possible, she kept her gaze on the handsome newcomer and carefully maneuvered her way across the crowded room.

She was fascinated by the man's easy movements while he casually worked through the boisterous group of men near the far end of the bar then rested his black boot on the footrail. With his knee slightly bent, he leaned forward on one muscular leg and said something of a jovial nature to Marcus, who immediately cocked his head back and roared with laughter.

While continuing to stare at the powerful lines of the newcomer's body—although most of the men in the room were powerfully built considering the work they did—Karissa found it increasingly difficult to catch her breath. At first she attributed the sudden feeling of breathlessness to the growing stench of tobacco smoke and unwashed bodies. But deep down, she knew better. She had managed to breathe just fine before that tall, rugged man with the pale blue eyes and long dark eyelashes had strolled in.

Problem was, she was not used to being around anyone of such apparent strength, and she certainly was not used to being around anyone quite that openly attractive. Judging by the way his gaze met everyone else's and by the confident manner in which he carried himself, she realized that here was a man of purpose. He was one who knew what he wanted and went after it with no qualms.

The muscles at the base of Karissa's throat tightened at the thought of being near such a man, which caused her blood to stir fast and hard while she instinctively fought to keep her lungs filled with much needed air.

Aware she was practically gaping at a man she did not even know, she tried to look away if for no other reason than to save her feminine pride. She was a Caine and a Caine did not gawk at strangers. But there was just something about the man that commanded her attention—and the attention of almost everyone else in that room.

Impressed by how enthusiastically he had been received at the bar, she wondered who he was and why he seemed so important to everyone. She next wondered if he was married, though she had no idea why that should matter to her at all. She certainly had no intention of making his acquaintance. She had too many other, more important matters to worry about while she was there.

"I was certainly sorry to hear about Big Thomas," she heard Marcus say when she was finally close enough to make out their words above the rest of the din. Now that the newcomer had taken his place at the bar, the noise level in the room had returned to its original state.

"Aye, it was a terrible thing," the tall man answered in a rich, deep voice that carried a lilting Irish brogue. "And to think they would try to blame Old Jack for his murder."

Murder? A sudden chill tremored down Karissa's spine until it reached the end then skittered back up again. She was not used to hearing people talk about such a dreadful subject quite so casually, as if it were no more important than yesterday's weather.

"Yeah, I know. I can't believe they actually arrested him and hauled him into jail for that. It was obviously just another one of their setups," Marcus went on to say, but when he noticed Karissa standing nearby, her wide eyes fastened on his, he excused himself and moved down to take her order.

Because the order was for only the one beer, Karissa waited while he quickly refilled the mug. She did not have the courage to look in the same direction where the tall stranger stood, but felt his eyes on her that whole time.

"Here you go," Marcus said, and held out the dripping mug to her. "And tell Pete McCrystal that's the last one he's having. I promised his wife I'd see to it that he got home early tonight. It's her birthday and she's got a special supper planned up."

As confused from having been told so many names in such a short time as she was rattled to be standing that close to the handsome newcomer, Karissa blinked while she tried to remember which of her customers was named Pete then realized Pete must be the man who had just ordered the beer. She nodded to let Marcus know she would deliver his message then braved a quick look at the attractive stranger still standing near the end of the bar at the same time she turned away.

Her pulses jumped when she discovered that he really was staring at her. Even though he was obviously talking to Deborah, who stood just to his right, his eyes were definitely on her.

Karissa knew she should glance away before he decided she was too bold, but for some reason she was unable to pull her gaze away. Something in the crystal depths of those unnaturally blue eyes held her captive, forcing her to stare at him like some mindless dolt.

Her blood raced when she realized just how handsome he really was. Unlike most of the men she had known, this one was even more attractive up close than he had been at a distance.

Because he was one of the few in the room who had bothered to shave, she was able to see every magnificent detail of his face. She noticed his skin tone looked healthier than many of the men in the room and that his face was shaped from much stronger lines. In addition to those commanding blue eyes, he had smooth eyebrows the same dark shade as his thick, wavy hair and a straight nose that flared ever so slightly at the end. His cheeks were lean and formed splendid ripples when he smiled—something she noticed he did a lot. Smiled so deeply, in fact, that the fascinating lines formed not only around his liberal mouth but at the corners of his eyes, too.

Mesmerized by what she saw, she continued to assess his appearance from only a few yards away until someone behind her bumped her right arm. The jolt caused the cold beer to splash across her hand, the shock of which finally broke her trance. Embarrassed to realize she had literally gaped at a man she did not know, she felt her cheeks burn while she turned and headed back the way she had come.

Eager to put distance between them, she continued to move across the large room, packed now with customers both seated and standing. While she worked her way toward the back tables where Pete awaited his beer, her thoughts remained on the incredible man at the bar. Everything about him had appealed to her, even the amused way he had lifted his dark eyebrows when he realized she was staring at him.

Feeling a little wild and reckless just because he had noticed her, she glanced back at him again and smiled shyly when she saw he was still watching her. Her heart shot skyward like a fireworks rocket on Independence Day when he returned her timid smile with a dazzling one of his own.

Glancing away again, for fear her heart would burst through her chest if she didn't, she decided God must have been at His finest when He created such a man — because he was certainly the most magnificent human being *she* had ever seen. Even Robert Edwards paled in comparison, and until now Robert had remained the handsomest man Karissa had ever met. That was one of the reasons she had been so quick to agree to marry him; that and he had seemed so terribly gallant. Little had she known there were other women who had also agreed to marry him, women who'd had no qualms about giving him whatever he wanted in exchange for a promised marriage.

She pushed the painful thought aside, not wanting to dwell on the horrible day she had found out the tawdry circumstances surrounding his death. Much to her disbelief and humiliation, Robert had been found lying in the ruins of his carriage late one moonlit night, dead from a broken neck — with a partially clothed woman he had been secretly seeing crumpled at his side. It still hurt when she thought back on that day — hurt to remember how much she had loved and trusted Robert and how horribly he had betrayed her.

The pain had been so severe, it had left her unwilling to fall in love like that ever again. Although she still went out with her gentlemen admirers on occasion, mainly because she enjoyed being with her friends and so many of the parties they attended required the women to have a male escort — she had not given her heart to another one of them.

She had decided long ago she would rather live the life of a simple spinster than suffer that sort of devastation ever again. Besides, she was happy enough without having any one special man in her life and she certainly did not need one to support her. Not when she had been born the daughter of one of the wealthiest industrialists in the nation. With arched eyebrows, she glanced down at her simple clothing and wondered what her friends would.say about her now. She also wondered why the man at the bar would give someone dressed like that a second glance.

"Here you are, Pete." She forced a cheerful voice when she set the tall, frothy mug in front of the frail little man who looked to be in his late thirties. "But Marcus told me to remind you that today is your wife's birthday. You need to be getting on home."

Pete grimaced as he ran a damp hand over his face, smearing coal dust across the portion of his cheek visible above his heavy black beard. "That it is. And I forgot all about buyin' her a present." He wrinkled his brow when he looked to the other men at his table. "What am I goin' to do to save me skin this time?"

The large man seated beside him nudged him with a meaty elbow then looked around to make sure he had the attention of everyone at the table before he answered in a loud, boisterous voice. "Go home and give her what every woman wants. Give her another baby."

All the men laughed so hard it forced most of them into coughing spasms while the one who had made such an absurd remark then reached out and grabbed Karissa by the arm. With one strong jerk, he pulled her down in his filthy lap and held her firmly in place.

"How about it, Pretty One?" he shouted in her ear, not caring that he nearly deafened her. He wanted everyone at the table to hear what he had to say. "How would you like for me to give *you* a baby?"

Karissa struggled to free herself but the big, ugly man turned out to be too strong. Her stomach clenched when she looked to the others for help and saw that they appeared eager for whatever might happen next.

"Please, sir," she said, sounding amazingly calm. "Let me go. I have work to do."

"Now don't ya go calling me sir again." His hot breath reeked of stale beer and boiled eggs when he bent forward and tried to steal a kiss, missing her mouth by only inches. "I told ya. My friends call me Robby." His sneer widened. "And I certainly plan to count ya as one of my friends."

When he then grabbed one of her breasts with his grimy hand and no one came to her rescue, she became truly frightened. She thought about the tiny pistol in her boot but realized there was no way for her to get to it. His arm prevented her from bending forward. She had to think of something else. "Please, sir. Not here. Not *now.*"

Robby's eyebrows jumped high into his forehead at such an unexpected response. He glanced around to see who all might have heard her. "If not now, then when?"

"Later. When we are alone," she said, knowing very well she would never allow herself to be alone with such a horrible man. Not only was he obese and homely, he was covered with black soot and smelled as if he had not bathed in weeks. "But not in front of all these other men. They don't deserve to watch."

117

Relief settled over her when she felt the fingers grasping her breast weaken, grateful that her words had registered somewhere in his liquor-dulled brain. "So please, Robby, my new friend, let me go for now. Before I get fired for not doing my job properly."

"Sure, darlin'. Anything you say," he replied with a loud, boisterous laugh. Finally he released his painful hold on her all together. His eyes widened then narrowed again when he glanced at something or someone behind her. "Just you remember where it was we left off when we finally are alone."

Leaping quickly away from him, she fought to regain her composure, aware now of the true danger she had just faced. Anger and humiliation washed over her when she glanced around and saw that everyone in the room was staring at her — even the handsome newcomer, who now stood only a few yards away. Many of those men looked disappointed. Obviously they had hoped their friend Robby would pursue the matter further.

Suddenly, Karissa was not so sure she had done the right thing by coming there. Maybe she should have listened to Lizbeth.

Chapter Seven

Although Karissa managed to keep out of most of the men's reach for the rest of the evening, by the time the last of the customers had left and Marcus was ready to call it a night, she was so exhausted she could hardly keep her thoughts in order.

Not only had it been a night of constant twirling and dodging to keep from being constantly manhandled, her head ached from having to breathe so much tobacco smoke and from having had to learn so many new names and faces so quickly. Especially if that name turned out to be the same as one of the four names Jacque had told to Madison and Franklin just before she left.

The trouble was that nearly a dozen of the men she had met or waited on that night had given her one of the four names she sought — including that incredibly attractive man with the pale blue eyes who never bothered to sit at one of her tables but had watched her the whole night like a hawk keeping an eye on its intended prey.

No matter when she glanced in his direction or

from where, she had found him always looking at her, as if studying her. Probably wondering what she had done to provoke Robby Drier into such crude behavior earlier. Which was another reason she felt so exhausted now. Just knowing that such a tall, attractive man was constantly watching her had kept her on pins and needles all evening. And had made it especially hard for her to concentrate on anyone else.

She had learned early on from one of her more talkative customers that the handsome man's name was Shawn McCowan, and as she had already guessed, he was very popular with most of the miners in that area. "There ain't nothing Shawn and his friends won't do for the others," she'd been told. "Not nothing."

It bothered Karissa to find out that such an attractive man bore one of the four names she sought. But he was not the *only* Shawn to come in that night. She had met at least two other men with the same first name.

Disappointed that there were at least three Shawns there in Black Hill, Karissa realized the search for her father's killers would take a lot longer than she had at first thought.

She had truly not expected there to be so many men in the small mining town carrying the names *Shawn, Thomas, Joey,* or *Jack*. Even the innocent-looking young man who had stood up and waved his arms so eagerly to capture Shawn McCowan's attention earlier was named Joey. Something she had been careful to remember.

Normally, she would have disregarded such a guile-

120

less-looking young man, but what had brought her attention to that particular Joey was the fact that when she had passed by his table while making her way to one of her own, she had heard him mention a cousin named Jack. True, it could be a coincidence that he had such a cousin and that he also had a friend named Shawn. *Or* it could be that she had already found three of the men she wanted.

But for some reason Karissa hoped those were not the three she sought. She especially hoped that particular Shawn did not turn out to be in some way involved with the murder of her father. She hated the idea of having to send such a strong, virile man to jail for the rest of his life — or worse — to the hangman's noose. But if it turned out he was the same Shawn that Jacque had overheard discussing her father's murder, she would not hesitate in having him arrested.

"So how'd you do your first night out?" Laura asked as she slipped into her bright red cloak. She looked every bit as weary as Karissa felt.

Karissa reached into her skirt pocket and pulled out a handful of coins. While she gazed at the half dozen or so coins and judged their weight in her hand, she felt a strange sense of accomplishment. She had never before done any work that had earned her money. The most she had done was act as a volunteer at the orphanage downtown.

"I made nearly thirty cents," she said, amazed at the men's generosity, especially after she had made it clear that she did not allow the same sort of casual touching the other two women allowed.

"Not bad for a first night," Laura agreed, then pat-

121

ted the tiny pocket centered in the front of her bodice. "I made nearly two dollars, but then I had some of Ireland's finest sitting at my tables tonight and they are always the first to part with their money."

Marcus paused on his way back to the bar with a tray of dirty glasses, unable to resist a comment. "That's partly because you have a very interesting little cash box there where you allow the men to deposit the money themselves."

Laura laughed then ran a hand through the length of her light brown hair to push it away from her face and lift it up off her shoulders. "Anything to make a dollar. I'm still planning to buy a place of my own someday." She bent forward to turn out one of the few lamps still burning. "Deborah's already left. I'll see you tomorrow."

Karissa watched her leave before she turned back to Marcus. "Do you want me to help you clean up some of this mess?"

"No. All I'm doing now is stacking the glasses in a pile. I have someone who comes in about noon ever'day and washes ever'thing for me. You're free to go. Just make sure you get back here by five o'clock tomorrow afternoon."

Sighing with relief, aware she had nearly seventeen hours to recuperate from such an exhausting night, Karissa picked up her handbag from behind the bar. She paused just long enough to deposit her earnings inside then headed immediately for the door.

Once outside, she noticed how cold and dark it had become in the several hours she had been inside the tavern. Crossing her arms to ward off the chill, she

122

made a mental note to remember her cloak and a lantern the following night.

She also noticed how quiet it had become. Earlier, there had been all the usual clanking noises of the three mining operations nearby, which included her father's. There had also been the sounds of dogs barking, horses neighing, and the trains that came and went; but now all those noises were gone. Everything was still. All she now heard was the clicking of her own boots as she hurried along the boardwalk and the distant chirping of nocturnal insects. The night air smelled of cedar, honeysuckle, and freshly mined coal.

Rubbing her arms with her hands to ward off the chill, she headed directly for the rooming house, eager to put that tiny bed in Kelly Waylan's attic to good use. Because she did not have to meet with Frank Neely until late that following afternoon, she would have plenty of time to get some much needed rest. She sighed aloud at the thought while she visualized herself in that tiny bed, snuggled beneath a thick, warm quilt. Sound asleep.

It was not until Karissa had stepped down off the boardwalk near a small leathercraft shop to cross a narrow sidestreet that the spooky feeling first crept over her. Although she had not seen nor heard anything out of the ordinary, it felt to her as if she were being followed at a distance. Rather than turn around and see who might be behind her, she hurried her pace forward. Her father had taught her never to show fear, even when her heart was drumming so hard and fast, it felt like it would burst right out of her chest.

123

Since there were no street lamps in Black Wall, nor did the businesses keep lanterns burning in their windows as they did in the city, her only light came from the fat slice of moon overhead. Because it was a clear night, the moon gave off just enough light for her to make out the silhouette of the small, closed restaurant ahead, but not that of the man who stood with his back pressed against it.

When she stepped up onto the opposite boardwalk, her thoughts were on the person she felt certain had followed behind her and not on whatever might lie ahead of her. A startled scream burst past her lips when suddenly the man stepped out of the shadows and blocked her path.

"I waited for you, darlin'," a deep, drunken voice proclaimed just before a pair of massive arms shot out and pulled her firmly against a very large body.

Karissa recognized not only the man's voice but also the rancid smell of his clothing and tried not to show her panic. "Robby? Is that you?" she asked in a surprisingly calm voice. "What are you doing out here?"

"I've come to collect the lovin' you promised me," he slurred then dipped forward in an attempt to plant his grimy mouth on hers.

Karissa turned her head in time to avoid the unwanted kiss while her mind raced, searching her wits for a possible way to escape him. She glanced behind her to see if the man who had been following her was in sight and saw no one. Whoever it was had gone on. "But I'm too tired for that right now."

"That don't matter with me none," he responded

happily, and tried again to plaster his lips against hers, this time landing his mouth and dirty whiskers against her cheek. The liquor on his breath caused her to wince, but he was too drunk to notice. "Darlin', I've got enough energy left in me for the both of us. All you got to do is lay there and smell pretty."

Karissa's heart continued to drum frantically, aware how very drunk the big man was and that there was no one around at that hour of the morning to help her. The nearest house was over two blocks away.

Again she thought of the derringer hidden in her boot and tried to pull free of his grasp long enough to make a grab for the hidden weapon; but his hold was too strong. She was firmly planted against his barrel chest with no room to bend forward or to the side.

"Don't you go tryin' to get away from me, you little harlot!" he shouted, displaying his first signs of anger. His grasp around her tightened until her breasts were flattened painfully against his lower chest and her face was only inches below his. "You promised me a roll in the hay and a roll in the hay is exactly what I plan to have."

Having announced his intentions, he snatched her up off the ground as if she were little more than a sack of grain. He carried her over his shoulder with one strong arm while heading out into the street, toward the livery.

Karissa knew it would do her little good to scream, for everyone but a very few, like Marcus, was already home and asleep by now; and the Lucky Choice was too far away for her new boss to hear any cries for help. Still she realized she had no other recourse and

125

screamed as loud as her compressed lungs would let her. She also started kicking Robby repeatedly in his stomach, though she wished she could land her blows a little lower. At the same time she pummeled his back and shoulders as hard as possible with her small fists.

None of which fazed him in the least.

"Let go of me!" she shouted. Her breath came in short, frantic bursts. It was hard to believe one man could be that strong, especially as drunk as he obviously was. "Let go of me right now."

"No. Not until I've got what I want from you." He tossed her easily from one shoulder to the other then reached for the livery stable door with the hand he had just freed. "I'm sure Sirus won't mind us using his hay loft for a few minutes. Not after he finds out what a pretty little thing you are."

Karissa was so terrified, she stopped fighting and started to cry—something she rarely did. But then rarely was she ever *this* frightened. "Please don't do this to me. Please."

"I wouldn't if you hadn't promised me," he said, his words so slurred they were hard to understand. "But you did promise me. And a promise is a promise."

"But I didn't promise you anything like *this*. All I thought you wanted was a kiss." She sobbed and again started flailing her arms and legs in an attempt to inflict enough pain to make him want to let her go.

"You knew what I wanted," he shot back, and rather than continue to take her constant blows, he slapped her hard enough in the middle of her back to knock the breath out of her. "So quit your complainin'."

Gasping for the breath that would not come, Karissa's panic grew. Soon she fell weak over his shoulder, her heart throbbing from the fear of what would happen after she had lost consciousness. It wasn't until the darkness that surrounded them had taken on a gray hue and she was about to pass out from lack of oxygen that her throat emitted a loud gasping noise and her lungs filled again with air. But by the time she had recovered, they were already inside the livery.

He carried her quickly to the back of the darkened barn, where all she could see was a faint light coming through the wide front door, which he had left partially open. The stench of horse dung and animal sweat inside was as prevalent as the odor of stale liquor and coal dust was on the man who carried her. She sobbed again at the thought of having her maidenhood taken from her in such a horrible place and by such a horrible man.

"Please let me go," she tried again. Her throat was so constricted with fear, the voice had not sounded like her own. "Please don't do this to me."

"You make it sound like I'm plannin' some sort of punishment for you," he complained, clearly not understanding why she was so upset. "If you'd just quit fightin' me like that, this could very well turn out to be the most excitin' night of yer entire life. I've been told by many a woman how good I am. Wait until you see the size of me."

Aware of his meaning, Karissa tried again to break out of his grasp only to have the steel-like grip around her ribcage tighten even more. While looking again at the partially opened door, wishing there was some way she could break free and make a run for it, she noticed another man enter. His silhouette had filled the door only briefly before slipping quietly into the darkness.

Aware now that Robby did not plan to keep her all to himself, that he had invited some of his tavern friends to join him, she gathered all the courage and what strength she had left then made one last wild kick for his groin. This time she met her target and he dropped her like so much dead weight.

Karissa hit the hay-strewn dirt floor already scrambling back to her feet. She tried to figure out the direction the other man might have taken before making a furious dash toward the door.

She went only a few yards then screamed again when she realized how quickly Robby had recovered from his pain and had caught her by her clothing. She felt the front of her blouse tighten against her breasts when his hold prevented her from taking another step. Knowing her choice was either to let him have the blouse or chance him to get his filthy hands on her again, she reached up and tore the blouse right down the front then tugged quickly out of the material. Once free of the garment, she hurried again toward the door.

"Dammit," Robby cursed when he realized what she had done. "Come back here!"

Karissa stumbled over something wooden lying on the ground but quickly recovered and was on her feet again within seconds. She was only a few yards away from the open door, only seconds away from freedom, when suddenly Robby had her again, this time by the hair. She shrieked from the resulting pain.

"You're are not leavin' here until I've finished makin' you mine!" He spun her around to face him then reached for her chemise and tore it open. Next he caught her flailing arms by the wrists and pulled her firmly against him to prevent her from striking him repeatedly.

Motivated by the stark white fear that tore through her, Karissa next tried biting his shoulder, but the muscles there were too bulky to let her get her teeth into him. And she could no longer hit him. But she could kick him again, which she tried to do, only to find he stood too close for her to get a good forward swing at him.

"Might as well stop that," Robby said, his hot breath against her cheek. He gave her wrists a painful twist. "I'm going to do what I came here to do. You might as well accept that fact."

Waves of revulsion washed over her, causing her to fight all the harder.

"Let go of her, Drier," came a deep, rich, determined male voice out of the darkness only a few feet from where the two now struggled.

Suddenly both Robby and Karissa stopped their struggles.

"Who's there?" Robby demanded. He let go of one of her wrists so he could circle an arm around her waist and pull her sharply against him. Certain he held her securely with that one arm, he then let go of the other wrist to give himself a free hand.

Karissa reached down and pulled the torn edges of her chemise together and waited to find out what would happen next. She saw nothing in the darkness but unmoving shapes.

"It's Shawn McCowan." He struck a lantern match so they could see his face.

Karissa recognized those angry blue eyes immediately and thought they looked especially threatening in the flickering shadows created by the long match he held. She wondered if Robby thought the same.

"W-what do you want?" Clearly Robby did not care to go up against the younger man.

"I want ya to let go of my woman," he responded with quiet authority then looked sternly at Karissa as if warning her to go along with him on this. "And I want ya to let go of her right now."

"Your woman?" Robby asked, clearly confused.

Karissa felt his ironlike grip weaken around her waist, but not enough for her to escape.

"Aye. *My* woman," Shawn repeated. A tiny muscle in the cleanshaven ruggedness near the back of his cheek pumped rhythmically, indicating a barely controlled rage. His dark, determined gaze remained fastened to Robby's startled face while he reached for a small lantern that hung on a nearby peg. "What ya planned to do to her just now, I've already done. Only with me, she came willingly. That pretty much makes her my property."

Karissa's mouth opened to offer an immediate response to such an outrageous remark, but instinct told her not to deny his claim. Instead of proclaiming him an outright liar, she snapped her mouth shut again and instead glowered angrily at the both of them.

When Robby did not let go right away, Shawn continued in a low, decisive tone. "I told ya. Catherine Sobey is my woman. And she has been for two days now. I met her this past weekend while I was in Pottsville. I'm the whole reason she came here." He paused for effect then opened the lantern and touched the match to the wick inside. Never taking his gaze off Robby's shaken face, he shook out the match just seconds before the flame would have reached his fingertips.

Quickly he adjusted the wick to allow a warm, steady glow then returned his right hand to his coat pocket where he had held it during most of their conversation. "And I don't think ya'd like knowin' what happened to the last man who tried to take a woman from me. But then ya probably already heard about that. Rumors do travel quickly around here."

Karissa felt a tremor pass through Robby's massive body and realized this huge man was truly afraid. Even though Robby Drier was twice Shawn McCowan's size and had to be equally strong if not more so, he trembled at the thought of having to go against the younger man.

"I didn't know she was your woman," he said, and promptly released her. He ran a filthy hand over his heavy black beard. "I swear I didn't."

Aware her safety lay with the tall man with blue eyes, Karissa hurried to his side.

"That's understandable," Shawn said, his anger having already abated, "considering I didn't get much chance to talk to her tonight. But then Joey and I had some pretty important *business* to discuss."

"Yeah, I heard about his cousin," Robby said, clearly wanting Shawn's attention drawn to something else. "It was hard for me to believe anyone thinks Old Jack could have done Big Thomas in like that. Why, those two were the very best of friends." His eyebrows dipped low into a sincere scowl, for although he was not a friend of Shawn's, he *was* a miner and all miners had a common bond. "It ain't right that Jack McGeehan should have to sit in jail for even one day over such a ridiculous claim."

"He'll be out soon enough," Shawn assured him then looked down at Karissa with a quick smile that caused his pale eyes to glitter in the soft lantern light. "Now, if ya don't mind. I'd like a little time alone with my Catherine."

Karissa's dark eyes widened when Shawn suddenly slipped a strong arm around her shoulders and drew her gently against his side. Aware it was in her own best interest to go along with the pretense, at least for now, she slid her free arm around his waist and returned his smile. While still clutching the front of her torn chemise, she leaned her head against his shoulder. She was amazed at how firm the muscles were beneath her soft cheek and felt a strong desire to press her fingers into him to see if he was that solid all over. She decided that working ten to twelve hours a day inside the coal mines had certain rewards.

Aware he had been dismissed, Robby wasted no time heading toward the door. When he reached forward to widen the opening enough for his large body to slip through, Shawn called out to him. "Oh, and Drier, do see to it that all the other men are informed that the beautiful Catherine Sobey already belongs to me so they will know to stay away from her. I wouldn't want to have to go usin' my pistol against one of my own."

Robby nodded his head vigorously to indicate he would see to it that everyone knew then quickly darted from sight.

"Thank you for saving me," Karissa said after she was sure Robby was well away from the barn. Her whole body felt suddenly weak with an overpowering sense of relief — until a few seconds later when she finally gathered the strength needed to pull away and discovered Shawn had no intention of releasing her.

Wondering why he continued to hold on to her like that when she obviously wanted to step away from him, she glanced up into his blue eyes and noticed that they had suddenly grown dark and menacing. Immediately her fear returned and she gripped the torn edges of her chemise even tighter. "W-what are you doing? Why don't you let go of me?"

Shawn's lips parted just enough to allow the tip of his tongue to slip through and dampen the lower curve of his mouth while his gaze slowly roamed over her, eager to take in every detail of her stunning beauty. Even with part of her long brown hair tumbling from its pins and her almond eyes stretched to their limits, she was the most exquisite woman he had ever seen. Everything about her spoke of perfection.

"I think I deserve a reward of some sort for what I just did," he answered. His eyes sparkled with sheer devilment when he dipped his head closer and grazed her cheek with the tip of his nose, thrilled by the deli-

133

cate scent of rosewater that lingered on her fair skin. She was soft, beautiful, and poised. A true woman in every sense of the word. Yet she was more.

Puzzled, he tried to figure out why someone who carried herself with such obvious dignity and grace, and who talked with such educated ease, had become a bar maid of all things. And in a small, isolated place like Black Wall.

Being one who made his living by observing and appraising others, he had noticed from the onset that she was far more refined than most women and quite unaccustomed to the boisterous ways of an Irish tavern. It was obvious to him she had not been a bar maid for very long. But if that was true, if she had not been born into such a life, then why was she working as a paltry bar maid now? Why wasn't this beautiful woman some wealthy man's wife instead?

It was his guess, she was there because she was hiding from something. *Or someone.* But from who or what? What could have possessed a woman like her to come to such a place and take such a job?

Whatever her reasons for being there, he knew it was just a matter of time before he knew them because he was just the man to uncover whatever secrets she had.

"I think what I deserve is a kiss of appreciation," he went on to say, and waited to see what her reaction would be. He could tell she was not the sort to share her kisses with just anyone.

A delicious shiver of awareness cascaded over Karissa while she studied him cautiously. He was close enough now for her to notice tiny flecks of silver in his pale blue eyes. A whole different kind of fear swept over her, this one aimed at something that had come to life inside her very own body. "Is that *all* you think you deserve?"

"Well, no, but it will do for now."

Karissa swallowed hard, knowing she would much rather kiss this man than fight him, especially after having used most of her strength during that frightening battle with Robby Drier. "All right. But only one kiss."

"Only one? After all we have already shared together?" he teased then stepped back long enough to set the lantern on top of a nearby barrel.

When he looked at her again, his blue eyes glittered with something Karissa could not quite identify. A floodtide of unfamiliar, tingling sensations washed through her body, causing her throat to constrict until she could barely squeeze any words through. "What have we shared?"

With his hands now free of the lantern, he moved toward her again, enjoying the discomfort evident in her eyes. "Why, don't ya remember how, just two nights ago, ya came to me *willingly?*"

Karissa stiffened at the sudden reminder of what he had told Robby Drier then lifted her chin to show her defiance. "I'll have you know that two nights ago, I was home and in my own bed—*alone.*"

"Glad to hear it," he commented with an off-centered smile, clearly amused by such a virtuous display of feminine temper.

Again he bent forward and brushed the sensitive curve of her cheek with the tip of his nose, causing a

135

wild array of sensations to scatter inside her. Her pulse raced at an unprecedented rate when she realized their bodies were again only inches apart. Although no part of him other than the tip of his well-shaped nose had touched her, she felt a very strong, very vibrant warmth radiating out of his body and into hers, causing a wonderfully languorous feeling of womanly need to steal over her.

His next words sounded soft and inviting yet terribly masculine when they fell with a gentle vibration against the sensitive lobe of her left ear. "Since ya seem to be so very proud of having been in bed alone Sunday night, I think it might be safe to assume that I am the only man in yer life right now."

"But you are not *in* my life," she protested, thinking him very bold yet at the same time wondering when he planned to take that kiss he wanted. She swallowed hard. Just knowing that his mouth hovered only inches from hers made it very difficult for her to concentrate. It also made it very difficult for her to breathe. It was as if someone had suddenly drained the stable of oxygen. "Just because you told that horrible man that I am some sort of personal property does not mean it is true." Although she had tried to speak with anger and conviction, her voice had come out sounding raspy and uncertain. "Why, I don't even know you."

He leaned closer until his lips were almost touching hers then gazed deeply into the large round eyes that peered up at him apprehensively.

"So you don't know me." While standing that near, he again let his gaze wander and again drank in the smoothness of her white skin, then noted the slight upward curve of her slender nose and the high cheeks that blushed slightly while he continued his bold perusal. He reached down to straighten the locket that had become twisted during her struggle with Drier. He noticed the initials CS engraved on the front and her full name carved into the back. "What does that matter?"

Her dark eyes stretched as wide as whole walnuts while she tried to bring her racing heart under better control. Wanting to put some desperately needed distance between them, she considered taking a step back, but for some reason her feet did not respond. She was paralyzed to the spot. "I-it matters a lot."

"Then I think it is time we got to know each other a little better," he said, and finally dipped forward to claim her lips in what turned out for Karissa to be the most powerful and the most persuasive kiss she had ever experienced. It was as if he possessed some invisible energy that when transferred to her had left her feeling momentarily weak yet at the same time vibrantly alive—and left her more breathless than ever. Especially when his hands moved from her shoulders to the small of her back and gently pressed their bodies closer together. She was overwhelmed by the wondrous feel of his firm body pressed intimately against hers and the fresh clean scent of his skin.

A strange, shimmering warmth developed in the vicinity of her rapidly pounding heart and spread quickly through the rest of her body, flooding her senses with its languid heat, making her feel instantly light-headed and unable to do more than persuade

137

tiny, raspy breaths into her lungs. Such a powerful response both amazed and alarmed her, for no other man's kiss had ever affected her quite so strongly, nor quite so completely. It was as if he had splashed her very soul with some form of evil, mind-controlling magic.

Although Karissa knew it was wrong for her to be standing in the middle of a darkened livery while allowing a man she hardly knew to kiss her in such an intimate manner, she could not quite gather the outrage needed to push him away. Instead, she slowly lifted the hand not clutching her chemise and used it to caress the strong muscles along the back of his neck. She immediately pressed him closer, allowing her a stronger measure of this strange new pleasure. For the moment, everything was forgotten but the wild yearning that had flared to life the second his mouth claimed hers.

While she futilely tried to sort through the many unbidden thoughts and wondrous sensations that had so quickly enveloped her, her body slowly relaxed, causing her to forget the torn edges of her chemise. Timidly, she let go of the rumpled fabric and eased that hand upward until it had joined the other one beneath the soft dark hair at the back of his neck. How very strong and virile he was. Nothing like the soft, idle men she had known before. She marveled at the feeling of such power and strength beneath her fingertips and wondered if she could ever get enough of such mindless pleasure.

It was not until a few seconds later when she felt his hands slip beneath her long hair to massage the sensi-

138

tive muscles at the base of her neck that a tiny voice echoed a warning from somewhere in the back of her mind, reminding her that even though this man had the ability to turn her insides to melted jelly, his name was still Shawn.

Knowing that it was quite possible he was the very same Shawn who had in some way been involved in her own father's murder, she finally found the strength she needed to push him away.

"There now," she said. Her next few breaths came in short, rapid bursts while she tried to calm the strange tempest still raging inside her. "You've had your kiss."

"And some kiss it was," he admitted, his eyes nearly black when they dipped down to take in the sight of her nearly exposed breasts beneath the parted edges of her torn chemise. Desire for her pulled at every part of his body and surprised him with its sheer intensity. He had truly not expected her kiss to affect him quite that strongly. He felt as if his body were on fire; and having glimpsed the tempting curves of her firm, young breasts only poured more fuel to that blazing fire. What he wouldn't give to snatch that chemise away and view the natural beauty before him.

With Karissa's senses still reeling from the aftereffect of what was supposed to have been a simple kiss of gratitude, and fully aware of where his darkened gaze had strayed, she gasped with indignation as she grabbed the edges of the torn chemise and again jerked the garment closed. She then glanced around to find out what had become of her torn blouse and saw part of it hanging from the loft where Robby had obviously flung it in anger.

Shawn noticed immediately where her gaze had gone.

"Here. Take my coat," he offered, still trying to recover from the burning aftermath of her kiss while he tugged out of the sleeves. Aware of the astounding effect she'd had on him, a small part of him wondered if he had made a terrible mistake by kissing her like that, especially knowing beforehand how attracted he was to her. A woman like her could prove to be a very dangerous distraction at a time when he really needed his sharpest wits about him.

But at the same time, another, more vital part of him decided there was nothing really all that detrimental in what he had done, not as long as he kept his desire for her under rigid control.

Just because he was a private detective who had been hired to infiltrate the Molly Maguires and expose them as being the murdering terrorists they really were did not mean he could not also enjoy the kiss of a beautiful woman occasionally. There was no law governing the state of Pennsylvania that claimed a private detective had to remain pure and chaste while working on an important assignment. As long as he did not let his attraction for the brown eyed beauty become a *dis*traction and thus get in the way of his work, he could see no real harm in pursuing her.

Surprised by the offer of his coat, Karissa watched while he reached into one of the front pockets, pulled out a small handgun and a leather pouch, then slipped them both into his waistband. Having thought his mention of a pistol earlier was an empty threat devised to frighten Robby Drier into easy submission, she tried not to look too startled to discover he really was armed. Instead she calmly held out her hand to accept the lightweight coat he offered. "Thank you again. I'll return it to you tomorrow."

"Good," he said with a brisk nod and a quick smile that formed long, curved indentations in his lean cheeks. Indentations that begged to be touched. "Return it to me tomorrow night while we are both at the Lucky Choice and I am surrounded by my friends. But don't act too surprised if I bend forward and give ya a friendly little kiss or two in front of the others. It will help convince everyone that ya really do belong to me."

"And why would I want them all to believe something like that? Especially after what you told Robby you did two nights ago to claim me." Her cheeks flushed at the thought. Now everyone would think her a tarnished woman.

"Because it will keep the other men from pesterin' ya like they did tonight."

"Why would it do that?" She studied his blue eyes carefully, wishing she could read his thoughts.

"Because most of the men in this area are afraid of me."

"Why are they afraid of you?" That still did not make sense to her. He was certainly not frightening in appearance. If anything, she detected a true gentleness in his eyes.

"Because someone convinced them I have a real mean streak in me."

Karissa tilted her head to one side, remembering how honestly frightened Robby had been, and knew he spoke the truth. "And who convinced them of that?"

Shawn's smile spread into a wide grin. "I guess I did. Which is why it would be toward yer own benefit to continue pretendin' to be my property."

"Just as long as *you* understand that it is only a pretense," she cautioned, then turned her back while she slipped her arms into his coat and tugged it up over her shoulders. When she turned around to face him again, she clutched the front of the oversized garment with both hands.

"Why do I get a strong feelin' ya do not trust me?" he asked, chuckling at the fact that her grip was so tight her knuckles were bloodless.

"Because I learned long ago not to trust *any* man," she said, then studied him a moment longer in the pale lantern light. Even with dim shadows covering part of his face, he was truly the handsomest man she had ever met. Too bad his name had to be Shawn. That meant she had no choice but to be suspicious of him, at least until she knew for certain he had not been involved in her father's murder. "But I still want to thank you for what you've done."

Shawn's blue eyes brightened and his endearing smile deepened when he took another quick step toward her. *"Again?"*

Sensing he was teasing and did not really intend to kiss her a second time, Karissa laughed. *"This time* the thank you is to remain strictly verbal."

"This time?" His dark eyebrows arched with immediate interest. "I guess that means I can expect for there to be a *next time.*"

142

"Only if you save my life again."

A dimple sank deep into Shawn's left cheek while he thought about that. When he spoke again, his eyes glimmered with some private thought. " 'Twasn't yer life I saved, Catherine Sobey. 'Twas yer virtue. And it could very well be that I saved it because I wanted it for myself."

Karissa cocked an eyebrow at him, warning him to be careful of his words, then dropped it again when she realized he had used her mother's maiden name a second time. "How do you know my name?"

"Simple. I asked Marcus back when I first saw ya," he answered with a slight shrug, then stepped forward and placed his hand gallantly against the small of her back, unaware of how wondrously that might affect her. "And because it is also inscribed on the back of your locket."

She reached up to touch her mother's locket, glad it had done what it was supposed to.

Shawn's eyes sparkled in the lamplight and drew her attention back to his face. "I knew from the very moment I set my poor, tired eyes upon ya that I wanted ya for myself. And since I *have* decided I want ya for myself, I won't be havin' other men puttin' their hands on ya. That's why I want everyone in Black Wall to know that ya already belong to me."

Karissa felt an odd sprinkling of apprehension cascade over her, raising tiny bumps beneath her skin when she heard the serious tone in his voice. But rather than spin about to remind him yet *again* that she did not in any genuine sense of the word *belong* to him and never would, she instead focused on keeping

143

her breathing under a much steadier control. Despite the inner turmoil his words had created, she offered an outward appearance of calm and indifference while she allowed him to escort her out of the livery and on to the rooming house.

Once there, he did not linger for another passion-filled kiss as she had expected, nor did he try to pull her into another close, intimate embrace. Instead, he simply opened the front door for her, waited until she had stepped inside, then bent forward to lightly brush his lips across her forehead, just below her wispy bangs, and left without comment.

Even the slight brush of his lips against her delicate skin was enough to set her blood racing again, making it almost impossible for her to drift off to sleep later after she'd finally climbed into bed.

Although she attributed her sudden sleeplessness to the muffled snoring drifting up from the floors below and to the fact she was not used to such a small, squeaky bed, she knew neither was the real reason she remained so restless. The truth was, she could not stop thinking about that unsolicited kiss in the stable and how dramatically it had affected her when such a thing should not have affected her at all. She was outraged, yet at the same time intrigued by how splendid his mouth had felt against hers. And it wasn't as if she had not been kissed before, for she had, many times; but *never* like *that*. Even Robert's kisses paled in comparison and until now she had thought her former fiancé quite accomplished in that area. But his kisses had never melted her resistance the way Shawn's kiss had.

Her cheeks stung with mortification when she realized how disgracefully she had responded to that one passionate kiss. She had always believed herself to be a woman of sound principle, a woman in control of every emotion. But the moment his strong arms had closed around her, pulling her body firmly against his, and his warm, hungry mouth had descended upon hers, she had lost all ability to think logically. She had behaved like a wanton fool.

Moaning at the shameful memory of how eagerly she had responded to his touch, she rolled over onto her side and stared at the fluttering lace curtain for a moment, then pressed her eyes closed.

She could not rid herself of Shawn's handsome image, even though the man had no business being in her thoughts at all. What she really needed to do was concentrate on the fact that she was now safely settled in Black Wall, and that it was only a matter of weeks if not days before she and Frank would know the names of everyone responsible for killing her father.

Nothing else should matter.

Chapter Eight

Because it had been so hard to force the bold and forbidding image of Shawn McCowan out of her head that night and because the bed was so small and unfamiliar, it was nearly dawn before Karissa finally fell asleep and early afternoon before she finally awoke.

Aware Karissa had missed both breakfast and lunch, Kelly Waylan had kept a plate of food in the warming butler for her, which Karissa ate ravenously. She was not sure if it was the invigorating mountain air or the fact that she had worked so hard the evening before trying to do her job right that had affected her appetite, but she ate nearly twice as much food that day than she normally did.

Even though it was common fare and not quite as flavorful as the food Lizbeth prepared, Karissa appreciated every bite. So much so, she decided to help Kelly with the dishes to show her gratitude. Washing dishes was something she had never actually done before, but she had watched Lizbeth on several occasions and understood the basic steps. To her amazement it was not all that tedious a task, and with Kelly there to talk with, they had the dishes and cooking utensils washed and put away in no time.

A little before four o'clock Karissa returned upstairs to get ready for work. She brushed her teeth then bathed herself with a damp cloth and the harsh, unscented soap she had been provided, then treated her rough, dry skin with rose-scented oil. With Shelly not there to help her with her long hair, she quickly shaped the heavy tresses into a simple twist at the back of her head and anchored it into place with two large combs. She then slipped into a blue and white cotton dress of simple design and headed off to work a little before five.

By six o'clock, when the bulk of Marcus's regular customers had shuffled noisily into the Lucky Choice for a much needed drink and a bowl of Marcus's famous Texas stew—famous because it was the only food he knew how to make and all that could be had at that particular tavern—most of the men had already heard the talk. The new girl working at the Lucky Choice belonged to Shawn McCowan.

Because the talk had spread so quickly and had been distributed with such aplomb, not one of the men who came in that night tried to grab at her or rub their body against hers as they had the night before. Most of the customers now treated her with considerably more respect; although a few, especially the older ones whom Karissa knew to be relatively harmless, continued to flirt with her shamefully.

By seven o'clock even Laura had heard the rumor and cornered Karissa at the bar to ask if it was true.

147

Rather than admit to the terrible incident which she had foolishly allowed to happen to her shortly after she had left work in the wee hours of the morning, Karissa decided to go along with the absurd story Shawn McCowan had concocted. At least for now.

"Is it really true, Catherine?" Laura wanted to know. "Are you really the spoken property of Shawn McCowan?" It was obvious by Laura's breathless tone and her wide green eyes that she was impressed.

"He seems to think so," Karissa answered while waiting for Marcus to fill two large mugs with beer and one small glass with whiskey.

Laura blinked then stared at her dumbfounded. "How can you sound so casual about something like that? Why, I'd give up my entire right arm to have a man like him lay claim to me."

"That certainly would make it hard to carry a large tray of drinks or stew," Karissa answered, not wanting to make anything phenomenal out of something so insignificant — and not seeing why Laura should react to such extreme. He was only a man, not some god set upon this earth to appease young women — though she was not so sure *he* would agree. Not after the arrogant manner he had kissed her in the livery — expecting her to swoon at his feet like some mindless child.

Which she shamefully did.

Even after having had all day to think about it, she could not understand what had happened to the usual calm inside her. What had possessed her to make her behave so foolishly? Never in her life had she reacted like that to a mere kiss.

Even now, just thinking about what had happened

in those few seconds their bodies had touched made her pulses react in a strange, rebellious way. Causing her whole body to tingle with renewed awareness.

And that made her angry. She was too used to being in complete and total control of her emotions. Except for those first few days after her mother had died and again right after her father was murdered, she had always managed to keep even her strongest emotions carefully regulated. *True ladies never allowed their emotions to run rampant. True ladies always held their composure.*

She frowned.

Did the fact she had not been able to control the desire she felt for Shawn McCowan mean she was not a true lady after all? She shuddered at the thought of what Lizbeth would have to say if she ever found out what had happened.

Dampening her suddenly dry lips, she glanced around to see if the object of her distraction had entered yet and felt oddly disappointed when a quick scan of the crowded room revealed he had not. Where was he? And why was he almost always one of the last men there each night, she wondered. Then she realized the answer. Because he was one of the few men who took the time every day to shave his full face and bathe away the day's collection of sweat and coal dust—one of the *few* traits she saw in his favor.

That and the fact he was the bold rescuer of women in distress. She shuddered at the memory of what Robby Drier had tried to do and how close he had come to success.

"Tell me," Laura went on, determined to have the

149

details of Karissa's relationship with the handsomest man in all of Black Wall. "Was that his coat you brought with you this afternoon?"

"Yes. I borrowed it last night because I was cold and I brought it with me tonight because I now have my own cloak and want to return it to him."

Laura sighed aloud with adulation, as if having worn Shawn's coat was the most wondrous thing she had ever heard. "How gallant of him to give up his coat just so you could stay warm. Not very many men are that considerate. You have to be one of the luckiest women alive."

Karissa looked at her strangely, for although his letting her have his coat had been the gentlemanly thing to do, it was not *that* awe-inspiring. "I suppose so."

"I know so." Laura's tinted face was alive with excitement. "The man is young and strong and extremely handsome. And he's obviously had some schooling because he can hold an intelligent conversation when he really wants to, and he bathes each and every day. What more could a woman want?"

Karissa tilted her head and thought about that. She wondered why a man of such obvious intelligence and aptitude was there in Black Wall working in a coal mine of all places. It certainly wasn't because he had a low opinion of himself!

Having overheard Laura's glowing appraisal of Shawn, Marcus looked insulted when he set the drinks to Karissa's last order on her tray then deposited the change. "It could be that she'd prefer to have a man who is not only strong, handsome, educated, and clean; but one who is *not* quite so young, therefore having a little more experience in pleasing women — and one who *owns his own business*."

Laura laughed and reached forward to pat his pouting cheek gently, as if to humor him. "I'm sorry. How could I have forgotten? We already have the perfect man right here."

Marcus tucked his thumbs under his suspenders and lifted his chin proudly though he continued to look deeply insulted. "That's very true," he said with more of a Texas drawl than usual. "And don't you go forgetting that fact ever again, little miss."

Karissa paused a moment to enjoy the playful banter between the two then lifted her tray and headed back across the room to where Frank Neely and several local gamblers were playing cards at one of her tables.

While she worked her way through the large room filled with loud, boisterous men shouting to each other in an effort to be heard over the din of the others, she thought about how obvious it was that Marcus and Laura had special feelings for each other. The problem was, neither would ever be the first to admit such deep feelings existed.

She shook her head at how childish that seemed and decided, if she did not already have so many other matters on her mind, she might consider playing matchmaker for the two. As it was, she needed to keep her thoughts focused on her one, main reason for being there. She had to know who killed her father.

Nothing else was important.

"Here you go, gents," she said, trying not to give

Frank more than a passing glance because, although they lived at the same rooming house, they were not thought to be friends. "Two beers and a whiskey."

"Set mine over here," Frank muttered without bothering to look up from his cards. "I really don't trust my new compadre there to keep his hands off my drink."

The man Frank had just referred to sat staring at him a long moment; as if trying to decide if he had really meant that. It wasn't until Frank looked up and grinned at him that it became apparent he was joking.

The other man's deep scowl turned into a wide, toothy grin when he then held out his hand for his own drink. "Don't you listen to him none. He's just pulling your leg. He knows I wouldn't never touch his stinking beer." He placed a heavy hand over his heart as if to pay homage to the drink she had just set before him. "I'm a whiskey drinker to the end."

"Keep drinking *that* whiskey and the end will come a lot sooner than you think," Frank quipped, causing everyone at the table to toss their heads back and laugh for Marcus was known for selling some pretty staunch rotgut.

Karissa would have stayed and talked with the jovial group of men longer, but when she glanced around to see if any of her other customers might be ready to reorder, she noticed Shawn saunter through the front door, dripping with his usual self-confidence and animal magnetism.

Even from across a smoke-filled room, Karissa noticed how he looked as tall and as handsome as ever in the light blue flannel shirt and black corduroy

152

britches he wore. Not having spotted her yet, for it was not his nature to study a room right after he had first entered, he nodded to several of his friends who had stood and waved for him to join them. But as was his custom, he headed toward the bar first.

Ready to give him back his coat and be done with it, knowing he planned to give her a token kiss in front of everyone so they would truly believe that she was his property, Karissa hurried across the crowded room to join him. Carefully, she worked her way toward the end of the bar, where he stood smiling and waving his arms about spiritedly while he talked to Marcus. She could not understand why her heart suddenly started to beat so rapidly. It was as if she was actually glad to see him when she knew there was no real reason for her to be glad at all. He was just another man.

But then it was hard at times to think of Shawn McCowan as just another man. Other than having the same first name as one of the murderers she and Frank sought—and having saved her from a perilous situation—his being there was of no real consequence to her. No more than *he* was of any real consequence to her. But that was not what the men surrounding them thought, most of whom were already watching them with eager speculation.

"Catherine!" Shawn stated in a loud, deep-timbred voice when he noticed her headed his direction. He clearly wanted to catch everyone's attention—which he definitely did. "Darlin', I've missed ya somethin' fierce."

Karissa felt a funny little leap of her heart and felt

extremely self-conscious when suddenly he flung his arms wide, prepared to greet her with a stout Irish hug.

"I have something for you," she said, and hesitated for a moment before heading toward the small shelf behind the bar where she had left his coat instead of into his open arms.

"And I've got somethin' for you, *too*," he said with a confident air then arched his well-shaped eyebrows to let everyone know his obvious intent while he waited for her to come back around the bar and into his awaiting arms.

Those men close enough to have heard him laughed loud and strong.

Swallowing back the embarrassment that brazen remark had caused her, knowing they all thought he had taken her to his bed nights earlier, she pulled his folded coat off the shelf then headed back toward him. When she looked to see his expression, he caught her quick glance with his amused gaze and held it captive a moment. Her pulses continued to race riotously, but now more out of annoyance than attraction.

Just because of the scandalous way she had reacted to his kiss earlier, he expected her to swoon at his feet forever. But her reaction last night had been that of a woman too tired to think properly. She'd had eight hours' sleep since then. "Here's the coat you loaned to me yesterday."

"Ya mean the one I loaned to ya early this morning when I walked ya to yer boardin' house?" Shawn slung the coat over his shoulder to move it out of his way then reached out to pull her quickly into his arms.

Knowing his plan, Karissa took a deep breath and steeled herself for the brief kiss that would undoubtedly send the whole room into a tempest of wild cheers and laughter.

But the kiss did not come immediately. While Shawn continued to hold her embarrassingly close, he looked out at the many expectant faces and shouted, "I want it known by one and all that Miss Catherine Sobey is now *my* personal property and has been for several days."

He glanced around to see if Robby Drier was in the room and frowned when he noticed that he was not. "I also want it understood that *any* man caught botherin' this little brown-eyed beauty in *any* way will have to answer to me and mine."

Having dressed in such plain clothing, Karissa was still a little startled by the fact he had just called her a beauty when, without warning, he bent low then kissed her long and hard, causing her to gasp for a much-needed breath when he finally pulled away. Despite his forewarning, she found herself ill prepared for the floodtide of sensations that had so suddenly washed over her.

While she tried her best to hide the unexpected stirring caused by his unwanted kiss, the room filled with ribald cheers and friendly heckles. Some claimed the poor lass did not know what she had gotten herself in for while others wanted to know when the wedding would take place and how many children the two would likely have.

Shawn shrugged off the mention of a wedding with a simple lift of his shoulders. He was far too obsessed with his work to ever again consider something as permanent as marriage and children, even to a woman as irresistible as Catherine. "How can ya be askin' me such a thing? Me? Shawn McCowan? Why, it should be well known by all of ya that I'm no longer a marryin' man. I've had my fill of that sort of thing."

Having just now gotten over the exhilarating impact of his kiss, Karissa frowned. She did not know which she liked the least: his announcement to one and all that he had no intention of marrying her, or the fact that he had obviously been married before. True, she had no intention of ever becoming seriously involved with this man, but still she did not like the thought of his having been married before. And she especially did not like all those men thinking she had given herself to him without first having obtained some sort of a lasting commitment from him. It made her seem so sordid and shallow.

Rather than allow everyone to continue believing the very worst of her, she turned her angry frown into the most pitiful of feminine pouts then looked up at him through sadly lowered lashes. "But that's not what you told me the other night, darling. You told me that you could hardly wait to make me your wife. That I was the best thing that ever happened to you. You said you could not live without me."

"I *what?*" Shawn's dark eyebrows arched high into his forehead at hearing such an absurd statement.

Seeing how truly startled he looked by what she had said, Karissa had a hard time keeping her own expression looking injured and forlorn. "You told me you wanted to marry me this September. Just as soon as you had a little money put away to buy us a small house."

The noise level in the Lucky Choice soared instantly with everyone speculating at once.

"You little minx," Shawn said under his breath in a voice so low only she could hear his words. "What was that all about?"

She looked at him with round, innocent eyes. "I realize it's *your* game and that *you* thought of it. But I really felt like it should be *my* move by now." She smiled sweetly while she gazed at him with what she hoped the others thought was an adoring expression. "It's high time some of those raised eyebrows were directed at you."

"A *game* is it?" he questioned, his blue eyes twinkling with pent emotions. "Is that how you see this?"

To Karissa's surprise, instead of slipping his stout hands around her slender throat and throttling her soundly, Shawn tossed back his head and laughed then quickly lifted those hands to indicate he had something more to say to everyone. As soon as the room had quieted enough for him to be heard again, he placed one arm across Karissa's slender shoulders while he used the other to emphasize his next words.

Karissa did her best to ignore the vibrant warmth that resulted from his touch while she waited to hear what he planned to say, already knowing it would be nothing to her advantage.

"Although I will admit to bein' a wee bit tipsy the other night when Catherine and I first discussed this

157

matter, I do recall my mentionin' somethin' about marryin' her come September, though it is all still a little hazy in my mind. But if that's what I said, then that's what I meant and I can assure ya, that's what I will do." He felt Karissa's body stiffen while he continued, which let him know she had not expected him to make the next move to this little game of theirs quite so quickly.

Aware she had no more intention of marrying him than he did of marrying her, he continued to play the scene for all it was worth. "As ya all know, I am not a man who ever goes back on his word. And since Catherine has already proved to me how very, very much she loves and adores me, I will be pleased to make her my wife."

Actually, the thought of marrying such a beautiful and conniving woman was far more than pleasing, it was downright intriguing. Catherine was far different from any woman he had ever known. She moved with a lot more grace and spoke with a lot more self-assurance than any other bar maid he had ever known. Truth was, if he were not already married to his work, he might actually consider such an interesting offer. As it was, he liked the idea of the others thinking he was engaged. It would give him a far more logical reason to behave oddly now and again. People suspected of being in love were known to do strange things.

Karissa stared at him a moment, bewildered by how easily he had just told everyone she loved him. How could he speak such lies without as much as batting an eye? Did he have no conscience?

Aware of the trouble she had just brought on herself, she hurried to counter that last move—before everyone in the room suddenly pronounced them man and wife. "But *not* until you have saved the money we need to buy our own house—like you promised."

"Which I should have by September easily," he said, and swept her into another bold hug, pressing the soft curves of her body intimately against his own while he gazed out at the others. "To tell ya the truth, I can hardly wait until autumn."

Karissa's stomach knotted with immediate apprehension while she wondered what would happen if for some reason he decided to try to force her into going through with such a ridiculous farce. Their improbable engagement would certainly raise a few eyebrows back in Pittsburgh should her true name ever surface. Her only comfort came in knowing that she and Frank should have the information they wanted long before September. By then they would both be gone from there without a trace. She found perverse pleasure in knowing that eventually Shawn would have to try to explain her sudden disappearance to these men.

Slowly, Shawn released her from his demonstrative embrace. Pleased by how effortlessly he had managed to turn her own little ploy against her, he shouted out merrily, "Mrs. Shawn McCowan. Has a nice ring to it, don't ya think?"

Determined to counter his every move with one of her own, Karissa lifted her left hand and displayed it for all to see. "No. I don't see that it has a ring to it at all. Looks to me like my finger is bare."

Shawn's gaze narrowed in begrudging admiration, aware the little minx had just tricked him into buying

159

her a promise ring. It was either that or admit to these men that he had fabricated the whole affair, which would cause him to lose a lot of credibility with them. "It won't be bare for long, my dear. That I promise."

Lifting his hand to her shoulder, he gave her a squeeze so gentle and so possessive it sent her mind racing in all directions at once. *What on God's green earth had she done?*

"Well, until I see that ring for myself, there will be no official engagement." She sighed with relief, aware she had just resolved the problem she had so unthinkingly created; but then tensed again when she wondered what would happen should he actually present her with the ring he'd just promised her. Would she then be *lawfully* engaged to this man? A man she hardly knew.

And if that did make her legally engaged to him and she did not go through with the marriage, would he then be able to sue her for breach of promise? Would he have grounds even though she had not used her own name while foolishly alluding to an engagement? She shuddered at the thought of what would happen should the newspapers ever get a hold of such a scandal and realized she now had *two* very good reasons not to let anyone discover her real name.

John Caine paced across the thick carpet in front of his lawyer's desk, infuriated by what he had just been told. "Isn't there *anything* I can do to break that will?"

Richard Goodman shook his head and handed the

160

family's copy of Lawrence's will back to him. "I've gone over every word and have found that document to be quite sound. But then Martin Michaels is one of the most competent attorneys in all of Pittsburgh. I really did not expect to find any weaknesses in it. He's far too thorough and too conscientious to make any casual mistakes."

"What about that opening paragraph that states something about Father being of sound mind and body? How could he possibly have been of sound mind and body? He was near death, for heaven's sake. Can't I contest the document on the basis of that?"

"There is a doctor's signature indicating that your father's illness had not yet affected his mind. He might have been in severe pain during that time, but he obviously understood what he was doing. John, you might as well reconcile yourself to the truth. As long as your sister, Karissa, is alive and able, she will be the one controlling your father's enterprises."

John closed his eyes and ran his hand over his face while he thought more about that. "You mean if for some reason Kari can no longer fulfill her duties as the administrator of father's estate, I'd be able to take over immediately?"

"Yes. If your sister should ever suffer either a physical or mental affliction that in any way interferes with the performance of her duties, and as long as she has remained unmarried and without children, then according to the wording in this will, she would have no other recourse than to relinquish those duties to you, his only son. And because there are no other siblings, if for some reason, God forbid, she should die before you do, you will probably inherit everything. Because unless she decides to make a will of her own stating otherwise, everything she owns would then go directly to you, her *only* brother. And should you die first, your father has it worded where she in turn gets everything. I gather by the way this was written that your father does not want Lana to have ownership of anything ever. It looks to me like he wanted to make sure everything stayed in the family."

John stared at Richard for a long moment. "Then all I can do is sit back and hope that Karissa either kills or maims herself?"

Richard grimaced. "For God's sake, John. You make it sound so serious. It's not as if you have been left destitute in any way. As long as your sister manages your father's investments well, you should receive quite a substantial sum of money at the end of each year."

"But not enough to satisfy Lana's needs," John admitted, his expression filled with misery. "She's threatened to divorce me if I don't come through with that grandiose lifestyle I promised her. And after having had a taste of what I thought our lives would be like after Father died, she is not about to settle for anything less. She's become too used to me giving her whatever she wants."

Which was true. During the six months he had been in charge of his father's enterprises, he had set himself a substantial salary, one that had afforded Lana an elegant touring carriage, the finest clothing, a store full of new furniture, and the start of one of the largest, most elegant homes ever to be built in the most fashionable residential district in Pittsburgh. "I'll lose her if I don't continue to do just that."

"It's not as if she's destined to live on the streets," Richard replied with a disgusted scowl. "Even if Karissa proves to be more conservative in her investments than you or your father, you will still collect enough at the end of each year to keep you and your wife comfortable for the rest of your lives. Your father's enterprises are worth millions, for heaven's sake."

"But Lana will not settle for being comfortable," he answered, waving his hands as if that might help Richard to understand. "She is determined to live a life of elegance." His voice dropped with shame when he then admitted, "To be honest, that house she has me building for her next birthday has already cost me all the money I have. I'm broke as a Baptist minister, and if I don't come up with another eighteen thousand by midsummer, that house will never be completed in time. What am I going to do? Karissa has taken away my power to sell anything, which means I can't sell something for one price but claim another like I have in the past when I needed extra money. And I can't bear the thought of Lana leaving me."

Richard appeared little impressed by his problem. "Do like the rest of us. Borrow at the bank."

"I can't. I have no collateral that isn't already under a lien. I've already borrowed all I can."

Richard leaned back in his chair and looked at him for a long moment. "Until your sister returns from wherever she went to work through her grief, you are still in complete charge of the family enterprises, aren't you?"

John nodded that he was.

"Then authorize yourself a substantial loan. Enough to finish the house and see you through till the end of the year. If your sister left you with full authority like you said she did, then about all she can do to rectify the matter is take that same amount out of your annual dividend this December."

John shook his head. "But what if that does not leave me with enough to live on next year?"

Richard looked unconcerned. "If you can't live on the four to six hundred thousand dollars you will probably have left over, then I think you have more of a problem than you realize. No woman is worth that amount."

John stared sadly at the wall just above Richard's head. "Lana is. I'd do *anything* to make her happy." He already had. Lana was the main reason he'd been so eager to stretch the company profits at the expense of his father's workers. It was to satisfy her needs that he had agreed to Clay Jones's suggestions and cut wages and maintenance costs in all his father's coal mines and increased prices at all the company stores. He knew other colliery owners had been getting away with those same tactics for years. It was also because of Lana he had agreed to cut the work force and the customer services of his father's railroads nearly in half.

His stomach coiled into a hard knot when he realized what Karissa would say after she discovered the sort of changes he had initiated during the past several months. She was too much like their father and would immediately do what she could to reverse most of those changes, which meant their profit margin would plummet back to where it was before.

H could not allow that to happen. He could not allow Karissa to come in and undo all he had done.

But then what could he really do to stop her? That will was ironclad.

Still, there had to be a way.

There had to be.

Chapter Nine

Karissa had to admit she was impressed with how eager the other miners were to remain on Shawn's good side. By his having simply announced to everyone that she now belonged to him, he truly had saved her from the future pawing of Marcus's rowdier customers. It was obvious that these men respected Shawn a great deal, if not by the way so many of them now treated her, then by the fact he had most of the men in Black Wall falling all over themselves in their eagerness to please him.

Even so, she was annoyed by the arrogant, domineering manner in which he had so proudly *laid claim* to her. It was as if she were little more than a small, insignificant piece of property to be easily owned or lost. She was too used to feeling important to let that set well with her.

Later that week, she became even further irritated when the pompous oaf suddenly started behaving as if he actually believed his own incredible lies.

The same night he had so arrogantly announced his *ownership* of her, he had stayed until after midnight then walked her home after she finished working, as if he had every right in the world to do so. And without bothering to as much as ask her permission first.

It had terrified her to suddenly find herself alone with him a second time. She was afraid the reason he had remained behind was so he could try to take another passionate kiss from her. But when all he did was walk her safely to her door then tip his cap to bid her a good night, she wondered what his true intentions could be.

It wasn't until she found Shawn outside waiting for her the following Saturday afternoon that she finally realized exactly what his intentions were.

She had left the rooming house early so she would have time to go by the company store to buy a few items she needed then by the train station to send a telegram to Lizbeth letting her know she had arrived safely. Unfortunately Shawn followed her, intending to aggravate her as much as he could. She had to do her shopping with him right behind her and had to forgo sending the telegram altogether. All because she could not convince him to leave her alone.

By Sunday, when he appeared unannounced at the rooming house shortly after noon dressed in his best corduroys and carrying a picnic basket in one hand and a small bouquet of flowers in the other, she realized his plans were to make a complete and utter pest of himself whenever possible. It was probably his way of getting even with her for having announced to all his friends that he had proposed to her, which she never would have done had he not insinuated an intimacy between them. It had been purely a reflexive action on her part.

167

She felt awkward enough having to work as a common bar maid in order to get the information she wanted, but to have everyone thinking her promiscuous as well had been too much to endure.

And now she had a whole new problem—getting Shawn McCowan to leave her alone so she could better concentrate on the real reason she was there.

"I'm sorry, Mr. McCowan, but I already have plans for this afternoon," she told him when she realized he had done it again. He had made plans to be with her without first asking her permission. Now she was glad she had promised the young boy who lived on the second floor a trip up on the hillside where there was a lot less coal dust so they could look for wild berries. She would much rather spend her time with a child who behaved like an adult than with an adult who behaved so much like a child. "I have already promised Tony Andrews I'd spend the afternoon with him."

" 'Tis a real shame, because now ye're faced with havin' to tell this Mr. Andrews y've changed yer mind," he said, as if that were her only choice in the matter.

He set the food basket he carried down on a nearby bench and, after she refused to take the flowers, laid them on top of it. That made her even more wary of him. Why the sudden need to free his hands? She glanced around to see who could come to her rescue should she need it and saw only Tony playing out in the yard.

When Shawn moved closer to get a better look into her splendid brown eyes, he noticed that for each tiny step he made forward, she took a precautionary step backward. His eyes glittered with the thought of what

168

her reaction would be if he continued stalking her like that until he had her backed against the heavy, wooden bannister that surrounded the veranda. He'd have her trapped with no choice but to try to run past of him. "I guess the best way to do that would be to explain to him how ye're now engaged to be married and therefore shouldn't be allowin' yerself to be seen in the company of another man." His eyebrows dipped low with mock seriousness. "After all, I have my reputation to consider here."

"But you and I have never become officially engaged," she reminded him, and lifted her bare hand to remind him of how easily she had maneuvered her way out of that one. He reacted by taking another small step in her direction. She did what she could to calm the inner turmoil his movements caused while she continued to back away, "Therefore I can and will see whomever I like."

She wondered what it was about Shawn that made her feel so ill at ease and decided she was simply reacting to the unsettling fact the man was so very good at twisting the truth. She had never met anyone who could tell such outrageous lies without as much as batting a lash. She herself had had a hard time looking anyone in the eye since she'd come there and had started pretending to be someone she was not — especially if those eyes belonged to Shawn. Every time anyone called her Catherine, she felt a little guilty.

"Ah, yes, ya did say somethin' about our engagement not bein' official until I produced a ring," he admitted. His blue eyes continued to sparkle with merriment while he slipped two fingers into his shirt pocket. "But as it turns out, I do have that ring I promised ya so I guess now we really are officially engaged."

Without giving her a chance to protest, he snatched the delicate hand she had just waved in front him and shoved a small ring made of gold and set with a small ruby onto the appropriate finger with lightning speed then stepped back to watch the fireworks. Oh, how he loved to torment this beautiful enchantress. It was worth every penny he had spent on that ring, which in this town was twice its value.

Karissa stared dumbfounded at the offensive object for several seconds then narrowed her dark gaze when she looked back into his smiling face and realized the only reason he had done that was to annoy her. She wondered then what lengths he would go to get back at her for having outsmarted him in front of his friends.

"Mr. McCowan, you know as well as I do that you never really asked me to marry you," she said with deliberate slowness, doing everything she could to keep her temper in check. She reached for the small ring and tried to wriggle out of it only to find the fit too tight. It would not go over her knuckle.

"That's true enough, *Miss Sobey.*" Shawn responded with a resolute nod, sounding all too agreeable. "But it doesn't matter to me that this whole marriage business was really yer idea — or that ya presented it while ya had me in front of all my friends so I couldn't say no."

He tilted his head to one side while he studied her more closely. "Most men woulda been very upset about such a thing, but y'll find I've decided to be a very good sport about this whole matter."

170

He then shook his head, delighted by the myriad of emotions that played across her face, bringing a high color to her cheeks and an intensity to her brown eyes. Oh, how he longed to take the pins from her hair and let the soft tresses fall down across her shoulders. "And to think, all I wanted was to protect ya from the local riff-raff, which by the way I have done. Until this Tony fella came along, no man in all of Black Wall has dared to do little more than ask ya for the time of day. Just who is this Tony fella anyway? Do I know him?"

Although it bothered him that there was someone in that town who obviously was not afraid of him when he had all but openly admitted to having committed a double murder, he tried not to sound all that upset. He also tried not to let on that it had also bothered him to find out that the beautiful, beguiling Catherine Sobey was now interested in someone else. Bothered him a lot more than it should. Still, it did not really surprise him for he had noticed the admiring way men stared at her when they knew her back was turned. It would have been asking too much to hope every last one of them had stayed away.

Karissa's mouth pressed firmly against her teeth while she continued to tug on the ring, growing more frustrated by the minute. "I doubt you'd know him," she finally answered. "He is not the type to frequent the local taverns."

Shawn's eyebrows arched questioningly, aware that had obviously been intended as an insult. Odd though, coming from someone who worked in one. "Oh? And what type is he?"

"The type who asks a lady's permission before

making plans for her," she answered then finally gave up on removing the ring. All she had accomplished thus far was to cause her knuckle to swell and the base of her finger to throb and turn red. For now, she had little choice but to wear it. She looked at him suspiciously and wondered if he had purposely bought a ring too small for her finger so she would be unable take it off right away. It would be just like him to plan something like that.

Shawn crossed his arms over his chest and shifted his weight to one well-muscled leg, aware both her last comments had been intentional barbs directed at him. Although he loved the fiery glint in her dark eyes, he did not care much for her sharp tone. "And is he also the type who would spend his time in the company of another man's betrothed?"

"I really don't think that sort of thing matters to him one way or the other," Karissa retorted with a forward thrust of her chin then tilted her head at an angle while she studied his arrogant stance. It wasn't easy maintaining her composure around him, especially when every time she met his gaze she was certain he was remembering the way she had allowed him to kiss her with such wild abandon. "What is it that you *really* want?"

Delighted she was on to him and did not take everything at face value, Shawn unfolded his arms and stretched his mouth into an easy smile. Long, narrow dimples curved around the corners of his mouth, drawing her attention to their endearing quality. "What any man would want from his intended."

He waited until her shoulders had stiffened in response before quickly adding, "To spend the afternoon basking in her fair beauty." His smile eased somewhat while he considered the rest of what he wanted to say. "And the chance to tell this Tony fella a thing or two right to his bloody face. I'd like for him to know exactly what he's dealin' with when he tries to spend time with my woman."

"First of all, I'm not *your* woman," she reminded him with a meaningful glower. "And I don't think he'd be very impressed even if I was." She glanced out into the yard beyond. "But if you really want to make a complete and utter fool of yourself, then go right ahead. He's right out there."

Shawn spun about, prepared for an immediate confrontation, then frowned when he noticed that the only person was a dark-headed boy with big green eyes and chipmunk cheeks who looked to be no more than six years old and who was busy poking holes in the ground with a sharp stick.

"*That's* Tony?" For the life of him, he could not figure out why he felt so relieved. He had been quite prepared to defend his claim against whatever foe—even if he really did not have that right. "That's who you plan to spend the afternoon with?"

"Yes," she answered with certainty, then took another small step away from him. When she did, she moved directly into the sunlight, which caught her long, upswept curls and brought out the golden highlights. "We made our plans yesterday right after lunch."

"And ye're in no way interested in sharin' a picnic with me instead?" he asked, wishing he could somehow change her mind. For once, nothing else pressed for his time.

"No, not today."

Shawn studied her determined expression. "Then what about next Sunday?"

Karissa's dark eyes stretched into an expression of obvious disbelief. "Are you actually asking me in advance?"

"Aye. That I am."

She turned her beautiful head to one side and lifted a skeptical eyebrow. "And you will abide by my answer no matter what that answer is?"

Shawn looked at her warily. "Aye."

"Then my answer is no. Just because the people in this town are foolish enough to believe you and I are engaged does not mean we should feel obligated to spend our time in each other's company. I'd prefer to spend the day alone. It is the only full day I have in which I can rest afterward because I don't work, and there are several things that I'll need to do."

Tiny lines formed at the corners of Shawn's blue eyes while he considered that response. "Ya don't like me much, do ya?"

"It's not that I don't like you," she answered honestly. "It's just that I don't trust you."

"Ahh, yes, that's right. Ya already told me. Ya don't trust any man." He tapped the tip of his finger against his forehead, as if he should have remembered. "But what I don't understand is why. What have men done to make you feel so unkindly toward them?"

"That really is none of your business," she answered, not about to relive the intense pain and humiliation that Robert Edwards had caused her. She had trusted him completely and he had made a mock-

174

ery of that trust, as had most of the other men in her life. Why, the only two men who had ever treated her fairly were her own father and Madison, their butler.

Shawn realized by the way her shoulders had stiffened he had struck a sensitive cord. Grinning, in hopes of easing the sudden tension that had sprung to life between them, he asked, "Will ya tell me *after* we are married then? Surely it would be my business once y've become my wife."

Karissa let out an exasperated breath, tired of pointing out the obvious fact that they were not really engaged, then motioned toward the front gate with a brisk wave of her hand. "Go. Now. Before I call Charles McAllister out here and have you physically removed from the premises."

"Y'd do that to yer own fiancé?" He tried his best to look deeply hurt instead of amused. "Y'd have him thrown out on his ear? Y'd do that to the man you love?"

Rather than respond to something so preposterous, she folded her arms firmly across her bosom and stared pointedly at him while she waited for him to comply — all the while fighting the strangest desire to grin. The man was impossible. "Go."

"Ye're certainly not very encouragin'," he muttered, pouting like a small child might. "All I wanted was a bit of your fine company." And the chance to take his mind off the danger and complexities of his latest assignment for an hour or so.

Karissa studied the little-boy expression for a moment and felt the odd urge to relent, but something inside her cautioned against spending the afternoon with him. She had enough to worry about without adding a tall, handsome, and extremely willful admirer to her list of concerns—especially when she remembered that this particular admirer might very well have been involved in her father's murder. His name was Shawn, and he had at least two friends who went by the names *Joey* and *Jack*. "If you'd like a little company, might I suggest you find yourself a dog? As I recall, there is one that hangs around the railroad depot almost every day. Perhaps you could encourage him to spend the day with you."

Having said that, and knowing how very close she was to giving in and asking him to join in their afternoon hunt for wild berries, she bid him a quick farewell then spun about on her slippered heel and hurried back inside the house.

Shawn stared after her, admiring her quick graceful movements while she sailed from his sight. Again he wondered what could have caused a woman of such obvious poise and refinement to end up as a common bar maid in a modest-sized tavern in a small mining town.

Having always been the inquisitive sort, by the time he had reclaimed the food basket and had headed back the same direction he had come, he was more determined than ever to resolve the mystery that surrounded her. He had to know why she was there.

Karissa was almost asleep when she heard a light tapping on her bedroom door—three quick raps followed by three slow.

Aware it had to be Frank needing a private word with her, she hurried to put on her wrapper before she opened the door at the top of the darkened stairway just wide enough to let him inside.

Because of the urgent need for secrecy, she did not bother to light a lamp even after she had closed the door and had moved back across the room; nor did she dare to speak above a soft whisper.

"What do you have for me?" she asked, knowing he would never have risked coming to her room unless he had important information. Even when it was well past midnight and everyone else living there had retired to their different bedrooms hours earlier, she and Frank had agreed to have contact with each other only when absolutely necessary. "What have you found out?"

"Nothing I can prove yet," Frank answered, also whispering, but in a much huskier voice, one that befitted a man in his late fifties. "But tonight I was told the names of two men who were probably involved with the murders — and it looks like your brother was dead right for once. Both men are suspected of being active members of the local Molly Maguires, though I can't really prove that about them either."

"Who are they?" She took a long, deep breath to steel herself against the coming answer for she now knew the names of more than half the men in town and had come to like a good many of them, especially those who came by the tavern early for one or two drinks then left because they had families waiting for them at home. Those men rarely tipped well, but they never caused any trouble nor did they become obnoxiously drunk like some of the others. And since money was never the reason she wanted the job, she did not care that those men kept most of their money to themselves and instead paid her with compliments and laughter.

Despite being surrounded by darkness, she closed her eyes and prayed the murderers would not be family men.

"One of the two is an older man named Jack McGeehan, who is already in jail for having murdered one of his own," Frank told her then paused a moment. "And the other one is that same man who keeps pretending to be engaged to you for all the attention it gets him. That tall, arrogant cuss who follows you around all the time."

"Shawn McCowan?" Although she had halfway expected it, she did not want to believe it. "Are you sure?"

"Not yet. Like I already told you, I don't have any hard evidence yet, but I'm already working on getting all the tangible proof I'll need to hang both him and his friends. I just thought you needed to be forewarned. That man is considered to be very dangerous by everyone who knows him. Just how dangerous I won't know until I've dug a little deeper into his past, which I'm having a hard time doing; but for now I think it would be wise for you to stay completely away from him."

Karissa felt a chill splash across her shoulders and spill down her back, causing tiny bumps to prickle beneath her skin. "When do you think you will know something more definite?"

"I can't really say. Because of the cautious nature of those even remotely involved with the Molly Maguires, it will take me a while to earn enough of their confidence to find out exactly what I need to know.

178

Meanwhile, I want you to continue keeping your pretty little ears open. Keep me informed of any unusual conversations you overhear, especially at the tavern. I'll want to know anything that might indicate Molly Maguire activity. Pay particularly close attention to anything Nathan Knight, Sirus Bebber, or Charlie McAllister say. It would help a lot if I could figure out their exact meeting place. I know it has to be somewhere up on the mountain because I've watched both McCowan and McAllister slip off into the woods during the oddest of hours, albeit always separately."

"Charles McAllister is one of them?" she asked, clearly surprised. He was such a likable man. How could he be involved with such a band of ruthless cutthroats?

"Appears so. Fortunately, he is not quite as secretive about that fact as some of the others are, at least not after he's had a bit too much to drink. Still, he'd rather talk about our pretty little red-haired landlord with whom he is definitely smitten than about any Molly activities."

"I'll do what I can," she promised, knowing that was exactly why she had come, to uncover the truth in any way possible.

"Good," he said, already reaching for the door latch to let himself out. "Guess I'd better get on back down to my room and catch myself a wink. I've got another long day ahead."

For several minutes after Frank left, Karissa stood in the middle off the darkened room contemplating all that he had just told her. She hated to think that Shawn could actually be one of the men who had killed her father, because in some small way she had started to like him, too; but if it turned out he was guilty, she would do everything possible to see that he was convicted. Even if it meant placing herself in further danger.

Aware she had one clear advantage over the private detective she had hired in that Shawn seemed very determined to get to know her better, she decided that rather than avoid the tall, handsome man as she had just been asked, she would instead actively pursue him to see what she could find out from him.

She had to do something. She had already been in Black Wall for nearly a week and had yet to discover anything about the Molly Maguires—or anyone else who might have had a hand in killing her father. In the six days she'd been there, she had made no noticeable progress, nor had she overheard anything that might help in some way. Although patience was considered a virtue, it was time to take more drastic measures, time to be more than a set of ears for the detective she had hired. It was time to take a few matters into her own hands.

But she knew better than to tell Frank of such plans. He would never approve of her purposely putting herself into such a dangerous situation. He might even become angry enough with her to threaten to quit and she did not have the time or the desire to interview any more private detectives. Besides, she still had the derringer, which she now carried where she could get to it. If Shawn tried to cause her too much trouble, she would simply shoot him.

With those thoughts still floating through her mind that following night after work, she did not try to ignore Shawn as she usually did when he appeared out of nowhere to walk her to her rooming house. Instead she greeted him with a warm smile while she did what she could to control her rapid heartbeat—which she now attributed more to fear than to the way the moonlight glistened from his dark hair and gave his handsome face an even more rakish look.

For some reason, it seemed unfair that a man with such a questionable reputation should look that appealing.

"Oh, there you are," she said as she handed him her lantern, a gesture that served two purposes. It let him know his presence was welcome and also freed her hands should she need to make a sudden grab for the derringer she now carried in her skirt pocket instead of her boot.

Her pulses continued to race wildly when she glanced at him. Although she was no stranger to the pleasures and triumphs of a passing flirtation, she had never before played the game for such high stakes. If he were to catch on to what she was doing, or if he were to find out who she really was, he might very well decide to kill *her*, too. *That is, if he really was one of the men involved*. "I noticed you did not come into the tavern at all tonight. You weren't off sulking somewhere because of the way I treated you yesterday, were you?"

"No. I just had somewhere else I had to be," he answered vaguely, then grinned dimple deep just before he fell into step beside her. "Don't tell me that ya actually missed me."

"No more than I missed several of the others who did not stop by tonight," she answered quickly, not

181

wanting him to think her too eager, then forced another flirtatious smile. "It's just that I was curious to hear how your picnic went."

"Ahh, the picnic. Y'll be pleased to know that the dog thoroughly enjoyed himself," Shawn answered with a curious arch of his eyebrows. He found the sudden change in her disposition a bit unsettling. "We had ourselves quite a feast."

He did not want her to know that he had actually taken the food basket back to his room right after he left her so he would be free to follow her later—nor that he had watched while she and the young boy filled their baskets with wildflowers and berries.

Being the type of man who never accepted anyone's word as fact, following her like that was the only way he could know for certain that she had told him the truth. It had also allowed him an opportunity to have a peek at the truly delightful woman behind that beautiful face. From his hiding place behind a thick stand of young cedar trees, he had witnessed her passion for children firsthand for she had laughed and played and danced about with the same exuberance as the young boy.

They had been two carefree spirits frolicking about the woods, happy as larks—which had caused Shawn to feel a little guilty for spying on them. It had also showed him what Catherine was like when all her barriers were let down and made him wish he could find a way to inspire that same sort of laughter and that same adoring smile from her.

"I'm glad to hear you found yourself a new friend. Dogs can become quite loyal after you've fed them a time or two," she said, then decided to see what she could find out about him by starting with a few insignificant questions then building up to that information she really wanted to know. "Did you ever have a dog when you were a child?"

"Not one of my own, but my grandmother, bless her, she had herself a fine dog. His name was Frisky and that was exact!y what he was. Frisky as a lamb, even when he was nigh on twelve years old." He laughed when he thought about the mindless black mutt with the eager brown eyes and gold tipped ears. "What about you? Did ya ever have a dog of yer own as a child?"

Karissa frowned. She did not dare mention the fact that they'd had several dogs, most of which were let loose on the premises at night to frighten prowlers away. That would be an odd response coming from someone who was supposed to be little more than a penniless waif. She had no choice but to lie.

"No. My family could not afford a dog," she said, and looked into the darkened windows of a nearby business to keep him from seeing into her eyes. Never having tried her hand at lying before coming to Black Wall, she feared he might be able to tell something was wrong just by looking at her. "My father said it would cost too much to feed one. They do eat a lot, you know."

Not knowing the true reason she could no longer face him, Shawn decided she was ashamed of having been so poor. But then he thought more about it and wondered how her father had afforded to give her such a noticeable education if he did not have the money to feed even one dog. Finally he decided the man must have really loved his daughter to save out enough to send her to what had to have been a very expensive private school. She was far too poised and far too educated to have gone to public schools. "Then I guess ya had no pets at all."

"No," she answered quickly, then wondered how to get the conversation turned back in the direction she wanted. It seemed they were forever talking about her, which was exactly what she did *not* want to do. She tried to decide how her father would handle the situation and for a moment had to fight the sharp stab of sadness his sudden image evoked. "Did you have any pets of your own?"

"Aye. Several," he answered, but did not elaborate because what he wanted was find out about her, even though he suspected by the way she continually turned away from him that at least part of what she told him was not altogether truth. He reached for her left hand and looked at the tiny ring still on her finger for a moment, but did not comment on the fact she had yet to find a way to get it off. He knew that would just make her angry again at a time when he did not want her angry at all. Instead, he let the hand drop back to her side and continued their conversation. "Ya are obviously not from around here. Where did ya do yer growin' up?"

Karissa's whole arm tingled in response to his touch and she wondered why he had held her hand so briefly.

"In Pittsburgh," she answered honestly, but she also did not elaborate. She wanted to keep the conversation centered on him. "Where did you grow up?"

"Mostly in New York the city, though I spent quite a bit of time visitin' my grandparents' farm when I was a lad. Where did ya go to school?"

"In Pittsburgh. Although my father was usually off working in the coal mines somewhere, my mother preferred to stay in the city," she answered, keeping to the story she had told Marcus that first day she arrived. "Where did you go to school?"

Shawn let out an annoyed breath. He was learning far less about her than he wanted. For every question he asked about her, she countered with one of her own about him. He had to break that trend by finding some topic that interested her enough she would be willing to discuss it at length.

"In New York, mostly," he answered, then quickly asked his next question. "Did you and yer new friend, Tony, enjoy yerselves yesterday?"

"Oh, yes," she responded with a bright smile, remembering exactly how much fun they'd had. "We had a wonderful time. We found out that if we climbed up high enough, we got away from most of the coal dust and mine smoke that blackens everything down here. We saw green trees and tall grass and some of the most beautiful wildflowers ever to grace this earth."

Relieved she had yet to counter by asking another question of her own, he pursued the matter further. But this time he was careful not to ask a true question. "I gather ya like children."

"Of course I do," she answered, thinking that an odd statement. "Everyone likes children. Don't you?"

Shawn closed his eyes briefly. They were back to discussing him again. "I suppose."

"Do you have any of your own?" she hurriedly added, keeping the conversation centered on him.

Shawn felt a painful tightening in his chest when he remembered the beautiful baby boy that had been stillborn, and how his dear Nicollette had died only hours later. "No. I have no children."

"But you've been married," she quickly put in, afraid he would change the topic again if she didn't keep at him.

He looked at her oddly. "How is it ya know that?"

"Because last week when someone first asked you if you planned to make an honest woman of me by marrying me, you said something about having had your fill of that sort of thing. I gather from having said that, your marriage ended unhappily."

Shawn took a deep breath to ease the black sorrow that still filled his heart on occasion. "Quite unhappily."

"Did she leave you?"

The surface muscles in his jaws hardened when the sharp pangs of regret pierced the very core of his soul. But Karissa had no way to know the reaction was anything but intense anger.

"Aye, she left me." Slowly he released the breath he had not realized he held.

Karissa felt something tug at her heart and wondered why any woman would ever leave such a handsome man then realized he must have done something so very horrible that she had run away from him out of sheer fear or in hate. The reason certainly could not have been because she had found a more appealing man to take his place. There could be no one more appealing than Shawn McCowan. "Do you ever see her?"

"No. She's dead now."

Karissa studied the rigid lines of his jaws a moment longer and wondered what emotion raged through him at that moment. Was it hatred or regret or perhaps intense anger?

"I'm sorry."

"Don't be," he told her, for she'd had nothing to do with that part of his life. "All that happened a long time ago." Hoping to turn the conversation back to her, he added, "I've learned that death is just another part of existence. Haven't ya ever lost anyone?"

A chill skipped down Karissa's spine, causing her to shudder. She could not believe how unemotionally he had just talked of death. Did he really have so little regard for that precious commodity called life?

"Yes, I have," she answered, for the first time being truly honest. "I have lost both my parents and all four grandparents." Her voice quivered and her lower lip trembled when the unbidden image of her beloved father lying dead in his own blood drifted before her. He had been such a warm, loving man. "And I'm afraid I don't look at death quite as casually as you do."

Aware he had hit upon an extremely painful topic, Shawn hesitated before asking his next question, not knowing whether he should pursue the matter or let it go for now. "Sounds like ya lost someone quite recently."

"I did. My father died just a few weeks ago." She could not stop the tears from spilling down her cheeks. She had not allowed herself to cry since the day of her father's funeral and had held her grief penned inside for far too long. "I lost *everything* when I lost him."

187

Shawn fell silent for a moment while he considered that last remark, thinking that explained why a woman who had obviously been brought up in a good family and sent to a prominent school was suddenly so destitute. After having already lost her mother for whatever reason, her father had died and left her nothing to live on. But what that did not explain was why she was out on her own instead of living with relatives or why she was not married like most women her age. Then he remembered. She distrusted men. And no wonder. Her own father had proved untrustworthy enough to have left her alone and penniless after his death.

"That's a shame," he said, thinking he had finally solved the mystery behind the beautiful young woman. Now he knew why she was in Black Wall working as a common bar maid. It was probably the first time she'd ever worked in her life, and having no developed skills, that had been the only sort of work available to her. "Do you have no other family?"

"Only a half-brother," she answered honestly, but knew she dare not mention his name. "But we are not close."

And he was probably left just as penniless as she, Shawn surmised. Suddenly, he felt very protective of this beautiful, brave young woman and slipped his left arm around her shoulders to comfort her. "That's *his* loss."

Karissa did not know what to think about such an unexpected show of tenderness. According to Frank, the man was very possibly a cold-blooded killer — a high-ranking member of those murderous Molly Maguires — yet he displayed such tenderness and warmth when he was around her. It was bewildering. And it set her pulses to racing again, this time with far more reason than just fear. Although she knew she shouldn't, she liked having him that close. Liked it very much.

"Yes, I suppose it is his loss. But it is also mine," she answered, and for the first time wished she and John did get along better. After all, he and Lana were the only family she had left now. They should band together and find comfort in each other instead of driving each other apart.

While she and Shawn walked the remaining distance to the rooming house in mutual silence, Karissa tried to figure out why it was she and John had never really gotten along—even when they were younger and lived in the same house—and decided the reason lay in their obvious differences of opinion.

Sadly, she realized that Lizbeth was right. She and John were just too different. They always had been and always would be. It was as if they had been born of one father yet existed in two entirely separate worlds. Although they might one day manage to set aside some of their stronger differences, they would never be what one would consider close. They just did not have enough in common for that to ever happen. The best she could hope for was a modest friendship and she would probably have to work especially hard just to obtain that.

By the time Karissa had reached such a dismal conclusion, she and Shawn were on the veranda and it was time to take the lantern back and tell him good night. Suddenly she felt so tired, her eyes felt heavy and her legs ached.

"How do you do it?" she asked, for the first time realizing that when Shawn left her each night it was usually midnight or later, yet he had to wake up in time to be in the mines by seven o'clock like everyone else.

"How do I do what?" he asked. His own thoughts had drifted back to a happier time, back to those days when his wife was still alive and there had been that magical promise of a child. How different his life would have been had she lived. He would have remained in the business world rather than looking toward jobs that included such danger and intrigue. Anything to keep his mind off the past.

She looked at him oddly. "How do you live with only five or six hours of sleep each night?"

Shawn shrugged. "I don't know. I'm just one of those people who does not need a lot of sleep." Which was true. Even when he was not working on an assignment that required so very much of his time and attention, he usually slept only five to six hours a night.

"It's hard for me to imagine someone getting by with so little sleep," she admitted. "I have to have eight or nine hours every night or I can't think clearly the following day."

Shawn's dimples appeared immediately. "Ah, then the secret to winning you over is to keep you up all night," he teased, then bent forward and brushed a fleeting good night kiss against her forehead.

It had been such a simple gesture and one that warmed her to her very toes. But the warm feeling was short-lived when she remembered what Frank had told her the night before. Shawn McCowan was one

190

of several men he now suspected of having helped murder her father. And until he knew for certain who was involved and who was not, she should not allow herself to care about Shawn.

"I'll see ya tomorrow," he said with a playful wink, then turned and sauntered away, leaving Karissa to wonder how such a truly likable man could ever be considered genuinely dangerous. She had seen the compassion in his eyes when she had mentioned the death of her father and had seen a glimmer of sorrow when he mentioned the death of his wife. Clearly, the man had too much heart to be a cold-blooded killer.

Chapter Ten

"Keep it," Sirus Bebber said to Karissa when she bent forward to place his change on the table. "I like you. You're different from those other two." A wide smile broke the dark tangle of beard that covered his thin face. "I guess that's why you are wearing Shawn McCowan's commitment ring. He realized right off that you were different from most of the bar maids we get in here. Besides, you kind of remind me of my little sister, Christina. She has big, innocent-looking brown eyes and piles and piles of dark brown hair just like you."

Karissa purposely ignored her body's intense reaction to the mere mention of Shawn's name that occurred even though she knew she wore the man's ring under false pretenses — or at least she *hoped* he understood they were false.

Instead, she focused on the coins in her hand.

"But this is fifteen cents," she pointed out, thinking Sirus may not have realized just how much change he had coming.

In the thirteen days she had been there, she had come to understand the honest value of the hard-earned dollar, especially after having discovered first-hand the outrageous prices charged by their own company store, where these poor, struggling miners had little choice but to shop. Most of those working the mines were paid at least half of what was owed them in store tokens whether they had agreed to such an arrangement or not.

It was a terrible injustice to those men who worked so hard to bring the coal up out of their mines, an injustice she intended to rectify the minute she returned to Pittsburgh and took over her duties as the new administrator of Caine Enterprises. She also planned to find out just whose idea it had been to entrap the miners like that in the first place and fire the man on the spot. And if it turned out to have been her brother's idea, she would make sure he never had the chance to make such decisions again.

She was just as determined to reinstate the widows' pensions and have mine safety brought back up to her father's earlier standards. She also wanted to see that these men were again paid an honest wage.

"I had me a darn good day at the livery," Sirus explained, his smile widening as he lifted his beer mug off the small scarred table and hoisted it to his mouth in preparation of taking that first, frothy drink. "And I should do even better this coming weekend."

"Why is that?" she asked, watching him down nearly a third of his drink in that first, long draw.

"Because the new head of Caine Enterprises is coming here for a few days and both he and the new local superintendent will want to rent my best carriages so they can ride up to the mines and inspect them in comfort."

"John's coming here?" she asked with a fearful constriction pulling at her chest, not realizing she had used his first name.

John had been told she would be up at Cresson during these next few weeks, trying to get over their father's death. It would ruin everything if he came to Black Wall and accidentally caught a glimpse of her while he was there. Not only would he undoubtedly call her by her real name, thus alerting everyone to the fact she was an imposter, he would find out why she was there and demand that she return home immediately.

But something was not right. Why would John be coming there of all places? Why would he make such a long, tiring trip himself when he could send one of their operations inspectors instead? She might have expected that sort of personal interest from her father, who had often randomly inspected the general operations of his own companies. But such deep concern seemed grossly out of character for John.

Her stomach knotted while she further considered his reason for coming. It was possible he was headed there because he had found out the truth and wanted to locate her and take her home. But how could he be certain where she had gone? Lizbeth was the only one who had been told her real plans and had sworn not to reveal them to anyone, even if Karissa failed to report in as she'd promised. "Why on earth would he be coming here?"

"Oh, and I suppose you know the man personally," Sirus put forth with a laugh, then winked gaily at the other men seated around his table. "You probably have dinner at the family table every Sunday. Am I right?"

"No, of course not," she responded in a sassy tone, having come to enjoy the easy banter of her customers and knowing that would be the easiest way to distract him from such an dreadful blunder. "I barely have time for breakfast before he rushes me out of there."

Delighted with the suggestive nature of that last comment, the men elbowed each other and laughed louder still.

"I can imagine," Sirus said, nodding appreciatively at her quick wit and reached up to wipe his dripping beard with his shirt sleeve. "I hear the man is quite married."

"Aren't *all* the rich ones?" she asked, then slipped the fifteen cents into her pocket, glad they had let the fact she had referred to her brother by name pass by so easily. Clearly, they believed she had picked up on the name while listening to casual conversation as the rest of them had. "Can I bring you gents anything else before I go over see what old Charlie wants?"

She gestured toward the back of the room where Charles McAllister, Frank Neely, and a young friend of Shawn's named Joey McGeehan sat playing a friendly game of cards. "He keeps looking around like he's ready for another beer."

"Go see what old Charlie wants?" Sirus repeated, already grinning over what else he had to say. "You mean besides the Widow Waylan?" His comment set off yet another round of boisterous laughter.

Karissa laughed, too, for it was common knowledge the big fellow was smitten by the short, voluptuous red-haired woman. "Yes, of course besides the Widow Waylan. Although I imagine I would earn myself a much larger tip if I could produce *her* at his table instead of a frosty cold beer or a hot bowl of stew, I do think I'd have a hard time actually doing so."

She waited until the laughter had died somewhat before she headed across the crowded room to the corner table where Charlie, Frank, and Joey sat contemplating their cards. While she stood nearby waiting for Frank to finish deciding his opening bet, not wanting to interrupt such a deep thought process, she overheard someone call out Shawn's name.

She felt an unaccountable rush to her senses that filled her with both excitement and wariness when she turned and watched him enter the noisy, smoke-filled tavern with his usual long, agile strides. As was always the case, the room quieted for a moment just before he headed toward the bar, making her wonder again why so many of these men admired him that much. Didn't they all know he and his friends were suspected of being cold-blooded murderers? Or was it possible that Shawn came across to them as being so much of a man's man, they just did not care.

"About time he got here," she heard muttered from the table directly behind her. Her eyes widened when she realized the derisive comment had been spoken about Shawn. Obviously not *everyone* inside the Lucky Choice that night revered Shawn's presence with the same depth as the others. Someone was very unhappy with the fact he had come in so late.

Karissa fought the temptation to turn around and

see who had spoken with such resentment. She was afraid that a curious glance might stop whoever it was from saying anything else, and was too curious to hear more of what he had to say about Shawn to risk it.

"How long can it take to run a simple errand like that? He should have been back here hours ago," the complaining voice continued. "It's after nine o'clock. I don't know about you four, but I am bone tired. I need to get some sleep tonight."

A cold, prickling sensation trickled down Karissa's spine while she waited to hear if anything would be said in response; but the voices from the surrounding tables escalated again, making it impossible to single out any one person's comments. While moving closer to Frank's chair, she gave a quick glance over her shoulder at the five men seated at the table behind her but could not tell who had spoken. What she did notice though was the way they nodded knowingly at each other, as if conveying some secret message.

"What will you gents have?" Karissa asked, looking directly at Frank to see if he had overheard the strange comment, but his eyes were focused on his cards.

"Beer," Frank responded without lifting his gaze. He waved his cigar about as if it were an important instrument of conversation. "For all three of us. And since most of the money on this table is now mine, I'm buying."

"Not for me," Charles put in, surprising not only Karissa, but Frank, too. Being temporarily out of a job, Charles McAllister rarely turned down a free drink. "I wouldn't have time to be finishin' it. I'll be leavin' out of here in just a few minutes."

Joey studied him curiously then turned to scan the room. When his green gaze fell on Shawn, he looked as if he suddenly understood why Charles would want to leave without having had that free drink. "None for me neither."

Frank glanced at the young man with his dark blue knit cap pulled low over a head of thick, sandy blond hair, then at Shawn standing near the bar across the room, then shrugged his shoulders. "Well, I guess you only need to bring over one beer."

"One beer it is." The uneasy feeling inside Karissa continued to build when she turned and headed toward the bar to place the order. She noticed that several of the men seated about the room were watching Shawn as if expecting something special of him. It was then she noticed it. A barely perceptible nod of Shawn's head followed by a quick cut of his blue eyes toward the side door.

One by one, the men who had sat casually watching him downed their last drink, made their excuses, and headed outside. By the time she maneuvered her way to the bar and had told Marcus she needed another beer for Frank Miles, eleven men had left the tavern. But Shawn still remained.

Curious to know why so many men had suddenly left, she walked to the far end of the bar where Shawn watched her while he sipped his beer. It made her feel ill-at-ease to find that he was studying her so closely.

"Why is everyone leaving?" she asked, then turned to look out at the room that was now dotted with empty seats before she returned her attention to him.

Shawn's eyebrows dipped slightly, as if he had not expected her to ask such a question, then he lifted them again when he glanced around at the fifty or so men who remained. "What do ya mean? No one is leavin'. Most everyone appears to be sittin' down and havin' a fine time."

"That's because those who suddenly saw a reason to leave have already left. I just watched nearly a dozen men get up and walk out within just minutes of each other."

"Maybe they didn't like the service," Shawn suggested with a light shrug, then took another casual sip of his beer, thinking next time the men needed to be a little less obvious about leaving. She was right. They had all gotten up and walked out at almost the same time, probably because he had been so late in returning.

Hurt by Shawn's intended insult, but not about to be distracted from what she wanted to know, Karissa set her tray aside and moved closer so they would be less likely to be overheard by those standing nearby. "The service in here is the same as ever. What's going on?"

"Best not to be askin' too many questions, my sweet," he commented, then bent forward to kiss her lightly on the cheek, pleased by the way her heavily lashed eyes always widened whenever he kissed her unexpectedly like that. "But if it will make ya feel any better, I'll go see what I can find out."

Having said that, he set his beer back down, pushed away from the bar, then strolled out as casually as he had entered, leaving Karissa to stare after him in total bewilderment.

"He's been in jail long enough," Charles McAllister

said, and slid off the large rock he had been sitting on. Just enough yellow light glowed from the one lantern that had been lit then placed in the center of the clearing to allow him to see the grim expressions of the others. "It's been over three weeks now. It's high time we got him out of there."

"That's right," Joey was quick to put in as he looked anxiously at the other men scattered across the wooded site. He'd yanked off his knit cap out of sheer frustration and his golden locks glimmered in the lamplight, making him look even younger than his twenty-two years. "The trial is this Friday. That's less than four days from now. We have to get my cousin out of there before then." He glanced at Shawn, who stood leaning against a tree with one knee bent, listening carefully to every word said. "If Jack's found guilty, they'll hang him that very same day. You know they will."

Shawn studied Joey's worried expression then looked out at the others. He knew they were all waiting to hear what he had to say. He said what they expected him to. "I'm game if Charlie is." And for once he was actually looking forward to taking the law into his own hands. These men were right. Jack McGeehan had no business being in that jail.

Charles smiled that big, crooked smile that had endeared him to so many. "Then it's settled. We'll spring him sometime Thursday night. Is there anythin' else we need to discuss before we start partin' company?" He glanced around to see if anyone looked as if he might have something more to say.

Sirus stood and leaned forward on his walking cane more as a way to get attention than steady himself. "I

200

know I'm not a voting member yet and I am really not supposed to say anything until I am, but I thought you might all want to know that John Caine is supposed to be here sometime this coming Friday or Saturday."

"Why's that? Do you think maybe he's coming to investigate his father's death?" Nathan Knight asked as if wanting to figure out why the new head man himself would come there when Black Wall represented only a small segment of Caine's many business concerns. He adjusted his eyeglasses with both hands while awaiting an answer.

"Don't really know what his reasons are for coming," Sirus admitted. "Could be he's coming because he wants to be here for Jack's trial. After all, it was his own father that Jack and Thomas were supposed to have killed just days before Jack was then to have turned on Thomas." Shifting his weight away from his cane, he shook his head at such a foolish notion. "All I do know for sure is that your new superintendent wanted to make sure I polished up the Stanhopes by Friday morning so a large group of them could ride up to the mines in comfort while the big man is here."

"If that's true then maybe we should get us up a committee of some sort and see if we can't have us a little talk with him while he's here," Joey suggested, looking for a way to take advantage of the new boss's unexpected visit. "Could be the son's not like the father at all. Could be he's more willing to listen to reason."

"Couldn't be hurtin' us none," Charles agreed. "We could at least let him know how we feel about all the changes that have been made these last few months.

Let him know we aren't goin' to put up with much more."

"Also, it wouldn't hurt for us to indicate that unless something is done to help our cause and soon, another member of the Caine family could end up just as dead as his father," Nathan put in with a knowing nod then thrust his jaw forward to show his determination.

Nathan might be a short, clean-shaven man and the only one in the group who wore eyeglasses, but he was clearly a man to be reckoned with. Shawn looked at him with a questioning frown. "Do you know somethin' about that murder that the rest of us don't?"

Nathan quickly shook his head then stretched his eyebrows until they stood high above the rims of his eyeglasses, wanting to make sure they gave his idea full consideration. "All I know is that the police still think some of us did it. Why not profit a little from such a fortunate misconception?"

Shawn grinned, and realized it was an idea worth considering since no one could get hurt simply by insinuating an idea. It was certainly better than Charlie's plan to blow up a large section of the mine if changes weren't made soon. "Might work at that," he said then nodded. "Might scare the man just enough to do right by us."

Although Shawn had been in Black Wall only eight months and was not really locked in to working mines for the rest of his life like the rest of them, he did sympathize with these men to a certain extent. In the few months since he had infiltrated the secret force known to most people as "those lawless Molly Maguires," he had attended enough of their meetings and had

202

worked in the mines enough days to understand that they really were being treated unfairly by the mine owners and that the mines where they worked really were unsafe.

Having nearly lost his own life when some of the new substandard bracing had collapsed a few weeks earlier, it was easy for him to appreciate many of the causes these men fought for. But what he could never appreciate were the ruthless actions some of them were willing to take in their attempts to get those wrongs righted—although at times he could understand *why* some of them had been driven to murder and violence. Many times these men were treated no better than animals, forced to work in areas that were either too hot or too cold for human endurance, or had filled with noxious gas that burned their throats and lungs because there was such poor ventilation.

If only there was some way to make the men understand that violence was not the right answer to their problems without making himself seem like an outsider. Then he might be able to solve some of the more serious problems both sides now faced. But because he needed this group's complete confidence to gather the sort of information Porterfield wanted, he had to pretend to be just as violent and just as angry as the rest of them.

If they ever found out that he had killed only once in his life and that had been in self defense back when he was working for the Pinkerton Agency, they would not treat him with quite the same admiration they did now. Nor would they allow him to make so many decisions for them, which had certainly been to his advantage. The more control he had, the less danger there was to him and those around him. He had a knack for convincing them to rethink some of their riskier ventures.

"Nathan, since Charlie, Joey, and I are takin' care of Old Jack's little problem, why don't ya and Sirus see if ya can arrange a little meetin' with Mr. John Caine?"

"Not Sirus," Charles put in quickly, then held up his hand to avert any comments until he explained why. "Sirus doesn't work in the mines anymore. Not since he lost part of that left foot. Now I realize he has a way of sayin' things in just the right way whenever we need him to, but our spokesman this weekend should be someone who's actually workin' in those mines. Someone who puts his life at risk every single day."

"Which would automatically leave you out," Nathan put in with a hearty laugh, not about to miss an opportunity to goad his large friend. "Ever since you told that new superintendent where he could put that pick ax, you've been above ground, too."

"Which is why I appreciate y' passin' the hat for me earlier," Charles responded, then scowled at the seriousness of his situation. "I really thought I'd be back on the payroll by now, but that new super has proved to be a very unforgivin' man." He took his hat off and raked a massive hand through his thinning hair, revealing the depth of his frustration. "It's hard makin' the rent when all I have is the few pennies I earn keepin' the coal dust swept off that bloody platform at the railroad depot."

Ralph Kilburn, a younger man who sat cross-legged on the large rock behind him, leaned forward and placed a supportive hand on his friend's large shoulder to let him know they understood. "I'll go with Nathan to have a word with this John Caine fellow. I'm sure between the two of us we can plead our case effectively."

"Good," Charles responded with a pleased nod. "Y'got a way of saying things right, too. Then it's settled. Nathan and Ralph will present our views to the new owner. Anything else?"

Nathan was first to glance at his watch then pushed himself up off the dead log where he'd been seated. "Since no one has any idea who really killed Thomas yet and it looks like we've been out here for nearly an hour already, I think we'd better be on our way. Before someone comes out here looking for us."

"Like yer wife?" Charles chuckled, also standing to leave. "I don't understand why that woman doesn't trust ya none. Could it be because yer always comin' in so late with such poor excuses about where y've been?"

Knowing they never let their meetings run for more than an hour no matter what issues were at stake, Shawn pushed away from the tree then brushed a few stray pieces of bark from his clothing while Charles stepped forward and picked up the lantern. "I think we've covered everything we needed to cover for tonight. Unless Charlie or I tell ya otherwise, plan not to meet again until next Monday night."

He waited in the center of the small clearing and watched while the others headed out through the woods in different directions. When he was certain no one had been out in the bushes listening, he headed back off toward Black Wall, wondering how he would explain everyone's disappearance to Catherine. She wasn't about to accept the fact that they had all suddenly decided it was time to go home, especially when some of them would undoubtedly stop back by three for another beer before heading off to bed. Nor would she believe they had all suddenly developed a strong hankering to head down the street and pay a quick visit at Miss Ruby's House of Sublime Entertainment, where women of lesser distinction took care of a man's needs for a nominal price. But what other excuse was there?

The fifteen-minute walk down the mountain into town gave Shawn time to think not only about what he might say to convince Catherine nothing peculiar had happened, but also about the problem that had arisen earlier when Joey suddenly announced that he wanted to help them free his cousin.

Unlike the other Mollies, who were all for it, Shawn did not want Joey to become such an active member of the group. He knew Joey had been lured into the Maguires only a few months earlier by his older cousin, Jack McGeehan, who had been a faithful member of that local chapter from its conception just over a decade ago.

It was apparent that Joey had become a member only because his cousin encouraged it. Obviously, the young man was as afraid to defy the man who had helped raise him as he was to defy the other members. Which was undoubtedly the reason Little Joey always did whatever he was told, whether it was a simple act of espionage or to cause major damage to someone's property. The young man simply did not have the courage needed to stand up and tell the others he did not want to participate, that he did not believe in handling matters in the same way they believed, or at least not to the same dangerous extent they did.

Shawn had sensed Joey's uneasiness from the very first day they'd met. And it was because the young man had not displayed the same depth of animosity as the others that Shawn had immediately taken him under his wing. He'd made certain Joey was rarely asked to do something that might put him in any real, lasting danger. Which was why it had bothered him so much when the boy suddenly volunteered to help them rescue Jack—knowing he had probably done so out of some deluded sense of family loyalty.

While Shawn headed back toward the Lucky Choice, where he would again be able to rest his tired, hungry gaze upon Catherine's beautiful face, he decided there had to be a way to change Joey's mind about helping them. What they planned to do was extremely dangerous. One tiny slipup and they could be killed. The boy was only twenty-two years old and Shawn wanted to make damn sure he lived long enough to see age twenty-three.

Although Robby Drier had not done anything that could harm Karissa physically since that first night she arrived in Black Wall, she shuddered when she realized he had been watching her for the past hour, his thick eyebrows drawn together in an angry, dull scowl. As was his custom, he had had far too much to drink as had the two men seated at his table.

"Laura, would you do me a favor and take care of Robby Drier for me?" she asked when she noticed him signal for her to come there. She was too tired to have to put up with his ugly glares and aggravating remarks any longer.

Laura pushed away from the bar where she'd been chatting with Marcus to see where Robby was seated. "Why? Is he giving you a bad time?"

"Let's just say he is not in the best of moods," Karissa admitted, then let out a weary sigh. "And I just don't have the strength to handle anyone like that right now." She had spent another sleepless night trying not to think about Shawn, and the past hour trying to think of nothing else, still wondering where he and the others had gone.

Laura shrugged then reached for her tray. "Since the place has pretty well thinned out, I guess I can take on an extra table."

Karissa glanced at the remaining customers. As was expected on a Monday night half an hour before closing, only a dozen or so men remained. And most of those were too drunk to care that they had to be up and at work by seven that following morning. The few who weren't that drunk had remained simply because they had nowhere else to go and they were not all that sleepy yet.

Surprisingly, Shawn was not among them. Which was why Robby's steady glower made Karissa so nervous. If Shawn were there, she would feel protected, for she well remembered the control he had over the huge, ugly man.

She glanced at the clock. It was almost time to close. Again she wondered where Shawn might be. He had not returned since his vow to find out where all those other men had gone.

"Marcus, what happened in here a couple of hours ago?" she asked, wondering if perhaps he knew and would tell her.

Reluctantly, Marcus pulled his gaze off Laura, who was now halfway across the room and looked at Karissa curiously while he thought over the night's events. "What do you mean? I don't remember anything happening."

"Shortly after Shawn came in here tonight, about ten or twelve men suddenly got up from their chairs and left. I was wondering why that had happened." She also wondered what Shawn had to do with the odd occurrence. Or *was* it an odd occurrence? She had been there only thirteen days. It was hard for her to judge what might be considered odd and what would be considered common occurrence in Black Wall.

Marcus's expression tensed when he reached forward. He took her hand in his, then rubbed it gently between his own as if coddling a small child. "Sometimes it is best not to ask too many questions."

"Why? Who were those men?" she persisted, although she already had her suspicions.

"Customers," was all he would admit, then smiled indulgently. *"Good* customers. All of them. And that's really all you need to know."

Karissa stared at Marcus a moment, wondering just how much he did know while she mentally reviewed the names of those men who had so suddenly left. All of the men Frank had told her to keep a careful eye on had been among them, which was why she now suspected that they were every one members of the Molly Maguires and had probably gone off to hold one of their secret meetings.

But what she did not know was if Shawn had left shortly thereafter just to find out where they had gone and why as he had said; or because he was supposed to be at the meeting, too. Then she remembered that Shawn had been the one they had all watched so carefully just before suddenly leaving. He was the one who had nodded ever so slightly toward them, as if indicating it was time for something to happen.

Even though Karissa had found no reason to doubt any of Frank Neely's assumptions thus far, still a tremor passed over her when she realized she had just seen visual proof that he was right. Shawn really was a secret member of that ruthless band of cutthroats. But how could that be? How could Shawn be involved with such a murderous group? When he was around her, he seemed like such an amicable person, always friendly, and always showing compassion toward his fellow workers. If he really was such a vile, treacherous man, how could he get along so well with everyone there—even the bosses?

It just did not make sense.

The Molly Maguires were evil. She had heard her father and his friends talk about them on many occasions. That's where she first learned that they were a select group of men, all low-wage Irishmen, mostly immigrants but some natural born, who had bonded together to look out for their own. She also knew that the Mollies did not care who they hurt or what they destroyed to get what they wanted or to right some wrong done to them by *anyone* who was not fortunate enough to have been born Irish. It did not matter if the person they attacked was a pit boss or a shop owner, or the member of a rival union group. If the Mollies thought a wrong had been done to one of them, there was always punishment to be dealt.

They proclaimed themselves to be a simple labor union like any other—only they refused to reveal their membership to anyone. But Karissa knew that what they really were was a pack of vile, ruthless men who were willing to murder or maim anyone who stood in the way of them getting whatever they wanted. Even women, children, and old men were not safe from their vicious attacks.

"Have you seen Shawn since all those men left?" she asked Marcus despite his warning not to solicit such information, then glanced at the door as if expecting Shawn to appear just because she had spoken his name. It had happened before.

"No. But then I haven't really been watching for him," Marcus admitted. He again patted her hand reassuringly while his gaze wandered off to find Laura again. Instead he noticed Deborah on her way toward the bar, an empty tray in hand. "Don't worry, he'll be here to walk you home. I'm sure of it."

Karissa's next breath caught deep in her throat while she stared at him. The thought of being alone with a person she now more than ever had reason to believe was a member of the Molly Maguires terrified her. Mollies were not to be trusted.

Yet at the same time she felt oddly compelled to see him again. She wanted the chance to question him again about what had gone on earlier that night. "You think so?"

"He hasn't missed a night yet," Marcus pointed out, then let go of Karissa's hand to take care of

Deborah's order. Though business had slowed to a trickle, he liked to be prompt at getting the drinks to his customers.

Karissa watched while Marcus quickly pulled a clean mug off the shelf and filled it with beer. She knew he had spoken the truth. Even on those nights when Shawn did not come in for a drink, he had not missed walking her to the rooming house. Nor had he missed the opportunity to kiss her lightly on her forehead and wish her a good night's sleep.

But then there might not have been any secret meetings of the Molly Maguires to get in the way of his seeing her until now. She knew if it came to having to choose between attending a secret meeting of the Molly Maguires or the chance to walk her that short distance to the rooming house just so he could kiss her good night and tease her a little, he would undoubtedly choose the meeting.

Still, she could not be certain that was where he had gone. Nor could she know how long such a meeting would last if it was where he had gone. All she could really do was wait to see if he returned to the tavern before they closed.

At fifteen minutes before midnight, Joey McGeehan entered through the front door, followed only a few seconds later by Nathan Knight. The two headed straight for the bar to order a couple of beers. Several minutes later, she heard the familiar thump-thump of Sirus Bebber's cane and he returned just as eager as the others to have one last, quick beer before the tavern closed.

To Karissa's relief, Robby Drier chose that moment to finish his last beer and leave, which meant she would not have to put up with him staring at her any longer. She watched while he and one of his friends stumbled through the front door and out into the darkened street. That left only the three men at the bar. Immediately, Laura and Deborah prepared to leave and within minutes both had offered their farewells and were gone. Karissa lingered behind, wanting to give Robby Drier and his friend plenty of time to be well on their way. Even though she now carried her derringer in her pocket, where she could reach it more easily, she did not want a confrontation.

"Pour me one more before I head on out of here," Nathan said, having been the first of the three remaining to finish his ale. He reached into his pocket to extract another coin, but scowled when all he came out with were a couple of worn-out store tokens. "I'm out of real money. Will you let me pay you with one of these instead?"

Marcus's expression turned deeply somber while he considered the offer. He did not like shopping at Caine Mercantile any more than the miners did; but he did not want to upset one of his more regular customers by refusing the token.

"Now, Nathan," he put forth in a friendly manner. "You know as well as I do, no one ever gets his money's worth at that particular store anymore. I do better sending over to Pottsville once a month for the things I need. But I'll tell you what I'll do. I'll go ahead and let you have one more beer, but I'd rather just wait and have you bring me the money for it tomorrow night."

Nathan nodded that he understood. "I'll place it in your hand first thing," he promised then put his token

213

away while he watched Marcus refill his mug.

Karissa felt a moment of guilt knowing Caine Enterprises was responsible for the worthlessness of those tokens, but knew there was little she could do until she was in a better position to take over.

"Joey, I hear your cousin goes on trial Friday," Marcus went on to say, his way of keeping the conversation alive while he set Nathan's beer in front of him.

"So they say," Joey responded with a wry lift of his eyebrows, then looked at Nathan and Sirus and cut them a quick grin.

Karissa watched while the three exchanged playful winks and jabs then she quickly turned away so they would not think her overly interested in their conversation. Aware these men had left at about the same time as the others, she thought perhaps they had just returned from a meeting and might say something that would indicate what had happened during that meeting or where it had been held.

"But don't you worry too much about that trial actually taking place," Nathan put in, clearly amused.

"Why?" Marcus asked but sounded only casually interested while he busied himself with collecting some of the dirty glasses and bowls scattered across the counter. "Have they found new evidence that will finally prove his innocence?"

Nathan glanced at Karissa to see if she was listening and noticed she was busily cleaning the sides of her lantern with a soft cloth, her gaze distant, as if lost in thought.

"No, they haven't come up with any new evidence; but that doesn't really matter. Jack will be gone before then," Nathan told him in a voice so low Karissa had

214

barely heard him. Then he abruptly changed the subject to the weather when they heard heavy footsteps scrape the floor across the room. He never turned to see who might have entered. It was enough for him to know they were no longer alone.

"Well, I guess I'd better carry myself on home," he said, speaking now in a much louder voice. "My wife will have my skin as it is." But when he turned to leave and saw that the person who had entered was Shawn, he made no actual move toward the door.

"Good. Ye're still here," Shawn said after he glanced around the room and spotted Karissa still behind the bar. "As late as it is and as empty as this place looked, I was afraid ya might have gone on without me and I'd miss my chance to kiss ya good night."

The men at the bar elbowed each other, clearly believing there was more to those good night kisses than a light peck on the forehead.

When Karissa did not immediately respond to Shawn's statement, Marcus took it upon himself to do so for her. "The truth is, she was free to leave about five minutes ago when the other two went; but she's been piddling around here ever since just waiting for you to show up."

Rather than admit that was the truth, at least partly, Karissa pretended she had not heard the comment when she lifted the lantern she had just lit and headed toward the door.

"Are you ready?" she asked, glancing at Shawn briefly.

Shawn winked at the other men before he, too, turned and headed toward the front door. "Ready, willin' and *able*."

Following behind her, he watched the graceful sway of her hips and took a deep breath to force his body not to react to his own lustful thoughts. The memory of how it felt to hold that soft, supple body pressed tightly against his with his mouth crushed hungrily over hers provoked a blaze of desire in him so intense, it actually hurt.

But it was a pain he would have to endure. There was no room in his life right now for that sort of a relationship to unfold.

It had proved distracting enough just being her self-appointed protector.

Chapter Eleven

Although Shawn knew it was pointless to try to dissuade Catherine from asking so many questions, that strong protective streak she always brought out in him prompted him to try. It was the same strong protective streak that had convinced him to walk her home each night after she finished work so that Robby Drier or others like him would leave her alone. Although he was not quite sure what it was, there was *something* about Catherine that made him want to be her champion. *Something* that made him want to keep her out of harm.

Perhaps it was because she was so new to Black Wall. She had no way of knowing that the seemingly innocent questions she had insisted on asking that night could place her in very serious trouble with the Molly Maguires. The group did not take kindly to newcomers who asked a lot of questions about them — no matter how pretty or innocent that newcomer might appear.

That was why he could not allow Catherine to continue placing herself in that kind of danger. He had to find some way to break that curiosity of hers before she ended up sticking that pretty little nose of hers into places where it would be easily cropped off.

"Just take my word for it, Katy, darlin'," he said, after suddenly deciding she needed a nickname. He held the lantern up high while they walked so she could see the sincerity in his expression. "There are several very good reasons I can't give ya the answers ya want," he said, wishing she would simply accept the fact she would not be getting an explanation and be done with it. "The most important reason of which is that it is none of yer business what these men do when they leave Marcus's tavern any more than it is their business what you do once ya've arrived at Mrs. Waylan's roomin' house."

"But it was such a curious thing," she persisted in her usual, headstrong manner. "Suddenly, about a dozen men just got up out of their chairs and left, some walking out the front door and some slipping out the side door. Why would they do that?"

She had repeated that question for a third time, determined to have an answer. She was tired of not being told what she wanted to know. Tired of getting nowhere with her attempts to find out who had killed her father. No matter what tidbit of information she sought, and no matter how cleverly she tried to obtain it, she always came away empty-handed.

Frustrated, she wondered why it was Frank who could get some of the locals to talk to him about those who were suspected of being a Molly, yet she could not persuade Shawn to give an honest answer to even one question. What was she doing wrong that Frank did right?

"I'm sure those men had their reasons," Shawn responded after a moment. The muscles along the backs of his jaws pumped in and out, indicating his patience had worn thin. The sound his workboots made on the rough-planked walkway became louder while his heels struck the surface with more clarity. "None of which would have anythin' to do with a beautiful sweet woman like yerself. Why is it so important that ya know such things?"

Determined not to be distracted by the unexpected compliment even though it had been most gratifying to hear, Karissa cut her gaze to the darkness around them. She did not want him to have a clear view into her eyes when she lied. "It's not all that important. I'm just curious to know what happened because I thought it was a little strange."

Shawn pulled his short-brimmed cap off and held it with his thumb and forefinger then ran his other three fingers through his thick hair as if that might help him to bring to the surface the words he needed. He continued holding the lantern in front of them with his other hand so they could see where they walked. "Ya *already* know what happened. Several men decided they suddenly had somewhere to go so they all got up from their chairs and left at about the same time. It's nothing to concern yerself with."

Annoyed to keep getting the same response, Karissa sighed, aware he had no intention of telling her anything beneficial. "Why is it such a secret where those men went?"

"It's not a secret!" He slapped his cap back down over his thick hair in a show of annoyance. Why did she have to be so mule-headed? "It's just not

219

somethin' ya need to know. Why is it ye're always askin' so many blamed questions? Some nights it seems that's all ya do."

"That's because I never seem to get any blamed answers," she replied with a resolute lift of her chin. "At least not from you." Then it dawned on her she was obviously asking the wrong person. Shawn was too stubborn to tell her anything; but perhaps one of the others would prove not so stubborn. Perhaps she should question young Joey. He was always looking at her with those big puppy eyes of his, as if wishing he were a couple of years older so he could ask to pay a call on her himself. Perhaps she could put that adulation to good use.

Since Joey was one of the men who had disappeared that night, it stood to reason he was also one of the Mollies, and because of his younger age, he would be much easier to manipulate. Another factor worth considering was that the young man's first name was the same as one of those on Jacqueline's list. It was possible that Joey McGeehan could turn out to be one of the men directly involved with her father's murder—though she found that very hard to believe. Joey might be twenty-two years old as he claimed, but he was still more boy than adult.

"That's only because ya ask the wrong questions," Shawn countered, then decided it was time to change the subject before they ended up in a nasty argument when the last thing he wanted to do that night was argue with the beautiful woman. "Now were ya to ask me what I think of yer new dress, then I'd feel inclined to tell ya it's quite pretty."

Karissa's forehead notched. She had not really expected him to notice. But after having grown tired of alternating those same four time-worn dresses when she was far more accustomed to wearing an outfit only a few times before tossing it aside, she had splurged and spent nearly all of her first week's earnings on a new dress that was a little more fashionable in design than those she had brought with her, though not by much.

For what she could afford to pay, and because of what the mercantile charged for finished dresses, she had barely been able to afford the azalea-pink broadcloth dress with a single, starched-crinoline lining that had struck her fancy.

Although the dress was not all that intricate in design, it had a three-inch banded waist made from dark burgundy silk that fit to her curves perfectly and had several rows of matching ruffles on the three-quarter sleeves. The neckline was deeply rounded but modest in cut compared to some of the dresses she had tried on, and the skirt had three stylish pleats in the back.

Although the pink and burgundy dress she had selected was much more colorful than the secondhand clothing she had been forced to wear since her arrival there and made her feel a little more feminine, it was still a far cry from the shocking garment Laura and Deborah had suggested she buy.

Having been in the store while she was trying on the small selection of dresses in her size, her two co-workers had done what they could to convince her to pick a garment that had been made mostly out of bright red satin and was tucked and flounced at the waist. The snug-fitted bodice, which was also made from bright red satin, had been shot through with tiny gold brilliants and had a daring enough neckline to have been a ball gown, though sorely lacking the proper skirt length. And as if all that were not enough to get the dress painfully noticed, it also had several tiny rows of black lace sewn at the hem and around the almost nonexistent sleeves. *Cap sleeves,* Laura had called them, *perfect for the warm summer months ahead.*

But Karissa did not have the courage it would take to wear such an outfit and had come away with the far more tasteful and less daring pink and burgundy dress. And now that Shawn had voiced his approval of that choice, she decided it was money well spent.

"Thank you for the compliment. For someone like me, new dresses are few and far between, but I did so long to have it," she said. "I guess I really should have spent the money on something more practical but I just could not help myself."

Reminded of his theory that her father had died and left her penniless, which was why she was as well spoken as she was beautiful, Shawn realized the misgivings she probably felt for having spent her money in such a frivolous manner.

"It seems only right that an attractive woman like yerself should have a lovely new dress from time to time." He stepped off to the side of the narrow gate that led to Kelly Waylan's rooming house to let Catherine pass through first then hurried to catch up with her, unaware her mind was on the fact he had complimented her again and no longer on the fact she had spent her money in such an imprudent manner. A soft breeze, cool and heavy with the scent of honeysuckle, pulled gently at the long strands of hair that had come loose from the twist she had arranged at the back of her head. The slight movement drew his attention to its silky texture.

"Ya know if you had snatched yerself a husband like most women yer age, ye'd probably be able to buy more such dresses for yerself," he told her. "Most husbands love to see their wives wearin' new dresses."

"But not all husbands can afford such things," she pointed out. Turning at the waist, she glanced back over her shoulder to make sure he followed while she continued along the short path to the front steps. "Some men have a hard enough time just putting food on the table."

Shawn fell silent. He knew that was true enough, especially for coal miners. "But the sort of husband you would attract would have plenty of money to spend on such things."

Karissa paused at the top of the steps to look at him, unaware of the way the silvery moonlight splashed against her skin.

"And do you have the money for such things?" she asked, knowing that as far as everyone else in Black Wall was concerned, *he* was her intended. She glanced at the small ring that still refused to come off her finger and knew that as soon as she returned to Pittsburgh, she would have to pay a jeweler to cut the blasted thing off. Then she would have to send it by special messenger back to Black Wall and make sure that Shawn received possession of it again.

Even though he had told her the ring was hers to keep for having put up with everything he had done, she would not feel right about keeping something so valuable from a man who worked at such a poorly paid, back-breaking job.

"I may not be a wealthy man," he answered, though not honestly, "but if I ever married again, I'm sure I could set aside enough money for my wife to have a new dress every now and then."

An old familiar ache filled his heart when he thought of the many dresses he had bought Nicollette in the two years they'd been married, especially those dresses designed to hide the fact that a baby was on the way so she would not feel like such a spectacle when she went out in public. How he had loved to lavish her with such gifts. "In fact I'd make a point of setting aside enough money for my wife to have many nice gifts."

"On a miner's pay?" she asked, clearly doubtful, unaware that his true earnings were over three thousand times what a typical miner made, that the only reason he worked at all was because he loved the danger and the intrigue. Loved the way it made him feel alive again.

Upon remembering she was supposed to be flirting with him to stay on his good side, Karissa curled her mouth into a timid smile and gazed up at him with wide, innocent eyes. "How could you ever afford it?"

He studied the beguiling way she looked at him for a moment, wishing he could crush her to him, then forced himself to answer. "If I loved a woman enough to marry her, I'd find a way for her to have nice things."

He felt an almost forgotten emotion wash over him while he continued to gaze down into Catherine's beautiful, moon-bathed face. Her dark eyes beckoned him like two jewels in a sea of glowing velvet. It had been a long time since he had wanted a woman as badly as he wanted this one.

"She would have nice things even if I had to go without."

It took great will for him to overcome the powerful urge to reach out and touch her delicate cheek. He knew that would be his own undoing. She had proved to be enough of a constant distraction without their becoming intimately involved with each other. He could imagine what it would be like if he ever let himself actually fall in love with her. But then he had managed to go this long without taking her into his arms again. There was no use spoiling all that now.

Still he was curious to know what she thought of him. "Do you believe that about me?"

Karissa looked at him a long moment and knew that he had spoken the truth. Shawn McCowan was the sort of man who, if he ever gave his heart to a woman, would give his soul and all his worldly possessions as well. Which was why it was so hard for her to imagine his first wife ever having left him. She still wondered about that, but then reminded herself there was a side to this man she had yet to see. The side that had allowed him to become a member of a violent group of terrorists like the Molly Maguires. The side that had allowed him to take part in her own father's murder.

If indeed he had.

Why was it she could not make up her mind about Shawn? Either he was a person able to commit murder or he was not.

At the moment, she preferred to believe not.

"Yes, I guess I do believe that." She studied the sincerity in his glittering blue eyes for a moment then realized how dangerously attractive he looked in the soft, yellow glow of the lantern he now held at his side.

A languid shiver spilled over her, causing her whole body to tingle with renewed awareness. He was truly the handsomest, most desirable man she had ever encountered. She crossed her arms to guard against the warm, quivering sensations that came over her when she realized just how handsome and desirable he really was.

Unaware of her physical response to him, Shawn ached his eyebrows in disbelief. He had expected another biting retort from her and now did not know what to think. But at the moment it was almost impossible for him to do anything more than gaze longingly into those wide, luminous brown eyes of hers — as if he were nothing more than a love-stricken schoolboy.

It was then, while she continued to gaze searchingly into his eyes, he knew he was going to kiss her again. Only this time not on the forehead nor the cheek. This time he planned to throw his earlier cautions aside and kiss her the way he had kissed her that first night — thoroughly and passionately. The way a man ought to kiss a woman.

Karissa watched the strange transformation on his face. A sudden heart-jolting current shot through her when she realized the reason his eyes had darkened so quickly. She had seen that same sort of response in a man's eyes before. She had seen it in *his* eyes before. That night in the livery.

Her heart drummed hard beneath the sensitive

226

walls of her chest, making it suddenly hard for her to breathe when she remembered the powerful kiss that had followed. It had been such a wonderful yet frightening experience for her.

"I-It's late. I should be going in now," she said, not knowing if she should let him kiss her again like *that* or not. She had responded so shamefully the last time, pressing her body ever closer to his as if she could not get enough of the pleasure he had wrought. She swallowed to ease the humiliation climbing her throat, embarrassed by the memory of her own bold behavior. What if she found herself unable to pull away yet again? What would happen then? She shuddered at the thought.

"No. Don't go in yet," he murmured in that deep, sensual voice of his that always made her want to close her eyes. He had already set the lantern aside and was bending forward to take that kiss he wanted before he spoke.

Aware that within seconds those splendid lips of his would once again be molded against hers, Karissa felt her next breath get caught deep in her lungs where it seemed permanently trapped. Her eyes grew very round as a result. She knew she should say something to him, something clever that would change his mind about kissing her, but the words simply would not form. Nor would her trembling legs carry her a cautionary step backward. It was as if she *wanted* him to kiss her, *wanted* to be overwhelmed by those same fiery passions he had aroused in her before. But that was ridiculous! Why would she want to put herself in such a truly dangerous situation again?

Holding Karissa's attentive gaze with his, Shawn

parted his lips while he continued to lower his exquisite mouth to hers. But rather than turn a stiff shoulder to him or back quickly away as she normally would have when faced with such brash behavior, she alarmed herself by leaning slightly forward to meet the kiss partway. Her heart raced with excitement and anticipation, causing a rushing sound in her head when their lips finally met in what started out as a surprisingly tender kiss.

Instantly Karissa was overwhelmed with a delicious sense of belonging, although there was no reason for such a feeling to exist. Slowly, she moved her arms out of the way and allowed him to pull her soft curves firmly against the hard, powerful planes of his body. Closing her eyes against the wondrous onslaught of desire and emotion, she listened to the gentle pounding in her ears while a strange, all-consuming warmth slowly entered her body from somewhere within and moved through her until it pervaded all her senses. She felt uncharacteristically weak and yielding, yet at the same time more vibrantly alive than she had felt in years.

After that, the kiss slowly deepened and her heartbeat grew ever stronger until her pulses throbbed in every part of her body with an alarming yet thrilling intensity. She had an immediate, overpowering desire to be closer to him even though it felt as if their bodies were already melded into one.

Pressing harder against him by shifting her weight to the very tips of her toes, she met the escalating kiss hungrily, eager to explore the passion that had swelled so unexpectedly inside her. What little apprehension she had felt during the onset had slowly dissipated until all she felt now was a turbulent desire to know more.

The tempest he had caused inside her had grown to all-consuming proportions and could no longer be compared to anything she had experienced in her life before. Overcome by emotions too powerful to subdue by sheer will, she responded to his every movement. Her lips parted beneath the gentle pressure of his while she slowly lifted her arms to encircle his strong shoulders. Pressing her hands against his back, she marveled at the brawn of muscles that had formed from years of hard work. She could sense the power behind each movement and moaned aloud in wonder.

Eager to take full advantage of Karissa's now parted lips, Shawn dipped his tongue into her sweet mouth, teasing the inner edges with quick, light thrusts, going ever deeper with each probing entry until she could not help but respond in kind.

Entering his mouth shyly at first, Karissa savored the tantalizing taste and enjoyed the shuddering response it had caused in him. She felt such a strong reaction to what she had done that it gave her a heady sense of power, making her forget for the moment that originally *she* had surrendered to him and not the reverse. *She* was the one who should have turned away when she first realized his intention to kiss her, especially when she knew there was still a very real possibility he was the enemy.

But it was very hard to think of Shawn McCowan as her enemy at the moment, not when he had aroused such a splendid longing inside her. It was simpler and easier to wonder what it would be like actually to fall in love with a man like him — a man of such strength and passion—than it was to think of him as the enemy.

Meanwhile Shawn made apt use of her confused state. He pulled out several of her hairpins then tugged at the long, shimmering tresses until they fell softly across her shoulders and down her back. Unable to resist, he then plunged his fingers into the soft mass and allowed the silky curls to caress his hands while he slipped them downward.

When Karissa did nothing to prevent him from that intimate action, his hands moved next to touch the inward curve of her tiny waist. While he held her pressed firmly against him with one hand, he edged the other hand slowly upward toward her breast. He noticed that her breathing became increasingly more ragged the closer he came to his treasured prize until he possessed it at last. He drew in a deep, shuddering breath when he found it was every bit as full and as firm as he had expected. The tiny moan that came from deep within her throat when he grazed the sensitive peak let him know that he was in command, which excited him more.

Overcome with the desire to see those glorious orbs at the same time he caressed them, and knowing everyone would be in bed by now, which would eliminate any chance of an audience, he continued to kiss her sweet mouth hungrily while he moved his other hand to the tiny pearl buttons that held the back of her dress and worked frantically to release them. His heart pounded with growing anticipation and his body stiffened with a need more intense than he had known in years when the back of the dress finally gapped enough to allow him to slip his hand inside and feel the velvety skin beneath.

It was when he first dipped his hand inside that an alarm finally sounded for Karissa, drawing her slowly back to sanity.

She was instantly appalled by what she had allowed to happen. Shawn was a dangerous man—a possible member of the treacherous Molly Maguires—and thus far she had done nothing but allow him the freedom to do whatever he wanted with her, no matter how corrupt or wicked.

Shame burned her cheeks. She was not completely innocent of the ways of men. She had known from the onset a kiss like that could easily lead to such intimate behavior, and she knew she should push him away before such uncontrolled passion carried them any further.

Clearly, everything Karissa held dear as a woman was at risk because his next move would undoubtedly be to step back into the shadows to remove her clothing entirely. Then once he had her naked and trembling beneath his touch, he would lower her into the grass or perhaps into one of the lounging chairs on the veranda and take whatever he wanted.

But, on the other hand, if instead of pulling away as she should, she instead followed her body's desire and give in to this intense craving that had so suddenly overtaken her, who would ever know? She was there under an assumed identity. Shawn had no indication who she really was. No one did. Everyone believed her to be someone else. They believed her to be the grieving daughter of a coal miner who had died just a few weeks ago. If she decided to have more of this wondrous pleasure, who would know of her failing?

Then she realized the answer. *She* would know. And if she ever changed her mind about what she wanted out of life and decided to marry, *her husband* would know. No, the proper thing to do would be to push him away, right now before it was too late, and shriek with virtuous outrage.

So why wouldn't her body heed those very commands?

At the same time she puzzled over her inability to do the right thing, Shawn struggled with a similar conflict. He knew he was far too attracted to this woman to think of their coupling as a mere rollick. And in his type of work, becoming emotionally involved with a woman as beautiful and beguiling as Catherine could prove fatal. While working to dredge up the evidence that would eventually destroy the Molly Maguires and thus stop them of their heinous crimes forever, he needed to have as few distractions as possible. If he made one mistake, if he allowed himself one tiny slip, not only would the Mollies continue along their merry way, he would end up just as dead as the other detectives who had tried to stop them but had failed.

Still, the desire to possess this woman was too strong. He had to finish what he had started. He had to know what it was like to make love to the beautiful and alluring Catherine.

"Shawn, we can't," Karissa said, her voice but a breathless whisper. It was her first vocal attempt to resist the passions that still raged inside her. "Not here. Not like this. Someone might see."

Though he knew there was no one else around, her

words struck him like a splash of cold water, making him aware of just how dangerously close he had come to losing control of his strongest emotions. He realized he was just a breath away from giving his heart to this woman, and if that happened, he would soon be thinking about her all the time. It was not like him to jeopardize an assignment like that, not when it was so very important he give it his full attention. "You're right."

Rather than chance finding a reason to continue, he pulled away and curled his hands into hard fists while he drew in several quick breaths to steady himself. His whole body felt weak when he gazed at her beautiful flushed face now framed by the riotous tumble of dark hair that streamed down to the middle of her back. "I apologize. I really did not mean for that to happen."

Which was true. He had tried very hard not to give in to his growing desire—as much for *her* sake as his own. She did not deserve to be involved with a man who could bring her only heartache and danger. A man who had lied to her from the very first moment they'd met.

"Then I guess the best thing to do is pretend it didn't happen," she said in an amazingly composed voice, glad for the chance to say it. She wanted to remain friends with him but without having to place her heart at risk every time he came near. At the moment, Shawn remained her only possible link to the Molly Maguires, though he had yet to prove cooperative in that capacity. Still, that was something she did not dare give up.

"That's a good idea," Shawn responded readily,

even though he wasn't completely sure he could pretend such a thing. That kiss had been too powerful and his need to touch her and to make love to her far too intense. "We'll pretend it never happened." He held out his hand in an offer of friendship. "Still friends?"

When Karissa extended her own hand and felt his strong, warm fingers close over hers and hold them gently for a moment, she felt the wild stirring inside her start anew. She closed her eyes to try to prevent the rapturous feeling from overtaking her a second time.

"Good night, Shawn," she said then forced her eyes open again. Quickly she pulled her hand free from his warm grasp, although wishing all the while she could find herself enveloped in his strong arms yet again, if only for a moment.

Bewildered that she could want such a thing from a man still suspected of having helped murder her father, she tried to figure out what had happened. She had set out that night to beguile him into telling her things he shouldn't by using her womanly charms against him, but somehow *she* had ended up being the one beguiled. What had gone wrong? Where had she lost control of the situation?

"Good night, Katy," he answered, then bent to place his usual light kiss upon her delicate forehead. When he noticed her heavily lashed eyelids flutter shut, as if wanting to enjoy the brief kiss to its fullest, it took all the restraint he had to turn and walk away.

If only he could have met Catherine Sobey in another place and during another time. Things could have been different for them. But as it was, because of the dangerous nature of his job and the importance of keeping his true identity a secret, every part of their relationship was based upon one deliberately told lie after another.

Sadly, he wondered exactly how angry she would be if she ever found out the truth about him — or the horrible things she would say if she ever learned about all the lies he had told her, even though he had told those lies out of necessity.

His heart ached at the thought of what that would do to them and realized that her finding out was inevitable. When this was all over, his real name would surface in all the area newspapers.

All he could do was hope that one day she would forgive him for all the lies he'd told. And give him a second chance.

Chapter Twelve

Karissa hurried to her room, horrified by what had nearly happened outside. She had never allowed such intimate behavior from anyone before, so why had she allowed it tonight and from a man like Shawn McCowan?

That sort of conduct was reserved for people who were deeply in love and committed to spending a lifetime together, which they definitely were *not*. Not only was Shawn not in love with her, she was not in love with him, or at least she *hoped* not. True, she was attracted to him in a way she had never been attracted to any man in the past, but what she felt toward him could not possibly be love. She had not known him long enough for such an all-important, all-consuming emotion to have developed.

So why then had she allowed him to touch her in a way no other man had, she wondered while she hurried to get undressed. Why hadn't she slapped his face soundly and told him never to touch her like that again? *Why?* Because deep down, she had enjoyed

236

the passion that had so suddenly flared between them. She had wanted him to touch her, to make her feel more like a woman than she had ever felt before.

Despite everything he was and despite everything he may have done in the past, she knew as she slipped into her white ruffled nightgown and pulled back the covers of her bed that some unknown part of her had wanted to know what it would be like for someone so strong and so terribly handsome to make love to her. And what was worse, she knew in some small way, she still did — even though she knew that allowing such a thing to happen would prove detrimental to everything she wanted to accomplish while there.

After positioning the mosquito netting around her bed then climbing in and settling onto the soft mattress, Karissa spent yet another restless night trying to sort through her jumbled feelings. She tried to figure out why she had behaved so shamefully yet a second time but, for the life of her, came up with no logical answer. There was just something about the man that drove her to madness, something that made all rational thought utterly impossible.

Finally, Karissa decided it would be better for her emotionally as well as informationally to stay away from Shawn for a while and focus instead on the younger and far less complicated Joey McGeehan.

That following night, when Shawn entered the tavern hours behind the others, as was common for him, she forced herself not to look at him. She knew to do so would only remind her how truly handsome he was, which could very well destroy her hard-fought resolve to stay away from him. All it would take was one glimpse of those remarkable blue eyes or those long, curving dimples of his and all would be lost. Her heart would immediately set to racing again and cause that rebellious desire she had to be near him to override her desperate need to stay away from him. She could not allow that.

Although not yet certain *why* he affected her so profoundly, she was well aware of the fact that he did. Perhaps he affected her like that because he was so completely different from any other man she had ever known during her short, somewhat sheltered life.

Shawn was a strong, powerful man in both body and action. There was nothing soft or yielding about him. He was truly a man to be feared by all. So why was it that the only time she ever felt afraid of him was when he took her into his arms to kiss her?

Her body quivered at the memory of how totally domineering that kiss of his could be, causing her to relinquish all form of basic logic or reason. Shame burned anew when she remembered how willfully she had given herself to his embrace, pressing her body against his with reckless abandon. Had the circumstances been different and her resolve only a little weaker, there was no telling what she would have allowed to happen. And that was what terrified her most about Shawn McCowan. Terrified her enough to cause her pulses to race uncontrolled at the mere thought.

"There's Shawn," one of her customers pointed out to her shortly after Shawn had entered the tavern and she had not headed immediately to greet him the way she normally did.

"Oh?" she asked, pretending she had not noticed the way everyone had quieted for a moment as they always did when he first entered, then slowly resumed their regular talk. Knowing some show of interest was expected of her, she glanced toward the bar where he stood, but purposely did not focus on his handsome face. It was distracting enough just to have glimpsed his tall, masculine body. "You're right. I guess I should go over there and say hello to him. But first I'd better see if Frank and Joey need anything else. We're not all that busy, but there is no sense making two trips when one will do."

Because she still hoped to persuade someone suspected of being a Molly Maguire to open up to her so she could finally start moving her investigation forward, she had shown young Joey McGeehan special attention all evening. So much so that he now straightened uncomfortably whenever she appeared at their table to see if he or Frank needed anything.

This time had proved no exception.

"Joey, your glass is almost empty," she said in a soft, sultry voice while standing only a few feet away from him. "Are you ready for another?"

Joey looked up at her with rounded green eyes and swallowed hard as if not sure what to make of her sudden interest. "No, ma'am. I've already had four and that's about as many as I dare have."

Thinking the more he drank now, the more he might be willing to tell her later, she fought the urge to admit how prudent it was for a man to know his limits and instead encouraged him to have one more. "A big, strong man like you? Why would you want to limit yourself to only four?"

Frank studied her for a moment, then smiled as if he suddenly understood why she was behaving so

239

strangely. "Ah, Joey, surely you can stand one more," he prodded. "What could it hurt?"

"After all, the night is young," Karissa put in, hoping to barrage him with plausible excuses.

Clearly smitten by her, Joey gazed up into her brown eyes and smiled a crooked little smile that reminded her of one of the children at the orphanage where she went once a week to read stories. She purposely ignored the pang that came from knowing she was using this young man for her own gains by reminding herself that he was not at all the young innocent that he seemed. Not if he was a member of those unscrupulous Molly Maguires.

"I guess another beer wouldn't do me no harm," he finally conceded, then reached into his pocket to see if he had another coin. He looked relieved to find that he had. "Sure. Why not? Bring me one more."

Aware money was a problem for the young man, who was still on the lower end of the miners' already low pay scale, Frank quickly leaned forward and slapped a coin on the table. "No. Make it two. One for each of us, and I'll pay." Then as if to explain his sudden generosity, he offered Joey a conspiratory wink. "I made myself quite a bundle off old Reggie last night after you and Charlie left. Enough to keep us in drinks for a week."

"Thank you, Mr. Miles," Joey responded, forgetting for the moment he had already been told to call the man Frank. He slumped back in his chair, glad to know he would not have to spend his own money for that fifth beer. "I appreciate that."

When Karissa went to the bar to get the drinks, she continued to avoid looking at Shawn and caught only

MORE PASSION AND ADVENTURE AWAIT... YOUR TRIP TO A BIG ADVENTUROUS WORLD BEGINS WHEN YOU ACCEPT YOUR FIRST 4 NOVELS ABSOLUTELY *FREE* (AN $18.00 VALUE)

Accept your Free gift and start to experience more of the passion and adventure you like in a historical romance novel. Each Zebra novel is filled with proud men, spirited women and tempestuous love that you'll remember long after you turn the last page.

Zebra Historical Romances are the finest novels of their kind. They are written by authors who really know how to weave tales of romance and adventure in the historical settings you love. You'll feel like you've actually gone back in time with the thrilling stories that each Zebra novel offers.

GET YOUR FREE GIFT WITH THE START OF YOUR HOME SUBSCRIPTION

Our readers tell us that these books sell out very fast in book stores and often they miss the newest titles. So Zebra has made arrangements for you to receive the four newest novels published each month.

You'll be guaranteed that you'll never miss a title, and home delivery is so convenient. And to show you just how easy it is to get Zebra Historical Romances, we'll send you your first 4 books absolutely FREE! Our gift to you just for trying our home subscription service.

BIG SAVINGS AND FREE HOME DELIVERY

Each month, you'll receive the four newest titles as soon as they are published. You'll probably receive them even before the bookstores do. What's more, you may preview these exciting novels free for 10 days. If you like them as much as we think you will, just pay the low preferred subscriber's price of just $3.75 each. *You'll save $3.00 each month off the publisher's price.* AND, your savings are even greater because there are never any shipping, handling or other hidden charges—FREE Home Delivery. Of course you can return any shipment within 10 days for full credit, no questions asked. There is no minimum number of books you must buy.

4 FREE BOOKS

TO GET YOUR 4 FREE BOOKS WORTH $18.00 — MAIL IN THE FREE BOOK CERTIFICATE T O D A Y

Fill in the Free Book Certificate below, and we'll send your FREE BOOKS to you as soon as we receive it.

If the certificate is missing below, write to: Zebra Home Subscription Service, Inc., P.O. Box 5214, 120 Brighton Road, Clifton, New Jersey 07015-5214.

FREE BOOK CERTIFICATE

4 FREE BOOKS

ZEBRA HOME SUBSCRIPTION SERVICE, INC.

YES! Please start my subscription to Zebra Historical Romances and send me my first 4 books absolutely FREE. I understand that each month I may preview four new Zebra Historical Romances free for 10 days. If I'm not satisfied with them, I may return the four books within 10 days and owe nothing. Otherwise, I will pay the low preferred subscriber's price of just $3.75 each; a total of $15.00, *a savings off the publisher's price of $3.00.* I may return any shipment and I may cancel this subscription at any time. There is no obligation to buy any shipment and there are no shipping, handling or other hidden charges. Regardless of what I decide, the four free books are mine to keep.

NAME

ADDRESS _____ APT _____

CITY _____ STATE _____ ZIP _____

TELEPHONE ( )

SIGNATURE _____ (if under 18, parent or guardian must sign)

GET
FOUR
FREE
BOOKS
(AN $18.00 VALUE)

ZEBRA HOME SUBSCRIPTION
SERVICE, INC.
P.O. Box 5214
120 BRIGHTON ROAD
CLIFTON, NEW JERSEY 07015-5214

a glimpse of his grim expression when she turned to leave again without having spoken to him first.

"Trouble in paradise?" she heard Marcus ask but did not look back to see if he had spoken to her or to Shawn. But obviously the words had been directed to Shawn because he was the one to answer.

"I guess so. I suppose I did somethin' last night that made her a little angry."

Even though that was not altogether true, because she was not really angry with him for what had happened that previous night, she continued on her way without as much as a backward glance. It made her feel a little guilty to be treating Shawn like that when what had happened last night had been as much her fault as his, if not more so. He had done nothing to make her all that angry at him. Still she decided it was to her own advantage to let him continue believing that he did. Especially when she intended for Joey to be the one to walk her home that night.

But by eleven o'clock, after nearly three hours of steady drinking, Joey was in no condition to walk anyone home. He could hardly hold his head up off the table, and when Frank sent Karissa to the bar to order Joey yet another beer, Marcus finally shook his head and refused to touch the empty mug. "He's had enough. I think it is time someone took that poor boy on home." He scanned the room, looking for someone who might do just that.

"I'll see him home," Karissa said, then turned to look at Joey with a worried expression while her heart pumped with eager anticipation. Leaving with Joey now would be perfect. Shawn would not be outside

241

waiting for her yet, nor would he be inside to watch them leave.

An hour ago, Shawn had left the tavern with Charles McAllister and some man she didn't know. If she and Joey could get out of there before the three returned, Shawn would not know they had gone until it was too late. "I feel partly responsible for the fact he has drunk so much tonight." She then looked back at Marcus. "I'll go if you think you can do without me."

Marcus glanced around at the few remaining patrons, none of whom looked much more capable than Catherine of getting Joey home, then nodded his agreement. "I guess it would be okay. We're not all that busy tonight. I'll have Laura and Deborah take care of your tables until you get back."

Karissa grimaced when she realized he expected her to return there after she'd had time to see Joey home. That would not give her the opportunity she needed to quiz him thoroughly. She glanced at Marcus then sheepishly admitted, "But I was sort of hoping not to have to come back here at all." She looked away when she realized she had no choice but to lie again to a man who had done nothing but treat her fairly since her arrival. "I have been feeling especially tired tonight and would really prefer to go on to bed if at all possible."

Marcus studied her a moment, then smiled as if he suddenly understood. "You don't want to have to face Shawn after work tonight, do you?"

Her eyes widened, aware that he was partly correct and she wondered where this man got such insight.

"You two had a falling out last night, didn't you?"

Knowing Marcus had just given her the perfect excuse not to return there so her supposed fiancé could walk her home, she nodded. "Yes, we did." She ran her hand along the scarred surface of the bar to avoid looking directly at him, knowing she had just piled on yet another lie. "And I really don't want to have to talk to him about it just yet."

"Then take off. I can help Laura and Deborah take care of your tables," Marcus said, then chuckled when he gestured toward the table where Joey's head had just plopped against the hard surface with an indelicate thud. "But you'd better hurry and get that poor boy to his cousin's house before he passes out entirely and has to be carried."

Rather than chance Marcus changing his mind, Karissa hurried to the table and nudged Joey gently with her hand. "Joey? You've had enough. It's time to go."

Joey muttered something indeterminate about his mother, but never bothered to lift his head up off the table.

Frank reached for his broadcloth coat, which hung over the back of his chair, as if he planned to go with them. He frowned, clearly confused, when she suddenly shook her head to stop him.

"Come on, Joey," she said in a low, coaxing voice. "Marcus has asked me to see that you make it home."

Joey's head popped up off the table as if it had been launched by a catapult. He stared at her in dazed disbelief. *"You?* You going to see *me* home?"

"Yes. That is, if you don't mind. Can you stand?"

Joey blinked twice, unable to believe his good fortune. "Sure I can stand," he said, and promptly pushed his chair away from the table. Finding sudden strength, he quickly propelled himself to his wobbly feet. "And of course I don't mind if you walk me home. Don't mind one bit."

Wanting to be off while Joey was still shot full of adrenaline and able to walk on his own, she held out her arm to him. "Then let's be on our way."

Joey looked at the arm curiously, as if he had no idea what to do with it. His eyes widened and his Adam's apple bobbed several times when she then reached out to take his hand.

"Come on." She gave the hand a gentle tug to encourage him to hurry, before Shawn appeared out of nowhere the way he tended to do at times. The thought of how easily this sudden stroke of luck could be turned into a complete disaster caused her a strong flutter of apprehension. "Let's go."

Joey took several quick, deep breaths then turned to look at Frank, his green eyes still stretched to their limits. Slowly that same lopsided grin he had displayed earlier stretched across his young face. "I'll see you tomorrow. Looks like I'm headed home."

Frank's forehead furrowed into a deep frown, clearly concerned over Karissa's decision to go it alone, but said nothing to stop the two from leaving together. Instead he reached for his mug and pretended to take another long drink, something he had done all night, which was why he was not nearly as inebriated as young Joey.

Karissa stopped near the bar to get both her lantern and her handbag before heading out into the dark with Joey. Knowing he lived with a cousin, but not knowing exactly where, she asked for directions as soon as they had stepped outside and away from all the noise.

"Up on the north end of town," Joey told her, indicating where about forty miners' shacks stood in uneven rows just off from the rest of town. "Ours is one of the first ones."

Not yet having considered she would be making the long walk back alone, Karissa held the lantern high in her left hand to light their way while she reclaimed his left arm with her right and headed off in the direction he had indicated. The sounds of dogs yelping in the distance drifted past but did little to distract either of them.

"Lovely night, isn't it?" she asked while they strolled slowly along the boardwalk, having decided to start with small topics then work her way to the more important ones.

"Sure is," he admitted, and nearly lost his balance when he gazed up at the night sky, where the stars twinkled through a thin haze of coal dust and machine smoke that still drifted down from the coal mines situated higher in the mountains. He immediately righted himself and made more of an effort to steady his walk.

Although he continued to weave a little from having drank far beyond his means, his gait was even and his speech clear while they slowly made their way down the street. If it were not for the dull look in his eyes and the difficulty with which he reopened his eyelids each time he blinked, Karissa would have thought him nearly sober again.

"Glad it turned off so cool. It seemed downright hot this afternoon when we first came up out of the mine," he said, as eager to keep the conversation moving as she seemed to be.

"You should have been out around noon," Karissa told him, remembering how uncomfortable she had been right after lunch. "I had to launder a few dresses and thought I'd perish from the heat. But I guess it stays pretty cool down in those mines."

"Some shafts are cool. Some are downright cold. And others are hot as blazes," he informed her, but did not bother to explain why that was. He stumbled slightly when they stepped down from the boardwalk onto the uneven street, but quickly recovered his balance and continued to stay at her side. "I don't mind working when it's hot as long as there ain't no gas to make me start feeling sick to my stomach. Although some men can tolerate the smell of it just fine, I ain't one of them. And I don't think it is right that I have to. Not when it makes me so sick."

"Is that why you joined the Molly Maguires?" she asked, hoping he would think it a natural question to ask after having heard such a complaint. "Did you join because you don't think it is fair to have to work in conditions like that?"

"It *ain't* fair," Joey said. The muscles in his young face tightened. "Why should I have to work around such foul-smelling gas when it would not cost that Caine family all that much to have the whole shaft ventilated."

Karissa bristled at the animosity in Joey's voice when he'd spoken her family's name, but she said nothing in their defense.

Aware he had not yet admitted to being a member of the Mollies, only that he did not like the environment where he worked, Karissa tried again, "So that's

246

why you joined the Molly Maguires? Because the shafts are not well ventilated?"

Finally realizing what she had said, Joey stopped so abruptly it caught Karissa off guard and she stumbled against him, causing him to have to catch her in his arms or let her fall. Whatever he had been about to say left him the moment he realized he held her close. "Goodness, you sure are pretty."

"Why thank you," Karissa responded, and fought the immediate urge to pull away. Although Joey did not reek as strongly as most the men who came up out of those mines each day, he did carry the smell of damp coal dust and stale beer, which made it very hard to breathe. "And you are very handsome."

"You really think so?" he asked, looking quite pleased to hear it. While he continued to hold her with one arm, he reached up with the other to snatch his knit cap off his blond curls as if suddenly realizing he was in the presence of a lady. He dampened his mouth while he quickly tucked the cap into his hip pocket. Off in the distance the sound of an accordion and laughter rode the gentle breeze—the same gentle breeze that now ruffled his hair.

Aware what Joey had on his mind yet not wanting him to kiss her, knowing how repulsive that would be considering the staleness of his breath, she nodded to show her sincerity.

"I know so. Why, if you were only a few years older and if I weren't already engaged to Shawn McCowan, I'd probably want you for my very own."

He looked crestfallen. "That's right. I forgot." Slowly, he let go of her and dipped his head as if ashamed of what he'd done then stepped away. "You

247

already belong to Shawn."

"But that doesn't mean we can't be friends," she put in quickly, not wanting him to sober up on her just yet. "Haven't you ever known a woman who was just a friend?"

"Sure I have. Why, one of the best friends I think I ever had was a woman who worked at the very same place you do," he said then looked at her with a twisted expression as if puzzled about something. "Until just a few weeks ago, she was always there for me when I needed someone to talk to. Always."

"What happened to her?" Karissa asked, wondering why he suddenly looked so bewildered.

"I don't really know. One night she was right there, working her tables just like she usually did, and the next night she didn't bother to show up. She had told Marcus she'd probably be late, but didn't say nothing about not showing up at all."

Karissa's eyes widened when she realized he was talking about her father's mistress, Jacqueline Lawler. If that was true, and if he was indeed involved with that group of men who had killed her father, he would now believe her dead. "What happened to her? Was she killed?"

Joey looked at Karissa curiously, as if he had not given that idea much consideration. "I don't really know what happened to her. It could be she's dead. After all, we did find most her things still in her room that next day when we went looking for her." He paused to think more about that possibility.

"When who went looking for her?" Karissa asked, thinking that at last she was getting somewhere. Perhaps whoever went with him to her room that following morning went there expecting to find her gone but had wanted to be sure.

"Me and Marcus. We thought maybe she was sick and went by that next day to see if she needed anything. But she wasn't there, and according to her landlady, she hadn't been there all night. As it turned out, she never did come back. Not even to get her things. As far as I know, Mrs. Waylan still has them stored out in her carriage house."

"Maybe the reason she never came back is because she *is* dead," Karissa said, still gauging his reactions closely. "Maybe she met with some sort of an accident while she was gone."

Joey shook his head, not willing to believe it. "No, what I think is that she finally got the courage to go tell the widowed man she's been seeing that he was the father of that baby growing inside her and he decided to do the right thing and take her in."

Karissa looked at him, stunned. "You seem to know quite a lot about this woman."

"I told you, she was a close friend of mine and had been since she first came here several months ago."

Karissa thought about that for a moment and felt oddly comforted to realize he had spoken the truth about having developed a close friendship with Jacqueline. It proved him innocent because Jacqueline had admitted she did not know any of the four men she overheard discussing Lawrence's murder. They had all four been strangers to her. That meant *this* was not the right Joey after all. He might indeed be involved with the Molly Maguires, which was why he had disappeared Monday night with the rest of them, but she was certain now that he had not had any part in her father's murder.

Aware they were far enough away from the Lucky Choice now to go unnoticed by anyone leaving or returning, she gestured toward a small wooden bench that stood in front of the leather shop. She decided this was the perfect opportunity to get to know the woman carrying her father's child a little better. "Tell me more about your friend. Who is the man who fathered her child? Do you know him?"

"No, she didn't talk about him much." Joey followed her suggestion by sitting where she had indicated. "All I really know about him is that his name is Lawrence and I think he probably works for the Caine Mining Company in some way."

"Why would you say that?"

"Because I accidentally saw a letter she wrote a few months back in which she asked if he knew that she was getting no more money from the widow's pension because of some new company policy stating that mining widows are now only eligible to get money equal to two months of their husband's wages and a plain wooden coffin. And because she'd already collected far more than that over the past years, she suddenly was to receive no more money. Having that pension of hers taken away from her was the whole reason she had to move here. With no more pension money coming in and no husband to take care of her, she had to do something to earn a living and was able to get a job working for Marcus pretty easy."

Karissa remembered Jacqueline having told her the same thing. "And this letter that you accidentally read, it didn't mention the man's last name?"

"No. Just his first name. But it's having read that

250

letter that makes me feel like maybe she finally went to see him, and after having told him what happened, he took her in, what with the baby coming and all. After all, what kind of life would it be for a youngster to have his mother gone off almost every night trying to make enough money just to put food on the table?" He paused while he thought more about it. "Still, I wish she'd write and tell me for sure that she's all right so I won't have to worry no more about that baby going hungry."

Remembering the generous trust fund that had been provided for Jacqueline, Karissa blinked back a sudden rush of tears. If only her father could have known how part of that money would end up being spent. "I don't think you have to worry. Your friend sounds like a very resourceful woman. She'll find some way to support her baby."

Joey nodded that he agreed then grinned. "I offered to marry her myself but she seemed to think she'd do better on her own. Said I was about ten years too young for her. But what I really think is that she was holding on to the hope that the father would somehow find out about the baby and marry her." His smile widened. "It's my hope that that is exactly what happened. She truly loves him, whoever he is."

Karissa's forehead notched while she considered just how very much Joey knew about Jacqueline's situation. She wondered if what he had just told her was common knowledge, and if so, who all might be aware of it and might have linked it to her father. "Who else knew about the father of her child?"

"You mean who all knew she was carrying a baby? Everyone. It was hard not to know," he answered, looking a little embarrassed when he held his hands nearly a foot in front of him. "Her belly was already out to here when she left."

"No, I mean who else knew the father's name and that he probably worked for Caine Enterprises?"

"Probably nobody. It was something she didn't like to talk about. And to tell you the truth, I shouldn't be telling you about it even now. She asked me not to ever tell anyone about him. She was afraid someone might figure out who he is and try to force him to do right by her and she was just too proud for something like that."

Karissa reached over to pat his hand reassuringly. "I promise your secret is safe with me. Besides, I didn't even know your friend so who could I tell?"

"That's true. Jacque left probably two weeks before you got here," Joey said, as if just now realizing that fact. "Too bad. You would have liked her."

"I'm sure I would," Karissa answered, knowing she already did. Then wanting to get away from such an emotional topic and back to the matters at hand, even though she now knew Joey was never involved in the murder itself, she asked, "Did Jacque know you were a member of the Molly Maguires?"

Joey blinked at such an unexpected change in the conversation. "What do you mean by that?"

"I don't know. I guess I was wondering since you seem to know so much about her deepest secrets if you in turn had told her any of yours."

Joey's face paled and he quickly looked down at the folded hands in his lap. It was as if suddenly they were the most interesting hands in the world. "But I have no secrets."

252

"Oh, come now." Karissa kept her tone friendly. "Isn't that where you and those other men went last night? To a secret meeting of the Molly Maguires?"

"No," he answered immediately, but could not bring himself to look at her. "Of course not."

"Then where did you and all those other men go?"

Joey pressed his lips together a moment, then parted them again when he finally dragged his gaze back up to hers. Karissa's heart rate quickened with expectation when she realized he was about to give her an answer.

"To a cock fight," he finally said, remembering that was what Nathan always told his wife whenever she bothered to ask where he had been. "We all went to a cock fight."

"A cock fight?" Karissa did not believe that for a minute. "Why would everyone be so secretive about going to a cock fight?"

"Because they are not lawful in Schuylkill county," he said then pursed his lips into a boyish scowl. "Not since all those uppity women up to the Presbyterian church started putting their noses into such matters. Said it wasn't right to be using God's creatures in such a way. But what they don't realize is that God is the one who made roosters to be such feisty critters in the first place. If he hadn't meant for them to fight like that, he would have made them much more sociable."

Not in the least interested in whether cock fighting was legal in Schuylkill county or not, Karissa hurried to question him further. "But it was my understanding that you all went to a special meeting somewhere. Isn't that true?"

Joey looked at her with a deathly somber expression. "Ma'am, I don't know who you've been talking to, but I'd advise you to stay as far away from that person as you can. He's obviously trying to get you into some very bad trouble. Maybe even killed."

"How?" she asked doubtfully. "By asking you a few questions about where you went last night? How can something like that possibly get me killed?"

"Asking *me* won't get you killed, 'cause I know you don't realize the seriousness of what you've just asked; but asking someone else those same sort of questions might." He hesitated then added in a hushed voice, "I'm not supposed to tell this to no one, but there are some men around here who do indeed belong to the Molly Maguires. But they don't want their names known to anyone outside their group because of some of the things they've done in the past and could be arrested for."

"What sort of things?" she asked, hoping he would not end their conversation without giving her at least some bit of useful information.

"Bad things like looting businesses, or harming people who have either caused them or members of their families trouble, or else just blackmailing them. Then there's also the deliberate destruction of those people's property, and even murder when they think it is necessary."

He spoke of the "necessity" of murder so nonchalantly, chills trickled down Karissa's spine. Tiny bumps formed across her delicate skin. "Murder? Who have they murdered?" She held her breath while she waited for the answer, wondering if he would admit that her father had been one of many the Mollies had killed.

Joey stood and abruptly stepped away, clearly upset with her. "I told you, you've got to stop asking so many blamed questions. It'll only get you in a lot of trouble."

"But how else can I know what's going on if I don't ask questions?" she tried one last time, aware he was about to walk away from her if she did not quickly engage him in further conversation.

"You don't need to know what's going on," he told her in a voice just as stern as Shawn's had been, then without further word, turned and stalked away, heading off in the direction of his cousin's house.

"Where are you going?" she asked, quickly rising from the bench. She reached down and lifted her skirts several inches in preparation to follow.

"Away from you," he said, and continued down the darkened boardwalk with long, steady strides. "Before I end up getting you into more trouble than you can ever get yourself out of."

Having said that, he started to run, determined to put as much distance as possible between them.

Karissa stared after him, dumbfounded, wondering what harm could possibly come from having asked a few questions of a half-drunken boy. Disappointed, she waited until she could no longer see his shadowed form then sighed and bent down for the lantern she had set on the planks beside the small bench. When she straightened back, she thought she saw a movement in front of the mercantile across the street; but as dark as it was that night, she could not be sure.

Rather than wait to find out if somebody really was out there, she tightened her grip on the lantern with one hand, hiked her skirts with the other, then headed off toward her rooming house as quickly as she could move and still appear to be walking.

Thinking it might be Robby Drier or someone like him, her heart pounded so hard against her chest it drowned any muffled sounds that may have been coming from behind her. She tried not to display any of the stark fear that held her. Still, she could not prevent a startled scream when she heard something topple behind her.

Rather than chance being overtaken like she had that first night, she set the lantern down just seconds before she broke into a dead run. By the time she reached the rooming house, she was out of breath and her side ached from having run so hard.

Aware Kelly Waylan always left the front door open for the latecomers, she quickly clambered up the front steps and hurried inside, clattering the door closed behind her. Knowing Frank was not yet home for she had not seen him pass, she did not bolt the front door closed like she wanted. Instead she went immediately to her room, where she quickly slammed and locked her own door.

Safe now from whoever had been out there, she hurried to her window and peered out onto the darkened street below. Nothing moved.

After several minutes of staring down at shadows that did not stir, she wondered if she had imagined the entire incident. Perhaps the noise had been a cat in reckless pursuit of a mouse or a clumsy raccoon digging through someone's garbage.

It was not until an hour later when Frank knocked at her door that Karissa finally learned the truth. Shortly after she and Joey left, Robby Drier rose from his chair and headed out the door. Aware of the grim manner in which Robby had been watching her that night, Frank then casually pushed himself out of his chair and sauntered out behind Robby to make sure there was no trouble.

"And did he follow us?" she asked. That same prickly feeling of fear she had experienced earlier washed over her again.

"Yes but he mainly stayed to the shadows," Frank admitted, keeping his voice low so as not to let those sleeping below know that he was in Karissa's bedroom. "But when young McGeehan suddenly got angry with you and took off running the way he did, Drier immediately emerged from the shadows and stumbled hurriedly in your direction. Then when you suddenly took off running, too, but in a different direction, he tried his best to keep up and did a pretty good job of it until an empty barrel got in his way."

"So that was the noise I heard."

"By the time he staggered back to his feet, you were too far ahead for him to catch up so he turned and headed back toward the tavern. Quite angrily, I might add."

Though she could not see Frank's face in the darkened room, she knew by his tone of voice he was grinning. Although she had never confessed the incident in the livery to him, he did not like Robby Drier any more than she did. "Do you think he saw you when he headed back?"

"No. He was too upset to consider the fact that he, too, might have been followed."

"Good. I'd hate for him to think that you had an abnormal interest in me. He might start asking questions."

"Don't worry. I was very careful not to let him see or hear me. I waited until he had gone back inside the tavern before I walked over and picked up your lantern for you. I left it downstairs by the door."

"Thank you."

There was a short pause, as if Frank was temporarily lost in thought before he finally spoke again. "I gather it turned out to be pretty much a waste of time for us to have gone to all that trouble to get young McGeehan drunk like we did."

"Why would you say that?" she asked. She did not want to come right out and admit total failure.

"Because, personally, I don't think the boy knows anything worth telling. At least not about your father's death. Although I still believe that Shawn McCowan was in some way involved with that murder, I don't think Joey McGeehan had anything to do with it."

"But I thought maybe since his name was the same as one of those my friend gave me—" Karissa started to say, but was interrupted.

"I know what you thought. And although I haven't quite yet figured out who the Joey is that your secret friend warned you about, I feel pretty certain it was not young McGeehan. That boy couldn't intentionally kill anyone, not even if ordered to. He just doesn't have it in him."

"But you do think he is a Molly, don't you?"

"Yes, but a reluctant one. Maybe his friend Shawn pulled him into the group hoping to make a man of him. It would be just like McCowan to do something like that."

"And what makes you so sure Shawn McCowan is like that?" she asked, feeling oddly defensive even though she, too, suspected his involvement.

"Because of what I've heard about him."

An icy wave of apprehension splashed over her, clenching her stomach into a hard knot. "Why? What exactly have you heard?" She reached for the bedpost to steady herself, not certain she wanted to hear the answer.

"Just that he himself has admitted to having committed murder." He paused a moment as if wanting that to sink in before he continued. "He admitted to some of his close friends that he's wanted back in New York for the murders of his own wife and her lover. Killed them both in a cold, angry rage. That's why he's so willing to stay right here and work such long hours down there in your father's mines instead of going out and finding a job that would be more suitable for a man with his education and experience. I've been told that his real name is not Shawn McCowan. It's Shawn Larsen, and I heard that he used to make pretty good money running a large freight company in New York. But now all he does is take whatever jobs will let him stay hidden from the authorities."

Though everything Frank said suited the situation, Karissa did not want to believe it. "Who told you that?"

"Several people. It seems to be pretty common knowledge around here," he admitted then headed toward the door. "Which is why I wish you would finally take my advice and stay as far away from him as you can. I can't get very much done if I'm always having to stay close to you so I can be sure you don't end up getting hurt in all this."

"I never asked you to watch over me," she reminded him. Obviously tonight was not the first time he had followed her.

"That's true, you didn't. But I do so for my own benefit. I'm no genius, but I do happen to be just smart enough to realize that you are the only one who knows I am here working for you; therefore you are the only one who will pay me when all this is over. That's why it is in my own best interest that you come out of this alive and able to write a bank draft."

He turned the doorknob but hesitated before actually opening the door. "Don't go getting a false sense of security by thinking I'm always out there protecting you, because I'm not. There are times when I *have* to be elsewhere, which leaves you entirely on your own. That's why I wish you'd quit spending so much time with McCowan. If you ever accidentally let it slip who you really are while you are off somewhere alone with him, you could be as good as dead. And if you let it slip that I am here working with you, I could be as good as dead, too. A man who can kill his own wife has no conscience."

Karissa waited until Frank had slipped out onto the darkened stairwell and had closed the door before letting those last few words register fully. Suddenly it felt as if someone had climbed inside her and was tying knots.

Shawn McCowan was a man with no conscience. He had willingly murdered his own wife. The woman he loved enough to have married. To Karissa, that meant the man was capable of doing just about anything.

A tiny shiver washed over her, forcing her to cross her arms protectively in front of her. She remembered how quickly after Shawn had declared her to be his property that the customers at the tavern had stopped pestering her and wondered now if the real reason they had suddenly decided to leave her alone had had more to do with stark fear than any sort of respect.

It stood to reason that if he had killed in a fit of jealousy once, then he could do so again. Only a fool would risk that sort of anger.

Karissa's whole body grew weak while she continued to pit what she now knew about Shawn against everything that had happened in the past. Suddenly it dawned on her that the real reason everyone stopped to take notice whenever Shawn entered a room had nothing to do with admiration. The real reason the men were so quick to notice him whenever he entered probably had more to do with a man's basic need for self-preservation. It made pretty good sense to be cautious of a man who had admitted to killing his own wife.

And now that she knew the truth—that there were obviously two very opposing sides to the man—she would be far more cautious of him in the future, too. From now on, she would take Frank's advice and stay as far away from Shawn McCowan Larsen as possible.

Tears filled her eyes, causing all the shadows to blend together into one dark mass when she realized just how close she had come to falling in love with a man like that. How could she have been so blind?

Swallowing to relieve the pain that so suddenly

261

filled her throat, she reached for the buttons of her dress and slowly began to unfasten them, unaware that at that same moment, outside, Shawn stood in the shadows staring questioningly at the house, wondering what interest Catherine could be to Frank Miles.

Chapter Thirteen

Shawn turned and headed back the way he had come, still wondering why Frank Miles had gotten involved with the night's events. He knew what the man was up to when he'd spotted him prowling in the shadows, following Robby Drier at a short distance, who was also slinking through the shadows but just not quite as adeptly as Miles. But Shawn had not realized Catherine was involved until he watched the two men settle into places where they could watch her talking with Joey McGeehan without being seen.

Shawn had wondered why Catherine and Joey would be out on the street together at that time of night when they hardly knew each other, but he was more curious to know why Drier and Frank had secretly followed them. At first he thought the two men were working together because Frank had followed so closely behind. But after Joey then Catherine suddenly took off running into the night, and Drier had stumbled off after Catherine, he realized Frank had to be working separately. He also noticed that Frank seemed far more intent on keeping an eye on Drier than he was on following Catherine or Joey.

Even after Drier had given up his bumbling chase and had turned around to stagger back toward the tavern, Frank had stayed in the shadows. Clearly, he had not wanted Drier to realize he had been followed any more than Shawn had wanted Frank to know *he* had been followed. But why? Why would Frank follow Drier of all people—unless it was to make sure he did not harm Catherine in some way? But why should he care what became of her? What could Catherine possibly be to Frank? As far as he knew, the two hardly knew each other.

Shawn shook his head, as confused as ever when he veered off toward Jack McGeehan's house. None of what had happened that night made any sense to him and probably wouldn't until he at least found out why Catherine and Joey were outside at eleven-thirty at night—alone. Or so they had thought, for neither had seemed aware of the fact there were three men squatting in the darkness watching their every move.

Although Shawn did not really think Catherine could be romantically interested in a boy who was years younger than herself, he still could not help but feel a sharp stab of jealousy when he remembered having leaned out to find out what had Drier's undivided attention and spotting his young friend holding her so caringly in his arms while she talked to him. He wondered what had brought on such a warm show of affection between the two, knowing that until tonight, Catherine had hardly spoken to the young man. He also wondered why rather than abruptly shove him away or slap his face for having held her so close she had gestured they sit and talk for a while.

Frowning, he pulled out his watch and saw that it was just turning midnight. Although he had promised to meet Charles back at the tavern before it closed, he continued in the opposite direction. He knew if he hurried he might still catch Joey before he fell asleep. He had to find out what happened. He also needed to talk with the boy about the change in Thursday night's plans.

Because Karissa had been nowhere near the tavern that previous midnight when it came time for Shawn to walk her home, and because of the way she had all but ignored him before that, she expected him to be truly angry with her when she saw him again. She was prepared to defend herself however she could against that anger when she saw him again and was a little taken aback when he entered the tavern that next evening and greeted her as cheerfully as ever.

"Ah, there's my beautiful Catherine," he said loudly then rather than wait for her to come to him, he walked over to give her his customary kiss on the cheek.

Having vowed to stay away from Shawn as much as possible, but not about to do anything that could make him want to do her any real harm, she accepted his friendly greeting with a cordial smile but did not try to engage him in casual conversation. Instead, she acknowledged his presence with a brief smile then carried her rapidly pounding heart as far away from him as possible.

Now that Frank had told her what a truly dangerous man he was, her heart had a whole new reason to react violently whenever he was near. The man had admitted murdering his own wife and her lover in a wild fit of jealousy. Yet even so, she was still oddly attracted to him and that frightened her even more. It did not make sense for her to be tempted by such a man.

That evening, for appearance's sake, Karissa continued to speak to Shawn whenever he was near, but she ignored any mention of his walking her home that night — or any other night thereafter. Every time he brought up the subject, she changed it. And when he questioned her about where she had been the night before, she told him it was really none of his business where she had gone and had promptly reminded him that he was not her keeper.

Finally, after two hours of being all but ignored, Shawn had taken enough of her cold treatment and pulled her none-too-gently off to one side. He bent close to her ear and spoke in a voice just loud enough for her to hear over the noise around them.

"Why are ya suddenly avoidin' me? Ya weren't here for me to walk you home last night and tonight you will hardly speak to me. Are you afraid to be alone with me because of what happened outside the boarding house the other night?" He really thought she had understood about the kiss. It was something he had not wanted to happen any more than she did.

"No. Of course I'm not afraid to be alone with you," she said with far more conviction than she actually felt while she brushed at the wrinkles he had made in her yellow sleeve. Truth was, she was terrified over the thought of ever being alone with him again.

Afraid of what might happen between them and the danger that presented. "It so happens I have grown tired of the little game we've been playing for over two weeks now. I think it is time we stop pretending to be engaged and let everyone know the truth."

Rather than chance their conversation being overheard by one of the other customers, Shawn grabbed her by the arm again and dragged her forcibly into the tiny back room where Marcus kept most of his overstock.

He waited until the door was closed and they had moved farther into the room before continuing. "I don't understand. Why are ya suddenly so determined for everyone to know the truth about us? Is it so you can openly pursue yer new friend, Joey McGeehan?" he asked, as confused as he was angry while he maintained a light, but possessive grip on her arm.

Although he did not truly believe that was the reason, for Joey was not exactly the type to make women swoon, the muscles in his jaw worked furiously at the mere thought that Catherine could be interested in someone else. He was too used to the idea of having his ring on her finger, and had even started to dream of the day when he could openly court her. After he finally put all that other business safely behind him, he hoped to find some way to make her a more permanent part of his life. Probably because all the recent talk about marriage and children had made him realize he did not really want to go through his remaining years alone. There would come a time when he could finally put this investigation behind him and would be able to enjoy a more normal life. He would have made enough money from this one job to retire

267

for the rest of his life. *If* he could truly convince himself that was what he wanted.

Karissa's eyes widened at the mention of Joey's name. "You heard about that?"

"Of course," he answered, not about to admit he had actually witnessed it. "Ya two havin' left here together was all the talk last night."

"Well, it shouldn't have been." She jerked her arm free of his grasp and rubbed the spot where she still felt his warmth while she stared up at him angrily. "Nothing happened between us that shouldn't have."

Shawn's eyes narrowed while he studied her beautiful face, wishing he could read the thoughts behind those sparkling brown eyes. "That's exactly what Joey said."

"You questioned Joey about it?" she asked, as appalled as she was worried that he would do such a thing.

"Let's just say he and I discussed it at length and now I'd like to discuss it with you." What he really wanted to do was to find out why she continued to ask so many foolish questions about the Molly Maguires even after having been warned twice of the danger. Why couldn't she get it through that pretty little head of hers that asking *any* questions about that particular group of men could eventually lead to trouble. For *both* of them.

"I'm sorry, but I don't have time to discuss *anything* with you right now. I have work to do."

"Then we'll discuss it later. When I walk ya home."

"Oh, but you won't be walking me home," she responded quickly. Her heart leaped fearfully at the thought of having to be alone with him while he was

268

that angry.

Shawn's body tensed at the adamancy he detected in her voice. "Why? Are ya plannin' to ask Joey to walk ya?"

"No."

"Then who?"

Karissa sighed with annoyance. "No one. I am quite capable of making it back to that rooming house all by myself."

"Oh, that's right. Ya proved that capability yer first night here."

Karissa glared at him for having reminded her of the terrible incident with Robby Drier. "That happened because I had just arrived and didn't know whom to watch out for. Now I do."

Shawn narrowed his gaze while he studied the forward thrust of her chin, and realized she was determined to push him out of her life. "And am I one of the ones ya suddenly feel ya have to watch out for?"

"Quite frankly, yes. You do frighten me."

Shawn's angry expression sobered. "I don't mean to."

"But you do."

His forehead notched in the center while he thought about that. "But just a few minutes ago ya said ya were not afraid of me at all."

"I lied," she admitted, then quickly brushed past him, eager to get away before he did something to justify her fear. She headed immediately toward the door.

"Catherine, come back here," he called after her, not ready to end their conversation so abruptly. He knew if he let her leave now, he would have a hard

269

time ever being alone with her again. "I thought we had an understandin' about what happened the other night. I thought ya understood that I did not intend for that to happen."

"I have work to do," she called back over her shoulder, then quickly opened the door and disappeared into the crowded tavern. She did not want to be reminded of her shameful behavior from two nights ago. Especially not now that she knew the truth about Shawn, that he was a man truly capable of killing someone. Just the memory of how eagerly she had melted in his arms, in the arms of an acknowledged killer, made her ache so strongly that by the time she returned to the bar to pick up that last order, she was near tears and trembling uncontrollably.

"My, what a pretty thing you are." She heard the deep male voice just as she turned away from the bar with her tray now filled with drinks. When she glanced up to see if that comment had been directed to her, she discovered a tall, well-dressed man she had never seen there before staring down at her expectantly.

"Excuse me," she said, not feeling up to any friendly bantering with the new customer just yet. She was still too shaken from her talk with Shawn. "I have to take these drinks to those tables across the room."

"No, excuse *me*," he said, and gallantly stepped back to let her pass. "I didn't mean to get in the way."

Not used to such overt politeness, she glanced at him again and this time noticed the man was as handsome as he was courtly. He was tall and clean shaven with thick, dark blond hair and gray eyes, and he wore a lightweight summer suit made from light blue twill. Clearly he was a cut above the rest of the men in the room and she wondered why a man of any means would pick a place like the Lucky Choice to have a drink or a bowl of stew when the town had such a nice restaurant only two blocks away.

"In this room, you have little choice but to get in the way," she responded with a sincere smile before hurrying past and across the room. Because she had talked with Shawn for nearly ten minutes and there were now several customers awaiting refills, she was too busy to give the handsome stranger any further thought. It was not until she later came across him seated at Robby Drier's table that she noticed him again.

"There's that pretty young lady I was telling you about," he said to the men seated around him, then to her amazement, he quickly stood and dipped his head toward her as if he thought it his gentlemanly duty to recognize her presence.

Karissa looked at him with a questioning expression. She had grown unaccustomed to such gallantry while in Black Wall. Had he not at that moment dipped his gaze to boldly take in every curve of her body, she might have believed him to be a true gentleman. She frowned with disappointment when she realized he was not. The package might look a little different, but inside the product was the same.

"Are any of you gents ready for refills?" she asked, glancing at their glasses and noticing that most were now empty.

"I don't know about the rest of them, but I am ready for another," the newcomer said in a deep voice, so richly cultivated Karissa had to wonder what a man like that had in common with Robby Drier and his lowly group of friends.

Stepping closer, she held out her hand to take his empty whiskey glass and money. When he purposely brushed his fingers across her palm, she felt an unexpected wave of repulsion. He then looked at her with such an unsettling gaze, she took a quick step away from him.

"Anyone else need another?" she asked while she deposited the empty glass and the coin he had given her on her tray.

"Sure, bring me another beer," Robby said in his usual growl, and nodded toward his mug, letting her know he expected her to pick it up for him. He then tossed his money on the table beside it. "And make it quick."

"As quick as I can," she assured him, and kept her tone pleasant despite his characteristically rude behavior. Smiling, she placed Robby's mug and coin on the tray beside the other man's, and when no one else asked for a refill, she hurried away.

When she arrived at the bar with the two empty glasses, she leaned forward and asked Marcus if he knew who the man was with Robby Drier.

"I don't have any idea who he is. I've only seen him in here a couple of times before and as far as I know he's pretty well kept his name to himself."

Karissa frowned. "How does he know Robby?"

"I don't know that either. All I do know is that he's not a miner like most of the men who come in here. You can tell that by looking at his hands." He glanced toward the end of the bar where Shawn stood watching them and looked quickly away, as if he felt guilty to be discussing the handsome newcomer with her. "That man hasn't had to work hard a day in his life. It's my guess he's a salesman of some sort. Or a gambler."

Pretending not to have noticed Shawn's angry scowl, Karissa waited for the glasses to be refilled then placed them on her tray and headed back across the room determined to find out the stranger's name.

"Here you go," she said with a cheerfulness she did not feel as she first set Robby Drier's beer in front of him then stepped laterally to place the stranger's whiskey in front of him. "I believe this twenty cents in change is yours," she said to the newcomer, reaching into her pocket to get the money Marcus had handed her.

"No," he said, smiling as again he stood to acknowledge her. It was almost as if he hoped to impress her with his height or perhaps what he wanted to do was intimidate her. "Keep it." He then lifted his hand to trail his finger down the side of her neck but she quickly stepped back and did not allow it.

"Thank you," she said, and quickly repocketed the money. Had he been one of the miners, she probably would have tried to talk him out of such an extravagant tip, but because he looked as if he could well afford to lose twenty cents, she accepted it with a polite smile. "I hope you enjoy your drink, Mr. —" She paused to give him time to supply his name. Having been told that he was a stranger who had been in the Lucky Choice at least once before made her wonder if he could be one of the four strangers Jacque had seen in there a few weeks ago.

"My name is Joseph Rourke," he supplied happily,

273

then cocked an eyebrow and smiled a very unsettling smile. "And I must admit that I am very pleased to make your acquaintance."

Although the men seated at his table made several spirited comments that warranted his attention, he did not take his eyes off Karissa to acknowledge them.

"And do your friends call you Joey?" she asked. Her heart made a frantic leap, aware she could very well have stumbled on to something.

"You can if you'd like," he said, and dipped his gaze to take in her curvaceous figure yet again. "That is if I can call you Catherine."

Knowing she had not given him her name, but aware any of the other men at his table could have supplied that information, she nodded her agreement. "Everyone in here does."

"Better watch it, Joseph," Robby put in, his face drawn into its usual tight scowl. "That one is already taken." He nodded toward Shawn, who seemed to show very little interest in them at the moment. "See that tall, arrogant-looking man at the bar? The one in the white shirt and blue neckerchief? Seems she's already engaged to him."

"Engaged is not married," Joseph quickly pointed out, and reached forward to graze her cheek with the tips of his fingers as if that was supposed to entice her in some way. "And nothing is ever final until the little lady finally says 'I do.' "

Karissa felt a second strong wave of repulsion and wondered why this man's touch affected her so adversely. Had Shawn been the one forcing such attention on her, she would be a quivering mass by now.

Aware that Joseph Rourke was a man obviously

very full of himself, even more so than Shawn Mc-Cowan, and wanting to indicate to Frank that he should keep an eye on this one, Karissa quickly bid the group farewell and went on to the next table to see if they were ready to reorder.

For the rest of that night Karissa felt two sets of eyes upon her: those of Shawn McCowan and those of Joseph Rourke. Both made the next few hours of work almost unbearable.

Between trying to avoid Shawn's angry gaze and Joseph's hungry one, Karissa suffered quite an uncomfortable Wednesday night and was glad when both men left the tavern within minutes of each other at about eleven-thirty.

By midnight, there were only a half-dozen patrons left, and to Karissa's relief, they all finished their drinks and left as soon as Marcus had announced it was closing time.

"I gather you and Shawn still have not patched up your differences," Marcus said to her in an offhand manner while reaching for a damp rag to wipe the counter, as if not wanting to pry but still curious to know.

"And I don't think we will," she told him while she picked up her handbag and felt inside for the small derringer. She had hoped to walk out with Laura and Deborah, but they had such a knack of being ready to leave just as soon as the last customer had cleared the door, she had missed her chance to go with them and knew she would now have to make the walk to Mrs. Waylan's alone.

"But you are still wearing his ring," Marcus pointed out, thinking that had to mean something.

"Only because I can't get the blasted thing off," she muttered, then frowned at her left hand. "I think he bought it two sizes too small on purpose."

Marcus chuckled. "Wouldn't put that past him." Then when he noticed her open her handbag and take the small handgun out, his eyes widened. It was the first time he had seen the weapon. "I gather he's not walking you home tonight either."

"Not tonight nor any other night," she told him as she quickly slipped the tiny gun into her skirt pocket, where she could get to it a lot easier if the need arose. "I made it quite clear to him that he was not to be outside that door come closing time."

Marcus reached up to scratch his jaw while he considered the implications. "You want me to close up long enough to see you home?"

Karissa smiled, grateful for his concern. "Don't bother. As you can see, I am well armed and the rooming house is not really all that far away."

Marcus perched his mouth to one side, not believing her to be quite as safe as she seemed to think. She was a very attractive young woman, and now that it was known that she and Shawn had suffered some sort of falling out, there could be a few men ready to step in and try to take Shawn's place—whether she wanted them to or not.

"Wouldn't be no real bother," he said, already reaching for the ties to his half-apron. "All I'd have to do is latch the windows shut and lock the door and I'd be ready to go."

Karissa knew he had not yet counted his money and put it away in his hidden safe, nor had he gathered up the dirty glasses so they would be ready for Carole

276

Minter to wash and set back on the shelves that next morning.

"I'm perfectly capable of making it home safe and sound," she said, then patted her pocket to remind him that she was not headed out there unprotected. "Women are not quite as helpless as you men seem to think." If they were, she wouldn't be there trying to solve her own father's murder.

"Well, I'll keep an ear turned to the window just in case. If someone tries to bother you, just give a loud holler and I'll come running with Old Shirley." He gestured to the small shelf under the counter where he kept a loaded shotgun.

"Will do," she promised, then picked up the lantern she had just lit and headed immediately for the door.

Before stepping outside, she held the lantern high and looked both ways. When assured no one was there, she turned to offer Marcus a final farewell then headed quickly down the boardwalk, her yellow skirts brushing against her boots in her haste. After having seen Marcus's concern, she was a little more apprehensive than before. Sometimes danger was unavoidable.

Keeping at a brisk pace, she was nearly to the first cross street when she first heard someone coming up behind her with long, steady strides.

Remembering that Frank had seen Robby Drier follow her the night before, she slipped her hand into her pocket and curled her fingers around the small ivory handle then quickly turned to face whoever was behind her. She was surprised to find Joseph Rourke headed toward her instead of Robby.

"Where did you come from?" she asked, wondering

277

how she could have missed seeing him when she first stepped outside. Without waiting for him to catch up to her, she turned and resumed walking.

"Philadelphia, originally," he commented, his tone casual when he finally caught up with her and fell into step. "But as of late, from a rooming house just down the street where I had to go to change coats after Pete McCrystal spilled his beer all over me. I had hoped to get back in time to walk you out, but I ran into an old friend when I passed in front of the Crimson Rose and I had a hard time getting away from him."

Karissa felt a icy shiver wash over her when she saw the way his gaze traveled so leisurely over her body, as if trying to detect what she might look like without her clothing. She quickened her steps.

"Well, there was no need for you to hurry back. I prefer to walk alone. It gives me a chance to think."

"Ah, but an attractive woman like you should not be out here alone at night," he said, in a clear attempt to be charming. "Aren't you afraid of what might happen to you?"

"No. For you see I am armed," she said, wanting him to know she had a viable means of protecting herself. She'd had enough abusive treatment from the men of Black Wall.

"Is that why you keep one hand inside your pocket?" he asked with a deep smile, clearly amused by what she had just told him.

"Yes. That way I am ready to shoot a hole in someone if I suddenly feel they deserve it."

Joseph chuckled as he pulled her to a sudden stop then reached down and clamped a hand over her pocket, squeezing her wrist with the other hand until he forced her to release the pistol. He then jerked her arm back and reached inside to take the pistol from her.

"Give that to me," she shouted, angry that he had just made such a fool of her. When he did not immediately oblige, she made a grab for her father's pistol and was further angered when he held it just out of her reach. "I said, give it to me, it's mine."

"In due time," Joseph answered, then quickly slipped it into his own pocket. "After I have walked you to your rooming house."

Karissa felt another chilling wave of apprehension. "And how do you know I live in a rooming house?"

"I asked some of the locals," he said, and reached for her elbow, as if he had every right in the world to take it. His amused smile faded when she immediately jerked her arm away. "What is your problem, Catherine?"

"My problem is you, Mr. Rourke," she said, placing both hands on her hips, so angry now she literally shook. That pistol had belonged to her dear father and she refused to let it end up in the possession of such an arrogant, overbearing boor. "I want my gun back. And I want it back now."

Joseph looked at her angry glare for a moment then shrugged as if the weapon were of no real consequence to him. "Very well." He reached into his pocket for the pistol; but before actually handing it back to her, he broke it open and removed the two bullets. "There. You have your gun back. May we proceed now?"

Karissa's eyes narrowed with further rage when he then pocketed the two bullets rather than handing them over. "Those are mine, too."

"*Those* you will get back after we've arrived at our destination. I don't want to take even the slightest chance that one of them could end up lodged somewhere inside my body," he told her, and again tried to take her arm only to have it snatched away.

"Why are you doing this to me?" she asked, still glaring at him. Angrily, she repocketed the pistol, aware it would be of little help to her now.

"Because I think you are an extremely beautiful woman and I want the chance to get to know you better without any harm coming to myself." He lowered his eyelashes as if he thought that might make him be more beguiling. "I am very attracted to you. That's why I am so eager for us to become much better acquainted."

"Well, there are better ways to go about it than this," she muttered, then spun about and started walking again. Her arms swung stiffly at her sides in military fashion while she hurried along, determined to be rid of him as soon as possible.

Joseph moved quickly to keep up. "Maybe there are better ways. But because I will be leaving Black Wall after only a few more days, I don't have the time to take a more conventional approach." He made another grab for her arm, this time catching it firmly in his hand. He then drew her up short and turned her to face him. "I don't want to have to wait until my next time through here to find out exactly what you are like. I'll bet you are a real hellion in bed."

Karissa looked up at him with a startled gaze. Although other men had made similar comments while she worked at the Lucky Choice, the phrase sounded considerably more threatening when presented outside while surrounded in darkness.

"I think you should know that all I have to do is scream and twenty men will coming running to my defense," she lied, hoping she was still close enough to the Lucky Choice for Marcus to hear her. Suddenly, she wished she had not brushed aside his offer to walk her home so readily.

"But you won't scream," he responded with confidence. He let his gaze dip downward again. "That's because you are as intrigued by me as I am by you."

"I am not in the least intrigued by you." Her dark eyes glistened with a combination of anger and disgust. "If anything, Mr. Rourke, I am repulsed by you. Now please let go of my arm."

"After I've walked you safely to your rooming house. And after you have started calling me by my given name, Joseph."

Karissa stared at him a long moment, aware her choices at that moment were very limited. At least he wasn't trying to drag her across the street to the livery. It was then she thought of Robby and she quickly scanned the shadows behind Joseph to see if the big goon had followed her again. Her stomach clenched at the thought, knowing that if she should end up in a struggle against Joseph for any reason, Robby would probably come rushing to *his* aid rather than hers.

"Okay, *Joseph,* if I let you walk me home, will you then let go of my arm and allow me to go inside?"

"After I've sampled the sweetness of your lips at least once," he said, his gaze centered on the fullness of her mouth, which at the moment was pursed into an insolent frown. "I will deserve that much for having seen you safely home."

Karissa already knew it would be a cold day in hell before she allowed his sneering lips to touch hers, but decided not to antagonize him further. At least not until she had Mrs. Waylan's front door well in sight, at which point a loud, piercing scream might indeed bring her the help she wanted.

"Well, then you might as well take the lantern," she said, and tried to hand it to him, knowing it would only hamper her should she decide to break free and make a run for it rather than scream and hope for help.

"No, I prefer to keep my hands free. You carry it." He made it sound more like an order than a suggestion.

"Very well, I'll carry it," she said, and started off down the boardwalk again, this time with Joseph's hand tightly gripping her upper arm.

At first they walked in silence, but after they had gone barely a block, he suddenly started to acquaint her with his wondrous male prowess by relating his many successes with women. According to his own assessment, most of the women he met considered him extremely attractive. Many went as far as to throw themselves at him wantonly—some married. While he regaled her with several of his more recent conquests, his grip slowly loosened, but never quite enough for her to jerk her arm free.

Rather than listen to his incessant gloating, Karissa tuned out his words and instead became engrossed in the way the light formed odd little shadows across the wooden planks that crossed in front of them. She had decided the man would never stop his ceaseless babbling and was about ready to place her hands over her ears when suddenly his words stopped short. His grip around her upper arm tightened again when he pulled her to an aggressive halt.

Confused by such odd behavior, Karissa glanced over to find out what had brought him to such an abrupt stop. He stared directly ahead with his gray eyes narrowed, as if he had spotted something extremely loathsome in the darkness ahead.

Puzzled, she glanced in the direction of his gaze and felt her heart suddenly cease pumping. Shawn stood just inside the lamplight. His expression rock hard. His body unmoving.

An icy tremor passed over her, making her feel instantly weak from her head to the very tips of her toes. Never had she seen anyone look so angry and yet so composed all at the same time. She wondered if that was how he had looked the day he killed his wife.

Chapter Fourteen

"Let go of her," Shawn told Joseph with deceptive calm, his right hand resting just above his coat pocket and not far from his right hip. "She happens to belong to me."

"Belong to you? And do you have papers proving that?" Joseph asked, not obliging in the least. If anything his grip around Karissa's upper arm tightened. "Is there a marriage license you can show me? Or perhaps you bought this brazen beauty on the black market. Do you have a receipt showing how much you paid for her?"

"I told ya to be lettin' go of her," he repeated, not about to be distracted by such babble. He shifted his weight to both his two well-muscled legs while he slipped the tips of his long, agile fingers into his front coat pocket that gaped open from the weight of the small weapon nestled inside.

Karissa's eyes widened. She realized he was getting ready to pull out the pistol he always carried and wondered if he planned to shoot them both.

Not certain which man frightened her more, she decided to do what she could to calm the volatile situation. "Joseph was just walking me home, Shawn. He did not want any harm to come to me between the tavern and the rooming house."

"Joseph, is it?" Shawn repeated. His blue eyes glinted with anger while he studied the two of them, his gaze lighting on the rough manner in which Joseph held Karissa's arm. "As I recall, just a few hours ago ya claimed to be quite capable of makin' it safely from that tavern to the roomin' house all alone. If that's so true, why then would ya turn to *this* man for protection?"

"I didn't exactly turn to him," she explained, wanting that point clear. She did not want Shawn to think she had encouraged Joseph in any way. "He just kind of volunteered."

Joseph snorted with indignation and pulled her closer to him, but she was not sure if it was his way of showing temporary possession, or if he planned to use her as a shield.

With Karissa held squarely in front of him facing Shawn, he curled his other hand around her other arm and anchored her firmly in place. "That's right, I volunteered. Do you have any sort of problem with that?"

Shawn's gaze narrowed, causing his handsome features to look all the more menacing. "As a matter of fact, I do have one wee little problem with that." He gestured toward her left hand with a quick nod of his head. "Do ya see that gold and ruby ring on her hand? I happen to be the gent who placed it there. I bought it, therefore it belongs to me. Which means that the woman wearin' it also belongs to me." He took a long, slow breath then spoke his next words as clearly and distinctly as his Irish brogue would allow. "Let go of her."

Joseph reached for Karissa's left hand with his. "A ring like that is easily removed and handed back."

When Karissa saw the black rage that filled Shawn's blue eyes, she quickly jerked the hand free. "No, don't touch it. You wouldn't be able to get it off even if you tried. It's too small for my finger and won't go over my knuckle."

"Ahhh, so the only reason you wear the ring is because you can't get it off?" Joseph questioned, wanting that truth made clear. His grip relaxed as if he no longer considered Shawn as much of a threat. "What you are trying to tell me is that even though you claim to be engaged to this man, you do not really love him."

"No," she responded quickly, then swallowed hard when she saw Shawn's gaze grow darker still. She wondered just when he planned to pull out that gun and kill them both. She could tell by the way he held his hand—tense and already inches into his pocket—that he itched to do just that. "No, that's not at all what I meant."

"Then you *do* love him?" Joseph asked, as if unable to believe such a thing. "This barbarian?"

"I didn't say that either," she injected, not wanting Shawn to think that she might actually care that deeply. She would have a hard enough time putting him out of her life—should he let her *have* a life. She did not need to complicate matters by having him believe that she loved him, not when most of what she felt toward him at this moment was fear.

"Then which is it? Do you love him or not?" Joseph pressed, obviously thinking her answer would be not.

Karissa looked at Shawn, whose gaze remained dangerously grim, then lifted her chin proudly. "How I feel about Shawn McCowan is my business and no one else's." That seemed a safe enough answer.

"And it is especially no business of yours," Shawn put in. His calm tone belied the fury still smoldering in his eyes.

"Ah, but I have made it my business," Joseph put in, clearly not impressed with Shawn's angry presence.

"Please, Joseph," Karissa pleaded, wanting him to stop his foolish goading. Obviously the man had no idea how dangerous Shawn really was, probably because he was from out of town. "Just do what he says and let go of me."

"Why? So you can move away and he can have a clear shot at me? I don't think I want that."

"He won't shoot you if you let go of me and then quickly walk away. I'll make sure of that," she promised though she had no idea how she could ever keep Shawn from killing the man if that was his true intent. She certainly had no intention of throwing herself into the line of fire just to save the likes of Joseph Rourke.

"No, *I'll* make sure of it," he said, letting go of her arm again so she could oblige his next request. "You just give me that derringer back and I'll take care of this myself."

"I will not!" she said, and turned to glare at him. "I've already told you, that pistol belonged to my father and I will not give it up."

"I'll give it back to you later," Joseph said through tightly clenched teeth. His gray eyes glinted with anger. "I only need it long enough to get safely away." He made a lunge for her pocket but she quickly grabbed his arm and shoved it aside.

"Don't touch my father's gun." She lifted her chin to show that she meant to keep that derringer.

"Listen here, you little—"

A deafening click brought them both to sudden silence. When they again looked at Shawn, he had already drawn his pistol and now held it with the hammer cocked back, ready to fire.

"Rourke, I will say this one more time, just to make sure ya understand exactly what it is that I am askin' of ya as well as what the consequences could be should ya continue to refuse me. If you have *any* desire to come out of this alive and whole, you really should let go of my Catherine's arm right now then turn and head back in the direction ya came as quickly as yer legs will allow."

He took several slow, deliberate steps in their direction until he stood only several feet in front of them. The gun remained pointed in the general direction of Joseph's head. "And if ya think I could possibly miss from this distance, y'll find yerself sorely mistaken."

Karissa stared at him, too frightened to speak. She felt Joseph's hands tighten around her arms just seconds before he suddenly propelled her forward.

"Here, take her," he said, already backing way. "She's pretty but she's not worth getting shot over."

Not having expected Joseph to shove her like that, Karissa stumbled forward, nearly dropping the lantern when she tried to keep from falling. She gasped with renewed fear when Shawn's free hand shot out and caught her by the arm in almost the exact same spot where Joseph had held her. He pulled her sharply to his side while he kept the gun trained on Joseph's rapidly retreating form.

Karissa felt like a helpless pawn, being forced from one terrifying situation into another. And that made her angry. But not angry enough to risk saying anything that could make Shawn want to shoot her. Above all else, she wanted to come away from the confrontation alive and with as few injuries as possible.

"You can let go of me now," she said with amazing calm, when after a few seconds he did not release her.

"Why? So ya can make a wild dash for Mrs. Waylan's?" he asked, though he kept his gaze trained on the blackguard who had just tried to force his attention on Catherine. He wanted to make sure Rourke did the intelligent thing and kept right on going. He knew from experience that men like him were not to be trusted even after having been threatened with death.

"I am not planning to run away," she said with a stubborn lift of her chin. She refused to give Shawn the satisfaction of knowing she was *that* frightened. "I'm just getting a little tired of people grabbing me by my arms and then holding me in place."

Shawn glanced at her to see if she'd meant what she'd said and decided she did. Slowly he let go of her arm then looked again to make sure Joseph had not turned around. He smiled when he noticed that the man was a good four blocks away. Thinking it now safe enough to give Catherine at least part of his attention, he nodded toward the livery with a sideward jerk of his head. "I want to talk to ya."

"In there?" she asked with rounded eyes. She looked at him again, trying to decide if he was still angry enough to harm her. "Why can't we talk out here instead?"

"Because the danger is not over quite yet. Yer latest suitor might have it in his head to go back to his room, get a gun, then come lookin' for me. If he does, I don't want to be givin' him an easy target."

Karissa's heart jumped when she realized Shawn was right. Joseph Rourke seemed like just the type to want to get even—*if* he thought the odds were in his favor. She bit deep into the outer corner of her lower lip while she thought about her current choices. She could demand they stay there on the street and risk Joseph coming back to exact his revenge and then have Shawn's death hanging over her for eternity, or she could go with him into the livery and chance him taking some of his anger out on her.

Not wanting to be responsible for anyone's death, she decided to take her chances in the livery.

"Would you at least put the gun away first?" she asked. She wanted every possible advantage. When he looked at her then, she was relieved to see that most of his anger was gone. Instead of glowering at her like before, his forehead notched questioningly.

"Why? Do ya think I intend to shoot ya?"

"To tell you the truth, after what you just did to Joseph, I really don't know what to think."

"Just get in the livery." He sounded more annoyed than angry when he obliged by quickly slipping the handgun back into his coat pocket.

Glad that much of his anger had abated, and not wanting to do anything that could trigger such rage again, Karissa decided for once in her life she would do exactly what she was told—*up to a certain point*. Slowly, she turned and started across the street on trembling legs.

"Turn out the lantern," Shawn ordered while he followed closely behind, his gaze drawn to the gentle movement of her hips. He bit back the sudden flood of desire he felt for her. "I don't want anyone to know where we are."

Seeing the wisdom in that, at least as far as the possibility of Joseph's returning was concerned, Karissa lifted the lantern and slowly rolled the wick down until there was nothing left to burn. By the time they'd reached the livery door and Shawn had lifted the heavy latch, they were shrouded in darkness. There was only a sliver of a moon that night to help light their way.

Barely able to make out the dark shapes inside, Karissa waited until they both had entered that same building where Robby Drier had carried her that first night before she bothered to ask any more questions. Setting the unlit lantern aside to free both her hands, she did what she could to single out his dark shape from the others. "May I ask what you hoped to accomplish by leaping out of the night like that?"

"I didn't exactly leap," he said after he had carefully closed the door. He headed immediately toward her though he could barely find her in the darkness. "But what I had hoped to do was exactly what I did do."

"Which was?" she asked, wishing he would stay where he was. Karissa was so frightened of Shawn's intentions and of the fact she could no longer see his face to judge his emotions that she let out a startled gasp when a horse suddenly shifted its weight in a stall somewhere behind her and whinnied to protest the late-hour intrusion.

"Which was to save yer virtue from certain ruin yet again."

Karissa could tell by his voice that he had already covered half the distance to where she stood.

"Save my virtue? From a man who wanted nothing more than to walk me home?" she asked, even though she knew that was not entirely the truth. Joseph had already admitted that his true intention had included far more than that.

"Ya know as well as I do, that is not all he wanted," Shawn stated matter-of-factly then came to an abrupt stop only a few yards away. "And what I want to know is why ya would let a man like Joseph Rourke come near ya, especially when for all intents and purposes ya are still engaged to me."

His tone was somber, but she had no way to know if his anger had returned. Fearing the worst, Karissa took several tiny steps backward. She stuck one hand out behind her to grope for obstacles. "I did not *let* him near me. He just sort of appeared out of nowhere like you seem to do." She waited until she thought she had moved well out of arm's reach before adding a truth she hoped would not enrage him further. "Besides we are not really engaged and you know it."

"Maybe I know it and you know it; but the people livin' here in Black Wall certainly do not know it. To them our engagement's quite real, thanks partly to yerself. That's why I cannot be lettin' ya go around makin' a mockery of me like ya have these last several days. I have a certain image to uphold around here and you are not lettin' me uphold it."

"How have I made a mockery of you?" she wanted to know, thinking herself unjustly accused. It was not as if she had *asked* Joseph to walk her home.

"By suddenly throwin' yerself into the arms of other men the way ya have been here lately."

"What?" She could not believe the accusing tone in his voice.

"First, it was poor little Joey McGeehan, and now Joseph Rourke, a man ya never even laid eyes on before tonight. Don't ya realize how bad it makes me look for ya to be seen out alone at night with either of those two?"

Although she still could not see his face, his tone reflected anger again; but for some reason his anger no longer mattered. Probably because now she was angry, too. "And just why should how *you* look matter to me?" Even though she knew he could not see her, she threw up her arms to indicate her frustration. She wondered how she had ever gotten herself into such a predicament. "This whole situation has gotten out of hand. I still think it is time we told everyone the truth."

"Why?" He closed the distance between them again. "So all the men in Black Wall will think it is open season on ya again? Are ya that eager to find yerself in the arms of another man?"

Frightened by the jealous tone in his voice, well aware of what Frank had told her he was capable of doing while in such a state, Karissa curled her hands into hard fists, prepared to defend herself against him, even though she had resumed backing away from him. Her heart drummed a frantic rhythm against the tender walls of her chest. If only she could tell exactly how much distance lay between them. "You make it sound like I'm cheating on you somehow."

"I guess because that's how it feels," Shawn answered honestly, unaware of her fear because of the darkness.

"But why would it when you know as well as I do that we're not really engaged?"

She could tell by the proximity of his deep-timbred voice and by the sound of the hay crushing softly beneath his boots, he was slowly gaining on her. She swallowed back the cold fear that squeezed her throat when she realized that without a weapon of some sort there was very little she could do to protect herself. Her stomach fluttered when she wondered if he had taken out his pistol again or if it was still tucked safely away in his pocket. If only she could see something other than shapes.

"I guess I feel cheated because ya still wear my ring," he admitted. "Whenever I catch sight of it glitterin' on your hand the way it does, it makes me feel as if ya really do belong to me. At least in some small way."

Panic filled Karissa's heart. His mind had twisted this into something it was not. Obviously he had decided she really was his.

"The only reason I still have on your ring is because I can't get it off," she quickly reminded him, then as if to prove her point, though she knew he could not see, she reached for the blasted thing and gave it a sharp

294

tug at about the same time she stumbled over something behind her in the darkness. She immediately righted herself but decided not to chance stumbling over the object again. The time had come to take a stand. "I have tried my best to get that ring off my hand but it is just too small to go over my knuckle. I have to wonder how you ever managed to get it on me in the first place."

"If ya really wanted that ring off, ya could have asked someone to cut it off for ya," he told her, not about to admit that he had dabbed the ring in butter just to make sure it went on. "All it would take is a good set of bolt cutters."

"And chance someone taking my finger off with it?" she asked, thinking that idea a little illogical. Bolt cutters were not exactly a precise tool. "No I think I'd rather wait until I can have a jeweler take it off for me."

He continued toward her, his black form growing ever larger in the surrounding darkness. "Catherine. Admit it. The truth is that ya have come to care for me, at least in some small way, but ya refuse to admit it or maybe ye're just afraid to admit it."

"Don't be silly."

"Ye're fascinated by the thought of bein' engaged to me and have been from the start. Just as fascinated as I am of bein' engaged to you—though only the good Lord knows why."

"No, that is not true," she stated, swallowing hard. He stood so close to her now, she could feel the vibration of his voice. There was no longer a chance for escape. Her only hope was to convince him of the truth. "The only reason I said anything at all about an engagement was because I was angry at the time and wanted to find a way to get even with you for some of the awful things you said about me. All I had hoped to do was make you squirm a little while you carefully worked your way out of it. How was I supposed to know that rather than be resourceful and find a logical way out of it, you'd actually go along with such a thing?"

Unable to be that close to her without touching her, Shawn reached forward to take her into his arms, surprised to find her trembling. His heart wrenched when he pulled her tenderly into the warm circle of his arms, making him wish he had never used her as a means to bring more attention to himself. He had needed to find some way to gain more approval from the men, and Catherine had unwittingly provided him with that. By pretending to be engaged to the most beguiling woman in that town, he had immediately earned himself a whole new form of male respect. It had also given him a good reason to be out late at night. Whenever anyone questioned him about his unusually late hours, he'd just wink and say he'd been with his Catherine. No one dared question him beyond that.

"Catherine, there are reasons I did what I did that day, reasons I cannot reveal to anyone just yet. Still, I think ya should know that what happens between us is no longer a game for me. Somewhere along the way, my feelin's toward ya turned very real. Although I cannot truly lay a proper claim to ya right now, my luv, I do hope to be able to do so someday in the future. I want you now more than I ever did."

Before she could say anything to ruin the moment,

he bent and kissed her gently, relieved when she did not respond by jerking her head away as he had feared she might. "Y've stolen my heart, Miss Catherine Sobey, and one day, when I am again in a position to do so without any harm comin' to ya as a result, I plan to steal yers in return."

Karissa was so confused by what he had said, and so weak with relief to discover he meant her no harm that, rather than push him away like she should, she allowed him to hold her close. It amazed her that a man who had shown such barely controlled rage toward Joseph Rourke only minutes earlier could hold her with such gentleness now. It was as if he were two different men.

"I never thought I would care this strongly about a woman ever again," he murmured close to her ear. His breath fell gently across her cheek, causing her to close her eyes temporarily in response. "But I can't help it. You are so very special to me."

"But you hardly know me," she reminded him, wishing he did not care so much, because as soon as she had the information she sought, she would be gone from there. She hated the thought of hurting him, especially after having heard the depth of sincerity in his voice. She also felt guilty for having lied to him about who she really was and why she was there, though she'd had a very good reason to lie. She knew if he ever found out the truth about her and it turned out he was *not* involved with the murder of her father, he would feel like a fool for having been so easily duped.

Even though she did not really fear him at that moment, for it was hard to fear a man who could show

297

such gentleness, she still did not like the thought of angering him like that.

"I know enough to understand how I feel," he admitted, then slipped a strong hand behind her head to hold it in place while he again brought his mouth down to possess hers, this time kissing her with more intensity than before. Now that he had admitted his feelings to her, at least partially, and she had not angrily rebuked him for having done so, he was suddenly consumed with the desire to make her a very real part of his life—even if only for this one night.

With the heated passion of a man who had for far too long denied himself something he had not even been fully aware he'd wanted until now, he pressed her soft, supple body against his while he devoured her with the hunger of a man half-starved.

Unprepared for such a kiss, Karissa was immediately caught up in the spinning vortex of pleasure the gentle pressure of his mouth had created inside her. She could not believe the intensity of emotion that had so suddenly sprung to life inside her and was temporarily unable to cope with its volatile strength. Her senses reeled and her pulses raced until she felt dizzy, causing her to lean against him just to keep her bearings.

Despite the fact she still had every reason to distrust this man and knew that she should shove him away and make a wild, frantic run for the door, she could not bring herself to actually do so. She could not even bring herself to offer a strong verbal protest. All she could seem to do while he continued to kiss her so masterfully was lean against him and marvel at the splendid feelings he had so easily aroused. She had to wonder why no other man had ever been able to elicit such a profound response inside her.

Obviously, Shawn McCowan had cast some sort of magical spell over her yet again—a dark, mystical spell that rendered her incapable of completing any rational thought. Never in all her years of dealing with men had she felt such an overpowering need course through her body, a need so strong and so basic, it made her ache inside.

Although she knew it was entirely the wrong response and she could hear Lizbeth's sharp voice in the hazy distance chiding her for such brazen behavior, she lifted her arms to encircle his shoulders. Shawn took immediate advantage of having her arms up out of the way and pressed her soft curves even more intimately against the solid muscles that covered his chest. As a result, startling shafts of white-hot desire rippled through her, causing her to feel more wondrously alive than she'd ever felt—yet at the same time dangerously weak.

While she fought to retain at least some semblance of her earlier sanity, Shawn's strong, demanding hands moved from her shoulders to the small of her back, where he pressed her body closer still. That brought her yet more waves of sensuous pleasure. She moaned softly in response, and although she knew it was wrong to continue with this madness, she could do nothing to stop him. Nor did she *want* to do anything to stop him. She was too lost to this strange swirling sea of emotions, too curious to know what else he could make her feel simply by touching her. Her usual common sense had completely abandoned her, allowing her womanly desires, now fully awakened, to take over.

Closing her eyes again, she leaned heavily against him, allowing him to part her lips with the gentle nudging of his tongue, amazed at the many new sensations *that* wrought. While she tried desperately to come to terms with *those* startling sensations, one of his hands moved from the small of her back, where it had helped the other hold her body pressed intimately against his, around to the outer curve of her ribcage. Then ever so slowly that same wayward hand edged its way upward until it gently cupped the underside of her breast.

Instead of pulling away and chastising him angrily for having dared touch that which no man had ever touched before, she responded to the sensations that intimacy had created by slowly sliding one of her hands across the hard contours along his back. She marveled over the noticeable differences between his body and her own and wondered if it was at all possible for her to bring him as much pleasure as he brought her. Did men react with that same volatile intensity or was this something reserved for women only?

Shawn was overcome by his own driving need. While trying to decide if he dared try to take her right there in the livery where anyone might come in and catch them, he pulled his mouth away from hers. He wanted to tell her how very much he desired her and to see what her response would be to the suggestion they climb up into the loft, where the fresh hay would provide a clean bed in which to lie.

"Katy, I want ya more than I've wanted *any* woman

since that dreadful, dreary day my wife died," he murmured, unaware that the mere mention of Nicollette would jolt her immediately back to reality. "But I need to know what yer thoughts are. I need to know if you are willin' because I won't force ya to do somethin' ya are not ready to do."

Reminded of her reason to fear him, Karissa quickly gathered the strength and the courage she needed to shove him away.

"You really want to know what my thoughts are?" she asked, gasping for needed air while she quickly moved several steps to the side, still blocked by whatever was behind her. "I'll tell you what I'm thinking. I'm thinking that you really have some nerve for trying to take advantage of me like that. Just because you happen to have whatever it takes for a man to make women swoon like a silly girl, you do not have the right to use that God-given power against every woman you find yourself alone with."

Confused by such a sudden and unexpected outburst, he reached out to try to calm her in some way, but the second his hands grazed her shoulders, she stepped farther out of his reach. For some reason he had frightened her. "I can assure ya I have not kissed a woman with that much passion nor that much need in quite some time."

"Oh and by that do you mean since before you killed your wife? Or was it perhaps after?"

So that was it. That was why she had been behaving so strangely these past few days. She had heard the rumors and believed them. But then why shouldn't she? *He* was the one who had started them to begin with. "Who told ya about that?"

"Everyone," she lied, not about to single out Frank. "It's all over Black Wall."

Shawn tried again to touch her but was rebuked by the quick slap of her hand. He closed his eyes against the painful stab to his heart, knowing what she must think of him. Oh, how he wished he could tell her the truth. That there was no reason for her to be afraid of him. But he couldn't. At least not yet.

"So now ya think I might be capable of killin' you, too," he said, aware it all made sense now. No wonder she had refused to let him walk her home. She was afraid of being alone with a confessed murderer. So, why was she alone with him now? Had she been *that* concerned for his welfare earlier? *That* afraid that Rourke would return and try to shoot him in the back? But why should she care what happened to someone capable of killing his own wife? Because she could never live with a murder on her conscience, even *his* murder.

Unaware of the direction Shawn's thoughts had taken, Karissa responded with a proud lift of her chin. "If you are capable of killing your own wife, then yes, I believe you are capable of killing just about anyone." Afraid his anger could erupt again at any moment, she continued to step slowly away from him.

"But what if I told ya there were extenuating circumstances?" he asked, wondering just how willing she was to believe him guilty of such a heinous crime.

"I've already heard the extenuating circumstances," she said, reaching her hand out to feel for obstacles while she continued to move away from him. "You

302

killed your wife because you'd discovered she'd taken on a lover," she said, though it was beyond her why the woman would have wanted anyone else.

"That's not all there was to it," he said, already trying to invent a logical reason for having done such a horrible thing. "The truth is, I had no choice. No, I take that back. I did have a choice. I could either kill her, or I could be killed *by* her. She happened to be holdin' a gun on me at the time."

"Why?" Karissa decided to hear him out. For some reason, she had to know the rest of the story. She had to know that she was not totally inept when it came to judging a person's character.

"Why was she holdin' a gun on me? Because I had refused to divorce her even though I knew she no longer loved me and she became very angry with me for that. She wanted to be free to pursue her lover openly, and by refusing her a divorce, I had refused to give her that freedom."

Shawn paused to consider what he had just said. It sounded plausible enough to him. "When I came home early one afternoon, I noticed that my favorite pistol was missin' out of its case and realized she was the only one who could have taken it and why. Not wantin' to be shot through with my very own pistol, I armed myself with another pistol and waited to see if she could really go through with it."

He was pleased with how the story had unfolded thus far so he continued, "That very same night, she and her new lover tried to murder me in my sleep; but because I was ready for them, I was able to defend myself and came out of it alive. Her bullet barely grazed my shoulder. But my wife was not so lucky."

303

He did what he could to sound deeply tormented. "She died right there in my arms. Her lover died only a few hours later at a local hospital."

Karissa frowned, not certain she believed such a ludicrous tale. "If that's true, then why are the police searching for you?"

Shawn thought quickly. "Because as it turned out, her young lover was also the precinct chief's oldest son. I figured that took away any chance I had for a fair trial."

The silence that followed let him know that she was seriously considering everything he had just told her. "So rather than face a certain hangin', I made a quick getaway and have been hidin' from the law ever since."

Karissa studied his dark form with a cautiously raised eyebrow, wishing she could see his eyes. "If all that's true, then why does everyone here believe you killed the two during some wild fit of jealousy?"

"Because that's the way it is with the men around here. They are always wantin' to believe the worst about a man. So rather than try to change their whole way of thinkin', I let them presume what they want." He waited for a moment before testing the result of such a quickly concocted story. "Ya do believe me, don't ya?"

Karissa did not know what she believed.

"It is possible you just told me the truth," she conceded, then tapped the corner of her mouth with the tip of her finger. "But it is just as possible that you invented that whole story just to confuse me."

"And *are* ya confused?" There was a trace of amusement in his voice.

"Very."

304

"Too confused to consider goin' with me to the picnic this Saturday?"

Karissa's forehead notched at the sudden turn in their conversation. "What picnic?"

"Haven't ya heard? This comin' Saturday will be the first Saturday of June and because of that there is to be a special gatherin' of the townsfolk in a clearin' just up the hill late in the afternoon. I'm not sure why that date is so important to these people, but I was told that everyone puts on their Sunday best and gets together for a big picnic on that day, and they have for years. Would ya do me the honor of lettin' me be the one to escort ya?"

Remembering what Sirus had told her earlier, that her brother, John, was due to visit Black Wall at some point during that coming weekend, Karissa knew she dared not risk being out in public like that. John might see her in the crowd and call to her by name, which would bring an immediate end to her investigation. He would also order her back home, to which there would no longer be a reason not to oblige. "No, I can't go Saturday. I already have plans."

"I take it you are still upset with me for what happened tonight." He moved toward her, hoping to touch her one last time before they left. "I know I indicated to ya that such as that would not happen again. Would it help if I apologized?"

"I suppose." It certainly wouldn't do any harm.

"Then I apologize," he said, and reached out to touch her cheek gently with the tips of his fingers. He knew better than to make a second promise that a kiss like that would not happen again. It was clear now that he could not help reacting like that whenever he was alone with her. Somehow she had found her way into his blood and that was driving him slowly insane. "Will ya at least let me walk ya home?"

Karissa closed her eyes in response to his tender touch then nodded her agreement. Having him standing that close to her again made her feel a little light-headed. The sooner they left there, the better. "If you will help me find my lantern."

Shawn let out the breath he'd been holding. He had worried she would refuse, worried she was still too afraid of him to risk being alone with him again. Within seconds, he had struck a match and located the lantern for her. He then relit the lantern and walked with her to the rooming house, glad she was so willing to give him another chance. And glad Joseph had not yet returned to exact his revenge.

Chapter Fifteen

By the time Karissa had pulled on her white ruffled nightgown and crawled beneath the black netting that surrounded her tiny bed, she realized she had two choices: believe herself to be so wanton that she could fall that willingly into a murderer's arms, *or* believe what Shawn had told her about his wife. That the murders of both his wife and her lover were more the result of circumstance than anything else.

Unwilling to believe that she had found such genuine pleasure in a murderer's kiss or that she had fallen so easily to his touch, Karissa decided to give Shawn the benefit of the doubt — at least for now. Still, she knew it was in her own best interest to remain cautious of him and to accept the fact that although he might not be the cold-blooded wife-killer everyone else in Black Wall believed him to be, he was still suspected of being a member of those malicious cutthroats, the Molly Maguires. Which meant Shawn was still one of the many suspected in her father's death.

Which was why she decided to follow Shawn when he left the Lucky Choice the following night. She had to know if he was one of them.

"Marcus, I'm still not feeling any better," she said, already reaching down to untie her apron from around her gray dress when she noticed Shawn heading for the door. She had chosen the dark color because it would be much less noticeable in the dark. "In fact, I think I feel a little worse."

Karissa had pretended having a stomach ailment for the past two hours just so Marcus would believe her excuse to leave when the time finally came to follow Shawn.

Because of all her earlier complaints, Marcus wiped his hands on a nearby rag then felt her face, which really was flushed, but flushed from the fear of what she was about to do and not from any stomach sickness. "You do look a might pink in the cheeks. Maybe you should go into the back room and lie down across some of those crates back there."

"No. I really think I should go on home before I get worse. Although I don't think I'm running any fever yet, it is probably only a matter of time until I do. And since tomorrow is Friday, which is always one of your busiest nights, I really do need to do what I can to get better by then. I'd hate to leave you short-handed on such a busy night."

Marcus nodded that he agreed. Fridays were certainly more crowded than Thursdays, probably because the men faced only a half day of work each Saturday and then would have Sunday free to do whatever they wanted. "It wouldn't hurt nothing to stop by the widow Kelly's room on your way in and see if she has some of that tonic for stomach ills. Could be something you ate."

Aware that the longer she stood there talking, the farther away Shawn would be when she left, she quickly pressed her hand over her mouth then widened her eyes as if she thought she was about to relieve herself of whatever was in her stomach right there in front of everyone. Hurriedly, she grabbed her handbag and her lantern, which she purposely did not light, and headed out the door.

To her disappointment, Shawn was already gone from sight when she finally stepped out onto the boardwalk and looked both ways to see which direction he had gone. Afraid Frank might have witnessed her sudden departure and decide to follow her instead of Joseph Rourke, she chose a general direction and started walking at a brisk pace. Because there was very little moonlight to brighten her path, she stumbled twice on warped boards and large stones that had found their way onto the darkened walk.

After having gone several blocks and still not catching a glimpse of Shawn, she realized her efforts were futile and sank onto a nearby bench to mull over the disappointing fact that she had already lost him. How could he have gotten away that quickly?

It was while she sat there in the darker shadows, staring absently at the buildings across the street, that she first noticed the sound of footsteps only a block or so away. Her first reaction was fear, thinking perhaps Robby Drier or Joseph Rourke had seen her leave and had followed her. She reached immediately for her derringer, which tonight she had kept inside her handbag for no other reason than the pocket on her gray dress was too small.

Gripping the weapon tightly, she pulled it out and rested it in her lap then glanced back in the direction she had come to find out who had followed her. She was surprised, and somewhat relieved, to see Charlie McAllister and Joey McGeehan headed down the planked walk across the street. Like her, they carried a lantern that was not lit and kept mostly to the shadows.

Unmoving, she held her breath and hoped they would not notice her. When they continued on without as much as glancing in her direction, she realized she had succeeded. She waited until the two were quite a distance ahead of her before setting her lantern aside then slowly rising off the bench and following quietly behind.

Staying in the darkest shadows as much as possible, she managed to keep up with the pair even after they left the main street and hurried toward a nearby wooded thicket. There they met up with Shawn, and together the three disappeared into the undergrowth.

Gripping the derringer tighter, she waited several seconds before attempting to follow. She never saw the three men again after that, nor did she come across anyone else lurking about the shadows. Eventually she gave up the search, and after stopping to retrieve her lantern, she returned to the rooming house, more confused and frustrated than ever.

The four men who had killed Lawrence Caine, Clay Jones, and Thomas Connolly stood in the alley waiting for the masked man to return. It was eleven o'clock, Thursday night, June 5, the night they had been promised the final payment for all their hard work; but with Clay Jones having been one of the three men they had been paid to kill, they were a little worried that they were about to be duped. Clay Jones was the one who had found them initially. He had been their only real contact. And now he was gone.

"What if he don't come?" the largest of the four asked, wondering what they could possibly do to get the money still owed them if the masked man did not show up as promised. "After all, Jones never did tell us just who it was we were workin' for, and now that he's dead, there's no real way for us to find out."

"Well, Patrick, I guess we should have thought of that before we actually killed him," the man to his right said with a slow shake of his head.

"Yeah, but it never occurred to me that would be creatin' such a problem."

"Maybe we should have asked for all the money up front as soon as we found out Jones was to be one of the ones killed."

The four fell silent again and resumed staring off

toward the street. Two stood slumped against a wall while the other two sank onto the tops of large, empty crates.

"I'm not worried," one of them finally said. "The man in the mask will be here. He promised us he would and rich men like him always keep their promises. *Don't they?*"

Again there was silence. Finally, after several long, excruciating minutes, a dark form appeared in the entrance. The four men let out a collective sigh of relief and headed immediately toward him.

"We was about to think you wasn't comin'," Patrick said as soon as he was close enough to the masked man to be heard.

There was just enough light glowing from the sputtering gaslamp across the street to illuminate their faces, which was why the elegantly dressed man who had hired the four henchmen wore a black silk costume mask that covered two-thirds of his face. He did not want his identity known even to them.

"Why wouldn't I come?" the masked man asked, already dipping his hand into the small valise he carried. "You did what you were told to do, didn't you?"

"Well, yeah, but we thought maybe you might have decided to cheat us out of that last twenty thousand." Clearly Patrick considered himself the spokesman for the four.

"Why would I do that? I could need your services again in the future. Besides, if I didn't come here and pay you the rest of the money I owe you, you might have found some clever way to let the authorities know that those three murders were in no way connected to the Molly Maguires. If the police ever found out those were all hired murders, I could end up in a lot of trouble. Too many people would realize that I had a very good reason for wanting those men dead."

"So this is hush money?" the largest man asked, his hand already extended for his share.

"In a way yes. That, and a gesture of goodwill to make sure you remain available to me for other such jobs."

Patrick's eyes lit with eagerness. "And will the pay for the next job be as good as it was this last time?"

"It's a little premature to discuss payment just yet. I'm not even sure I'll be needing someone like you again. At this point, I just want to make sure you four are happy with me just in case I do need you again."

The large man held the packet of money up close to his face so he could see the denominations then chortled. "I couldn't get much happier than I am right now. I never had so much money at one time."

The others chimed their agreement, each accepting his payment in turn. Only the shortest man actually bothered to count the money and smiled when he found all five thousand to be there.

"I'm glad you're happy," the masked man said, looking quite satisfied when he closed his now empty valise and tucked it up under his cloak. "And I think you should know that I was very pleased with your work. You did exactly what you were told to do."

"We even remembered to talk like Irishmen and used those four names Jones gave us to help throw the suspicion off of us and onto those other men." He patted his large chest with a meaty hand then grinned wide enough to reveal several gapped teeth. "I pretended to be Thomas. Was kind of a kick when I later ended up being the one to kill the real Thomas."

"And it's a good thing we remembered to use those names," another said, already tucking his money into his underdrawers. "What with the way that red-haired woman showed up there in Pittsburgh at the last minute like she did."

The masked man stiffened. "A red-haired woman?"

"The same one who was workin' at that tavern where we made our final plans for the first two murders. I guess she overheard what we was up to and decided it might be worth her while to try to warn Lawrence Caine about us. Probably figured there had to be some money in it for her somewhere."

"Yeah, lucky for us she got there too late."

"No. What's lucky for us is that George fired off that last shot when he did. If she'd lived long enough to tell the authorities what she knew about us, we'd all be in a hell of a fix by now."

"Then you know for a fact that she's dead now?" the masked man wanted verified, clearly upset.

"As a doornail. While the rest of us caught the

train back to Black Wall to take care of Jones, Heath stayed behind to make sure she was dead and watched with his very own eyes when the coroner's men carried her out just a few hours later."

The masked man nodded, as if they had just confirmed something for him. "Then there are no witnesses to what you men did?"

"None that I know of. Why, even old Jones himself is gone now and he's the one you sent out to hire us."

"And you have no idea who I am?"

"Don't really care now that we've got our money." Patrick chuckled then signaled to the others that it was time to leave. "And if you decide that you do want to hire us again, you know where to find us and you know who to ask for."

"Patrick Moore," the masked man confirmed then waited until the four men had left the alley before he slipped the small pistol out of the hidden holster and turned to follow. He knew this was not the sort of neighborhood to be alone and unarmed in that late at night.

It was all anyone wanted to talk about in Black Wall. That Friday morning, when the authorities went to the jail to get Jack McGeehan and walk him across the street to the church where the trial was to be held, they found his cell empty. Empty despite the fact there was no sign of forced entry on any door and the man they'd hired to guard him had stayed in the front office the entire night and

315

claimed to have been awake that whole time. Yet when he searched his pocket for the key he had been given in case of some emergency, he found it was not there.

It was as if the devil himself had snatched the key right out of his pocket then used it to let Jack McGeehan out of his cell. No noises were heard and nothing looked to have been touched. Which made the local authorities feel like absolute fools and made John Caine so angry he threw his coffee cup right through a stained glass window. He had just arrived in town and had stopped by a restaurant for a cup of coffee and something to eat while he sent his secretary and the two Pinkerton agents he had hired on to the jail to find out if the trial was still scheduled to begin at ten o'clock as the telegram had stated.

"What do you mean he just vanished?" he asked, looking from his frightened secretary to the two local lawmen who had walked over with him to explain what had happened. The Pinkerton men he'd hired had wisely chosen to remain outside, but John's voice was so shrill with anger that even they heard his every word. "How can anyone just *vanish* out of a locked cell?"

"We really don't know how the man escaped," the taller of the two admitted, his gaze darting from John's angry face to his companion, who refused to look at John at all. "All we know is that he was there when we left last night but when we decided to walk him over a little early so the newspaper could take some pictures, he was gone. Oddest thing, his cell was still locked, but the man himself was gone."

"Well, it is obvious he had some help." John raked his hand through his thinning hair. He had counted on them finding Jack guilty and hanging him that very same day while he was still there to watch. "Do you have any idea who might have wanted to help him escape?"

"About half this town would. The man was well liked among his mining friends."

"But he was a *murderer*." John's voice rose another octave until it sounded more like a woman's shriek than a man's shout. "He not only killed one of his own friends, but according to the man sent here by the Pittsburgh police just this past week, it is very possible he had a hand in killing my father as well."

"The miners don't see it that way. They feel like Old Jack was framed," the taller man said, then took a tentative step backward, as if not certain what John might do next. "To tell you the truth, Mr. Caine, I'm not all that sure he wasn't framed. I know Old Jack McGeehan and I knew Big Thomas Connolly. They were too close of friends for either of them to have wanted to harm the other."

John glared at him for a long moment but decided to let such a ludicrous statement pass. The evidence was clear. "What are you doing to find him?"

"Everything is possible. I have one group of men conducting a house-to-house search for him while others are combing the woods and even checking some of the larger caves in this area. If Old Jack is still anywhere around here, we'll find him."

"You sure as hell had better," John said, then wagged his finger only inches from the lawman's stony face. "I want that man found, tried, and hanged before I have to go back Monday. Don't make me have come all this way for nothing."

The two lawmen exchanged doubtful glances but said nothing to enrage the young industrialist any more than he was already. "We'll do what we can."

"Ask the two Pinkerton men I hired to help you. They've had a lot of experience hunting down just such criminals."

The two lawmen nodded then headed immediately for the door.

John waited until they had both stepped outside and he was alone in the restaurant with his male secretary and the one waitress who had not fled the room the second that coffee cup crashed through the front window.

"Well, what are you staring at?" he shouted to her, aware she stood frozen to the spot.

The waitress was not the sort to be easily intimidated. Rather than flinch as some women might, she shifted her weight to one leg and crossed her arms over an ample bosom. "I'm not staring at nothing, sir. I was just waiting to see if maybe you wanted another cup of coffee. I felt like you were probably finished with that other one." She then nodded toward the jagged hole in the restaurant window.

"All I want is to be left alone," he muttered, then

turned his attention to his secretary as if to let her know she was of no further importance to him. "Looks like we are going to be stuck here awhile. Go see to a couple of rooms at the hotel."

The short, thin man dressed in a dark blue pin-checked suit and a bowler hat lifted his chin as if in an attempt to bolster his own courage before responding. "Sir, I was told there is no hotel in this town."

"Then where in the hell are we supposed to stay while we are here?"

"There are two rooming houses with vacancies, both a stone's throw from here."

"I am not staying in some rat-infested rooming house. Go find that man I hired last month to take Clay Jones's place. Tell him I want his house for the weekend. Let *him* be the one to stay at a rooming house."

Nodding sharply, James Munn quickly backed out of the room. When he stepped outside and saw how many people had gathered around the broken glass to peer inside at the wealthy owner of the Black Wall colliery, he could not help but grin. He knew by their wide eyes and gaping mouths that his boss had made quite a first impression. He just hoped they had the good sense to stay out of his way until that McGeehan fellow was found. John Caine could be a real bear when he was angry.

Karissa did not hear about Jack McGeehan's un-explainable escape until midafternoon, shortly after she had finally come downstairs to eat something.

319

Having awakened with a slight headache and having heard that her brother was supposed to arrive in Black Wall that morning, she had decided to stay in her room until it was nearly time to leave for work. It was while she ate the ham and egg sandwich that had been left for her in the warming butler that she found out what had happened the night before.

"Can ya believe it?" Kelly asked, her green eyes wide with Irish wonder. "It's as if that old man just slipped between those iron bars and walked right out the front door without bein' seen."

An uneasy feeling crept over Karissa while she listened to what Kelly had to say. There obviously had to be much more to the incident than that, making her wonder if Shawn McCowan, Charles McAllister, and Joey McGeehan had had anything to do with the man's sudden disappearance. "And no one saw anyone lurking about the jail at any time during the night?"

"Not that I know about. Even the man they paid to guard the front office di'na see anyone and he was awake all the night. Ask Mr. Miles. He's the one who was in here earlier tellin' me about it. Seems the whole town tis in a real stir. I hear that at least half the miners have refused to go down in the shafts today because they're so eager to stay atop the latest gossip."

"Where is Mr. Miles?" Karissa asked, eager to find out what he did know.

"I think he went on back down the street to see what else he could find out. But then I imagine y'll be seein' him later at the Lucky Choice. He said somethin' about takin' his supper there."

Eager to find out more and hoping Frank would stop by early, Karissa set what was left of her sandwich aside then hurried back upstairs to finish dressing for work.

By four-thirty, she was on her way across town to the Lucky Choice, all the while keeping an eye out for Frank. She felt that if anyone had even an inkling about what had happened, it would be him. He seemed to know almost everything that went on in Black Wall, which was why he believed he was now very close to getting the information he wanted concerning the Molly Maguires.

Still hurrying, Karissa became so intent on finding Frank in among the many people milling about that at first she did not notice that John stood only a few yards away from the jail, talking with a small group of reporters. She was only a few hundred feet away before she realized who he was.

With her eyes stretched to their limits and her heart hammering painfully in her chest, she spun about in search of a place to hide and was startled to see Shawn standing in front of the Crimson Rose, watching her curiously.

"Catherine," he shouted to her, waving to make sure that she saw him. "Over here."

Knowing she dare not stop for a conversation on the street, not with her half-brother standing less than a block away, she turned and hurried back the way she had come, her heart pounding so hard and so fast she felt certain it would explode right out of her chest.

Shawn frowned and watched while she practically ran from his sight. He also noticed that she kept cutting her gaze back toward that small group of reporters who stood in front of the jail talking with John Caine, and only once looked back to see if he had followed her.

Frowning, he wondered why she was so concerned with the reporters' whereabouts. He also wondered why as soon as she had ducked into a nearby alley and well out of everyone's sight, Frank Miles moved to follow.

Curious to find out the connection between Frank and Catherine, Shawn pulled his cap down low over his face and headed off in the same direction. It was not until he spotted two Pinkerton men standing near the alley entrance that he abruptly changed his mind.

Afraid one of them might recognize him from his own days with the agency, he veered off in a different direction then kept right on going until he was just another part of the crowd.

That night, Shawn stood in his usual place at the end of the bar waiting for Marcus to hand him his first beer when the four lawmen entered the Lucky Choice. He watched, showing little concern even after they headed directly toward him.

Karissa's forehead notched when she noticed the four lawmen she had never seen before working their way through the crowd toward Shawn. Curious to find out what they wanted, she set her tray down and headed in that same direction. She arrived at his side just seconds before they did. Her stomach knotted when it then occurred to her that they might be there to arrest him for the murder of his wife and her lover. If that was so, they would handcuff him right there and haul him away to New York to stand trial, where he would probably be found guilty and hanged. The thought of Shawn having to die for something he had been forced to do brought a sharp pain to her heart.

"Mr. Shawn McCowan?" one of the four lawmen said after they had gathered in a line to face him.

"Aye," he responded with a casual nod, then reached out to accept the beer Marcus held out to him. "I'm Shawn McCowan. And just who might ya gents be?"

"I'm Sam Evans," the spokesperson of the group said, and answered Shawn's slow, easy nod with a brisk one of his own. He gave Karissa a quick glance before continuing in a voice filled with self-importance. *"State Deputy Sam Evans."*

To Karissa, it felt as if her whole world was falling apart. A state deputy had the authority to make an arrest anywhere within the boundaries of his state and then take that prisoner to wherever in the United States the crime had been committed. Shawn could be on his way back to New York within the hour. She curled her hands into tight fists to keep from revealing her fear.

But Shawn remained amazingly calm. So calm, that he stretched his left arm out and pulled her

323

gently to him as he often did when standing at the bar.

"Can I do somethin' for ya, Deputy?" He bent to press a quick kiss on Karissa's forehead, as if to reassure her somehow that everything would be all right.

By now they had the attention of everyone in the tavern and the man looked at Shawn grimly. "You can tell me where you were early this morning, say at about one or two o'clock."

Karissa's fear took a new turn. These men weren't there because of what happened in New York; they were there because they thought Shawn was in some way connected to Jack McGeehan's mysterious disappearance. Obviously, these outside lawmen had been brought in to help recapture the old man and at the same time find out who had helped him escape.

Her heart twisted with apprehension when she realized that they would want a witness to prove where Shawn had been and knew he was probably still off with Charles and Joey at that hour. But doing *what* she did not know. Her whole body felt suddenly weak. What if he *was* guilty of helping Jack escape? What would they do to him for something like that?

Shawn paused long enough to take a quick drink of his beer, then responded in a still casual tone, "I'm afraid I can't answer that."

The deputy's shoulders tensed just before he narrowed his gaze as if with warning. "You can't or you *won't?*"

"Take your pick," Shawn offered with a shrug, then took another drink of his beer. If Karissa had not felt the muscles in Shawn's arm grow suddenly rigid while he continued to hold her close, she would have thought him completely unaffected by their questions.

There was a long moment of silence before the deputy spoke again. "Why don't you save us all a lot of time and trouble by telling me where you were?" he said, then reached into his jacket and pulled a small handgun from a holster hidden just above his waist. Although at no time did he actually point the weapon at Shawn, his intention was clear. He wanted to intimidate him by offering an unspoken threat. "We'll find out eventually anyway."

Not knowing if the deputy was the type to follow through with such a threat, Karissa moved instinctively closer to Shawn, as if that might help protect him in some way.

Again there was a long pause while the four men waited for Shawn's response. When there was none, the deputy's nostrils flared and the muscles in his neck pumped angrily. "Come on, McCowan. Be a man instead of some sniveling coward. Tell us the truth about where you were."

When Karissa felt Shawn's arm loosen from around her shoulder, her heart slammed hard against her chest. She remembered the pistol he carried in his coat and feared with his hand now free, he might make a grab for the gun and be killed on the spot. There was very little chance he could out-draw all four men.

325

"He doesn't want to tell you where he was because he was with me," Karissa blurted out. She could not bear the thought of witnessing Shawn's death, especially at the hands of bullies like these.

The deputy's eyes widened at the unexpected response as if he had dismissed her presence entirely. "And who the hell are you?"

Karissa held up her left hand so he could have a clear view of the ring. "I am Catherine Sobey, the woman Shawn is engaged to marry. And the reason he wouldn't tell you where he was last night is because he is trying to protect me. He knows it would hurt my reputation for such a thing to be told."

The four men stared at her for several seconds, blinking several times but not saying anything. Clearly that was not what they had hoped to hear. Finally the deputy spoke. "So what you are claiming is that he was with you all night last night?"

Karissa crossed her arms and leveled her gaze at the man so he would not realize it was a lie. "And *most* of the morning."

"Are you willing to swear to that under oath?" He narrowed his eyes as if thinking that might intimidate her in some way.

"It's the truth," she responded with a determined lift of her chin, wondering all the while how she was able to tell such a blatant lie with hardly any feelings of shame or remorse. Perhaps it was because she knew she was saving a man's life. *Shawn's* life. "He was with me in my room until nearly dawn when he had to leave to go to work."

"He was in your room until nearly dawn?" The deputy slipped his pistol back in its holster then placed his fists on his hips while he continued to stare at her, clearly doubting every word: "Doing what?"

"That is none of yer damn business," Shawn ground out, and slammed his beer down and took a menacing step toward the deputy. Several of the other men near him did the same.

Able to see the anger on the deputies' faces from where she stood just a few feet behind Shawn and the other men, Karissa closed her eyes, afraid of what might happen next. She was surprised when instead of hearing more angry words or the sickening sound of flesh striking flesh, the deputy quickly apologized.

"You're right. It is none of my business what you and your lady friend did. I'm sorry to have bothered you."

Karissa opened her eyes again in time to see Deputy Evans tip his hat toward her. "Pleased to meet you, Miss Sobey. I'm sure I'll be talking with you again real soon. I'll probably be wanting a sworn statement out of you."

Karissa stood with collapsible knees while the four lawmen turned in unison and headed back the way they had come, nodding at those men who continued to glower angrily at them. It was not until they were completely out of the tavern that Karissa finally released the breath she'd been holding and fell weakly against Shawn.

"Why did ya do that?" Shawn asked, bending close so that his words were heard only by those who stood close by.

"Do what?" she asked, then smiled up at him, not certain who in that room was to be trusted. Because of the trial that had been scheduled for that day, there were quite a few strangers in town, many of whom looked especially eager to hear what they had to say. "Why shouldn't I admit that we were together last night?" she stated loudly, knowing her words would be overheard. "I'm not ashamed of my feelings for you. After all, I will soon be your *wife*."

For one brief moment, she wished that part of her statement were true, but knew it could never be. They were from two different worlds. Even should it turn out he was not the Shawn involved in her father's murder, a marriage between them would never work.

Shawn stared down at her with those penetrating blue eyes of his for several long seconds before finally shrugging his shoulders and reaching for what was left of his beer. "I guess I owe ya one."

Now that the initial danger had passed, Karissa was so relieved she felt giddy. "We can discuss what you owe me later, when you walk me home tonight." She awaited that suggestive lift of his eyebrows she had come to adore and felt an icy wave of apprehension when instead he dropped his gaze and stared idly at his now empty beer mug. "I won't be walkin' ya home tonight," he said, his voice so low she barely heard him. "Joey will."

"What? But I thought you were to walk me home."

Not wanting to discuss the matter in front of the

others, he pulled her gently toward the back room. He stopped just short of the door to offer her a long, dizzying kiss, mostly for the benefit of those carefully watching them, before he quickly tugged her on inside and closed the door.

"I don't understand," she said as soon as the door was closed and she had her equilibrium again. "I thought you didn't want me to be seen alone with other men because of the poor way it reflected on you."

"Tonight is different. Tonight I have to be somewhere else at midnight; but just because I can't be here to walk with ya home doesn't mean ya should have to chance it alone again. Especially not with there bein' so many strangers in town." He paused as if considering whether to tell her the rest of it or not. "I think ya should know, when Joey shows up outside to walk with ya, he'll be wearin' these clothes."

"Shawn, what's going on?"

"Nothin' to worry yer pretty head," he assured her then slipped his arms around her for a second kiss that left her just as weak and wanting as the first one had. When he spoke again, it was in a far more serious tone. "Katy, I want ya to know that whatever happens to me durin' these next few days, I do love ya."

Karissa stared at him unblinking, too frightened by the finality of what he had just said to respond to the fact he'd just confessed his love for her. A cold wave washed over her when he then let go of her and stepped away.

"I'll see ya tomorrow afternoon durin' the picnic." At which time he would ask her about her strange behavior on the street. He was still curious to know what had frightened her but knew it could wait until then.

"But I'm not going to the picnic," she reminded him, finally finding her voice. She couldn't. Not with John in town.

"Neither am I," he said with a wry wink. "But everyone *else* is." Without giving her a chance to respond, for fear she would tell him not to come, he headed immediately for the door.

Chapter Sixteen

Now that the incident involving the four lawmen was over and Shawn was safe, Karissa felt guilty for having lied to them about where Shawn had been that previous night and decided to find out for herself if he had been involved. If it turned out he was guilty of having helped Jack McGeehan escape, she would have little choice but to right the wrong she had done and tell the authorities the truth. Just not *those* particular authorities. She would tell someone whom she felt could be trusted to take Shawn to jail without harming him in some way.

But first she needed to find out where Shawn and his two friends really did go that previous night and decided the best way to do so would be by trailing him again that night.

Remembering that Frank was still angry with her for her attempt to follow Shawn the night before, Karissa wondered if she dared try to do that same thing again. She knew if Frank saw her leave the tavern early for whatever reason, he would be right behind her. And when he found out she really was dis-obeying his orders yet again, he would do what he could to stop her.

But she remembered his plans for that night were to keep an eye on Joseph Rourke, who it seemed had some pretty strange dealings going on in and around Black Wall. If she could somehow convince Joseph to leave early, then Frank would follow him and she would be free to leave early, too. But how could she possibly trick him into something like that?

Remembering his professed desire to be with her, and knowing that Shawn could leave at any time, Karissa pretended to have her tables confused when she stopped at the one where Joseph was seated and asked for his order.

"What will I have?" He repeated her question, looking at her with immediate interest. He cut his gaze to Shawn, who was busy talking with Charles McAllister at another table, then straightened his shoulders as if having found sudden courage. "What if I said I wanted *you?*"

To keep the other men at his table from hearing her response for fear it would quickly make its way back to Shawn, she bent close to his ear and responded. "Then I'd say you would have to be at my doorstep shortly after midnight when I arrive home."

Joseph's eyes widened while a slow grin stretched the width of his mouth. "What about — ?" He nodded toward Shawn to indicate whom he meant.

"He has other plans for the night," she said with a playful pout that revealed none of the heart-pounding fear that poured through her.

She knew that if either Shawn or Frank ever found

out what she had told this man, they would be furious with her. Frank would be furious because of the risks involved, and Shawn would be furious because she'd shown an interest in another man again, the same man from whom he had already rescued her once. Her stomach knotted at the memory of what Shawn was like when he was that angry but she ignored the resulting pain.

"Why, he doesn't even want to walk me home," she whimpered pitifully.

"Then I'll do the honors," Joseph volunteered, his gaze dipping down to take in the curves hidden beneath her dress.

"No," she whispered quickly. She knew that would ruin everything. "You saw how angry he gets when I'm with other men. A black rage comes over him that makes him do terrible things. That's why I don't want to take the chance of any of his friends seeing us together. You just be there waiting for me when I arrive, because if you are not there, I'll think you are not coming and go on inside without you." Having said that, she quickly straightened, then in a normal voice she asked the other men at the table if they needed anything.

Since Laura had just brought them new drinks, they shook their heads and Karissa was able to go along her way unnoticed by everyone but the men at the table.

Shawn could not wait around to help Joey finish changing. He had to be on his way if he was to meet Richard Porterfield at the RP mining offices at exactly midnight then head up the mountain with Jack McGeehan's horse in tow by one o'clock.

"Now remember to keep that hat of mine pulled low and yer face turned away from any light," he said to Joey, hoping for both their sakes the young man was not recognized by anyone. He knew the authorities would not take too kindly to such a deception.

"I will," Joey vowed while he worked with the many buttons on Shawn's trousers, trousers which looked about two inches too large for his skinny frame.

Though there was not much moonlight, Shawn could see the comical look on the young man's face after he had finished with the last button then let go of the trousers to see how they fit.

"It's a good thing you thought to wear your suspenders tonight, Shawn," Joey said, tugging at the waist. "I doubt I would be able to keep these things up without their help."

Shawn frowned. Because the boy always wore such bulky clothes, he hadn't realized just how different they were in build. "Just ya remember to keep to the shadows as much as possible."

"I will. And you remember to tell my cousin hello for me when you see him. You got the money he needs?"

Shawn patted the pocket on the black shirt he now wore then winked. "There's enough here to get him where he plans to go and then back again. And Charlie put a small pistol, some food, and two changes of clothes in the saddlebags on the horse."

"Do you think that'll be enough for him to get by until we can find out who really killed Big Thomas?" He looked up at his new friend with hope-filled eyes.

Shawn nodded, although by this time he wasn't sure they would ever know the truth behind Thomas Connolly's death.

"I'd better be off if I want to be gettin' that horse on up to Jack and be back here before dawn," he said, then slipped through the bushes with the agility of a cat. After gazing up at the wind-whipped clouds and deciding it was not going to rain as Charles had predicted, he headed first west in the direction of the ridge where Jack's horse waited so Joey would think that was where he was headed, then cut back to the north. He would deliver the animal as promised, but only after he had kept that meeting with Richard.

Karissa's heart raced as much from fear as it did from exertion. To keep from making any unnecessary noise, she had wadded the bulk of her gray skirt into one large ball which she held pressed against her waist with her left hand while she used the right to push branches out of her way. She hurried through the dark woods in stockinged feet, ignoring the sharp rocks that pricked her feet and the limbs that made angry swipes at her delicate skin and tugged at her hair. She had almost lost Shawn twice already and was afraid if she did not stay close behind him, he would elude her yet.

Karissa did not want to think about what might happen if she lost him. She was too determined to know why he and the others kept slipping off into the woods late at night. For her own peace of mind, she had to know if he really was involved with those hideous Molly Maguires as Frank thought; and if he was, she would also want to know if he had had a part in freeing Jack McGeehan.

She had a feeling that if it was true, if he was really involved in Jack's escape, he would now be headed to warn the others that the authorities were on to them. He would want them to know the sort of questions he had been asked and the answers that had been given. Which was why she halfway expected to be led right into the middle of a Molly Maguire meeting.

Either that, or Shawn had a very strange need to tramp through the woods during the wee hours of the morning. Which she supposed was a possibility.

Like a deer that senses a hunter, Shawn froze when he thought he heard a twig snap behind him. Nothing moved but his pale blue eyes for several minutes, then he moved only his head. After several more minutes, when nothing had emerged from the darkness and he saw no one lurking in the wind-tossed shadows behind him, he continued on, but at a more cautious pace.

Although Charles was supposed to keep anyone from leaving the tavern directly behind him and Nathan was supposed to make sure the police did not follow him, there was a chance, however slight, that someone had managed to get by one of them unnoticed. But when he did not hear any more suspicious sounds and did not develop any real sense of danger, an instinct which had kept him alive during the past several years, he decided he was letting his imagination run away with him. No one had followed him. The noise had probably been caused by an animal or a falling branch. It was obvious he had been working that one particular job too long. It was time he started making a little more headway. If only there was something he could do to hurry matters along. He was eager to put the entire investigation behind him so he could spend more time getting to know Catherine better.

Twelve minutes later, Shawn had the mining offices in sight, and even though he felt pretty sure no one had followed him, he again waited several minutes before heading toward them. As expected, one of the back windows had been left open and it was no trouble for him to slip inside.

"You are a few minutes late." Richard's deep voice sounded from somewhere across the room. "Did anyone follow you?"

"I wouldn't be here at all if I thought I had been followed," Shawn responded, thinking it a ridiculous question. As was always the case when he was with Richard, he dropped the Irish brogue and spoke in his natural voice.

"Good," Richard said, then struck a match and lit a white candle that illuminated only a small area around his desk. He indicated for Shawn to take the chair across from him with a quick dip of his hand. "I've ordered my body guards to come back for me at exactly twelve-thirty so we don't have much time. What have you found out about Lawrence Caine's death during these past two weeks?"

Shawn waited until he had settled comfortably into the chair before bothering to answer. "Just that the deed was done by outsiders and not by the Molly Maguires."

"Outsiders?" Richard leaned forward in the chair and frowned. He rested both elbows on the desktop but continued to move his hands freely while he spoke. "What makes you think it was outsiders?"

"Marcus Wade, the man who owns the Lucky Choice Tavern in Black Wall, remembers having seen four strangers in town the day before Clay Jones and Lawrence Caine were murdered."

"So there were strangers in town," Richard replied with an annoyed huff, clearly rankled by such flimsy evidence. "There are almost always strangers in that little mining town."

"Yes, but those particular four asked Marcus a lot of questions about Clay Jones. They wanted to know things like where he lived and at what hour he usually went to work and home again. At the time, Marcus thought the reason they were asking so many questions about the man was because they planned to ask him for jobs at the mines and wanted to know the best time to approach him. But when they did not show their faces again after that night, he started putting two and two together."

"And came up with five," Richard snapped. "It appears to me you have no proof that these men actually did anything."

"No real proof. At least not yet."

"Yet? Why? What *have* you found out?"

"Just that the four of them had arrived together by train the same day Marcus saw them then left again the following morning headed for Pittsburgh. That same afternoon, just about dark, three of the four returned to Black Wall, again by train, but were never seen again after that, at least not by the man in the ticket office, who fortunately believes it is his life's calling to keep up with everyone who passes through his train station."

"That doesn't mean those men killed anyone. Maybe what happened is that after returning from some quick business they had in Pittsburgh, they accidentally witnessed Jones's murder. Maybe they were then themselves killed as a way to keep them from telling anyone. The Molly Maguires are well known for ridding themselves of any witnesses."

Shawn let out a provoked breath. "And maybe you are reaching for something that just did not happen. I know you were hoping to be told that the Mollies were in some way involved with the Jones murder so you could finally nail a few of them, but it just didn't happen that way. Obviously there was someone *else* out there who wanted Lawrence Caine and Clay Jones dead."

"What about Thomas Connolly?" Richard put in, his tone clearly argumentative. "You do know that whoever killed Lawrence Caine and Clay Jones killed him, too, don't you?"

"And I think the only reason Big Thomas was murdered was to help throw more suspicion on the Mollies. That's why the clues that were planted on Thomas's body all pointed directly to Jack McGeehan, who we both know is innocent because he was with me that morning."

"Speaking of the innocent," Richard said, temporarily changing the subject. "Do you happen to know who is responsible for McGeehan's rather timely escape?"

"I am, among others."

"You? But *why?*" His dark eyebrows pulled together in a deep, scowling frown. Clearly he was angry that Shawn had been involved. "Don't you realize what might have happened if you'd been caught?"

"Wasn't much chance of that, not with the guard being such a heavy drinker. By the time we entered that jail after having left a full bottle of whiskey inside the main office, he was so drunk we were able to take the key right out of his pocket without his ever knowing we were there."

Richard's expression was rock hard as he continued to glower at Shawn. "But still, you shouldn't have meddled in something like that."

"It was a good way to gain the group's confidence without having to kill or maim anyone."

"There had to be other ways to go about such as that," Richard insisted, so angry now that his whole body shook. "You didn't have to help set that man free."

"Why are you so upset? It's not as if Jack was really guilty. Remember? He was with me that morning he was supposed to have killed Thomas."

Richard's green eyes narrowed then darkened with hatred. "Still, he was an active member of the Molly Maguires. That means he deserves to hang. If not for Thomas's murder, then for others he undoubtedly committed."

"Not all members of the Molly Maguires are killers," Shawn told him, thinking of tender-hearted Joey. "And not all the members really want to be members. Some joined simply because they were afraid of what would happen to them if they didn't go along with their friends."

"Doesn't matter if they joined because they wanted to or not. A Molly is a Molly," Richard stated, then raked his hand through his thinning hair while he continued to glower furiously at Shawn. "If it weren't for those blasted Molly Maguires, I'd be making a lot more money in my mining operations. But as it is, every time any one of my coal mines gets a little ahead, those Mollies either blow up a mine shaft or set fire to a breaker house, which takes most of my profits to rebuild. Don't they realize that they are costing themselves when they do that? Don't they understand that I have to make up the money lost the only way I can by cutting back their wages? That without any real profits there is no money to modernize like they want?"

"No, they really don't see the connection between your profits and their well-being," Shawn admitted. "All they see is a way to get even for the substandard working conditions they are already suffering."

"What substandard working conditions?" he asked, then muttered, "Those men don't even know what substandard working conditions are."

Shawn studied Richard for a long moment before finally responding to that last comment. "Have you been down inside your own mines lately?"

"No. Why should I? I have inspectors who do that," he responded angrily as if Shawn had somehow personally insulted him.

"That's what I thought," Shawn said with a disgusted toss of this head. "That's why it is so hard for you to understand their anger. You haven't been down there to see what it is like. I have. And some of their complaints are legitimate. You don't know what it is like to have to breathe that foul, damp air all day and worry about whether or not the bracing over your head is enough to keep several hundred tons of earth from coming down on top of you. I don't know how you mine owners get those men to go down there day after day for what little you pay them. If I weren't making several thousand times more a week than they are, there's no way I'd go back down there."

"But you haven't even been inside *my* mines," Richard responded with a puckered pout. He straightened in his chair as if that helped prove his integrity. "You've only been down in Lawrence Caine's mines."

"That's true, but the way I hear it from the men, your mines are in far worse condition than his. That there for a while, Lawrence Caine was keeping his mines in fairly good shape."

"My mines are not any worse than his. If they were, young John Caine wouldn't be trying to buy me out like he is."

"What are you talking about?" Shawn asked. He knew from the start that Richard was disgusted with his mining operations, mainly because of the problems the Maguires had caused during the past few years, but he was unaware the man had reached the point he had considered selling.

Richard looked insulted to have to explain his reasoning. "Now that John Caine has control of Caine Enterprises, he's offered to buy me out at a very reasonable price. He wouldn't do that if he thought my mines were in such poor shape like you say."

"Why not? As long as he thinks he can squeeze a profit from them, what does he care if they are safe or not?"

"Because John Caine is young, which means he's still out to prove himself as a good businessman. He would not purposely buy faulty merchandise."

"Maybe he doesn't realize just how faulty that merchandise is. Has *he* been down in your mines?"

"Well, no, but his inspector has. As has mine. And they both told me my mines are every bit as sound as his."

"Which isn't saying much," Shawn muttered with disgust, knowing that when this job was over and he'd accomplished all he'd been hired to do, he'd have a thing or two to say to Richard and John Caine about the manner in which they ran their operations.

Richard was so angry over Shawn's insinuations that he stood and leaned heavily against his desk. "Why are you insulting me like this?"

"I'm not insulting you. I just think that the Mollies do have a few legitimate complaints when it comes to their present working conditions is all."

Richard's hands curled into fists atop the desk. "I'm not paying you to side with them. I'm paying you to expose them for the cold-blooded murderers and cutthroats they are."

"And a bonus if I find out who murdered Lawrence Caine," Shawn reminded him. "All of which I still plan to do. In addition to finding out who really killed Thomas Connolly."

"How? By running around letting prisoners out of jail?"

"If it helps to gain the others' confidences, then yes. But that's not all I'm doing. I have two men I trust explicitly trying to find out who those four strangers

343

were. I wired them much of the information they'll need just last week."

"Just don't rule out the fact that it might have been someone connected to the Molly Maguires."

"I never rule out anything," Shawn assured him, then ran his hand over his strong chin while he continued to study Richard's angry expression. "Including the fact that it might even have been someone like you. Someone who could have profited in some way by Caine's death."

"What?" Richard's eyes widened at such an affront. "Are you implying that I may have murdered one of my own friends just so I could sell those troublesome mines to his son?"

Shawn studied the veins bulging in Richard's neck for a moment, then shook his head. "No. To tell you the truth, that thought never occurred to me. But it does make for an interesting motive, don't you think?"

"Get out!" Richard said, pointing toward the still open window with a trembling finger. "Get out before I get so angry with you, I decide to fire you on the spot."

"You won't fire me," Shawn replied calmly, although already rising from his chair. "You have too much money invested me." He nodded a polite goodbye then headed immediately for the open window but stopped when he heard his name called.

"What do you want now?" he asked, and turned to face Richard again. Now that he was away from the small island of light surrounding the desk, he was little more than a tall, black shadow in the surrounding darkness.

"To remind you that I want to meet with you at least once more before I leave again next Wednesday."

"Then I'll plan to meet you back here early that same morning. But make it two o'clock instead of midnight. There is something else I'd rather do at midnight."

"Planning on releasing another prisoner?" Richard asked with a sarcastic wag of his head, his body still stiff with anger.

"No. There's someone special that I plan to see safely home."

"Oh?" Richard's eyebrows arched. He was too curious to remain angry. "Male or female?"

Shawn grinned while he considered the answer to that. "Oh, definitely female." He then laughed as he headed again for the window. "Truth is, I can't imagine any woman being more female than her." He paused with one leg inside the window and one out. "You can whistle for those high-priced body guards now. I think you'll find them napping over by the breaker house." He chuckled again just before he dropped to the ground and headed immediately for the brush.

Karissa limped back toward town, more confused than ever. Shawn had not slipped off to meet secretly with possible members of the Molly Maguires after all. He'd slipped off to meet with Richard Porterfield, a man who had been one of her father's closest friends. But why? Richard Porterfield could not possibly have been involved with the disappearance of Jack McGeehan. Or *could* he?

But then why would a respected businessman like Richard be involved in something as shady as that? And if he was involved with Jack's escape in some way, did that mean he was also involved with her father's death?

No, she told herself resolutely, *that was impossible.* The two might have been in direct competition with each other in several areas of business, but no matter what conflicts arose between them, they were always, above all else, very good friends. Richard was not the type of man to become involved with anyone suspected of being a member of the Molly Maguires.

But what other reason could there be for Shawn to have met with him alone in his offices like that, and after midnight?

She was still without answers when she returned to the area just outside of town, where she had pulled off her boots and dropped her handbag so she could follow Shawn more quietly. It was while she tried to shoved her swollen feet back into the stiff leather that she realized that the only way she would ever find out the truth about that meeting would be to admit to Shawn what she'd done and ask him straight out what his involvement was with her father's good friend.

But because she was not sure what Shawn might do to her once he'd found out that she'd followed him and why, she decided it would be best to wait until she knew for sure that Frank Neely was somewhere nearby. Which meant tomorrow afternoon would be out of the question. Frank had already promised to go with Charles and Kelly to the picnic and they might think it a little odd if he backed out of that at the last minute. Besides she wasn't sure she should tell Frank what she had done. He had already threatened to quit once, right after he had found out about the first time she tried to follow Shawn. It might be better to wait until normal circumstances caused him to be nearby.

That meant if Shawn did come by the rooming house tomorrow afternoon as he had hinted that he might, she would have to be exceptionally careful not to let him know what she had done. He would not accept being told she had followed him simply because she'd had nothing better to do. He would want to know the real reason why, and might not stop questioning her until he did.

But for now she had something entirely different to worry about and that was how to get back into the rooming house without Joseph Rourke or Frank Neely seeing her. Even though it had to be well after one o'clock by now, Karissa had a feeling Joseph was just stubborn enough to still be there waiting on her; and if that was true, then Frank would still be out there, too. Watching and waiting. And slowly putting all the clues together.

Sighing when she realized she would have to climb in through a back window as tired and sore as she was, she slipped her arm through the strings of her handbag then headed back toward the area of town where she had left her lantern.

Chapter Seventeen

Because it was hotter than usual that day, Karissa wore only a cotton chemise under the lightweight pink and white summer dress she had selected then waited until everyone had left for the picnic before she emerged from her room in her stocking feet. Limping to avoid putting pressure on a badly scraped heel, she went immediately to the kitchen to see if Kelly had left her anything to eat.

It was not until she discovered a baking pan with four fat biscuits with a jar of honey sitting nearby that she realized just how very hungry she really was. Because of everything that had happened to distract her the day before, all she had eaten since Thursday afternoon was a part of one small sandwich with which she had drunk one glass of milk. Having eaten so little and after the previous night's trek across the wooded hillside, she was now starved. So starved that the four biscuits did not nearly satisfy her hunger.

Finding half a loaf of bread and a few pieces of ham left in the cooler, she decided what she really wanted was a nice hot ham and egg sandwich like the one Kelly had made for her the day before. Thinking it could not be all that hard to scramble an egg or two, she hurried to see if there might be any left in the henhouse out back.

While still limping to avoid the tender area of her foot, she opened the mesh door and hobbled across the back porch. Rather than cover her stockings with dirt and grass, she sat down in one of the wicker chairs long enough to remove them both before gently tiptoeing across the yard. When she finally arrived at the henhouse, she was so delighted to find three freshly laid eggs that she did not at first notice any sounds other than those she usually heard this time of day. It was not until she was halfway back to the house carrying the prized eggs that she first sensed someone nearby.

Her heart slammed hard against her chest when she glanced up and noticed Shawn on the back porch waiting for her. He was dressed in a new pair of black corduroys and his best blue cotton shirt, which he had left unbuttoned at the collar for comfort. His broad shoulders were accentuated by a pair of black and brown suspenders.

"What happened to yer foot?" Shawn asked, glowering down at her angrily.

"I cut my heel," she answered, not about to admit the whole truth to him when there was no one around to come to her aid. *Especially when he already looked ready to kill her.*

"When did you cut it?" He narrowed his blue eyes and stared at the injured foot, as if trying to detect blood while the afternoon breeze tugged gently at his thick brown hair, lifting it away from his angry face.

"I cut it last night," she said when she realized he thought she had meant just then in the henhouse.

"On what?"

"On a piece of glass," she lied, thinking that sounded reasonable. She ran her tongue across her lower lip while she quickly devised what else she planned to say. "Last night, when I was cleaning up a broken beer mug, I accidentally stepped on a large, jagged piece that sliced right through the bottom of my boot. Happened not very long after you'd left."

Shawn tilted his head as if considering the possibility of that. "Is that why ya weren't there when Joey showed up there right before midnight to walk ya home like he had promised?"

"Yes, of course," she replied, thinking that to be as good an excuse as any. She glanced down at the eggs in her hands so she would not have to look directly into his accusing blue eyes. "Didn't Marcus explain to him that I'd already left?" She lifted her gaze to his briefly only to be reminded of his anger.

"Ya know he didn't."

Although Shawn had spoken in a carefully controlled voice, Karissa knew from his dark expression that he was furious with her, but she tried not to reveal any resulting fear while she again met his gaze. "And why not? Marcus may have been very busy when I had to so suddenly leave but I scribbled a quick note letting him know that I was leaving early so he wouldn't worry when eventually he noticed I was gone."

She tried not to look uncomfortable about how very little she had written on that note. All she had said was that something unexpected had occurred and that she had to leave. She did not mention what the emergency was or why it was so important she go right away.

Mainly, because she had not had the time to come up with anything believable. Shawn had already pulled on his hat and his summer coat and was making his way toward the door by the time she'd thought to write her excuse to Marcus rather than admit to his face that she was leaving. If Marcus ended up being so angry with her for what she had done and she lost her job because of it, then so be it. At least now she knew that Richard Porterfield and Shawn McCowan were somehow involved in something together. That was more than she had known before she followed him.

"That's all well and good for Marcus," Shawn went on to say. "But the note did little to help Joey, who could not very well go inside and ask where ya were. Not while dressed in my clothes the way he was. People would have noticed what he had on and wanted to know why."

Thinking it a good opportunity to change the subject — before she said something that might raise further suspicion at a time when she wanted no suspicion at all — she quickly asked, "And just what was Joey doing there in *your* clothes anyway? You never did explain that to me. Nor did you explain to me why you would not be the one to walk me home like you usually try to do."

"Yes I did," Shawn said with a resolute lift of his chin. "I told ya that there was somewhere else I had to be."

"But you didn't tell me where that was." Feeling at a disadvantage to be standing barefoot in the middle of the yard looking up at him like a scolded child might, she headed immediately for the back steps. "Where did

351

you have to go that was so important you could not walk me home first?"

Shawn fell silent for a moment, then slowly smiled while he watched her ascend the steps then turn to face him squarely. "We aren't even truly engaged yet and already ya sound like a nagging fishwife."

The word *yet* in that last comment struck Karissa as awfully odd, then she remembered what he had said to her in the livery just two nights earlier. *Although I cannot truly lay a proper claim to ya right now, my luv, I do hope to be able to do so someday in the future.*

She remembered something else he had said, something that now made her wonder exactly what he had meant. *You've stolen my heart, Miss Catherine Sobey, and one day, when I am again in a position to do so without any harm comin' to ya as a result, I plan to steal yers in return.*

She should have asked him right then what he had meant by such an odd remark. But that had been just before he had kissed her, and any comment she may have considered at that point had immediately left her. Forced aside by the wondrous sensations from his kiss.

Karissa's body shivered lightly over the memory of that last kiss. It had been the most powerful, most compelling kiss she had ever experienced. And something she would be better off not thinking about at that particular moment.

"I may sound like a nagging fishwife," she said after subduing the sudden emotions that had filled her heart. "But at the moment I feel more like a small child who has just been scolded for having done something very wrong when the truth is I don't really understand what it is that I did. Why was it so important I be there last night?"

Shawn took his gaze off of her and looked out across the small yard. "It's not that it was all that important. It's just that ya left Joey with a very awkward situation. He ended up hidin' away in the shadows waitin' for ya to finally appear for quite some time."

"But why was he hiding?" she asked, wishing Shawn would tell her the truth. That way they could discuss what had happened last night without her having to admit what she had done. "And where *were* you?"

Shawn shrugged then smiled when he held open the back door for her. "It doesn't really matter where I was. What matters is that I am here now. With you."

Karissa looked at him questioningly. His anger had abated far too quickly, probably because he did not want to admit that he had slipped off in the night to meet secretly with Richard Porterfield.

"You don't happen to know how to scramble eggs?" she asked, deciding to let the matter drop for now. She knew it would be better than chance him questioning her again about her own activities during the night before.

"Of course, everyone knows how to scramble an egg." He looked at her oddly.

"No. Not everyone," she admitted, and handed the three eggs to him.

For the next two hours, while Shawn was there, she made it a point not to discuss where she had been the night before nor question him about where he had been. She wanted to wait until she had her pistol with her and Frank was somewhere nearby, then she would confront him with what she knew point blank.

"There are two men outside who want a word with you, Mr. Caine," the large detective said shortly after having returned from the front door. Although he wore his usual three-piece suit, he had loosened the necktie and undone the top button of his shirt to make the day's heat more bearable.

John Caine glanced up from the elaborate meal he'd had sent over from the restaurant. Because there had been threats made by several of the locals since his arrival in Black Wall, he had decided to keep at least one Pinkerton man at his side at all times. The other, when not sleeping, was out helping find Jack McGeehan so they could get the man tried and hanged as soon as possible. With both Thomas Connolly and McGeehan dead, there would be only two men left to see hanged. After that, his father's death would be properly vindicated, four Molly Maguires would be dead, and he would finally be free to get on with other matters just as important.

"Two men? Who are they?" he asked. He was not expecting company.

"A Mr. Knight and a Mr. Kilburn," the Pinkerton agent informed him.

John noticed the detective looked a little annoyed to be carrying out the duties of a personal secretary but did not really care. "Ask them what they want with me."

"I already did. They said something about wanting to talk to you about the conditions of your mines."

John glanced toward the door worriedly. "Were they armed?"

354

"Not that I could see." The Pinkerton man waited several seconds more then asked. "But they didn't look any too happy. Do you want me to check them for weapons then send them on in?"

"No. What I want you to do is send them on their way. Tell them that I am eating supper and do not have time to bother with such matters."

"What about tomorrow?" the detective asked, obviously wanting answers to questions the men outside would eventually ask. "Will you want to see them then?"

"No. I plan to be gone by tomorrow. In fact, I plan to leave on the last train out of here tonight."

"Because of those two?" The detective looked at him doubtfully.

"No, of course not," he snapped, narrowing his brown eyes. "It just so happens I miss my wife. I want to be home by the time she returns from the opera tonight."

"But what about McGeehan?"

"I plan to leave you and Ronald behind to continue looking for that low-life, and as soon as you have found him, just send word when the trial will be, and I'll come right back. That's the only reason I came to this godforsaken place in the first place. To watch that man hang. That and set up a meeting with Richard Porterfield while he was here overseeing some problem at one of his mines."

"Will James be going with you?" he asked, a little too eagerly.

"Of course," John responded. "He's my secretary, isn't he? He has to be with me."

"Good," the large man muttered, then headed back

toward the door to give the two men the bad news.

Knowing how his jabbering secretary seemed to get on both the detectives' nerves, John did not question the burly man's response. Instead, he returned to eating his meal, which he had demanded be served to him on the restaurant's finest china. That was the way it was with John. He loved all the lavish trappings that came from being wealthy. It was why he had always yearned to be the richest, most powerful man in both Pittsburgh and New York; but it was not until he met Lana that he became so truly driven. It was because of her that he had been so willing to take Clay Jones's lucrative advice because not only did he want his wife to have the very best, she had threatened to leave him for a wealthier man if he did not provide the high quality of life she wanted.

Fortunately, Clay Jones had proved to be a veritable fountain of money-saving ideas. It had been Clay's suggestion that he cut the widows' pensions until now a woman received practically nothing in compensation for her husband's death. John had immediately seen the wisdom in such an idea, knowing that as soon as the other policies were put into effect, there would be many more widows in need of those pensions.

Because of all the substandard bracing they were now using in those coal mines and the lack of proper ventilation in some of the newer areas, he knew there would soon be twice as many mining widows as before. Widows who would want to collect what they could from Caine Enterprises, though they had done nothing to deserve the money other than marry a fellow destined to die.

But now, those widows would discover that all they

had coming in the way of compensation was a plain wooden coffin and two months' worth of wages, which was one month more than some mines paid.

It was also because of John's awareness that the mines were becoming more and more dangerous as a result of the many policy changes that he had refused to go down and inspect them with the man who had taken Clay Jones's place. Not about to risk being buried alive, he'd sent his secretary in his stead, claiming to want a detailed report when he came out. A detailed report that he intended to tear up and toss into the trash the moment it was handed to him because he had no intention of making any changes. Not when those coal mines were finally showing a noticeable profit.

He could hardly wait until the end of the month when that first trainload of Orientals arrived from out west. Orientals were well known for working cheaper than most other men, and doing so without a lot of complaints. That would mean an even greater profit all the way around because he would then be able to cut all the miners' wages yet a third time. Then when he finally bought Richard Porterfield's mines and, without anyone being aware, put them in his own name, he should finally start making enough money to pay off the unofficial loan he had taken from the company and still be able to buy Lana whatever she wanted.

Lana. Just the memory of her beautiful face and voluptuous young body made him all the more eager to hurry home.

After having learned that her half-brother had caught the six o'clock train back to Pittsburgh the evening before, Karissa saw no reason not to accept

357

Shawn's offer to escort her to church that Sunday morning. It was not until she had put on the same dress he had complimented weeks earlier, tucked her mother's Bible under her arm, then headed with Shawn toward the church down the street that it dawned on her the mistake she might have made.

There was no way for her to know if Richard Porterfield had left, too. And if he hadn't left, it was possible he might decide to attend one of the local churches. She knew if he did decide to attend church, it would probably be the Presbyterian, since it was more like the Lutheran church he normally attended than the Catholic would be.

Aware it was too late to turn back, and knowing if Richard did come he would probably arrive late and sit near the back, since he was one of those men who valued his time and was always in a hurry, she decided to go directly inside and sit as close to the front as possible.

To her relief, Richard was not there when she arrived, nor did she see him when they left. And since Shawn was willing to take her straight home afterward, she thought she had gotten by without being seen by her father's friend at all. That meant her identity was still safe. At least for now.

For the following two days, Karissa continued to try to pull as much information out of Shawn as was possible without admitting to him what she had done. But little progress was made because the more important her question, the less detailed his answer.

It was becoming more and more important that she arrange to be alone with him, yet with Frank somewhere nearby, so she could finally confront Shawn with the truth about what she had done and what she now knew as a result. The problem was that she was still afraid to tell Frank about what she'd done to make sure he followed her, and knew that the only time she and Shawn were really alone was when he walked her home at night. And because Frank was too caught up with trying to find out where Joseph Rourke went after hours, he had not yet followed them again.

But Karissa had heard that Joseph Rourke was supposed to leave town sometime Wednesday morning. That meant Frank would finally be willing to turn his attention to other important matters. Perhaps Wednesday night, when Shawn again walked her home, Frank would decide to follow just to make sure she was really as safe as she claimed to be while in his company.

"What are ya thinkin' about?" Shawn asked Karissa when he looked over at her while walking her home just before midnight Tuesday night and noticed that her brown eyes were focused somewhere in the darkness beyond. He held the lantern higher so he could see her better. "Ya look as if yer thoughts have slipped a thousand miles away."

Karissa came aware with a start, not having expected him to speak. Ever since his meeting with Richard Porterfield, Shawn had become very quiet during their walks, giving her much more time to think.

"I was remembering those eggs you scrambled for me Sunday," she lied, stating the first logical thing that crossed her mind. "Wherever did you learn to cook like that?"

Shawn lowered the lantern again and smiled at the fond memory that question evoked. "From Nicollette," he admitted as he, too, focused on the darkness in front of them. "There were several days there while she was so heavy with child that I had to do the cookin' and eggs were always so fast and easy to make."

Karissa's brown eyes widened at such a surprising revelation then narrowed again when she looked at him questioningly. "While she was heavy with child? I thought you said you had no children."

Shawn's stomach clenched when he realized the mistake he had just made. He had grown so comfortable with Catherine during these past few days, he'd temporarily forgotten that he was supposed to lie to her. "And I don't have any. The child she was carrying tried to be born too early." Which was close enough to the truth to cause him a sharp stab of anguish. "The baby was a stillborn."

When Karissa glanced at him then and saw the pain reflected in his pale eyes, her heart went out to him. "I'm sorry. I didn't realize." She slowed her pace. "How horrible that must have been for you."

"It was horrible. It is also something I don't like to talk about." He turned away so she could not see the dampness collecting in his eyes.

While Karissa let Shawn have a moment to recover, she wondered how different his life might have been had that child lived. Surely his wife would not have gone looking for another man had Shawn been the father of her living child. Family would be too important to her.

The sadness that engulfed her as a result of that realization was enough to cause her to reach out and touch his arm gently. "I'm sorry. I didn't mean to pry like that."

"You didn't?" he asked, and turned his head to look

at her, obviously surprised. The tears that had glistened in his eyes only moments earlier were gone. "Then why have ya been barragin' me with so many questions these past few days if ya don't mean to pry?"

Karissa's heart skipped. She had hoped he hadn't noticed. "Because I want to know more about you." Afraid of where their conversation was headed, she picked up a faster walking pace, glad now that her foot was so much better.

"Ya already know enough about me." He glanced out into the darkness again, but this time to make sure no dangers lurked. He'd been extremely cautious of shadows and sounds ever since that angry confrontation with Joseph Rourke.

"No I don't. I hardly know anything about you."

"How can ya say that?" he asked, glancing at her again, puzzled. "Ya know where I was born. Ya know where I grew up. Ya even know about my beloved old grandmother and her dogs. What else is there to know?"

Karissa decided to give it one more try. "I still don't know where it was you went the other night when you sent Joey to the tavern to walk me home."

Shawn let out a short, annoyed sigh. The muscle at the back of his well-defined jaw twitched. "Are we back to that now?"

"Yes. It bothers me to know that you keep secrets from me."

"Why?"

Karissa was caught off guard by such a direct question and blinked several times while she tried to think of a believable answer. "Because I thought we had become better friends than that." When that did not seem to come across as a good enough reason, she quickly added, "And because I'm jealous."

Shawn pulled up short and looked at her with suddenly raised eyebrows. "Jealous, are ya? And why would ya be jealous?"

"Because I was told the reason you weren't around to walk me home that night was because you were busy walking someone else home. Only with this someone else, *walking* wasn't all you had on your mind."

"And who would be tellin' ya such tales?" Shawn looked truly concerned.

"Someone who wanted me to know the truth," she answered vaguely, knowing he might decide to question the person if she were to name a name, and he would then find out she was lying.

"But it's *not* the truth." He pushed his hat to the back of his head, which allowed the shorter hair around his face to fall forward. Because he hated to have his hair in his eyes, he had not allowed the top part of it to grow long. Only the back.

"Then what is the truth? Where *were* you that night?"

Shawn's dimples sank into his cheeks, obviously very happy over her supposed confession. "Now I don't want ya to go gettin' the wrong idea, but I can assure ya I was not with another woman that night. Truth is, I was off with another man."

"A man? Who?" Karissa held her breath, thinking at last he would tell her the truth.

"An old friend who wanted to see me about something important."

"An old friend?" Karissa pressed, not about to give up yet. "Who was it? Anyone I know?"

362

Shawn continued to look at her, amused now by all the questions. "No, it is no one you would know and I promised I would not tell anyone about having met with him."

"But why not? What harm could it do to tell me? Especially if I don't even know him?"

"Isn't it enough to be told I wasn't out with another woman?" he asked, and tilted his head while looking at her questioningly.

Aware she had already reached the limit of what he was willing to tell her that night, she nodded and reluctantly agreed. "I guess it is enough."

The two resumed walking and it was several minutes before Shawn again broke the silence between them. "Were ya really jealous, Katy?"

"I said I was," she answered abruptly, annoyed over the fact that again she had not gotten the information she had hoped.

"Good." He offered a brisk nod. "That means that I still have a chance with ya. The way ye've been actin' toward me here lately, I was startin' to think that maybe yer feelin's for me had cooled considerably."

"And just what kind of chance is it you want?" she asked, intrigued by the playful glimmer in his pale blue eyes.

"Why the chance to finally win yer heart, of course."

Karissa couldn't help but grin. "And what would you do with my heart if you were to win it?"

By this time they had reached the small gate in front of the rooming house and Shawn paused to let her pass through first.

"Good question," he answered, his brow furrowed with thought, then he chuckled while he followed her through. "I guess that what I really should be hopin' to win is yer lips."

Karissa tried to return to a somber expression while she waited for him to catch up with her again. "And what would you do with my lips if you were to win them?"

"I was hopin' ya'd be foolish enough to ask that," he said, already bending for the kiss he had been dying to give her all evening.

Aware of his intention, Karissa felt her breath catch in her throat, and her brown eyes grew very round. But no word of protest escaped her lips. Rather than chastise him for what he was about to do, she tilted her head back to offer him easier access — of which he took quick and complete advantage.

While his lips descended over hers, his free hand came around her to draw her closer to him. That now-familiar heart-shaking current his kiss always caused shot through her, warming her to the tips of her fingers and toes. She moaned softly in response and wondered why it always felt so right to be in his arms. Even though she knew so very little about him.

"That is what I'd do with your lips if I were to win them," he muttered between short, rapid breaths after finally finding the willpower to pull away. If it were not for the fact that he was due to meet with Porterfield in just over an hour, he would have tried to carry that kiss a whole lot further. Despite his promise to both her and himself to keep his hands off her.

Karissa stared at him with her delicate eyebrows drawn into a puzzled frown. His kiss had scattered her thoughts to the point where it was hard to concentrate on his words. Hard to concentrate on anything other than the beguiling way his pale blue eyes glimmered in the lamplight.

"I can see that ye're tired. I'd better be off so ya can get yerself some sleep," Shawn said, knowing if he did not leave at that very moment, he would miss his meeting with Porterfield altogether, and his work was too important to let his desire for this woman get in the way.

Karissa continued to stare at him blankly. *Tired?* How could he think that when the truth was she had never felt more exhilarated? "Will I see you tomorrow night?"

"Same time, same place," he said with a brisk nod, already handing her the lantern. *And with Rourke finally gone, without the same worries of being caught off guard.*

Sadly, Karissa watched Shawn from just inside the door until he reached the gate then reluctantly she turned to go upstairs. Once in her room, she hurried to the window hoping to catch one last glimpse of him, but it was too late. He was gone. Unhappily, she turned away from the window and wondered why she suddenly felt so disappointed.

Chapter Eighteen

"I received a very strange telegram this afternoon," Richard Porterfield told Shawn as soon as he had lit the small candle that sat on his desk and they had settled into the same chairs they had occupied just four nights earlier.

"Oh?" Shawn asked, glancing around the room as if barely interested in what Richard had to say. As before, he was dressed all in black, making his blue eyes seem all the lighter. "And what did the telegram say?"

"It was from someone named Lark and it said something to the effect that the four Welch men I wanted to meet were waiting for me in Pittsburgh."

Shawn smiled when he brought his attention back to Richard. "Welch, are they? That means they can't possibly be members of the Molly Maguires. The Irish and the Welch don't get along that well."

"*Who* can't possibly be members?" Richard asked then leaned back in his chair, clearly confused.

"Those four men who I still think had something to do with Lawrence's murder. My man Larken obviously thinks he has found them," he said then ex-

366

plained. "I told both of the agents I'd sent out looking for them that if either of them found out anything worth reporting before noon today, they were to try to send a telegram through you. Otherwise, they were to wait until I could get over to Pottsville again and wire them."

"And what good does it do you to know where they are if you can't get away to question them?"

"My men will question them then let me know what they find out. They are good men. I've worked with them before and I trust them to find out exactly what I need to know."

"And how will they let you know what it is they find out? By sending another telegram?" Richard asked acidly. It was clear he did not like the idea that Shawn had asked for outside help.

"No. Of course not," Shawn responded calmly. "One of them will come here and report in person."

"And what if it turns out that the four men they've found are not the ones you wanted?"

"Then I'm back where I started," Shawn said with a light shrug while he studied Richard's brooding expression. "You're still hoping I'll find out that the Molly Maguires were somehow involved, aren't you?"

"I just want to find out who killed Lawrence so I can know who to watch out for myself."

"But you hope it was the Mollies."

Richard studied him for a moment, then admitted, "It would make things simpler if it was."

"Ah, yes, you'd be solving two problems with that one bit of information, wouldn't you?"

"And *you* would be free to go back home and live a more normal life," Richard pointed out. "It must be hell having to go down in those mines almost every day and work eight to twelve hours straight."

The strong lines defining Shawn's face hardened. "But at least I'm being well paid for my work. It bothers me to know that those other poor men are doing the same back-breaking work and receiving only about ten to twelve dollars a week. I really don't see how they manage to live on that."

"There you go siding with them again," Richard said, his voice filled with warning. "That doesn't do you any good."

"Doesn't do me any harm either," Shawn answered, stating the obvious. "Besides it doesn't matter what I think, just as long as I do my job."

"That's true," Richard agreed, then leaned his short body quickly forward as if something very important just occurred to him. "By the way, I saw who you were with Sunday. What's Karissa Caine doing up here in the coal mines?"

Shawn stared at Richard blankly for a moment while he let the peculiar question register in his mind. "What do you mean?"

"I saw you on Sunday walking at a fairly brisk pace with Karissa Caine at your side. What on earth is she doing here? And why was she dressed like some penniless little pauper? Why, my housekeeper wears better clothing than that."

Shawn waited several seconds then responded by asking a question of his own. "Where were you?" Having been a private detective for several years now, he was far too used to being hit with the unexpected to let that last bit of news rattle him. Rather than insult Richard by asking if he was sure of what he saw, he had to assume the man knew Karissa Caine well enough to recognize her on sight.

"My body guards and I were headed into town to get something to eat about the time church let out. I must admit, it surprised me to no end to see Karissa Caine here. I thought she was supposed to be at some private resort trying to get over the death of her father. At least that's what John told me before he left Saturday." Richard paused a minute, then added in afterthought. "I wonder if her brother even knows she's here. Surely he does. But why would he lie about where she was when I asked? And *why* is she here?"

Shawn waited until all that Richard said had soaked in and made some form of sense before he finally answered. "She's here to find out who murdered her father." Having reached the only logical conclusion, he hurried to caution him. "But she's here under an assumed name so I'd appreciate it if you did not mention having seen her here to *anyone*."

"Why? Are you working for her, too?" Richard frowned, clearly not pleased with the idea that Shawn might be accountable to someone else. He slumped back in his chair again to contemplate how he should handle such a situation if it was true.

"No, I'm not working for her at all. I learned years ago that working for two people at the same time caused too many conflicts of interest. Besides she doesn't have the faintest idea who I really am. She knows only what I have told her. Like everyone else around here, she thinks I am someone who is forced to work in the coal mines because I am hiding from the law."

Richard knew better than to doubt Shawn's word.

"So you are using her to get information? Is that it?"

Shawn decided to be open with Richard about Karissa; but not so open he would admit that until just a few minutes ago he had honestly believed her to be the destitute daughter of a dead coal miner. How ironic. He had fallen for her story every bit as willingly as she had fallen for his. "No, I'm not out to get information from her. The truth is, I'm very attracted to her. She happens to be an *extremely* beautiful woman."

"Oh?" Richard's eyebrows arched with interest as again he leaned forward. "Is she the one you wanted to see safely home tonight? The reason we had to put off our meeting until two?"

"Yes. Because of where she works and the sort of people she has to deal with there, it is not all too safe for her to walk home alone that late at night. A fact which unfortunately has been proved more than once. I've already had to save her pretty little neck twice."

Richard's green eyes rounded with curiosity. "Why? Where does she work?"

"In one of the local taverns."

"In a tavern? *Karissa Caine?*" He sat back with his mouth agape. Clearly he found that hard to believe.

A smile stretched across Shawn's face. Suddenly he felt very proud of her. "She's a very determined young lady."

"Obviously." Richard fell silent for a moment then asked, "How long has she been here?"

"A little over three weeks," he answered aloud, but to *himself* he added, "Which is just long enough to have planted herself firmly in my heart — no matter what her real name or who her father was." It was odd though for him now to have to think of that beautiful, beguiling woman as the wealthy and courageous Karissa Caine instead of the poor and forsaken Catherine Sobey.

"What has she been able to find out in that time?" Richard wanted to know. "Does she have any idea yet who might have killed her father?"

"No, I don't believe she does." His smile widened when everything started to make more sense to him. *Why that clever little minx!* No wonder she had been so willing to put up with his antics. She was trying to get information out of him. "But I have a feeling she suspects me."

"*You?* Why?"

"Why not?" Shawn asked. He turned his palms up to indicate what an obvious conclusion that was. "Almost everyone else around here thinks I had a hand in those murders. I'm still one of the state authorities' primary suspects."

"Then Karissa's no closer to finding out the truth than you are," he surmised, and lifted one eyebrow in thought.

"Evidently not."

Richard rubbed his chin while he considered all he had just learned at length. "Is she here in Black Wall alone?"

Shawn shook his head and laughed out loud when he realized the answer to that. "No. I don't think she is. There's an older man here who I am pretty certain is working for her. If not, he should be. He certainly has shown an exorbitant amount of interest in her welfare these past few weeks." His dimples sank deeper still. Everything made sense now. Frank Miles

371

was there to protect her. And possibly even to help her garner some of the information she needed. No wonder he was always watching her. She was his employer.

"Who is this older man?" Richard wanted to know. "Do you know him?"

"No, I don't know him." Shawn answered the second question while he purposely ignored the first. He did not feel right about revealing the older man's identity—not when he obviously was there to help. "I've been around him but I've never had the actual opportunity to meet him."

"Do you at least know his name?" Richard asked, wanting more than the fact the man merely existed. "No," Shawn answered. His forehead creased in thought, knowing Frank Miles probably wasn't his real name anyway. "Can't say that I do know his name."

"Then find out."

"Why do you want to know?"

"I want to have him checked out. Karissa is the only daughter of a man I considered to be one of my closest friends. I want to make sure she's safe."

"Don't worry. He's not the only one protecting her. She has several friends here who help watch over her, including her boss at the tavern. Plus, I keep a pretty close eye on her myself," he attested. "As long as we are around, no real harm should come to her."

"But there may be a time when one of you isn't around," Richard pointed out, his brow furrowed with concern. "Maybe I should pay her a little visit before I leave. I might be able to convince her to forget this foolishness and go on back home where it's safe."

"She wouldn't go," Shawn responded proudly.

"She might if I threatened to expose her true identity. She wouldn't be able to accomplish very much if any of these people ever found out who she really was."

Shawn's look of amused adoration turned into an immediate scowl. He jabbed a finger in Richard's direction. "Don't you do that to her. Don't you dare take away the only opportunity she may ever have to solve her father's murder."

Richard tossed up his hands as if to indicate he didn't understand the importance of her quest. "It's not as if there aren't others out trying to uncover the very same information. In addition to you, there are two law enforcement agencies trying to find out what happened as well as the two Pinkerton men John brought with him and left behind. There's no reason for Karissa to continue putting herself in such danger. She should let the others take care of this matter."

Shawn curled his hands into tight fists and shook them gently to emphasize his words while he spoke. "You don't understand. This is something she has to do for herself." Quickly he pushed himself to his feet, eager to be alone and think more about this amazing turn of events. "Promise me you won't go see her and that you won't mention to anyone who she really is."

Richard ran a hand through his thinning hair while he considered the request. "As long as you promise she will be safe."

"She's probably a lot safer here pretending to be someone else than she would be in Pittsburgh living as herself. It is very possible that whoever murdered her father might want to murder her, too." So much a possibility that he would now watch out for such as that. Thinking they had discussed everything they needed to discuss, Shawn headed toward the same open window he had used before.

"All the more reason to find out who murdered Lawrence Caine," Richard called after him, and slammed his hand down across the desk with finality. "Those men must be found."

"I agree, and I promise I'll work even harder to find out who was involved," Shawn said before he quickly slipped through the opening and dropped lithely to the ground.

Smiling again over what he had just learned, he checked to make certain no one else was around then ran spritely across the small yard and into the woods. He could hardly wait for the opportunity to confront "Catherine" with what he now knew about her. But first he planned to use what he had just learned to find out exactly how she felt about him. If there was any chance at all that she cared for him even half as much as he cared for her, he had to know.

"John!" Richard Porterfield shouted when he spotted him and his wife entering the Bellomy Restaurant just a few dozen yards away. He stood up on tiptoe and waved his arm to be seen over all the people crowding the mason sidewalk that Wednesday evening. "John Caine, over here."

John glanced up just as he and Lana were about to enter. When he saw who had called to him and that he was already headed toward them, he gently pulled Lana back away from the door and waited. "Richard, what are you doing back in Pittsburgh so soon? I thought you would be stuck up there in those bleak mountains until at least the end of the week."

"I have an important meeting in the morning so I had to get back," Richard explained. "I was headed over to the Hotel Royale Restaurant to join some of my friends for supper and saw you headed into Bellomy's. I thought you might want to know that I was back. Just in case you have any more questions you'd like to ask me."

"About those coal mines?" John asked, glancing around to see who might be near enough to overhear, then spoke in a voice just loud enough for Richard and Lana to hear above the usual street clamor. "Yes, I might be ready to talk more about particulars by the end of the week. Will you still be in Pittsburgh then?"

"Yes. I should be here until the middle of next week," Richard assured him, glad John was that close to making a decision. After all the problems he had had lately with those blasted anthracite mines, he was more than ready to be rid of them. "Next Wednesday, I'll have to make a short trip to New York to check on a problem with one of the railroads my son and I just bought then I'll probably stop back by Black Wall on the way back to see if they've made any progress in finding McGeehan. I'll check on your sister, too, while I'm there."

John's forehead wrinkled. "While you are in Black Wall? Why would you do that? Cresson is probably two hundred miles from Black Wall."

Richard winked to let John know he knew the truth. "Well, actually I think Cresson is more like a

375

hundred and fifty miles from Black Wall; but that really doesn't matter when I already know she is not in Cresson at all. I saw her while I was in Black Wall Sunday so there's no more reason to pretend otherwise with me."

John's whole body tensed. "You saw her in Black Wall?" He and Lana exchanged questioning glances. "Are you sure?"

"Of course, I'm sure. I was only about a block away when I saw her," he answered, looking from John's round, almost nondescript face to Lana's perfectly sculptured face, perplexed. "Didn't you know she was there?"

"No. The last I heard she was going to Cresson for a few weeks to relax and try to get over the horror of having witnessed our father's death."

"Well, obviously she didn't *stay* in Cresson," Lana put in. Her dark blue eyes narrowed. "I wonder what could have lured her to Black Wall." She looked up at John with an intense frown. "Maybe Lizbeth sent word that you were going there to watch one of those men who killed your father hang and she decided she wanted to be there, too. Or maybe she needed to find you for some other reason. Perhaps she had something important to tell you, but arrived too late. By the time she got there, you'd already left."

"No," Richard interrupted, and held his hand out to stop all the rambling guesses. "Her going there had nothing to do with wanting to see that man hang or with needing to find John. According to a man I have had working there since last November, Karissa has been in Black Wall for at least three weeks. Maybe four."

John's puzzled frown deepened. "You mean she was already there when I arrived last weekend?"

Lana rolled her pretty eyes skyward as if annoyed with John for having said something so incredibly stupid. "Richard told you he saw her last Sunday and that she's been there for at least three weeks. That means that, yes, she was already there when you arrived and was still there when you left. She was probably hiding from you on purpose, which is why you never saw her." Her eyes narrowed again while she tapped a delicate finger against the corner of her mouth. "I wonder why she's there, and why it is she doesn't want us to know she's there."

"She's there to find out who killed your father," Richard supplied, thinking there was no reason they should not know. They were her family.

"She's what?" John replied, so surprised he pressed a hand against his chest as if that might help steady him somehow.

"She went there because she wants to find out who killed your father," he repeated, then like John, cut his gaze to those around them to see who might be listening. He took a step forward to assure further confidentiality. "Obviously she knows that the money token the killers dropped was one issued from your own company, so that's where she went to see what she could find out. According to what I was told, she's very determined to see that whoever shot your father is found and made to pay dearly for what they did."

"I should have *known* she was up to something." John closed his eyes while he thought back to the last time he'd seen her then opened them again to look stonily at Richard. "When I suggested she go away for a while to try to get over some of her grief, I should have noticed that she was just a little too receptive to the idea. Normally Karissa pays no attention to anything I have to say whatsoever." He let out a disgusted breath. "It's pretty obvious she was not listening to me when I told her to let the authorities handle that whole investigation."

"Then it's a good thing I stopped you," Richard said, wanting full credit for what he had done. "You'd have gone on believing she was somewhere she was not. Now, if she ends up in need of help and wires you to let you know, you'll have a better understanding of what's going on."

"Yes, thank you for letting us know," John said. Again he and Lana exchanged glances. "We appreciate what you've done."

"Oh, and you'll be pleased to know that the man I have working for me there in Black Wall has agreed to keep a close watch over her." He grinned. "Truth is he's really quite smitten with her."

John turned one ear toward Richard, as if eager to hear every tiny sound he made. "And who is he? One of your supervisors?"

"No. He's not connected with my mining operation at all. He's a private investigator from New York who I had already hired to look into another matter, but have since ordered to find out about your father's murder. Like Karissa, I won't rest easy until we know who killed him." He did not bother mentioning that the original reason he had hired Shawn was to infiltrate the local Molly Maguires and force a disbandment by exposing and bringing down as many members as possible.

"And who is this detective? Anyone I know? A Pinkerton man perhaps?"

"No, he's not a Pink, and I doubt you'd know him. But take my word for it, he's the very best New York City has to offer. And if he says he'll keep a close watch over Karissa, he will do just that. She'll be safe as long as he's around."

"That's good to hear." John spoke in a strained voice, clearly concerned over everything he had just learned. "Tell me his name and I'll send him some extra money to make sure he does just that."

"Don't worry. I'm already paying him plenty. Besides, he's working under an assumed name as a coal miner in one of your mines and doesn't need anything like that drawing attention to him."

"Well, if I can't send him money, tell me his assumed name and I'll see to it that he gets easier treatment by the pit boss. I'll tell Philen that he's a cousin of my wife's or something."

"He doesn't want special treatment. Besides, he shouldn't be there all that much longer. I think he's pretty close now to finding out the truth. He's already traced four of the men back here to Pittsburgh," he said, revealing none of the disappointment he still felt. He had so hoped the Mollies had been involved; he would have a reason to send a few more of them to the gallows. "He should have the name of whoever fired the fatal shot within a matter of weeks."

John reached up a trembling hand to push an errant strand of brown hair back off his forehead. Suddenly he was very pale. "He's that close to finding the murderers?"

"I told you, he's the best New York has to offer," Richard said proudly. "And I've spared no expense on this matter. None at all. Why, this man stands to earn over half a million by the time he's through."

"You are very kind," Lana said, watching her husband curiously. "It's nice to know Mr. Caine had friends like you."

"I'll let you know when I find out more," Richard promised then patted John vigorously on the shoulder. "But it will probably be the end of next week before I hear anything else. I won't be meeting with him again before then and he refuses to send out telegrams of any kind. Doesn't want to take the chance of being found out."

"I'd appreciate any information you can give us," John said with a brisk nod, then smiled weakly at Lana. "We're as eager to know what has happened as you."

John waited until Richard had said his goodbyes and had headed on off toward the Hotel Royale before motioning Lana toward the door again.

"That sister of mine! I never know what she will do next," he said, trying his best to sound merely annoyed by what he had just learned.

"And to think, your father left *her* in charge of everything," Lana replied, her expression as bitter as her tone.

"Well, there's nothing we can do about that now," John said as if having resigned himself to the fact, even though he knew it was not true. There *was* one thing he could do. The *one* thing that would solve all his problems. But he wasn't sure he had the courage to try something like that a second time. "Let's get on inside before they give our table away."

For the duration of their meal, John remained too preoccupied with what Richard had told him to keep up his end of the conversation. Finally Lana became annoyed with him for paying so little attention to her and tossed her napkin into her plate much like a spoiled child might.

"What's wrong with you?" she asked, provoked. "Are you *that* worried about Karissa?"

"Yes, I guess I am. I've been to Black Wall. I've seen the sort of people who live there. I really think I should go back and try to find out where she is then find some way to force her to come back home with me."

"If that's what you think you should do, then do it," Lana said as if it were really just that simple. "Go first thing in the morning."

"I can't. I have two very important business meetings tomorrow afternoon. I don't dare miss either one."

"Then go as soon as your meetings are over or else the first thing Friday morning. If Black Wall is as small and lifeless as you said it was, it shouldn't take you too long to find her. If you left early enough Friday morning, you could probably be on your way back home late that same afternoon."

John nodded his agreement. "And I'll bring her back with me if I have to tie her up with rope and toss her on the train myself. I will not allow her to stay there and make fools of herself and our family any longer." He lifted his chin to show his determination. "I will leave first thing Friday morning."

He let his narrow shoulders relax a degree, knowing

that would give him tomorrow and tomorrow night to try to find those men again and arrange the death of a certain private detective.

And his sister, too, if necessary.

Chapter Nineteen

Shawn smiled while he watched Karissa from across the room and wondered how he had ever believed that beautiful young enchantress to be the penniless waif of some destitute coal miner. Although she was certainly dressed the part in faded blue cotton with her long, dark hair pulled into a simple twist near the nape of her neck, she moved with considerably too much grace and laughed and talked in a voice too refined to be that of a common girl. Not even one who had been fortunate enough to be sent to a private school.

How had he ever convinced himself otherwise? He was normally such a suspicious person and was usually very quick to recognize whenever someone had purposely lied to him. Why hadn't he detected such lies in her? Why had he accepted everything she told him at face value?

He shook his head when he realized the answer to that. He had believed her because he *wanted* to believe her and had uncovered no grounds not to believe her. Which was probably the same reason she had so readily believed everything he had told her. *If* she had believed it. Truth was, he had no way to know what she did or did not believe about him. The only thing he knew for certain was that she asked lots of questions about him whenever they were together and seemed a little too pensive whenever they were alone.

But at least he understood the reasoning for that now. She not only thought him to be a man capable of killing his own wife, she had probably heard some of the other rumors going around that falsely connected him to her own father's murder.

That also explained one reason why she was so hesitant to admit that she was even partially attracted to him. She was not at all the person she had claimed to be yet thought that *he* was. She had no way of knowing the truth about him or his situation. Therefore she had to believe that even if it turned out he was innocent of the two murders he had been accused of committing, he would still never fit into her world.

Suddenly it was very important to him that he get her to admit her attraction to him while she still believed him to be Shawn McCowan, even though he would not allow her to make love to him as such. If or when they ever made love, he wanted her to be doing so to the man he really was—to Shawn Madden. Not to Shawn McCowan. But that would mean trusting her enough to tell her the truth. Trusting her not to become so angry with him for having told so many lies to her that she would ruin the whole operation by revealing to the others who he really was out of sheer spite.

His whole body tensed when he realized just how angry and hurt Karissa could become. Angry enough to want to harm him, or worse yet, force him out of her life forever. It was obvious that she already did not trust men as a whole. What would she feel after finding out that he, too, had lied to her? He shuddered to think.

Karissa was disappointed when, shortly before eleven o'clock, Frank Neely suddenly got up from his table and left the tavern. It meant he would not be following her that night either, which also meant she dared not question Shawn McCowan yet about his mysterious involvement with Richard Porterfield. She would have to wait longer still.

Frowning, she headed toward the bar, following a route that would not take her anywhere near Shawn's table. She did not like the intense way he had been staring at her that night, as if he already suspected her of having done something terribly wrong. It gave her the eerie feeling that her time in Black Wall was about to come to an abrupt end, whether she wanted it to or not. He was not about to let her stay there and continue following him around.

"You want to take off early?" Marcus asked when she set her tray on the bar yet had no order for him. "It's your turn again, you know."

"No," she answered, wanting to put off being alone with Shawn for as long as she could, then realized if she left earlier than expected, she might be able to slip off without his even being aware. She could always come up with some logical-sounding excuse later on like she had that night she'd followed him to Richard's offices. "I mean, *yes*. I would."

"Fine. I'll go tell Shawn," Marcus put in, then stepped from behind the bar to go do just that.

Aware it would raise questions for which she really had no answers, Karissa did not try to stop him. Instead she remained where she was and watched with growing trepidation while Marcus bent to give Shawn the message.

Shawn immediately rose from his chair and headed toward her. As was usual for him, he was dressed in dark corduroy trousers with wide pleats that lay flat against his waist and hips along with a loose-fitting cotton shirt, unbuttoned at the collar. He also wore black workman's boots and a pair of black and tan suspenders that tucked the shirt in at his shoulders and down the center of his back, emphasizing the contour of his strong, muscular body. His long, dark hair had been quickly washed and brushed away from a freshly shaven face. But in the past hour most of the front had dried and fallen forward over his forehead, giving him a rakish look that set Karissa's heart to thudding.

"I hear we are leavin' early tonight," he said. His eyes sparkled their usual crystal blue clarity when he stepped behind the bar to gather her lantern and handbag for her.

Karissa tried not to reveal her growing apprehension. "Yes. Marcus has offered to let me go on since there are not that many customers tonight and it is my turn to leave first."

"Good. I've been lookin' forward to bein' alone with ya all evenin'," he said, then lowered his eyebrows as if accusing her of something when he stepped back around the bar to rejoin her. "After all, ya haven't put together enough time to say two words to me all evenin'."

"I've been busy," she said, hoping he would let it go at that. She did not want to admit that his watching her the way he had that night had made her extremely nervous.

"Are ya sure it is because ye've been busy? Here lately, ye've been actin' almost like ya have some reason to be afraid of me," Shawn baited then watched her carefully for a reaction. When there was none, he marveled again at what a fine actress she was. No wonder he had never suspected her of being anyone other than who she claimed to be.

"What reason would I have to be afraid of you?" she asked, trying to sound as if she truly did not understand then motioned toward the door. "Come on. Let's leave here before Marcus changes his mind."

"Y'll get no argument from me," Shawn said, quick to follow. He waited until they were both outside and well away from the noisy tavern before offering the suggestion he had waited all night to present. "It's such a nice night, why don't we take a nice long walk first? It'll give us more of a chance to talk."

"Talk?" A tiny chill skipped across Karissa's spine. Did he plan to question her whereabouts last Friday night? Or did he perhaps already know? There was always the possibility someone had seen her. "What's there to talk about?"

Aware of her reluctance to go with him and the reason behind it, he decided to offer her something too tempting to resist. "There's something about me I think you should know."

Karissa looked at him with a mixture of caution,

distrust, and curiosity. "Oh? And what would that be?"

"I can't be tellin' ya out in the open like this. Someone might overhear. But if ya'd agree to go with me to somewhere more private, I'd gladly tell you what it is I think ya should know."

Karissa studied him a moment and decided the request was genuine. He really did have something important to tell her. "Where would we go?"

"We could take a walk through the woods. Or better yet, we could go across town to my bedroom. There's a door that opens directly to the outside so no one would ever have to know that's where we went."

Karissa's brown eyes widened until she reminded Shawn of a frightened puppy. He fought the urge to gather her into his arms and hold her close.

"But why the woods or your bedroom? Why not somewhere a little closer?" Somewhere where she would be able to make a quick run to safety should he become angry with her for any reason. There was still the possibility he had found out she followed him.

"Because what I have to tell ya is too important to chance *anyone* overhearin'." He offered a reassuring smile. "If ye're worried that I plan to do ya some sort of harm, don't be. If ya choose to talk in my bedroom, where it is certain we won't be overheard, y'd be comforted to know that two other men live in the same house with me. They would come runnin' in an instant if they were to hear a woman's scream," he assured her, though he knew that was not altogether true. Jeremiah Clark, the older man who lived in the room directly adjacent to his was as deaf as a man could be. He wouldn't hear a fire siren if one was to be set off in his very own bedroom. And George Sanford, who also lived there, was known to be a very sound sleeper, which was why Shawn was able to slip in and out so easily.

Karissa tapped her foot while she considered his request. "Is what you have to say to me *that* important?"

"I wouldn't ask ya to go with me to my bedroom if it were not."

"Okay, I'll go on one condition—that you promise to leave the door open," she said, thinking that would still leave her a means of escape.

"I can't be promisin' ya such as that. Someone might be lurkin' about outside and overhear. I can't take that chance."

Karissa continued to tap her foot while she considered what to do. She knew that what he had to tell her might have something to do with her father's death. Or it could be he planned to tell her about his involvement with Richard Porterfield, which would mean being able to find out what was going on without having to admit what she had done. Finally, she made her decision. "Okay, I'll go with you, but say what you have to say quickly because I'll stay only a few minutes."

"A few minutes is all I ask," he said, and smiled again, knowing full well what he intended to accomplish in those few minutes. "Come on. Let's take the long way just in case we are bein' followed for some reason."

Although he felt certain Frank was busy trailing Charles and Joey through the woods, there were always those two Pinkerton agents who sometimes followed him at a distance. Tonight, he did not want to take any chances. What he had planned would not come to pass unless they both felt completely alone.

While Karissa walked alongside Shawn down a darkened side street, she did what she could to convince herself that she had made the right decision. The whole reason she had come to Black Wall was to find out who had killed her father, *no matter what the risks;* and by having agreed to go with Shawn tonight, she might manage to uncover some very important information. Information she was becoming very impatient to have.

In the month she and Frank had been there in Black Wall, the most they had learned was that the local group of Molly Maguires met at least once a week out in the woods somewhere and that Shawn had to be one of them since he always disappeared at about the same time the rest of them did. And even though it was hard to think of Shawn as being capable of anything so terrible, it was still possible that he was involved with the murder.

She had to know the truth.

Still, she wished he would agree to talk somewhere other than his bedroom. *Anywhere else would do.*

"You look a little nervous," Shawn commented, hoping to calm her with conversation while they walked.

"That's probably because I am," she responded, then glanced at him briefly, her heart fluttering when she saw how intently he was watching her. "I'm not exactly accustomed to going into men's bedrooms."

"Glad to hear it," he said, and offered her one of his knee-melting smiles. His dimples sank deep into his cheeks while he continued to watch her beautiful face for reactions. "I'd hate to think I had gotten myself engaged to someone so wanton."

Glad for the playful banter, she smiled back then responded in kind; "I'd think you would be hoping just the *opposite* about now. After all, we are about to be *alone* together in your bedroom." Her smile quickly faded. Having said such a thing made her suddenly aware of a whole new danger. A danger that had absolutely nothing to do with the possibility that he had found out the truth about her or that the truth might come out during their conversation. Knowing how weak her resistance was where Shawn was concerned, her pulses raced uncontrolled at the thought of what might happen should he attempt to seduce her while she was there alone with him.

"You're absolutely right," he answered with an intrigued lift of his dark eyebrows that made her pulses race all the faster. "I obviously have my priorities confused."

Aware their conversation was headed off in a very perilous direction, she hurried to change it. "So, what does this confession of yours have to do with me? Can you at least tell me that?"

"I'm afraid y'll have to be patient and wait until I am certain we are alone to find that out," he answered while he fought a very strong urge to touch the velvety skin along her ivory cheek. Any other time and he would have acted on such an impulse, but he did not want to do anything that might frighten her from entering his bedroom. What he was about to say to her was far too important.

Karissa studied him a moment, then noticed he still carried her handbag. Aware she might need the derringer inside before their *talk* was finished, she held out her hand. "Don't you think you look a little silly holding my handbag? Here, give it to me. I'll carry it."

"That's okay," he said, purposely ignoring the offer. He had already felt of the contents to see if the tiny handgun was inside and found that it was. "I don't mind carrying it for you."

Aware he meant to keep the handbag, she decided not to make an issue of his having it. Instead she changed the subject again, thinking to put her hands on the small bag the moment he set it down inside his bedroom.

"How much farther?" she asked. She did not want him to know that she already knew where he lived, and had for weeks. It would make it seem as if he was more important to her than he was.

"It's that next house." He nodded toward a small frame house near the southernmost edge of town.

There was just enough moonlight peeping over the mountain for her to see the house with its small, overgrown front yard. "That's where you live?"

"For now," he said, then paused several dozen yards away to turn the lantern out. He waited until he had glanced in all directions before guiding her through the side gate. When he spoke again, his voice was barely above that of a whisper. "I don't want anyone to know where we've gone."

Karissa felt very uncomfortable with the way he expected her to sneak across the side yard and into his bedroom, but said nothing of her discomfort. She was too curious to find out what it was he wanted to tell her. She waited until they were both inside and

Shawn had closed the door before daring to speak again. "I can't see anything."

"That's because it's dark in here," Shawn said, stating the obvious. His voice had come from somewhere near the door.

"I know that," she responded flatly. "Would you please light the lantern again so we can at least see each other?" And so she could see where he had placed her handbag. She knew she would feel much better about being alone with him if she knew she had that small derringer within her grasp.

Shawn struck a match and relit the wick, but turned the flame so low it barely allowed any light into the sparsely furnished bedroom.

"There," he said. He still held the lantern while he placed the handbag on a high shelf alongside several books where he knew she would have a hard time reaching it. He then removed his coat and placed it there, too. He did not want her using his own gun against him either. "We can now see each other, but without the lantern creatin' enough reflection to prevent me from bein' able to see out the windows."

He wanted her to think danger was his motive for keeping the light dim when in truth he was setting the mood for what he hoped would follow. He drew in a deep breath to help contain his anticipation.

Casually, he set the lantern on a small cluttered table that stood near the door. It let off just enough of a glow for him to see her worried expression when he headed toward her. "I want to thank ya for comin'."

"What is it you wanted to tell me?" she asked, eager to get on with it. Deciding the tiny glimmer reflecting in his pale blue eyes was a bit too intimidating, she took a precautionary step back and wished she had been more demanding about having her handbag turned over to her. "What is so important that it must be said in private?"

"The fact that I now know that I love ya," he answered candidly while he continued his slow advance. "I wanted ya to know that I love ya more than I have loved anyone in a long, long time; and that I don't like playin' all these games anymore. I really *do* want to marry ya."

Caught completely off guard by such a statement, Karissa's brown eyes widened to their limits. She swallowed hard and took another step back, unaware she was headed directly for his bed. "You *what?*"

"How can I say it more plainly? I love ya, Karissa Caine." He waited for her to notice that he had just used her real name while he continued moving steadily toward her.

"B-but you don't even know me . . ." she stammered—more conscious of the fact he was coming toward her than what he had said—then she came to a sudden stop. She blinked twice with confusion. "What did you just call me?"

"Karissa Caine. That is your name, isn't it?" he asked though he never paused in his advance on her. Because the room was small and the bed only a few yards behind her, he knew he would be upon her in less than a minute.

"H-how did you find that out?" she asked, having quickly decided it would do her no good to deny the truth now. He was obviously on to her.

"Someone who knows ya mentioned havin' seen ya

with me last Sunday," he answered honestly, but without giving away any names. Although he intended to tell her the truth about who he was and why he was there, he did not plan to tell her everything. He felt the less she knew about certain matters, the better.

"Someone who knows me? Who was that? Richard Porterfield?"

Now it was his turn to blink with confusion. He paused, just two feet away. "You knew he was here?"

"Yes," is all she was willing to answer. She swallowed again, this time capturing only air. Aware he was now well within striking distance should that be his intention, she considered taking another few steps backward, but decided instead to stand her ground. "What do you plan to do to me now that you know I lied to you?"

"Just this," he said in a low, ominous voice, his eyes darkening when he took one more step, effectively closing the distance between them.

Before she really understood what was happening, he pulled her into the warm circle of his arms for what turned out to be a very long and very persuasive kiss.

Having expected angry retribution for having lied to him, Karissa was as relieved as she was surprised to be kissed so tenderly. His lips moved gently yet powerfully against hers, creating instant havoc inside her. While she tried to calm the sudden stirring so she could better think, he moved his hands to cup the back of her head as if afraid she might try to break away. But the effort was unnecessary for Karissa had no desire to pull away from something so warm and so completely arousing.

Those same splendid sensations she had felt before when he'd kissed her had invaded her yet again, spreading through her body quickly and leaving her feeling suddenly light-headed and physically weak. She had little choice but to lean against him while she wondered again what strange power Shawn McCowan held within his grasp. Why did his kiss leave her too muddled to do anything more than marvel at the amazing effects it had on her?

Responding much as she had before, she pressed against his strong, powerful body, too overwhelmed with the desire to discover more about the pleasure he gave her to consider pulling away. Instead, she waited eagerly to find out what might happen next, not quite sure what to expect. To add to her confusion, Shawn suddenly broke their tender kiss—but not the caress. His arms stayed around her, holding her gently in place.

"Admit it, Karissa," he urged in a deep, sultry voice, his mouth but inches from hers. "Admit that ye're attracted to me. Admit that ya want me every bit as much as I want you."

"But I can't be attracted to you," she answered, trying to deny even to herself the importance of what she felt for this man. "I just can't."

"Why? Because you are incredibly wealthy and I am not?" he asked, then tensed while he awaited her answer. It was important that she accept him no matter what she thought his station in life might be.

"No," she answered, her head still spinning from having been so soundly kissed. Her gaze fell on his wide, virile mouth and she knew she wanted more than anything for him to kiss her again. "Money has nothing to do with it."

"Then is it because I am suspected of havin' helped three others kill yer father?"

The image of her father with trails of blood trickling down his face and neck swam before her eyes, causing tears to spring immediately forth. "And did you?"

Unable to bear the thought that he might, she pulled her gaze off his handsome face and looked down at the buttons holding his shirt. She was so emotionally distraught that her whole body trembled.

Shawn placed his hand beneath her chin then gently lifted her face so she had to look at him again. "No, Karissa. I had nothin' to do with the death of yer father."

Although it was tempting to tell her everything at that point so she would more readily believe him, he resisted. He wanted her to accept what he had to say without first being told all that. He wanted her to believe him because in some small way she trusted him. After having learned how very little she trusted men as a whole, having her trust was important to him. "I was nowhere near Pittsburgh the day yer father was killed."

Karissa blinked away the tears while she studied the sincerity in his blue eyes. Something inside her wanted to believe him. "How do I know that's true? What proof do you have?"

"Just my word. And the word of my co-workers, which I'm afraid does not carry too well with the authorities. They want to believe I'm guilty because they know I'm a member of the Molly Maguires."

Karissa studied the candor in his eyes a moment longer. "You admit to being a member of the Molly Maguires?"

"Yes," he answered, and continued to meet her gaze. "But there is no crime in that."

"That depends on what you do for them," she said, still finding it hard to believe he had actually told her. Her heart raced with the thought of what else he might be planning to tell her.

"I don't murder for them, if that's what ya think," he said, then waited a few seconds before asking, "Do ya believe I am innocent like I say?"

"Of having helped kill my father?" she asked, still studying the sincerity in his blue eyes. She waited a long moment, then nodded. "Yes, I believe you are innocent of that."

"Then there is no reason for ya to continue denyin' how ya feel about me," he said, determined to have a confession of love before he told her the rest.

Karissa looked away for a moment to consider her answer but returned her gaze to his before answering. She deliberated asking him about his involvement with Richard, but decided not to chance angering him yet. Not while they were still being so open and honest with each other. "No. I guess there's not."

Shawn waited for her to say more then decided she needed further encouragement. "Then tell me how ya feel. *Are* ya as attracted to me as I am to you?"

She continued to stare at his handsome face, trying to peer into his deepest thoughts. "Did you mean it earlier when you said that you loved me?" Her pulses raced while she awaited his answer, knowing it would hurt her deeply if he answered no. "Or did you just say that to catch my attention."

Shawn did not hesitate answering. "Of course I meant it." Thinking she needed more convincing, he bent forward to place a brief, tantalizing kiss near the outer corner of her mouth. "I don't know how it happened or exactly when, but somewhere durin' these past few weeks I fell deeply and insanely in love with ya."

Refusing to let the tingling response to his kiss muddle her thoughts, she tilted her head back and notched her forehead. "Did you love me even when you thought I was Catherine Sobey, the daughter of a penniless coal miner? Or was it finding out who I really was that caused these sudden feelings?"

A dimple sank deep into his cheek when he dipped his head forward to kiss the opposite corner of her mouth, causing yet another current of mind-dazing warmth to shoot through her. Already she felt weak again and was glad to have his strong arms to prevent her from sagging.

"Karissa, don't ya remember me tellin' ya days ago how y'd already stolen my heart?"

Swallowing hard, she nodded that she did remember. Remembered it well.

"Well, I had no idea who ya really were then."

"You also said something about harm coming to me as a result. Why was that?"

"Answer *my* question first," he responded, still determined to know how she felt about him before telling her the truth. "Are ya attracted to me?"

"Very much," she finally admitted, and looked away, feeling suddenly very timid.

"Enough to make love to me if I asked ya?"

Karissa cut her gaze back to him again, startled by such a direct question. "But we are not married," she said, avoiding a real answer.

"*Ah,* but we are engaged. For some people that is enough."

"But we are not *truly* engaged," she reminded him. "We only say that we are to keep all those other men from bothering me."

"But we *could* be truly engaged if we wanted."

She felt an odd surge of exhilaration at the thought, but quickly pushed the feeling aside. She was not there to find a husband. She was there to find her father's killer. "But we are *not.*"

"Kar-is-sa." He said, sounding out all three syllables as if to issue a warning. "I need to know exactly how ya feel about me."

"Why?"

"Because I have something else to tell ya, but I don't want to tell it until y've told me exactly how ya feel."

She wondered if what remained to be told had anything to do with Richard Porterfield. "If you're asking whether I'm in love with you, I can't say. I really don't know that much about love. At least not the kind of love you mean."

Shawn grinned, unable to resist the comment, "That's okay, I can teach ya whatever ya want to know."

He bent to place another tantalizing kiss upon her, this time at the tip of her nose.

Karissa felt all resistance melting away. She yearned to have those lips pressed hard against her mouth. "Then teach me."

That response had been so unexpected, it startled even herself.

Shawn responded with a low, lustful growl just before he claimed her mouth in another long, hungry kiss. When he pulled away the second time, his eyes were nearly black with desire. "I still have somethin' I have to tell ya."

"Can't it wait?" she asked, too consumed by the passion his kiss had wrought to care what else he had to say. She was too eager to be taught about love to hear any more of his confessions.

"No. It can't wait. There are things ya need to know about me first. Things ya must swear never to tell anyone y've heard."

That had sounded so ominous, it brought Karissa immediately out of her muddled state. "Does this have anything to do with Richard Porterfield?"

Shawn looked at her questioningly. "Before I answer that, ya have to promise not to tell anything I tell ya tonight to anyone," he reminded her. "My very life is at stake here."

Karissa's forehead notched with immediate concern. "Why would your life be at stake?"

"Because of who I am."

She looked at him strangely. "And who are you?"

"First, yer promise."

Karissa studied the deep concern that shadowed his handsome face for a long moment and realized he had meant every word he'd said. His very life was at risk. "Very well. I promise. Whatever it is, I won't tell a soul."

Shawn let out a relieved breath then dropped his

arms and stepped away so he could better decide how to tell her. When he spoke again, it was from several yards away and without a trace of his earlier brogue. "I am not who you think I am."

"You're not?" she said, as confused by the sudden elimination of his Irish accent as she was by his words.

"No. My name is not Shawn McCowan."

"I know. Your name is really Shawn Larsen and you are hiding from the New York police. But I already know about that, remember? We discussed all that a while back."

Shawn shook his head. "My name is not Shawn Larsen either."

Karissa looked truly baffled. "Then what is it?"

He hesitated, hoping she would not feel betrayed when she found out about all the lies. "My name is Shawn Madden. Shawn Weston Madden. I am a private investigator from New York who was hired earlier this year to infiltrate those Molly Maguires living here in Black Wall and uncover enough information to have the more malicious ones brought to trial for crimes they'd committed, and the rest disbanded forever. I am also supposed to be finding out who killed your father."

"A private detective?" Karissa repeated, clearly surprised. "Working for Richard Porterfield?"

"Why do you keep bringing up that name?" he asked, still looking at her questioningly. "Just because you saw the man in town a few days ago does not mean he is the one who hired me."

Karissa felt it was time for her to tell the truth. "I followed you late last Friday night—or should I say early last Saturday morning. I saw who it was you went all that way to meet. Are you by any chance a Pinkerton man?"

Shawn's eyebrows shot up, surprised that she had managed to follow him that far without his knowing. "I used to be. But Allan Pinkerton and I had too many differences of opinion about how certain situations should be handled. Despite the strong code of ethics that was supposed to be in place, some of his operatives proved to be every bit as cruel and malicious as the criminals they sought. I didn't like being associated with men like that so I quit and ventured off on my own."

"How long have you been a private detective?" she asked, as intrigued as she was shocked by his confession.

"For nearly five years," he answered, relieved that she had yet to show any anger. "Before that I was a business broker on Wall Street."

"Whatever made you become a detective?"

"My need to get into some form of work that would help me take my mind off my wife. After she died, everything about my life changed."

Karissa looked startled. "You mean that part of what you told me was true? You really did have to shoot your wife?"

"No. My wife died in childbirth," Shawn admitted. "We had been married for about two years."

"So practically everything you've told me about yourself until now has been a lie," she realized, aware she would have to start all over getting to know him.

"Not everything. But a lot of it was lies. Necessary lies. Like those you had to tell me. But what I think you need to understand now is that I really have put my very life at risk by telling you who I really am. If anyone involved with the Molly Maguires ever catches wind of the truth before this project is completed, I could very easily end up just as dead as all those other detectives who have tried to do virtually the same thing."

"Why *are* you telling me?" She looked truly puzzled.

Shawn smiled then stepped toward her again. "Because I don't want any secrets or misinformation between us when I tell you again that I love you."

"Is that what you are about to do? Tell me again that you love me?" Warmth and giddiness washed over her.

"Yes," he said as he slipped his arms around her again. "I love you, Karissa Caine; and I do want us to be married someday. Just as soon as I have finished here and can get back to leading a more normal life. I want you to know that being a private detective is just something I do; it is not something I was *born* to do. I'd gladly quit and do something else with my life if it means we can be together. Besides, I've always liked Pittsburgh. It seems like it would be a very nice place to raise children."

He paused to look into her luminous brown eyes a long moment before continuing, "I know this has all been very sudden for you and I don't expect you to decide anything so important right away. But I do want you to think about everything I've said to you while I kiss you again."

Karissa's heart vaulted to instant heights. Not only did he love her and want her to love him, she was about to be soundly kissed again. Happily, she leaned forward so he would know the kiss was wanted.

While she watched his mouth slowly descend toward hers, her heartbeat grew stronger with each beat it took, until her pulses throbbed throughout her body with alarming intensity.

When his mouth finally met with hers yet again, her lips parted and her arms slowly lifted to accept his loving kiss. Overwhelmed by an immediate need, she met the resulting embrace with a hunger she had never known before. It was all so extraordinary. No wonder she was having such a hard time believing him to have been involved in her father's murder. Her instincts had been right all along. Shawn really was the kind, honorable man she'd thought him to be. And he was a man who had just proclaimed his love for her and wanted to marry her. All she had to do was say yes and all this would be hers forever. *He* would be hers forever.

Suddenly, she knew that was exactly what she would say. She would say yes to his proposal of marriage. She would become Mrs. Shawn Madden and spend the rest of her life making him happy.

Unaware he had already won her, Shawn pulled away just enough to be able to meet her muddled gaze. "I want to see your hair down," he whispered, his voice husky, then released his hold on her long enough to slip the pins and combs from her hair. Using his fingers, he freed her long tresses from the simple twist, allowing them to fall gently over her shoulders.

Karissa closed her eyes while he raked both hands through the silken mass, as if hoping to physically capture its softness. The feel of his strong fingers gliding through the length of it caused a delightfully sensuous feeling to build then cascade over her like warm water.

"You are so very beautiful," he said, then moved his hands first to her soft cheeks then down and around to gently draw her body closer to his.

Karissa leaned forward, effectively luring his mouth downward once again. Although she thrilled at hearing his praises, words were not what she craved. At that moment all she wanted was to feel his embrace about her and explore the wondrous magic of his kiss. To find out at last what it was to be a real woman.

Like before, Shawn dipped his tongue lightly past her parted mouth and teased the sensitive inner edges of her lips, each time going deeper and staying longer, until finally she responded in kind. Karissa closed her eyes to savor the tantalizing taste she'd discovered when she allowed her tongue to follow his and enter his mouth.

It was like nothing she had ever experienced—to explore such intimate recesses and feel his lightly shuddering response. It gave her a sense of power and made her eager to discover yet more about him. Driven by a maddening hunger, she brought her mouth harder against his, dipped her tongue deeper, and pressed her body nearer, all the while wishing she could find some way to bring them closer still.

Shawn realized the passion inside Karissa was fully ignited and now raged deep within her, controlling her. He felt certain he could take her then and she would let him, but he chose instead to proceed very slowly. He let his lips linger over her sweetly demanding mouth while he eased his hands down the curve of her back then around to her rib cage. He was well aware that her breathing became more and more labored with each new exploring touch, and it delighted him that he had created such a powerful response in her.

There was a beautiful sense of accomplishment in knowing he was capable of giving her such true and basic pleasure. He held back his own response while he worked to bring her to one new height of arousal after another.

Unhurriedly, he moved his hand ever upward along the smooth surface of her dress, until he was at last able to grasp the undercurve of her breast. She did not brush his hand away as he feared she might. Instead she leaned eagerly into his hand, letting him close his fingers around the precious find.

Gently he played with the tip through the layers of her clothing until he felt it grow rigid with need and heard her gasp aloud over such unexpected pleasure. He waited several seconds before unfastening the buttons that ran between her breasts and held the front of her outer garment together. Instead, he allowed his hand to continue its hungry prowl along the outside of the faded dress — ever seeking, ever searching, but never again quite finding.

Driven mad by such teasing, Karissa became instantly lost in the deep, swirling torrent of emotions that resulted. Liquid fire coursed through her veins while her arousal spiraled ever higher, until the need for more possessed her entire being.

Slowly, Shawn turned his attention to the many

buttons. While working with them carefully, his fingers dipped inside the garment and brushed against the swelling curves of her breasts, movements which sent even more delicious waves of white-hot ecstasy rippling through her body. She trembled with further anticipation when he stepped back enough to pull first the outer garment then what few undergarments she wore up over her head.

He allowed himself a leisurely view of her thrusting young breasts while he tossed the unwanted garments aside and found her every bit as exquisite as he had known she would be. Amazed by such true beauty, he stared at her a long moment more before he gathered her into his arms again.

After lifting her easily off the floor, he carried her the short distance to the bed. His eyes grew darker as his lips found hers yet again before he gently lowered her onto the soft mattress. He broke away for only a moment to gaze longingly at her again, watching her magnificent breasts rise and fall with each labored breath.

While he continued to marvel at her beauty, her eyes drifted partially open and she looked at him expectantly. Eager to fulfill those expectations, he stripped himself of his own clothing and proudly revealed his body to her.

When Shawn moved toward the bed that second time, he was breathtakingly naked yet Karissa felt no desire to look away. Instead, she slowly smiled and lifted her arms to receive him. Receive the man who would one day be her husband.

Lying down beside the woman who had so completely stolen his heart, Shawn lifted up on one arm to claim her lips once more while he gently slid his hand over her bare skin, eager to memorize and explore every curve of her body. It took increasingly more effort for him to keep her pleasure before his needs, especially when he knew he could take her at any moment and find complete fulfillment.

Instead he continued to torment her by trailing his fingers lightly over her skin. He teased and taunted, coming ever closer to the sensitive peaks of her breasts with slow, circular motions.

Unable to bear the gentle torture, Karissa arched her back and thrust her breasts higher, wishing frantically that his hands would hurry and reach their destination. She wanted to feel that same wondrous feeling she'd felt earlier when they had touched her outside her clothing.

When moments later, he again broke off the kiss to gaze again at her writhing form, she moaned aloud her disappointment. How could he bring her to such a state of madness and not fulfill her needs? Not knowing why he was treating her like that, she moaned again and reached out to bring his mouth back to hers.

Shawn obliged her with another long, ravaging kiss, but then pulled his lips away again. Only this time it was to trail feathery kisses down her body, until he finally arrived at one of her thrusting breasts. Gently he closed his mouth over the tip and drew deeply. Karissa could not believe the wondrous effect that had on her.

While his lips held the hardened tip in place, his tongue deftly teased the end with short tantalizing strokes, nipping and suckling until she again cried aloud with pleasure. Then when she felt sure she could bear no more, he moved directly to her other breast. Again, he brought a cry of ecstasy from her lips.

Karissa was not certain how long she could endure the tender torment and grasped his shoulders to make him stop his delicate torture and bring her the release she so desperately sought. Still, his mouth continued its assault. She shuddered from the delectable sensations that continued to build inside her, until she felt certain she would burst. A luscious ache had centered itself low in her abdomen, and her whole body craved release from the sensual onslaught that burned uncontrolled within her.

"Shawn," she called to him softly, only vaguely aware she had spoken aloud.

Relishing the sound of his name from her sweet lips, Shawn suckled first one breast then the other one last time before moving to fulfill her. Carefully, he eased through the barrier that proved he was her only lover, and with smooth, lithe movements, brought their wildest longings, their deepest needs to the ultimate height. When release came for Karissa, it was so wondrous and so deeply shattering, she gasped aloud with pleasure. Only a moment later, the same shuddering release came for Shawn.

Once their passions were fully spent and the bond of their newly found love made complete, they lay perfectly still, listening to the steady rhythm of each other's heartbeats, bound together in each other's arms. Together, they drifted into the warm depths of satisfaction, both in awe of what had just happened between them. It had been so astound-

410

ing, it compared to nothing else in their lives.

While settled contentedly at Shawn's side, Karissa marveled over the fact that this exquisite man wanted to be her husband. Such extreme happiness was to be hers forever.

For that moment, while she considered what her life would be like married to someone so wonderful, she refused to let any other thoughts enter her mind. She refused to consider the very real dangers they both still faced. Refused to worry what would happen should the truth about either of them ever become known to the people in Black Wall.

For now, all she wanted to do was bask in the warm aftermath of their wondrous lovemaking and enjoy the feel of her future husband at her side. For the very first time in her twenty-four years, Karissa felt blessed, truly blessed. Shawn Madden loved her and wanted to marry her. She refused to dwell on anything else.

Chapter Twenty

John had already told Lana he was leaving for the office and was waiting near the entry for his driver to bring the carriage around when someone rang the bells beside the front door. Rather than wait for Eldon to come all the way from the back of the house to answer, he stepped over and opened it himself. He was surprised and a little confused to see the city coroner standing there with his hand still on the bellcord.

"John Caine, I am so glad to find you home," Samuel Alexander said in his usual quiet voice, and held out his hand in greeting. "I hate to trouble you this early in the day, but I do need to get this rug out of my office." He gestured toward the small, rolled area rug held by the two young men who stood behind him. "I've tried twice now to deliver it to your sister, but she's never home. And today, even the servants were not there. I stopped by just twenty minutes ago and rang the bells then knocked but no one ever answered the door."

"That's because it's Thursday. That means Lizbeth and Franklin will be the only ones working today and they were probably still at the market," John explained, looking at the three men oddly. "Madison wasn't there because he always has Thursdays off, and ever since Father's death, after which Karissa took off for Cresson, there has been no real need to keep a full staff. Lizbeth has been handling the house pretty much by herself these days." He saw no reason to reveal Karissa's true whereabouts.

"Karissa's in Cresson? Well, no wonder I haven't heard from her. I really expected her to send for this rug before now; but if she's been gone all this time, that explains why I haven't heard from her."

"I don't understand. Why would Kari want you to bring her a rug?" John asked, clearly confused. The city coroner was certainly no delivery service.

"Because that's her rug. It's the one she had me carry out the day your father was killed. The one that was supposed to represent the body of the woman she wanted to save. Didn't she tell you about that?"

John frowned then answered evasively. "Not about the rug."

Samuel smiled, as if finally understanding John's strange behavior. "Well, then let me explain what happened. When your sister asked me to pretend to take two bodies out of the house that day instead of just one, I had to have something to put under the other drape that would be about the right size. So I decided to roll up one of your father's rugs and make it look like a woman's body. My attendants here then covered the rug with the drape and carried it out on a stretcher. Then just before I left, your sister agreed to have one of her servants stop by after a few days to pick up the rug so it wouldn't be in my way. Well, it's been over a month now, and as you can see, I still have the rug. Or should I say I still have the *unidentified female*." He chuckled softly at his own wit.

John looked at him, his face drawn into a questioning frown, then waved the two younger men inside. "Set that thing down anywhere. I'll have two of my servants carry it over there later," he said, his hands trembling when it finally occurred to him what had happened. Karissa must have realized that the men who killed their father were still outside, watching the house, waiting to make sure the woman who had overheard their conversation the night before was out of their way for good. They knew they had shot her, but until they actually saw a second body be removed from the house, they could not be sure she was dead

That was why Karissa had asked Samuel to pretend to carry a second body out, so those men would think the woman they had shot was indeed dead, when she obviously was not.

His heart vaulted hard against his chest when he realized that the woman Karissa had wanted everyone to think was dead was the same woman who could prove that the four men he and Clay Jones had wanted accused of the two murders were not the same ones she had overhead discussing their plans in that tavern the night before. They did not even match a similar description.

And knowing that his sister and some unknown private detective that had been hired by Richard Porterfield were in Black Wall at that very moment working against him, his legs and arms suddenly grew very weak while his pulses raced frantically. According to Porterfield, they were already very close to the truth. He had to do something to stop them. He had to keep his name from ever coming to the surface.

"I am truly sorry to have to leave it here with you like this," Samuel said, obviously thinking that John's serious expression meant he was annoyed by the inconvenience. "But it really was starting to get in my way and I didn't know what else to do with it."

"That's perfectly all right," John said in an attempt to sound quietly reassuring. He clasped his hands together to keep Samuel from noticing how they shook. "You were kind to do the family such a favor. It certainly isn't your fault that Karissa forgot to send for the rug before she left like she promised."

"I'm glad you see it that way," Samuel responded, smiling again as he waved his men toward the door. "We'll get out of your way now."

Although John's heart continued to drum frantically against his chest, he tried to appear outwardly calm while he walked with Samuel and his two attendants outside. He waited until the three had climbed back into the wagon and had driven off before turning to his driver, who waited patiently atop John's shiny new Stenhope carriage.

"Get down off there," he shouted abruptly. His breath came in quick, short bursts while he waited for the startled driver to do as told. After what Samuel had told him, he was no longer headed for his office and did not want anyone else to know. "I'll drive myself today."

Hiking his worsted trousers, John clambered up

into the front seat as soon as the driver had vacated it then snatched up the reins and snapped them hard against the horse's back. He was in a hurry to speak with Lizbeth.

Within minutes, he was at his father's house, although to John those minutes felt as if they had taken forever. Without bothering to tether the horse, he climbed out of the carriage and headed straight for the front door.

He waited until he was well inside the house before shouting Lizbeth's name. Although he had never really understood why, he knew the large black housekeeper had always been his sister's closest confidant. If anyone knew where Karissa had gone and why, it would be her.

"Lizbeth!" he shouted a second time, hurrying toward the kitchen, since that was where she spent so much of her time. "Lizbeth, where the hell are you?" It was after eight o'clock. Surely she was back from the food market by now. She had only three mouths to feed these days.

"You calling me?" Lizbeth shouted just seconds before he burst through the kitchen door and found her standing just a few feet away from the back door with a large wooden box in her hands. As usual, she was dressed all in black, including the black turban she'd wrapped around her graying head.

"Yes, I'm calling you," he responded angrily. "Why didn't you answer me."

"Because I didn't hear you until I came inside the house," she said, indicating the door that still stood partially open. "I just now got here."

"Where's Franklin? Didn't he drive you?" he asked, then peered outside to see where that tall, lanky son of here was.

"Yes, but he's not here right now." She looked at him questioningly. "I sent him on to the ice house to get us some more ice. We are about out. I also asked him to drive on down to the docks and see if he could get hold of some fresh fish, so he might not be back for a while. Why do you need him?"

John stepped away from the door, relieved that Franklin was not there to get in his way. That young man could be awfully protective of his mother at times. "I don't need him, I need you. Or rather there's something I need to ask you."

Lizbeth waited until she had set the box of food on the counter then turned to face him. "Just what is it you want to know?"

Aware by the wary expression on her dark face that his impulsive behavior had frightened her, he forced himself to appear outwardly calm. "I need to know where my sister is. I know she's not in Cresson like she led me to believe."

Lizbeth drew her forehead into a puzzled frown. "Why you asking me?"

"Because I happen to know that Karissa tells you everything. If anyone knows where my half-sister is right now, it's you."

"You wrong about that," Lizbeth said, then spun about to start unpacking the produce she had just bought. "Right now, I don't rightly know *where* she is. I haven't heard from her but once since she left here and that was just to let

417

me know she was all right."

"Don't give me that. I can tell by the way you suddenly turned your back that you are lying to me."

Lizbeth's body stiffened but rather than turn to face John again, she continued taking the vegetables out of the box and setting them on the counter to be washed. "I ain't lying to you none, Mister John. Right now I don't know where she is. I don't happens to keep up with every move that child makes."

"But you do know where she's staying," John said, aware he had made the mistake of making it sound as if he was trying to pinpoint her whereabouts at that exact moment.

"No, I don't. She never told me *where* she ended up at," Lizbeth said, scowling to indicate how deeply insulted she was by his accusations while she continued to sort the vegetables.

John was too angry to let her get by with lying to him about something so important. "You impertinent woman, you turn around and look at me when I'm talking to you."

Lizbeth filled her lungs with a slow breath, then turned around to face him squarely. "Okay. I'm looking at you."

"Now I want you to stop all your lying, and tell me what you know," he shouted, forgetting the need to remain calm. He leaned forward, putting his face directly in front of hers so she had no choice but to look into his angry eyes. "Where is Karissa?"

Glowering, Lizbeth pressed her lips together then crossed her arms over her ample bosom as if to signify she had nothing to say.

"I won't take this from you!" John bellowed then in a fit of rage struck her soundly across the face with the back of his hand. "Tell me exactly where my sister is."

Lizbeth never as much as flinched while she continued to glare at the angry man, nor did she bother to try to straighten the turban he'd knocked askew. "I already told you. Missy never did say exactly where it was she was going."

John hissed through his tightly clenched teeth. "Then tell me what she did say to you."

Lizbeth thrust her chin forward defiantly. "No."

John's whole body shook while he tried to regain control of his rage. He refused to let this woman get the better of him. "It doesn't really matter if you tell me or not because it just so happens I already know," he informed her with a tight-lipped sneer. "She's gone to Black Wall to try to find out who killed our father. Even after I told her not to go, she went anyway. All I really wanted from you was to find out where she was staying so I could find her quicker and what she might have found out thus far. *And* to find out exactly what happened here that day Father was shot."

"What do you mean?" Lizbeth asked. Her black eyes grew wide with concern.

John knew he had struck a cord with that question. "What I mean is, who was the woman who came to this house just before Father was shot?"

Lizbeth swallowed hard then dropped her gaze to her hands, still wet from the fresh vegetables she had unpacked. Since she wore no apron, she wiped the excess moisture on her black skirt. "I'm sure I don't know what you are talking about, Mister John."

"And I'm sure you do," he said, then caught her face in a ruthless grip and forced the large black woman to look at him again. His lips tightened into a thin, white line while he squeezed the pulp of her cheeks with all the strength he had. "I'm talking about the woman the city coroner and his men pretended to carry out of here that day on a litter. The one who was shot by the same men who shot my father, but evidently not seriously enough to die. Who was she and where did she go?" He curled his fingers, causing his fingernails to dig into her cheeks. "And don't you dare try to convince me she was never here. I've already had a long talk with Samuel Alexander and he told me everything."

"I-I was never told her name and I have no idea where she went after she left here." Her voice trembled with fear. She winced from the painful hold he had on her face, knowing he would gladly break her jaw if he thought he had to. "All I know is that she was a friend of your father's."

"That's a lie. She was a bar maid of some sort and you know it, John ground out, then slowly squeezed his hand tighter, letting his fingers dig deeper into the bruised area where he had struck her only minutes earlier. "Now stop all this lying and tell me the truth. Who was she and where is she now? It's important. I have to talk to her." He had to know exactly what she did know about his father's murder — whether she had overheard anything that could in anyway implicate him.

Lizbeth was in such pain now she peered at him

420

pleadingly, clearly fearing what he might do next. "I wasn't told who she was or where she went to and that's the truth. Missy, she didn't want me to know. She didn't want none of us to know."

"You are still lying to me!" John shouted, then suddenly let go of her face so he could strike her again, this time on the opposite cheek, using his opposite hand. The force of the blow sent her turban to the floor. "You know damn well who that woman was but won't tell me because you hate me. You have always hated me."

"No, sir, I don't," Lizbeth said, her voice now pleading with him to believe her. She feared enough for her life now that she was willing to say anything. "I ain't never hated you and I wasn't told nothing about who that woman was. All I can say is that she was shot by somebody while she was outside the house then taken out of here shortly after I tended her."

"Liar!" John shouted with savage fury, so angry now his narrowed eyes smoldered with black rage. If he did not get the truth out of Lizbeth, he could lose everything. Lana included. And she was the whole reason he'd decided to have his father murdered. So he could gain control of his father's money and buy her all the things she wanted. How could he know that hurrying his father's death along would not help his situation as he'd thought? How was he possibly supposed to know that Karissa had already wormed her way into controlling everything? Damn that meddling sister.

With veins bulging, he leaned forward again so that

his angry face was barely inches from Lizbeth's. "You know who that woman was! I know you do. You know everything that happens in this house. But you are just too damn stubborn to tell me what I want to know." Curling his hand into a hard fist, he pulled it back and struck her squarely across the jaw. The blow knocked her back against the kitchen cabinets with a hard jolt. "If you value your black life at all, you'll tell me who that woman was and where she went from here. Did she go to Black Wall with Karissa?"

"Please, Mister John, believe me," Lizbeth cried. "I wasn't told what that woman's name was nor where she ended up running off to. Missy wouldn't tell us none of that. It was her way of protecting the woman from more harm."

"Liar!" he shrieked, striking her again each time he spoke the word. "Liar! Liar! Liar!"

"I ain't no liar, Mister John," Lizbeth sobbed, cowering against his repeated blows. With one eye already swollen shut and bleeding, she held up her hands to prevent him from striking that part of her face again. "I wasn't told what you need me to say. Honest, Mister John. I don't know nothing."

"Liar!" Suddenly aware he was getting nowhere by beating Lizbeth senseless, he grabbed his head between his hands and started looking around, as if he hoped to find the answers he sought somewhere within the walls of that kitchen.

"You *know* and you won't tell me," he continued to babble, though without the same rancor as before. "But that's because you don't understand. You don't know how important it is. I *have* to find her. I have to find her before she tells someone else what she knows. Before she reports what she overheard that night. I can't let her do that. I can't let them know I am the one responsible. They will send me to jail. I know they will. Because they won't understand either."

Lizbeth sank to the floor in one large, trembling mass and watched while John continued to rant and rave, all the while holding his head as if that would help him think better.

"No one will understand that I had no choice. I had to do it," he continued, his voice low and breathy. "But they won't understand that. Especially not Karissa." His eyes widened. "Why does that spoiled little brat have to interfere in everything? Doesn't she know what she's done?" He dropped his hands limply at his sides then looked directly at Lizbeth, as if pleading with her to understand. "Doesn't she know that now I have to kill her too? I have no choice. I can't let them put me in jail. I can't be with Lana if I'm in jail. I have to be with Lana."

Aware of the implication, Lizbeth gasped with horror, but said nothing to try to stop him from his rantings. She was too afraid to bring further attention to herself. Too afraid he would start hitting her again.

John's eyes widened as if suddenly comprehending. "Kari already knows everything that woman knows, or else she never would have tried to save her like that. And *that's* why Karissa went to Black Wall. She went there to search for those four men. That's because she doesn't know they really are from here. There's no way for anyone to know that, is there?"

An eerie smile crept across his face, as if the perfect

solution had just occurred to him. "So all I really have to do is go to Black Wall, find Karissa and that woman, then have them both killed." He blinked several times while his awareness deepened. "I'll also need to find out who Porterfield's man is and have him killed him, too. Yes. That would solve everything, wouldn't it? Of course it would."

He cut his eyes from place to place, then focused again on Lizbeth's trembling form. "But I don't have time to try to locate those men again. That would take too long. No. I'll have to take care of this myself."

He took two steps toward the door as if planning to leave then curled his hands into fists, shook them in the air, and started raging anew. "Why couldn't that meddlesome half-sister of mine have married some wealthy fop like she was supposed to? Why did she have to stay here and become interested in the family business? Everything would have worked out fine if she'd just had the good sense to be like other women."

He looked at Lizbeth again, but it was as if he did not really see her. "This is your fault, you know. This is all your fault. You encouraged her to be like she is. If you'd made her behave more the way she was supposed to behave, she'd be married by now and living somewhere else. She'd sure as hell be out of *this* house."

Gnashing his teeth, he charged at Lizbeth again and, because she was still on the floor, started kicking her with a vengeance. "Damn you, tell me who that woman was and if she went to Black Wall with Karissa. I have to know what I'm facing."

Lizbeth screamed with pain when she felt her ribs

424

splinter from the violent impact of his foot; but that yelp of pain only angered him more. It was not until she finally lost consciousness that he stopped his merciless beating.

Still in a crazed furor, aware of the very real danger closing in all around him, John backed away in horror. Panicked further by what he had just done to Lizbeth and deciding to make it look like she had been beaten to death in a robbery, he spun about and started ransacking the house.

Frantically, he grabbed up a laundry sack and started filling it with whatever valuables he could find, all the while muttering to himself that Madison might know if that woman had gone to Black Wall with Karissa, or whether she had gone somewhere else. Even after he'd gone upstairs and started rummaging through the bedroom, he continued to mutter to himself about Madison. Knowing how his father's butler loved to stick his skinny nose into other people's affairs, he realized that was who he should question next. Since Lizbeth didn't know, Madison must. Someone had to know something!

Because Madison liked to visit his cousin, Maxwell, on his days off, he decided to go there just as soon as he was through here. But first, he needed to finish ransacking the house then go back downstairs and make certain Lizbeth was dead. He could not have her telling anyone the truth about what he'd done.

While John was still upstairs tearing the house apart and filling his sack with valuables, Madison returned through the back door after having forgotten his pipe and tobacco. He was just about to call out to

Lizbeth when he spotted her lying on the floor.

"Oh, my heaven," he gasped, and hurried to kneel at her side. Gently he lifted her bloodied head and placed it in his lap. "Lizbeth, what happened?"

When all she did was moan in response; he wiped his bloodied hand on the turban he found lying beside her then patted her swollen cheek. "Lizbeth, wake up." He sucked in a frightened breath and rolled his eyes toward the ceiling when he heard something crash upstairs. "Lizbeth, wake up. Whoever did this is still here. We have to get away."

Frantically, he patted her cheek again. This time she moaned a little louder then slowly opened her one good eye. "Madison," she said, her voice choked with fear. "It's Mister John. He's gone mad. We have to get out of here before he tries to kill us both."

Gritting what was left of her teeth, she rolled over onto her side then tried to get to her feet. But the attempt caused her too much pain and she fell back.

Madison looked toward the ceiling again, aware the sounds had suddenly stopped, then looked again at Lizbeth's bruised and bloodied face, and realized she was right. It would be suicide for them to stay there.

"Lizbeth! Lizbeth, you have to get up!" he told her in a hushed but strident voice while he quickly stood to help her. Bending at the waist and with a strength he did not know he possessed, he slipped his hands up under her arms and pulled the large woman to her feet.

Dizzy from the blows she had taken in the head, she leaned heavily against his small frame and together they headed toward the door Madison had fortunately left open.

Once they were outside, Lizbeth was able to gather just enough strength to climb unassisted into the small carriage Madison had borrowed for his own use that day before she collapsed again in a bloody heap. She bit deep into her swollen lip in an effort to remain conscious.

"We have to warn Missy," she said between short, painful breaths. "Mr. John. He plans to kill her."

"But why?"

"Says she knows too much. I'm not sure about what, but I think it has to do with Mister Caine's murder. I think Mister John had something to do with that."

Madison gasped, his face turning as pale as his hair was white. "But how can we warn her? We don't know where she's gone," he said, already slapping the reins hard against the horse's rump.

Lizbeth grimaced at the pain the sudden lurch of the carriage caused her. "I do. She's gone to Black Wall. She's there using her mother's maiden name. But I don't have no way of getting a message to her. I don't even know where she's staying. You'll have to go there and warn her. Warn her that her brother has lost his mind. Warn her that he intends to kill her and some man working for Mr. Porterfield. Also warn her that he wants to kill the woman who came to warn us about Mister Caine, too."

"I will. Just as soon as I've gotten you to a hospital," Madison vowed. "I'll stop by my cousin's house and borrow enough money from him to get me there. I'd better borrow a change of clothes, too. People

427

might wonder about the bloodstains on this one."

"Just do it right away. The way that man was talking, he knows he done killed one person. He's got nothing to lose by killing himself two or three more."

Chapter Twenty-one

Because Karissa had not gone home right away, preferring instead to lie for hours in Shawn's arms and marvel at her newfound happiness, and because she had also stopped by Frank's room and told him some of the information she had found out, it was well after two o'clock before she finally awoke that Thursday afternoon.

Remembering afresh the glorious event that had kept her occupied so late, she lay snuggled in her bed with the silliest of grins on her face. When she glanced down at the tiny ruby ring on her hand, it was with a whole new perspective. No longer did she oppose having the telltale circle of gold on her finger.

"Mrs. Shawn Madden," she said softly, testing the name that was soon to be hers. "Mrs. Shawn Weston Madden."

Her smile widened when she remembered Shawn's reaction when she had finally admitted she wanted to marry him. He had pulled her into another strong embrace and literally kissed her breath away. It was not until she had caught that breath again and had settled back into the warm crook of his arm that they discussed any details.

Because of the danger they both still faced should their true identities become known before their goals were accomplished, they realized they would not be able to make any real, lasting plans right away. Out of necessity, they would have to wait until Shawn had completed his assignment and she had found out the names of those who had murdered her father first. Even so, they had both agreed on one thing right away. They would not wait the customary year. They would be married just as soon as it was safe to do so. They were too much in love to wait any longer than that.

Meanwhile it was agreed Karissa would continue pretending to be Catherine Sobey the bar maid; and Shawn would continue pretending to be Shawn McCowan a murderer turned coal miner. Only now, instead of working against each other and being suspicious of one another as they had in the past, they intended to work together in getting whatever information they both needed. That way they could attain their separate goals and be married a lot sooner.

Determined not to worry about how long it might take to gather the evidence they needed to accomplish everything they needed to accomplish, Karissa closed her eyes to relive the previous night's events more clearly. How wondrous his words of love had all been. And how resplendent the outcome. She was now engaged to a man she loved very much.

A sudden wave of sadness swept over her when she realized her father would never know the man she had finally agreed to marry nor would Shawn ever have the chance to know what a truly wonderful man her father had been. Not wanting to dwell on such sad thoughts, she quickly blinked back the tears and forced the heart-wrenching thought to one side, then laughed right out loud when she realized what Lizbeth's reaction would be when told about the engagement.

"What you mean you're getting married?" she would say, her dark face drawn into a tight scowl. *"Who is he and what do his family do?"*

Karissa wondered if she should first tell Lizbeth some wild story about him to make her eyes bulge out, then realized that just telling her the truth would surely do that. How many men could claim to be a high-ranking member of the famous Molly Maguires? She laughed again. She could hardly wait to drop that little piece of information on the conservative housekeeper. Lizbeth's eyes would stretch so big after hearing that Shawn was a member of the Maguires, they would probably explode right out of her head.

What a sight that would be.

Since Madison had no baggage to claim, he straightened his brother's jacket just so then headed directly toward the main part of the small mining town at a brisk pace as soon as he had stepped off the

431

train. Having already lost two hours getting Lizbeth admitted into the only hospital in Pittsburgh that accepted Negroes and then waiting for his cousin, who of all days was not home when he first went by, Madison was in such a hurry to find Karissa, he felt panicked.

"Excuse me," he called to three men seated on a long bench in front of the only mercantile in town. There were no other men on the street that particular afternoon. Not wanting to draw unwanted attention to himself, he tried not to look apprehensive when he sauntered over to speak to them. "I was wondering if one of you three gentlemen could help me with something."

"Gentlemen?" the largest of the three said with raised eyebrows. Suddenly they all burst out laughing. "Us?"

Madison frowned. He was not used to being laughed at, especially by the likes of these three. By looking at them, they had to be the town loafers. He arched his shoulders to show that he was not someone to be ridiculed. "Yes, you. My name is Madison Busch and all I ask is that you give me one moment of your time."

"Well, time certainly is something we got to give," the older of the three said, looking up at Madison as if he did not quite believe what he saw. "My name's Frank Miles," he continued, but did not offer his hand. Instead he simply nodded toward his companions. "And these two laggards are friends of mine." He looked at the larger man seated to his right, the one who had thought being called gentlemen was so hilarious, then continued his introductions. "That big one there is Charles McAllister and the skinny one on the other side that smells pretty much like the inside of a horse barn is Sirus Bebber."

"Pleased to meet you," Madison said with a polite nod, trying not to let them know his heart was pounding so hard he could barely concentrate on anything the man said. "Now, if you don't mind. I do have a question I need answered by someone who lives around here."

"A question, is it?" Frank responded with a inquisitive frown then looked at the other two. "I suppose we can handle at least one more question today. But first you have to answer one of ours. That's the rules around here."

Madison tried to remain patient. He did not want to rouse any unusual notice. For Karissa's sake. "If I can."

"Where are you from? It's obvious by that funny-looking suit you got on that you're not from around these parts."

"I'm from Pittsburgh," Madison answered, wondering why his origin should matter to these three. He also wondered what was so funny looking about his brother's suit. Not only was it new, it was cut from quality cloth. Only the best for Maxwell, who worked for the famous Andrew Carnegie.

"What do you know about that? We got us another one from Pittsburgh," Sirus said with a playful wink then reached up to stroke his thick beard thoughtfully.

"And what might *your* question be?"

"I am trying to locate a friend of mine who moved here very recently and was wondering if one of you might know where I can find her. Her name is Catherine Sobey."

The three men looked at each other questioningly. "That little lady sure is popular today, isn't she?" Frank said to the other two before looking back at Madison with a raised eyebrow. "You say you're a friend of hers?"

"Yes, I've known her since she was a child."

Frank studied him a moment longer. "Then your best bet is to try Mrs. Waylan's rooming house, but you probably should wait until a little later. I imagine Catherine's still asleep at this time of day."

"But it's after three o'clock," Madison said, thinking they must have no idea of the time.

Frank nodded that he was aware of the hour then shrugged. "That's the way it is with Catherine. She gets to bed pretty late so she doesn't get up until pretty late. Never in time for lunch. To tell you the truth, it might be better if you waited until five o'clock then caught her on her way to work."

Madison tried not to look surprised. Before now, the only work Karissa had ever taken on was volunteer work at the orphanage. "And where does she work?"

"At the Lucky Choice," Charles supplied, pointing down the street toward his favorite tavern. "She's a bar maid there."

"She's a *what?*"

Frank looked particularly amused by Madison's

434

startled reaction. "She's a bar maid. Didn't she tell you? She's been working at the Lucky Choice for about a month now."

Madison's forehead twisted into a perplexed frown. "Obviously we are not talking about the same woman."

"I think we probably are," Frank supplied, being the only one of the three to know how that news would surely surprise anyone who knew who Catherine really was. He narrowed his gaze while he continued to look closely at Madison. "Do you know that you're the second stranger today to ask us about her? The other man didn't seem to know her name, but had a picture of her that left no doubt whatsoever about who he was looking for."

Madison swallowed hard, but tried not to look too worried. "Was he a tall man with brown hair and brown eyes with sort of a round face?"

"That was him all right. Stopped by here just about an hour ago shoving that picture in front of our faces and demanding to know where she lived and if she had a short, red-haired woman living with her."

"And I suppose you told him the same thing you just told me," Madison surmised, feeling sick inside. That had to have been John. He had gotten there first after all. Damn his cousin for not being home when he'd needed him most.

"Only the part about where she worked and that the only red-haired woman in all of Black Wall was her landlord, the Widow Waylan," Frank admitted with a snort. "We didn't care too much for the way he approached us. Came stalking over here in his expensive clothes and fancy boots like he owned the place. Acted like the three of us had been put here just so we could answer his questions. Because of that, we didn't tell him where she lives. Though I guess he could get that information from just about anyone else around here. This is a very small borough. Most everyone around here knows Catherine. Isn't that right, Charlie."

Charles narrowed his eyes and rubbed his chin as if suddenly deep in thought about something else. "Y' know, I still think that I've seen that other man somewhere before."

"And where would you have met someone like him?" Sirus quickly bantered, unaware how desperate Madison was to ask more questions.

"I've been around," Charles argued, then pursed his lips forward as if he'd been insulted by his friend's remark just moments before he lifted his eyebrows with a new thought. "Shawn sure isn't goin' to like hearin' how all these strangers have suddenly started comin' to Black Wall and askin' around about his woman." He looked at Madison and grinned, thinking his comments were what made the priggish man squirm so. "He'll probably end up shootin' the both of y' clean through, just like he did the last man who tried to come between him and the woman he loved."

Madison pressed his hands together to keep them from shaking. He knew that if John was an hour ahead of him, there was every chance he had already found Karissa. He could be knocking on her door at that very moment. His only hope was that John would not want to kill her there in town where there might be witnesses. He would probably try to convince her to leave with him first. That meant she would have to pack her things before they went anywhere. And if that was true, there might still be time to save her.

But how could he possibly hope to go up against a man like John Caine alone? Especially when John was probably well armed and he was not. What he needed was some help. Someone who would be willing to risk his life to save Karissa from her own demented brother.

"This Shawn fellow you mentioned, where can I find him?" he asked, thinking that if the man was truly in love with Karissa as these three had just implied, he might be willing to help save her.

Frank looked really surprised by that question. "At this time of day, he'd still be down in the mines. Last I heard he was working shaft seventeen."

"And how do I get to this shaft seventeen?"

"Why? You planning on going down there yourself?" Frank asked, clearly skeptical. "Dressed like *that?*"

Madison sighed aloud his impatience. Time was too important to continue conversing with these men. "Let me worry about the suit. You just tell me how to get there."

Frank studied him for a long moment, then finally stood. "I've got nothing better to do. I'll show you the way."

"What business you got with McCowan?" Andrew Philen asked after Madison had politely requested to see the man. Like most pit bosses, Andrew was a big man with big shoulders who enjoyed being rude and intimidating.

"Personal business" is all Madison would say, not about to reveal the truth.

"Important enough he's willing to go down there all by himself dressed like that," Frank put in, thinking to help. He knew that the sooner this little man was on his way down into the mines, the sooner he would be free to slip on over to the rooming house and talk to Karissa. He was eager to find out who the two new strangers were and at the same time let Karissa know there were people out there looking for her—one who had her photograph in his pocket and the other who knew her assumed name.

"And who are you?" Andrew asked Frank, looking at him with a curiously raised brow.

"Just someone trying to help out a stranger," he answered with an apathetic shrug then reached into his shirt pocket. "What if I gave you some money. Would you be more willing to let him go down then?"

"Depends on how much money," the large man responded, watching Frank's hand closely. When it opened to reveal several coins, he smiled and glanced toward the closed door behind him, as if afraid someone might come out of one of the inner offices and catch him. "I guess it won't hurt anything for him to go on down for a few minutes." He snatched up the coins and put them in his own pocket. "But I don't have time to take him. There's someone pretty important in there at the moment so I don't dare leave." He nodded toward that same closed door to indicate where. "Your friend will have to jump on one of the coal cars headed down and find McCowan on his own."

"That's fine with me," Madison said. "All I ask is to be pointed in the right direction."

"I'll show him where the coal cars are," Frank offered, already headed out of the small office.

Minutes later, Frank was on his way back down the path eager to talk with Karissa, and Madison was seated inside an empty coal car headed down toward a large black opening cut in the side of the mountain. On his head he wore an oversized metal hat with a tiny oil lamp attached and in his hand he carried a small square lantern like those he had seen used by the railroad. In his heart he held on to the hope that he would be able to find this Shawn McCowan and convince him to come with him to help save Karissa's life. Before it was too late.

John Caine rubbed his eyes while he studied the stacks of papers that had been handed him. The fact that it had been days since he had had any real sleep had finally started to take its toll. Between the ongoing fear of one day being found guilty of having hired those four men to murder his father, and the haunting memories he carried of his father's smiling face, he had not slept soundly for weeks.

If only he had never been told how well his father had felt that day, then perhaps he would not feel so guilty about having taken away the man's last few months of life. But then he'd really had little choice. He needed the money or else chance that Lana would follow through on her threat to leave him. If only he had known that Karissa was the one being left in charge. He would have seen how futile the murder was and let his father live, at least long enough to convince him to change his will back the way it was. But there was nothing he could do about all that now — except try to keep anyone else from finding out what he'd done.

Which was why he was there in the mine office poring over employee records rather than out on the streets trying to find out exactly where his sister and that red-haired landlady of hers lived. He wanted to get the most dangerous of his three adversaries out of the way before turning on the other two. But with any luck, he might be able to arrange it so he could kill all three of them at the same time — which was how he hoped to work it.

After having found out from his own company storekeeper that the woman in the photograph was using the name *Catherine Sobey,* which he remembered had also been Karissa's mother's maiden name, he had been able to learn a lot about her in a very short time from those willing to take a dollar in exchange for information.

The most interesting fact he had turned up was that she was supposedly engaged to someone named Shawn. But the man he had questioned about that did not know Shawn's last name or where he lived. Only that he was a coal miner and frequented the tavern where Karissa now worked.

Remembering that Porterfield's investigator had come there in November pretending to be a coal miner, and was also considered to be close enough to Karissa to be able to keep a careful watch over her, he decided the man he needed to kill could very well be the fiancée. That was why he had walked up to the Caine offices and asked to see the files on every man who had started to work in any part of the Black Wall operation during that month.

He studied the papers, knowing that if any of the men who had joined on in November had done so using the name *Shawn,* he had him. All he would need to do then would be to look for his address, find out where the house was located, then be waiting for him when the time came for the miners to leave work.

John's eyes lit with a combination of relief and trepidation when in the fourth file he searched, he found the name he sought: *Shawn McCowan.* He glanced farther down the page and discovered that this particular Shawn had not worked in the coal mines before, was originally from New York, and now lived in a small rooming house on Union Street. He also noticed in the lower margin of the page a small handwritten notation stating that this particular Shawn was suspected of being a member of the local

Molly Maguires. It was then that the name *Shawn McCowan* registered in his mind. Shawn was one of the four that Clay Jones had wanted blamed for the murders.

Checking the rest of the files to make sure there was not another Shawn among the twenty or so who had started last November and finding none, he realized he had found his man. His stomach knotted with mounting apprehension while he folded the page and tucked it into his coat pocket. It was already nearly four — he would have to move quickly if he wanted to be there waiting for him when he finished the day's work.

Madison waited until the empty coal car rumbled to a sudden stop near a small group of men deep inside the mountain before he attempted to stand again.

"What have we here?" one of the miners asked, clearly surprised to find human cargo inside the car.

Madison wasted no time on introductions as he swung his legs over the side closest to the men. "Where can I find Shawn McCowan?"

"McCowan? He's down that cavern there," one of the men responded. He pointed toward the middle of three large openings.

Madison headed immediately in the direction indicated. He sloshed through water and mud six inches deep while the yellow wooden supports creaked ominously overhead. Unable to breathe without coughing spasmodically, he placed his handkerchief over his face to help keep the black dust out of his mouth while he hurried along.

When he reached the end of the small shaft and found four tall, muscular men hard at work with pick and shovels, he called out Shawn's name. He was pleased when the strongest-looking of the four turned around and pulled off his safety goggles, revealing two of the palest blue eyes Madison had ever seen set in a face covered with black soot.

"Are you Shawn McCowan, the man who is in love with Catherine Sobey?" he asked, wanting to be sure he had the right man before saying anything more.

Shawn tilted his head at an angle and lowered one eyebrow while he studied the strange little man before him. "I am."

"Good. I'd like to have a word with you. It's terribly important." He then met the annoyed expressions of the other men with a obstinate lift of his chin. "Your pit boss said it was all right for me to talk with you."

Shawn glanced back at the others, who had all three paused in their labor to find out what the little man wanted. "I'll be just a wee minute."

Madison waited until the tall man covered in a thick layer of sweat and black coal had stepped closer before saying what it was he had come to say. When he did speak again, it was in tones low enough only the man in question could hear.

As soon as Shawn had heard that Karissa was in danger, he dropped the pick he carried into the mud at his feet and headed immediately in the direction Madison had just come. He did not answer to the calls of his co-workers, who wanted to know where he was going.

"Wait for me," Madison called after him then hurried to keep up with the taller man's longer strides. "You need to know exactly what we are up against before you do anything."

"You already told me what I'm up against," he said as he tugged off his heavy leather work gloves and tucked them into his belt. "You said that Catherine was in danger. That her brother is here in Black Wall and wants to kill her. That's enough for me."

He already understood just how much danger Karissa was in because, just by having been told that her own brother wanted her dead, everything else had suddenly fallen into place. John was the one who had hired those four assassins from Pittsburgh. It was possible he had wanted his father dead so he could claim an early inheritance, or perhaps the man had cut him off financially. And then obviously during the past few days, he had found out that Karissa was in Black Wall attempting to uncover the very information that could eventually send him to the gallows and had decided to stop her from causing any further trouble.

Shawn scowled when he realized how John must have discovered where Karissa was. Richard Porterfield had to have told him. No one else, other than one of Karissa's housekeepers who she claimed could be trusted implicitly, knew where she had gone.

Doing all he could to keep up, Madison waited until they had both climbed on top of a loaded coal car and were headed toward the mountain's surface before giving his new friend the rest of the details as he knew them, including the fact that Catherine Sobey was not Karissa's real name.

"I already know all about that," Shawn said, staring at the tiny hole of daylight ahead, wishing that large metal chain pulling that particular coal car would do the job at a much faster pace.

When the car finally did burst out into the open and started rolling immediately toward the breaker house, where the large chunks of coal would be crushed into a more manageable size and any slate removed, it took Shawn a few seconds for his eyes to readjust to the sunlight. As soon as they had, he shouted for Madison to jump before he ended up being tossed into the breaker bin. About the time they both hit the ground rolling, the burly pit boss came running out of the main office shouting and waving his arms wildly.

"McCowan, what the hell do you think you're doing? It's only four o'clock. It's not time to quit yet."

Shawn pretended not to hear him. Instead he tossed his helmet onto the ground and started immediately down the mountainside toward Black Wall.

"McCowan, get back here right now or I'll dock you a whole week's pay."

"Then dock me," he shouted back.

After tugging out of his own helmet, Madison continued trying to keep up with the taller man, who was obviously used to the rough terrain. "Where are you going?" he asked, when it became apparent he was not headed toward the rooming house Frank Miles had pointed out during their walk up there. Instead, he was headed toward a whole different part of town.

"To get my gun," Shawn answered simply. "I'm not about to face that deranged brother of hers empty-handed. Not after hearing that he is capable of beating a woman senseless." It did not dawn on Shawn that he had failed to use his Irish accent while he continued to explain, "And if you plan to continue following me everywhere I go, you'll need a gun of some sort, too." He glanced over at his shoulder at the tiny man, who tried his best to keep up. "Can you shoot?"

"Of course I can," Madison lied, afraid he would be told to stay behind if he answered truthfully. He had come too far to be put out of it now.

"That's what the rumor is," Kelly told Karissa while she sat across the table, watching her eat. "I've heard it twice now. John Caine has hired himself a whole trainload of Orientals to come in here and work for half of what he is now paying the rest of them. And according to Charlie, that means only one thing. He plans to cut everyone else's wages yet a third time."

Karissa paused with her fork halfway to her mouth and tried not to show just how angry that made her. "Well, you tell Charlie he worries too much. Tell him that I have a feeling those Orientals will end up being paid the same wage as everyone else if and when they get here. In fact, I have a feeling that everyone working in the Caine mines are due for a substantial raise

446

very soon."

"Dream on, lassie," Kelly said with a short sigh and a quick shake of her head. "It'll never happen. I hear John Caine is even worse than his father. I hear he—" She cut short whatever else she had to say when she heard someone approaching hurriedly down the main hall toward the kitchen, where Karissa had come to eat her late meal so she would not have to be all alone in the dining room.

"Who's there?" Kelly asked, already reaching up to push stray strands of red hair into place. "Is that you, Charlie?"

"No, it's Frank," came the response though he was still halfway down the hall. "Is Catherine here?"

"Aye, she's seated right here eating me out of house and store," she said, then waited for Frank to appear in the doorway.

Frank paused for only a moment before nodding politely. "Do you mind if I have a word alone with Catherine before she heads back upstairs and starts getting ready for work?"

Kelly looked surprised by the request, but immediately stood and headed toward the back door. "No, I don't mind. Truth is, I need to be bringing in my laundry anyway. Those clothes have probably been ready for hours now."

Frank waited until Kelly was well away from the house before telling Karissa about the two men in town.

Karissa grimaced when she recognized the description of John then looked puzzled when Frank next de-

447

scribed Madison. "I can pretty well guess why John is here, especially knowing how he wanted me to let the police handle everything; but I wonder what made Madison come all this way?"

"He's probably hoping to do the same thing your brother came here to do," Frank suggested. "He probably wants to convince you to go on back home."

"But I can't. Not when I'm finally getting so close to finding out who killed father."

Frank looked at her with an arched eyebrow as if not quite certain what to think. "Yes, and I'd still like to know how last night you managed to trick McCowan into telling you so much of what he knows."

"I have my ways." Karissa smiled but refused to reveal her secret even to Frank for she had promised to tell *no one* who Shawn really was. "It's just a good thing the Maguires have started their own investigation in hopes of clearing their own members," she said, remembering the excuse she had given Frank for knowing that the four men who had killed her father were actually hired assassins from Pittsburgh.

"You're just lucky McCowan was feeling so talkative," Frank put in with a begrudging smile. "Even so, it might not be a bad idea for you to pack your things and go on back with either your brother or the butler. Especially when you realize how close they've come to finding out where you are. All we need is for one of them to see that you really are Karissa Caine then convince someone else of that and you won't be of any use here anyway. No one will trust you after that."

"Then I'll just have to make sure neither of them tells anyone," she said with a determined lift of her chin. "Madison won't be any problem. That sweet man wouldn't do anything that would hurt me. But I can't say the same of John." Her forehead creased while she realized just how little she did trust her half-brother. "Do me a favor. Find my brother and tell him I know he's here and that I want to have a talk with him in private. Tell him not to come to where I work, but instead to meet me inside the Caine offices shortly after midnight — alone."

"Do you really think you can convince him to let you stay?"

When she saw how truly concerned Frank was, she offered a wily grin. "Yes, I do. After I tell him how very close we are to finding out the truth, he should be more than willing to let me stay. *Especially* if I remind him that as long as I am here gathering all this information, he doesn't have to worry about me being there wanting to take over my duties as the new administrator of Caine Enterprises."

Chapter Twenty-two

Because Shawn did not want to be seen by anyone on the streets, knowing they would want to know why he was not in the mines, he skirted the main part of town and came up on his rooming house from the back. Hopping the fence with ease, he did not consider the fact that Madison would have to go around to the nearest gate while he headed immediately for the side door that led into his room.

He was too upset by what Karissa's butler had told him to pay close attention to his surroundings and did not note that one of the windows he'd closed just before he left for work that morning was now open. He did not notice anything amiss even after he unlocked the door and headed across the room to the small chest of drawers where he kept both his pistols.

Despite the deepening shadows of late afternoon, Shawn did not stop to light a candle to help him see. Instead, he depended on the light from the open door when he yanked open the drawer and reached inside to pull out both pistols. He frowned when his hand did not come into contact with either one.

"Looking for these?" he heard from inside the

room, and spun around in time to see a hatless man dressed in a dark blue business suit emerge from the corner behind the door. There was just enough light coming through the doorway to allow him to see that the intruder held one of his pistols in each hand. He also held all three boxes of Shawn's ammunition under his arm.

"Who are you?" Shawn asked, not wanting to let on that he already knew, then glanced outside to see if Karissa's butler had heard the voices and understood he should not come inside.

"My name is not important," John responded, then aware of Shawn's interest in the open door, stepped over and closed it. "What is important is that I already know your name. I am also aware you work for Richard Porterfield." He decided not to mention that he knew about his association with the Molly Maguires because he wasn't quite sure how he could use that to his advantage just yet. "You're the private investigator he hired from New York."

"And where would ya be gettin' a ridiculous idea like that?" Shawn asked, knowing a denial was expected of him.

"From Porterfield himself," he responded then sneered. "I guess you could say he's the one who sent me here."

"To steal my pistols?" He tried to look as if truly perplexed by what had happened—yet not frightened. He knew better than to show any fear to a man like John Caine.

"No, to stop you from continuing with your investigation."

451

Shawn tilted his head, his mind already racing, looking for possible ways to outsmart him. "Then why didn't he come himself? He knows what to do to get in touch with me."

"Because *I'm* the one who wants the investigation stopped, not him," John stated as a matter of fact. A sinister smile stretched his mouth when he then pointed the larger of the two pistols he held directly at Shawn's head. "And I have one sure way to make certain it is. But that's only if you don't cooperate."

"Cooperate? How?"

"First by sending a note to Karissa telling her that you need to see her about something very important. Tell her to be sure and bring her landlady with her."

Shawn looked at him questioningly, unable to figure out why he would want Kelly Waylan there. The woman was certainly not a part of their operation.

"Who is this Karissa?" he asked in an attempt to stall for time, hoping that Madison had enough sense to figure out what had happened and go for help. It was his only chance to come away from this alive.

His gut then clenched into a hard, painful knot when he considered the possibility that the little man might not go for help at all. He might decide the fiancée was expendable and head off to warn Karissa instead. *Or worse,* decide to try to save him without going for help first. A fainthearted little man like Madison wouldn't have a chance against someone as cruel and as determined as John Caine. "Do I know her?"

"Don't give me that innocent routine," John

snapped. His dark eyes glimmered with anger—eyes the same color as Karissa's. "I am already aware that you know who she really is because you told Porterfield that you would keep a close eye on her while she was here. Therefore, cut the performance and do what I tell you. Find some paper and a pencil. I want you to write that note telling her and her landlady to meet you over here just as soon as they possibly can."

"Why?"

"Because *I* want them here with us and because I am in a big hurry. And because if you don't, I'll shoot you right where you stand."

Shawn doubted that. A gunshot would be heard for blocks. He wouldn't risk taking a shot at him unless it became his last resort. "And if I do write the note?"

"Then maybe I'll be so grateful to you for having cooperated that I'll let you live to see another day."

Shawn knew that wasn't true either. What John wanted to do was kill as many birds with one stone as he possibly could by getting them all to perch on the same limb. If only he could figure out why Kelly Waylan was to be one of those poor birds.

"What do you want me to say in that note?" he asked, having dropped the Irish accent as a show of faith. He would pretend to go along with John until he could figure out the best way to gain the upper hand. But he would not let the man actually send a note to her. He would not allow John Caine to lure Karissa to her own death. He would do whatever was necessary to stop him, even if it meant taking a bullet himself.

* * *

When Madison discovered that the three men he had talked with earlier were now gone and that no one else was outside at that time of day, he ran as hard as his mud-caked shoes would let him toward the rooming house Frank Miles had pointed out to him earlier. He had to find Karissa and tell her what had happened. He had to warn her she would be next.

"Karissa!" he shouted when at last he had the large, white frame house in sight and noticed that she had just come through the front door and was headed toward the main gate. Relieved to have finally found her, he continued toward her as fast and as hard as he could run. "Karissa. Over here."

Karissa looked at him with a meaningful frown then glanced back at the house to see if Kelly was where she might have heard the name.

"Sir, I'm afraid you've made a mistake," she responded in a loud voice, more for Kelly's sake than Madison's. She came to an abrupt halt. "My name is Catherine Sobey."

"We don't have time for that right now," he insisted just before he shot through the gate and closed the final distance between them. Aware she was concerned about being overheard, he lowered his voice accordingly as he tugged at her arm to start her walking again in the direction of the gate. "Your brother—has come to Black Wall—with plans to kill you—and that private investigator who works for Richard Porterfield," he said, getting as many words out as possible between breaths. "It looks like he also—wants to kill your landlady, too, although I have no idea why—and

I didn't want to stay long enough to find out."

Karissa's forehead notched, not quite sure she had heard him right. She was as baffled to learn that Madison seemed to know all about Shawn as she was to hear that he thought John had come there to hurt her. "I don't understand. You didn't want to stay where long enough to find out what? And why would my brother want to kill anyone?"

"I don't know the reason he wants to do away with the landlady—but according to Lizbeth, he intends to murder you and Shawn McCowan because you are both too close to finding out the truth about who murdered your father." Slowly he had caught his breath and spoke more clearly. "He's determined that doesn't happen."

Karissa's face paled at the implication and she temporarily slowed her pace, "Why? Who *did* kill him?"

"According to Lizbeth, John is responsible for the whole thing," Madison told her, then looked at her imploringly while he continued to pull her hurriedly down the street. "But we don't have time to discuss any of that right now. We have to do something to help Mr. McCowan. And we have to do it now."

Karissa's body felt as if it had suddenly been impaled on sharp spikes. The danger had come on too suddenly to comprehend it fully yet. "Why, what's happened to Shawn?"

"Your brother has him. He was there in Mr. McCowan's room waiting for him when he went in to get his pistol just a few minutes ago."

"His pistol? But why would Shawn want his pistol?

455

And what were you doing there?"

"I'll explain all that later. Right now we have to find someone who can help us. When I left, your brother was holding two guns on Mr. McCowan and making him write some sort of note that was supposed to convince you and your landlady to come over there. Once that note is written, your brother might not have any further use for him. Could be he'll kill him right then rather than wait for you. Does this town have a sheriff or a constable of some sort?"

"Not one who would help us," Karissa muttered. She knew the authorities were all still angry with Shawn for the way he had treated those four state deputies several weeks ago.

"Then we have to find someone else to help us, or your Mr. McCowan soon will be a dead man."

Shawn made a long, drawn-out production out of first washing his hands then his face after John had told him to get rid of some of the coal dirt. He did not want him dotting the letter with black smudges that would let her know that he had actually been at work most of the day instead of home sick as the letter was to suggest. But he also did not like how much time Shawn took removing that dirt.

"Hurry up. I don't have all day to stand here and watch you bathe."

"I am hurrying," Shawn said, but continued to move slowly while lighting a lamp and finding a suitable sheet of clean paper. Finally, after gathering up everything he thought he'd need, he sat down at the table to write. After scribbling only a few words, he paused with a deep frown as if trying to come up with just the right wording when what he wanted was to stall for yet more time.

"What reason should I give for getting her to come over here?" he asked when he glanced back at John, who stood watching him at a distance with the larger of the two pistols still pointed at his head. "It's not going to be easy to convince her to come to come over here. Not to my bedroom. She's not that type of woman."

"I already told you," John responded with an angry scowl. "Tell her you are sick and need her to come here to nurse you back to health. I know Kari. She'd jump at something like that." His eyes widened when he realized the full potential of that idea. "And because she is so proper when it comes to being alone with a man, suggest that she bring her landlady with her as a chaperon."

"I really don't understand that part. Why are you so determined to get Kelly Waylan over here?"

"Because of what she did," John answered evasively. "And because of what she knows."

Shawn pursed his mouth while he wondered what Kelly Waylan could possibly have done to anger this man. Was there some deep dark secret about the woman he did not know? "But if I tell Karissa I'm sick, that means I can't be the one to deliver the note. How do you plan to get this to her?"

"You let me worry about how I get it to her," John answered with a determined thrust of his chin. "You just do what you're told."

Shawn shrugged his wide shoulders as if it really

didn't matter to him one way or the other. He then bent forward over the table and quietly crafted the letter John wanted written. After several minutes he sat back and looked down at the page as if extremely pleased with what he had written.

"Come read what I have here, see if it meets with your approval," he said, still glancing down at the paper. He held his breath while he waited to see if John would be foolish enough to comply. He knew that John would have to set one of the guns down to be able to take the paper and read it. It was then, while John held only the one gun and his attention was on the letter, that Shawn planned to tackle the man and wrestle the remaining gun out of his hand.

"You certainly are being cooperative," John said after he took several cautious steps toward Shawn. "Why is that?"

"Because I have every reason to want to live," he answered, keeping his gaze on the paper so as not to alert John of any danger. He listened carefully to the sound of John's boots grinding against the unswept floor while he continued to hold the letter up off the table, as if waiting to hand it to him. "At the moment I have over a quarter of a million in the bank from the money Porterfield paid me up front, and I happen to have very definite plans about how I want to spend it. Problem with having such plans is knowing that dead men can't spend money."

"How true," John said with a soft chuckle, and took a few more steps in Shawn's direction. "Oddly enough, I reached that same conclusion not too very long ago. Dead men *can't* spend money. Nor can men who have been slapped in jail for the rest of their lives."

Knowing John stood right behind him, Shawn's heart raced riotously while he waited for John to reach over his shoulder and take the letter from him. Though he tried to look unconcerned, his body remained tense, ready for action. "Is that where you're headed if you don't find a way to get rid of this Karissa Caine and her landlady? To jail?"

The last thing Shawn remembered after having asked that question was the splintering crack of something hard slamming into the back of his skull. Flashes of white and blue light clouded his vision just seconds before everything suddenly went black.

By the time John had stepped out onto the street again, he knew exactly what he planned to do and laughed out loud at the simplicity of it all. Not only would he soon be rid of that investigator, his meddlesome half-sister, *and* the woman who had overheard what the men he'd hired had to say the night before the murders, he would be able to put the blame of all three deaths on the local Molly Maguires in the process.

All he had to do was convince Karissa and the short, red-haired woman to go with him to Shawn's house without letting any of the locals see him, then promptly pull out the knife he carried and murder them both.

After that, he would certainly not need Shawn McCowan again, and could then finish him, too. And to make it look as if the local Molly Maguires were the ones who killed them, all he had to do was toss Shawn's personnel file down beside his body after first adding the simple notation that he was a private investigator hired by Richard Porterfield to break up the Molly Maguires.

To an outsider, it would appear that a member of the group had somehow gotten his hands on the private file and in doing so had discovered that Shawn was a traitor to their cause. Everyone knew what happened to anyone caught double-crossing the Molly Maguires. But to make absolutely sure the desired conclusion was reached, he planned to write word *traitor* on the floor in Shawn's own blood.

Now if that didn't sound like something the Maguires would do, nothing did.

Again, John cackled with glee. How perfect the plan was. And how clever he was to have thought of it.

Because Karissa had no idea where Frank might have gone and knowing that most of the other men in town were still down inside the mines at that time of day, she set her lantern aside and headed directly for the Lucky Choice with Madison following closely at her heels.

"Marcus is the only one I know in town right now who might be willing to help," she explained while they hurried toward the empty tavern. She held her handbag tight in her hands so she would not risk losing it in her haste. "And he's the only one I know with any kind of a gun."

Madison did not question her decision. As rapidly as they walked, he would not have had the breath to question her even if he'd wanted to. He was not used to so much exertion.

Not caring who saw her ankles or the fact that she wore two different stockings with her boots, Karissa held her skirts high enough to be out of her way while she continued along at a brisk pace. Although she realized Madison was gradually falling behind, She did not slow her steps and ended up entering the tavern several dozen yards ahead of him.

"Marcus, Shawn's in trouble," she said with surprising calm only seconds after she had scanned the room to make sure no one was there to overhear what she had to say. She knew it was quite possible her brother had brought more Pinkerton men with him — only this time she would have no way to know who they were. It was definitely a time to be cautious of all strangers.

"What kind of trouble?" Marcus asked, already setting aside the tray of clean glasses he held.

"Serious trouble. There's a man in his bedroom holding a gun on him who I think plans to kill him."

"A man with a gun?" Marcus repeated, already bending to get his shotgun from behind the bar. "Do you know who he is?"

Rather than risk Marcus asking a lot of needless questions when there was no time for any answers, she lied. "No I don't. But I do know whoever he is, he's serious about wanting to kill Shawn."

Marcus did not wait for any further details. He checked to make sure the shotgun was loaded then headed toward the door, surprised when he came face to face with a tiny, gasping man dressed in a pin-striped suit and mud-caked shoes.

Karissa did not waste time on introductions. All she said to Madison was, "Marcus has agreed to help."

Marcus glanced down at the man curiously, but said nothing while he followed Karissa out the door. Nor did he take the time to lock his tavern or even remove his apron.

Running as a group, the three raced down a nearby sidestreet so they would come up on the house from the back. They paused behind a large clump of bushes a half-block away to devise their plan.

Because Karissa knew John would recognize Madison right away and wonder why he was in Black Wall, she ordered him to stay well out of sight while she went to the door to try to draw his attention.

"But you can't just go up to the door like that," Madison argued while keeping his voice low. "He'll shoot you on the spot."

Karissa pushed her hair back out of her eyes. Because it had turned out to be such a windy day, part of it had come lose and billowed in her face. "No, he won't shoot me out in the open like that. He knows someone on the street might see him do it. And by my walking straight up to the door like that, Marcus will have a better opportunity to slip up to the back window without being noticed. Besides, I'll be armed." She patted her handbag. "I have Father's derringer with me and I'll already be holding it in my hand behind my back when I go to the door."

"What do you want me to do after I get to that window?" Marcus asked, eager to hear the rest of her plan.

"Since it is all one room, you should be able to see the side door through that window. Wait until you feel certain I have his attention, then break the window and try to take him by surprise. Fire once into the ceiling to let him know how serious the danger. Knowing John, he'll drop his weapon immediately rather than risk getting shot."

"John?" Marcus asked with sudden caution. "I thought you said you didn't know this man."

"I lied, but that's because I don't have time to explain everything to you right now. We have to hurry and save Shawn."

"If that's what you plan to do, you have even less time than you think," came a surprising response from several dozen yards away.

All three turned to see who had spoken and Karissa gasped with immediate fear when she saw John standing behind them with Shawn's pistol already pointed at her. She looked around to see who else might be witness to the fact that this man held a gun on them and felt a tight knot of dread to see that the streets were still empty. There was still half an hour or more before the mines would let out.

"Who's that?" Marcus asked her, frowning when he saw that someone had the drop on them.

"That's the man who was holding Shawn hostage," she answered in an emotionally choked voice. Her heart twisted when she realized why John would be outside rather than inside watching over Shawn. Obviously Shawn did not offer any further threat.

"But what's he doing out here?" Marcus wanted to know. "Where's Shawn?"

John's mouth stretched into a chilling sneer. "That's a very good question. Why don't we all go inside and find out?" He then motioned toward Marcus with a slight wave of his free hand. "But first, unload that shotgun and toss it over here."

Marcus wasted no time complying with that demand. He knew how dangerous it could be to refuse an armed man, especially one who already had his weapon drawn.

"Good," John said with a delighted nod when Marcus had tossed the empty shotgun to within only a few feet of him. He knelt to pick up the weapon then pitched it up on the roof of a nearby building. "Now keep your hands out in clear view while we go see whatever became of Shawn McCowan."

Chapter Twenty-three

Rather than risk angering her half-brother more, Karissa decided to do exactly as told. She held the handbag out so John could see it and her hands while she preceded Marcus and Madison down the street and across the yard, toward the door she knew led directly into the bedroom. She wanted to wait until she had actually seen Shawn before attempting to do anything else to try to stop her brother from his deranged quest. She had to know if Shawn was still alive.

Steeling herself for what she was about to see, she stepped into the room ahead of the others and quickly searched the area for a glimpse of Shawn. Her heart ached with disappointment when she saw that he was not even there. John had lied to them. They were not to know Shawn's fate.

Originally Karissa had planned to make a grab for her derringer just as soon as she had stepped well inside the room, but not about to harm John until she knew exactly where he'd taken Shawn, she instead turned and waited for him to follow Marcus and Madison inside. It was then, while John was carefully closing the door behind him so no one could see inside, that she spotted a small puddle of blood on the floor near the table. There were several more droplets a few feet away. Her heart wrenched with renewed fear when she realized it had to be Shawn's blood.

"Where is he?" she demanded, needing more than ever to see that Shawn was still alive. She glared angrily at her brother while waiting for him to answer, already moving her handbag to where she could get to her father's derringer easier. "What have you done with Shawn?"

John's face drew into an immediate frown then paled as he, too, quickly scanned the room.

"He was right here," he said, indicating the area of the floor near the table then cut his gaze to first the window, which he'd been foolish enough to leave open, then the door. Panic filled his voice. "He was right here. He was still unconscious and bound with plenty of rope when I left not ten minutes ago." His face twisted with bewilderment.

"Well, he's not here now," Madison felt brave enough to point out, obviously aware John was too panicked to harm anyone just now. "Looks like he escaped. Probably gone to tell the authorities all about you."

"As hard as I hit him? He won't get far," John said with a determined shake of his head, as if trying to reassure himself it was true.

Hoping Madison was right, that Shawn had escaped with his life, Karissa glanced again in the direction of the blood droplets, curious to see if they led to the open window. Her heart leapt immediately to fill her throat when instead she spotted Shawn lying under the bed, part of his hair and face wet with blood, working frantically to untie himself.

Aware how easily seen he was from that side of the unmade bed, and fearing that John would notice the droplets of blood leading directly to him, Karissa purposely stepped forward and put her boot in Shawn's still wet blood then started tramping about the room, waving her arms and handbag wildly, eager to draw her brother's attention away from the bed.

"John, tell me what you did with Shawn!" she shouted, making sure she tromped the blood in several directions so there would be no definable trail. "I have to know what you did with him!"

John looked at her with angry confusion, his eyes round with disbelief while he kept Shawn's pistol pointed toward his sister, knowing the two men would not do anything that might cause him to shoot her. "I don't know what I did with him!" he shouted back at her. "He was right here a few minutes ago. He must have come to while I was out looking for you and untied himself." He glanced at the door fearfully, his whole body trembling. "He could be anywhere."

"That doesn't help me," Karissa said, and continued to march about the room flailing her arms and the handbag, aware how successfully those movements had distracted John. "I want to know where he went."

Finally John became so flustered by her erratic actions, he cocked the hammer back on the pistol and shouted angrily, "Sit down! I have to be able to think."

Aware she had pushed him nearly to the edge, and that she would be of little help to Shawn dead, Karissa did as told. She sat down in the very same chair Shawn had used earlier.

"John, you should have done your thinking a long time ago," she said while trying not to show any of the very real fear that gripped her. Although she did not like the thought of enraging John more, not while he still had that hammer cocked, she had to know the truth. She had to know if Lizbeth was right. "You should have done all your thinking *before* you had Father killed."

"So you *do* know!" John nodded that he had expected as much. "And here you are, already judging me for what I did. You are not even taking into consideration that our father was already a dying man or the fact that he was in extreme pain more days than not."

"Is that why you killed him? To put him out of his misery?" she asked, though doubtful. John was not that noble.

"No, I killed him because I had to." He looked at Karissa as if pleading with her to understand. "Lana was going to leave me if I didn't."

Karissa stared at him a moment, wondering if he was serious or if he had finally gone over the edge and started talking nonsense. "Lana wanted you to kill Father? But why?"

"It's not that she wanted me to kill him. What she wanted was for me to hurry up and finish that house so she could move in and start entertaining her friends. But don't you see? I couldn't do that. I was out of money. I'd already spent every penny I had."

Karissa felt her skin crawl at the realization of what John had done. "You had Father murdered so you could collect your inheritance?"

"I had to have the money," John repeated then scowled darkly. "It was important."

Karissa was too shocked by that revelation to say anything more. She fell into stunned silence, her arms limp at her sides, her handbag dangling from her wrist.

"But everything went wrong after that," John continued, thinking she should know just how badly she had ruined his life before she died. "It turned out Father had not left me in charge of everything after all. He'd left *you* in charge. Suddenly, I had no way of getting the money I needed at all. Not with you refusing to let me sell anything."

"So that's why you want to kill me?" she asked, trying to make sense of his continued rantings. "To finally get your hands on Father's money?"

"No. I have to kill you because you know too much," he stated matter-of-factly, then turned to look at Marcus and Madison, who stood side by side staring at the gun in his hand as if fearing it had a life of its own. The hammer was still cocked and his finger lay right up against the trigger. "And now that these two dolts know what happened, I'll have to kill them too. Then I'll have to find out where that meddling detective went and kill him, too. If he's not already dead by now. And then I'll have to find your landlady. I have to kill her too." He talked as if making an ordinary list of things to do then shook his head as if annoyed to have to go to that much trouble. "Then I have to go back to Pittsburgh and make sure Lizbeth is dead."

Aware John had gone beyond all reasoning, Karissa pulled her handbag into her lap, and while John continued to keep his unblinking gaze on Marcus and Madison, she started carefully loosening the ties. As long as John continued facing the other two, who both stood against an empty wall, she had a very good chance of getting that gun out.

Marcus saw what she was doing and, realizing she must have that little derringer with her, stepped forward to make sure John continued looking toward them instead of glancing over at her.

"You don't have the guts to shoot us," he said in a taunting voice then took another step toward him. He glanced at Karissa and saw that she had the handbag open and was ready to reach inside. "You'd have already shot us if you did."

John's eyes stretched to their limits as he turned the gun on Marcus instead. "Get back where you were. Get back or I'll shoot a hole through you right now."

"You don't have the nerve."

Whether John intended to shoot Marcus or not, suddenly the gun fired and a bullet tore through Marcus's right shoulder, throwing him backward.

Karissa screamed in response to the unexpected gunfire and, after only a moment's hesitation, frantically felt inside the handbag for the tiny pistol. By the time her fingers finally closed around the ivory handle, it was too late. John had spun around to face her again. His pistol pointed directly at her heart.

"What do you think you are doing?" he shouted, staring pointedly at the hand now hidden from his view. "What's in that handbag?"

"Nothing," she answered, then swallowed hard, aware he was about to take their only hope of getting out of this away from her. "Just the usual things."

John continued to aim the pistol at her while holding out his other hand. "Give it here. I want to see for myself."

Karissa stared at him, wondering if she dared risk pulling the derringer out when suddenly Shawn rolled out from under the bed, making enough noise to wake the dead. Clearly, he wanted to draw John's attention away from her.

Reacting instantly, she yanked the derringer out of the handbag and pointed it at John just as he fired haphazardly toward Shawn. Realizing he had missed that time but might not the next, she pointed the gun at John's chest, closed her eyes, and squeezed the trigger.

When she reopened them, John had straightened back around, looking as if he did not believe what she had just done while he aimed his pistol again at her. Aware by the murderous gleam in his eye, he meant to kill her, she fired again. This time John fell to the floor, jerked twice, and did not move again.

Still unraveling the rope that had held his wrists together behind his back, Shawn hurried to take her into his arms while Madison knelt to examine Marcus's shoulder wound.

"I thought I was about to lose you," Shawn said, pulling her out of the chair and into his arms then kissing her face repeatedly. Tears of relief streamed down his face. "I don't know what I would have done if he'd killed you."

So emotionally wrought over what had just happened, Karissa leaned against him and started shaking uncontrollably. "Someone had better go get the police. I've just murdered my own brother."

Shawn looked at Madison, who understood and went immediately to find help. They were all surprised when Joseph Rourke was among the first to arrive. Never would they have guessed him to be a state investigator trying to find out what had really happened to Lawrence Caine. He admitted that the only reason he had tried so hard to get close to Karissa was because she was so close to Shawn. When he'd failed to do that, rather than risk getting killed by a man he had truly suspected of being guilty, he'd simply turned his investigation in a new direction.

By the time the rest of the state and local police had arrived and carried John's body away—and Marcus had been placed in a wagon headed for the nearest doctor, which was twelve miles away—Karissa had had time to calm down and think through what had happened.

Now that she had explained John's death to the authorities and had heard everything Madison had to tell them about what had happened earlier in Pittsburgh, she felt better about what she had done. Had she not killed John, he really would have killed them all. He had gone past the point of realizing that he would never have been able to get away with committing that many murders, especially with Lizbeth hidden away in a hospital under an assumed name, still very much alive and able to testify against him.

Sadly, Karissa waited until everyone had left and she was alone again with Shawn inside his bedroom before turning to him for further comfort. Because she needed to feel his gentle warmth surrounding her, she went immediately into his arms and stood there with her cheek pressed against his chest, listening to the gentle pounding of his heart for several long seconds before saying anything. "You know what is really sad about all this?"

Shawn could name any number of things, but decided to let her be the one to talk. "No, what?"

"My brother did all those terrible things—not only had my father killed but then came after every one of us—all because he was in love with such a cold, selfish woman."

Shawn closed his eyes while he continued to hold her, relishing the fact that she was still there to hold. "Men have been known to do some pretty strange things while under the influence of love." He pulled away just far enough to be able to gaze down into her beautiful, sad brown eyes. "Some have even been known to give up everything they ever worked toward just to please the woman they love."

Karissa bit her lip and looked away. "I'm sorry your investigation is ruined."

"I'm not. To tell you the truth, after seeing what those miners are really up against, I had started to feel largely unjustified in what I was doing. Though I don't agree with some of the tactics a few of the Maguires use, I do understand why they are so angry. This is not a case of lazy, worthless men wanting more than they deserve like I had been led to believe. After having been down in those mines and having worked alongside them, I know how hard they work and truly believe those men are being flagrantly mistreated." He shook his head. "If Porterfield wants their membership exposed and the group disbanded, he'll have to hire someone else to do the job. I'm washing my hands of the whole ordeal. I can't see punishing these men any more than they've already been punished."

"Neither can I," Karissa agreed. "Which is why there will be some significant changes around here, starting just as soon as I can get back to Pittsburgh." She smiled then looked at him coyly. "Now that you are unemployed again, perhaps you'd be willing to work with me. I could certainly use someone with a good, moral business sense who I know I can trust."

"You *trust* me?" he asked, clearly surprised by that revelation.

"With everything I own," she answered honestly.

"But I'm a man," he pointed out, remembering that she had once claimed not to trust anyone of the male species.

"Don't I *know* it," she answered, her smile widening while she ran her hands lightly across the solid muscles of his back, wishing he had not bothered to put on a fresh shirt after his quick bath. "So how about it? Do you want to work with me or not? That is as soon as you have finished clearing Jack McGeehan of Thomas's murder charges and feel up to making the trip back to Pittsburgh. I realize you have quite a gash there on the back of your head."

Shawn reached up to touch the tender spot, his hair still damp from having just been washed.

"Me? Work for you?" he asked, one eyebrow arched as if he could not comprehend such a proposal. "In what capacity?"

Karissa's smile widened while she continued to run her hands across the hardened muscles of his back. "Does the title 'husband' still interest you at all?"

Shawn let out a playful little growl and pulled her hard against his chest. "More than ever," he said as he dipped his mouth for the long, ravenous kiss that would seal their happiness forever.

Epilogue

"It really is the best of all worlds," Karissa said to Jacque while watching Weston toddle off after a large yellow butterfly. Because Shawn had insisted on having more grassy area in their yard than gardens, Weston had plenty of room to run and play. "Most days I get to stay home and help Lizbeth take care of Weston, yet I still have a hand in what goes on with the companies."

"That's because that husband of yers insists on going over the reports with ya at least one a week," Jacque said teasingly while she continued cutting the prettiest yellow roses in the garden and placing them into the large basket she had brought with her. She then glanced over to where Shawn lay in the grass on his stomach, happily dividing his attention between the two women and the two boys, who were now both in determined pursuit of the fat yellow butterfly. Although Lawrence was nearly four and Weston was barely three, the two boys were almost the same size and enjoyed playing the same games. "That husband of yers never lets a week go by that he doesn't bring home those reports."

"Well, you can't expect me to make *all* the decisions,"

Shawn said in ready defense then slowly pushed himself to his feet. "After all, the company is still called Caine Enterprises and I'm not exactly a Caine."

"But then neither am I anymore," Karissa pointed out, turning her adoring gaze to him. She then gestured to the tiny gold and ruby ring that was still on her finger, the same ring she had insisted be used for her wedding ring. "I'm a Madden now."

"Your name may be Madden," Shawn countered, bending to brush the grass off his trousers and shirt, then stepped over to retrieve his coat off a nearby chair. "But you'll always have very definite Caine traits. Like that stubborn streak of yours." He looked over at Jacque and winked. "I've never known a woman more hard-headed than that one."

"I'm not hard-headed," Karissa responded with a determined gleam in her brown eyes. "I'm just one of those people who likes to have her way all the time."

"Which is why we were both in Black Wall all last week," Shawn said, still looking at Jacque. "She was determined to be there when Laura and Marcus were finally married. It didn't matter that I had to miss a very important board meeting. All that mattered was that Marcus had finally proposed to Laura and we had been invited to the wedding."

Jacque laughed, knowing how hard it had been for Marcus finally to get up his nerve. "Well it *was* a rather historic event. Besides, it gave ya both the chance to be seeing old friends and checking on yer mining operations up there. Ya have to admit it was nice seeing what a fine difference those reforms made."

"There you go, siding with Karissa again," Shawn complained good-naturedly then called to Weston and

Lawrence. "Come on, boys. It's nearly time to go to the cemetery and put these flowers on your father and grandfather's grave." He then held his hand out to Karissa and helped her up out of the lawn chair. Glancing at her protruding stomach, he frowned. "Are you sure you are up to this, sweetheart? You know what the doctor said. This is your final month. You really should be taking it easy."

"Yes, I'm sure," she said, then looked at him with sad but convincing round eyes. "This is the fourth anniversary of Father's death. I want to help Jacque arrange the roses like I always do."

"I just don't want you overdoing," he cautioned, then bent to kiss her cheek. "You know how worried I get about you."

"I know. And I appreciate your concern but this is something I have to do." She then leaned against her husband, finding instant solace in the warmth of his arms when they circled her.

Jacque smiled as she set the basket of roses aside then knelt to straighten Lawrence's new velvet jacket and ruffled shirt. "My, what a handsome little man ya are today," she said with a mother's usual pride. "I must say, ya look more and more like yer father everyday."

"I'm a handsome fellow, huh?" Lawrence responded then wagged his head proudly, causing everyone to laugh.

"Me, too," Weston said with an instant pout, and held up his arms to his mother.

Knowing she dared not pick him up with Shawn right there standing watch over her, she bent to kiss his long, dark curls. "Yes, dear, you too. In fact, you are *very* handsome."

Aware the boy wanted to be held, Shawn quickly scooped his son up into his arms. "How could you not be?" he asked, gazing at his son's face proudly. "Look who your father is."

Karissa and Jacque groaned at such a pompous remark then Jacque picked up the basket and they prepared to leave.

"Daddy?" Weston said after they had gone only a few feet toward the house. He gazed into his father's blue eyes with a most concerned expression. "Will I also be smart and strong?"

"Of course you will be smart and strong," Shawn said, already laughing as he slipped his free arm around his wife's shoulders. "After all, look who your mother is."